HIDEOUS BEAUTY

HIDEOUS BEAUTY

KINGDOM WARS SERIES

BOOK ONE

JACK CAVANAUGH

an imprint of
GILEAD PUBLISHING

Hideous Beauty: Book 1 of The Kingdom Wars series
Copyright © 2007, 2018 by Jack Cavanaugh

Published by Enclave, an imprint of Gilead Publishing, LLC

Wheaton, Illinois, USA.
www.gileadpublishing.com
www.enclavepublishing.com

ISBN: 978-1-68370-167-5 (printed softcover)
ISBN: 978-1-68370-168-2 (ebook)

Cover design by Kirk DouPonce, www.DogEaredDesign.com
Interior design by Beth Shagene
Ebook production by Book Genesis, Inc.

Printed in the United States of America.

18 19 20 21 22 23 24 / 5 4 3 2 1

Acknowledgments

SPECIAL THANKS TO CLINTON E. ARNOLD AND GREG BOYD FOR your excellent studies on principalities and powers and the nature of spiritual conflict as portrayed in the Bible. Your books have been a source of enlightenment and inspiration for this work.

Special thanks to Alton Gansky, a constant friend and sounding board for all things theological.

Thanks to Brett Burner for valuable suggestions that developed the story during rewrite.

Thanks to Steve Laube, agent, cheerleader, and friend.

And thanks to my wife, Marni, and children, who bring such joy and laughter into my life.

For our struggle is not against flesh and blood,
but against spiritual forces of evil
in the heavenly realms.

—HOLY BIBLE

For how shall I relate
To human sense th' invisible exploits
Of warring Spirits?

—JOHN MILTON

Let us suppose that this everyday world were,
at some point, invaded by the marvelous.
Let us, in fact, suppose a violation of frontier . . .

—C. S. LEWIS

Before the clock of cosmic time was wound,
In heaven, fresh made, there dwelt a holy race.
Conceived in light for worship we were cast
To walk in luster and eternal grace.

Until a fatal wickedness was found
Hidden, a cancer deep within a soul.
Thus Lucifer turned thought to plan and deed,
With dragon's breath set heaven's fields aflame
With war. He scorched the Father's pristine realm,
Laid waste unblemished joy.

Defeated, he and all the host who loved him,
Cast down to worlds new born. Archenemy now,
Confined in time, a cosmic spectacle.
The rage that ravished heaven's brotherhood,
Now terrorizes earth with lies and strife.
Its borders breached, the warring hoard descends,
And what began in heaven now scourges man.

—ABDIEL, SERAPH OF HEAVEN

CHAPTER

1

"NIFTY LITTLE TALK, MR. AUSTIN."

The kid's eyes mocked me from the recesses of a hooded gray sweatshirt. I'd used the word earlier to describe a research app that had proved helpful to me. The kid was throwing the word back in my face. I chose to let it go and focus on the larger insult.

"Speech. It was a speech," I corrected him. He was playing to his buddies a few feet away.

The kid smirked. "And that prize thing . . . like, wow!"

"It's the Pulitzer, son, not some whistle ring you pull out of a box of Cracker Jacks."

"Yeah, whatever . . ."

I walked the open hallway. Ten years separated me from my graduation. This wasn't my high school anymore. The buildings were the same, but the occupants had changed. Everywhere I looked there were hooded sweatshirts. Since when had my alma mater become a school for Unabomber groupies?

Swept along in a river of adolescent angst—an endless stream of tattoos, piercings, colorful swatches of hair, studded leather chokers, and black lipstick—I tracked the smart-mouthed kid as he passed.

He joined his pod of friends, casting himself as the hero who'd gotten under the skin of some old geezer. They looked my way and laughed.

What is it about high school that brings out the worst in the human species? All my teenage insecurities, like faithful old dogs, were waiting for me when I stepped on campus, and had been nipping at my heels all morning.

I had an overwhelming urge to grab the kid by the scruff of his neck and take him on, to teach him a thing or two about respect.

Instead, I told myself I wasn't going to sink to his level. What difference did it make if some identity-challenged adolescent didn't appreciate the magnitude of my literary achievement? I told myself to let it go. I was the mature one here.

Breaking eye contact with him, I turned forward and walked smack into a metal pole.

A pair of coeds, one plump and one rail thin, gasped. Their hands flew to their mouths, at first in shock, but then to hide their giggles.

A wiry-haired boy with a serious acne problem laughed openly. "Ouch! That's gotta hurt!"

He was just glad it wasn't him.

"Are you all right, sir?" the plump coed asked.

"Do you want us to take you to the nurse's station?"

I cringed as the image flashed in my mind. Me, with a coed under each arm, being assisted out of the fast lane.

I assured the girls I was fine. I struck a fine pose—more than fine, robust, virile—and continued on my way, eager to put them, the pole, and the incident behind me.

A buzzer sounded. The corridor cleared rapidly as students disappeared into open doorways like water pouring down drains.

With the hallway to myself, I rubbed my forehead and wondered if the pole had left a mark. A familiar spring breeze swirled past me. And without the distraction of students, my thoughts turned nostalgic.

The outdoor stucco walls were the same mud-brown color I remembered, the doors aqua-blue. The open central corridor still stretched the length of the campus, with alternating wings of class-rooms and grassy lawns on each side.

Approaching one of my former classrooms, I peered inside. A small, redheaded woman with a hairstyle that predated my lifetime stood in front of the classroom. She wielded a wooden pointer like it was a broadsword. Behind her was a map of Gettysburg with red and blue arrows indicating troop movements.

"Reminiscing?"

I turned toward the voice behind me to find a smiling, horse-shoe-bald Hispanic man with a thick, black mustache. He held a sheaf of papers in one hand. Extending his other hand, he intro-duced himself. "Carlos Ruiz Mendoza." His smile widened, reveal-ing a gold tooth.

"Grant—"

"Austin. Yeah, I know. The assembly. Congratulations, by the way. The Pulitzer. Quite an achievement."

I shrugged modestly but didn't disagree. "Are you a teacher?" I asked.

"Remedial reading." He said it like he was apologizing. "The way I see it, if I do my job, by the time my students complete the course they'll actually be able to read your book. They won't, of course."

We both laughed.

"It's not exactly *Game of Thrones*," I admitted.

Mendoza motioned toward the classroom. "Do you know Rose?"

Inside the classroom the teacher, Rose, had leveled her broad-sword at a sandy-haired student who slumped in his chair and stared at her defiantly.

"I haven't had the pleasure," I said. "This was Coach Walker's room when I was here."

"Walker . . . quite a character from what I hear," Mendoza said.

"He passed on two years before I arrived. Stories still circulate, though."

I laughed. "Believe them. Walker knew only one way of doing things—as a football lineman coach. History, football, it was all the same to him."

"Were you on the team?"

"Football? No. Tennis was my sport. But Walker coached it too. The man didn't know a foot fault from a double fault, but he had us in great shape. We were the only team in the district doing bear crawls on the courts."

Mendoza laughed.

"But I learned some valuable life lessons from him," I added. "If nothing else, Coach taught us to hustle. I learned that hustle can beat superior talent; not always, but often enough."

"Good lesson."

"Got me where I am today."

By silent agreement, we continued down the corridor.

"I didn't have the smarts for scholarships," I explained. "Worked my way through college throwing baggage around at the local airport and pinching pennies."

"Ah, the Cup o' Noodles degree," Mendoza said.

I grinned. "You too?"

"Midnight shift at a 24-hour convenience store."

I liked this man.

With matching strides, we walked in silence for a moment, then he said, "You've come a long way since your microwave soup days, Austin. The Oval Office. Air Force One. The G-8 Summit in Paris. Few men get to see the things you've seen."

"I'm glad someone was listening to my speech."

Mendoza gave me a sideways glance. "Was school assembly behavior all that different when you attended?"

"I guess not," I admitted. "In one the music teacher stopped his orchestra mid-concert because we started batting a beach ball in the stands."

Mendoza nodded. "Some are better than others. Last month we had a band . . . a rhythm group, actually. They beat on trash cans, banged lids, swished brooms, that sort of thing. They were good. The students loved them."

"So you're saying if I want to make a hit with teenagers, I need to bang trash can lids together."

"Of course not," Mendoza scoffed. Then, with a twinkle in his eye, "But it wouldn't hurt."

"I'll take that under advisement."

"Seriously, Grant—long after the din of trash can lids fades away, what you have done will be remembered and revered. The Pulitzer Prize, son! They don't hand those out in Cracker Jack boxes!"

"Seems I've heard that somewhere before."

"You are, without doubt, the most famous alumnus this school has produced."

I thanked him as humbly as I could. But, truth was, I'd traveled the width of the country to hear those words. If only Myles Shepherd had heard them, my day would have been complete.

"Coming back here," Mendoza continued, "after all the exotic places you've been, all the famous people you've met, this must seem rather mundane to you."

"I don't know," I replied. "Singing Hills High will always be a part of who I am."

Mendoza pulled up in front of a door labeled faculty. He offered his hand again. "I'm glad I had this chance to chat with you, Mr. Austin. Something to tell my grandchildren someday."

Before he disappeared through the door, I said, "One thing more, Mr. Mendoza, where is Myles Shepherd's classroom?

"Shepherd? Sure. First room on the last wing."

I thanked him and continued down the corridor, my spirits much improved. There's something satisfying about hearing a teacher call you "Mister." I made a mental note to send Mendoza a signed copy of my book.

Upon reaching the last wing, I peered through the louvered windows and caught my own reflection. I was grinning like a man about to burst at the seams. And why not? I'd waited a decade for this day to arrive, and I wanted to savor every second of it.

This morning, as I dressed for the assembly, I told myself I wasn't going to gloat, that I was going to take the high road. But now that I was here, all I had were low-road thoughts.

I peered into the room. It was empty. In the front right, a door stood open. The teacher's office. A light spilled out from inside.

Shepherd was in there.

I was almost surprised. It would have been just like him to deprive me of my moment of triumph.

The door was unlocked. I let myself in.

The threshold proved to be a time portal. As I walked between the rows of desks, I was seventeen again with books under my arm and worries that I'd forgotten to do my homework swirling in my head. I trod the same scuffed, green-tile floor that I'd stared at while straining to remember answers to test questions. Even the assignment on the chalkboard could have been one I'd copied down years ago—

Chapters 45–47 for Thursday
TERM PAPERS DUE IN TWO WEEKS!

I ran my fingertips across the top of a desk. Suddenly, the past gave way to a sobering thought.

Mundane.

Mendoza had pegged it, hadn't he? The room. The studies. The students. The repetitious routine. All of it was ordinary. Commonplace. Mundane.

I couldn't believe that for years I had allowed myself to be haunted by Myles Shepherd's teaching success. For what? For this? Look at it! Shepherd's grand kingdom consisted of nothing more than row after row of graffiti-marred desks with chewing gum stuck to the undersides.

"Grant? Is that you?"

I approached the office door of my old nemesis and poked my head inside. My first impression? Cramped. Books defined the decor. Books squeezed vertically and horizontally into every inch of shelf space. Books stacked on top of shelves, on chairs, on the floor, on other books. In the center of the room, a gray metal desk dominated the floor space. Binders and folders of every color formed what looked like a New York city block of towers. On the working side of the desk was a small stack of papers, which were being graded. The top sheet was heavily slashed with red marks.

"Grant! Welcome to my snuggery!" Myles Shepherd half rose from his chair. He extended his hand across the desk. His grip had no more warmth than that of a car salesman.

"Sit! Sit!" he cried. "Just move those books anywhere."

He motioned to two student chairs with identical three-ring binder towers. I managed to relocate one of them to the floor without toppling it or setting off an avalanche.

I situated the chair in front of the desk and sat. The chair was smaller than it looked. I felt like Papa Bear sitting in Baby Bear's chair.

Looking down on me, Shepherd made no attempt to hide his amusement. I didn't care. There was only one Pulitzer Prize winning author in this room and it wasn't him.

"So, you took the time to stop by," Shepherd said. "I wasn't sure you would, now that you're famous."

"And miss this opportunity to see you? I've been looking forward to it." And that was the truth. "You're looking good, Myles."

It was an understatement. He looked great. Tanned. Fit. Not only had he not lost any hair, but his neatly trimmed style looked fuller and thicker than it had in high school.

He still had that killer combination of pale blue eyes and dimpled smile that turned women's knees to butter. The cleft in his chin sealed the deal. He looked more like a movie celebrity than a high school teacher. He was one of those guys who looked better in person than in his publicity pictures.

A tweed sports coat was draped over the back of his chair. Blue oxford sleeves rolled midway up muscular forearms. His collar was unbuttoned and his red tie loose.

"I suppose congratulations are in order," he said.

He swiveled around so that the back of his chair was facing me. I could hear three-ring binders toppling. When he swiveled back, he was holding a thick book which he plopped onto his desk. I recognized it instantly.

Lionheart: The R. Lloyd Douglas Story by Grant Austin.

Instinctively I reached to autograph it, then stopped myself. I settled back into my undersized chair.

Let him ask.

"Have you read it?"

Shepherd replied by picking up the book and thumbing through it. He took his time, pausing at every chapter.

He took so long my attention wandered to the display on the wall behind him. He'd hung his master's degree from Yale along with three framed news clippings—

**Myles Shepherd Turns Down Yale Offer
to Teach at Local High School**

**Myles Shepherd:
California Teacher of the Year**

PARADE MAGAZINE
Trendy Teacher Inspires Teens:
Myles Shepherd, Role Model Extraordinaire

Something familiar caught my attention. Prominently displayed on top of a mustard yellow file cabinet was a tennis trophy—Most Valuable Player.

On the night of the award ceremony, Coach Walker confided in me that his decision to give the award to Myles had been a coin toss. Myles had edged me out. That's the way it had always been between us.

I couldn't help but wonder if the trophy normally resided atop the file cabinet or if Myles had placed it there in anticipation of my visit.

As I continued to look around, I sensed there was something odd about the room. At first I couldn't put my finger on it. Then I did.

Conspicuously absent was any kind of student homage to Shepherd. For an award-winning teacher, that struck me as odd. There were no pictures of Shepherd surrounded by laughing students. No nostalgic teacher plaques or knickknacks, the kind gift stores sell by the case at graduation time. In fact, there were no apple-for-the-teacher mementos of any kind.

"Your book is certainly getting you a lot of attention," Shepherd said, breaking into my thoughts. "The New York Times bestseller list, for what? Three weeks now?"

"Thirteen weeks."

"Thirteen! Are you sure?"

"Thirteen. Trust me. An author knows. And you still haven't answered my question. Have you read it?"

Shepherd paused in his page thumbing. He silently read a sentence or two and grinned. "It's pedantic," he said, "but adequate for our purposes."

"Pedantic?" I blurted, louder than intended.

"Unimaginative, pedestrian, bookish—"

"I know what 'pedantic' means."

"Sorry. Teacher's habit."

But he wasn't sorry. He'd baited me and I'd bit.

Shepherd slapped shut the cover and tossed the book onto the desk, this time back cover up. I found myself staring at myself and wincing. I'm one of those guys who doesn't look as good as his publicity picture.

"What exactly about the book do you find pedantic?"

Shepherd smiled that smug, insufferable smile of his. "Jana looked good at the assembly this morning, don't you think?" he said.

The change of topic blindsided me. "Jana? Jana was here?"

"You didn't see her?" Shepherd sniffed. "Given your past involvement, I would have thought she'd get an exclusive interview."

"Last I heard she was in Chicago."

"KTSD. For about a year now."

Local station. That would explain it. "The White House staff handles all media arrangements," I said. "They give preference to the national networks."

"So much for old friends, huh?"

I ignored the cheap shot. My thoughts were on Jana. The last time I saw her was the day she walked out on me. I was a cad. She cried. The worse part was that she left me for Myles.

Shepherd slapped my book with the flat of his hand. "You know what amazes me about historians?" he said, changing the subject again. "The way they interpret events to suit their own purposes. Doesn't that strike you as dishonest?"

I didn't hear him. I was still wading in waters of regret, the romantic kind.

"Of course," Shepherd pressed, "you could make a case for the argument that all recorded history is essentially a collection of legends, half-truths, and lies."

"What are you talking about?"

"Don't get me wrong. I'm sure you did the best you could, given your limited access and understanding of the forces at work."

I'd had enough of this.

"Sour grapes, Myles?" I snapped. "It's beneath you. You know fully well that for a project of this scope I had to be granted complete access both to records and to people. My research was extensive. I've logged hundreds of hours interviewing the president, his family, his staff, and world leaders. My work is meticulously documented."

Shepherd chuckled. "Don't get defensive, old boy. I'm sure you dutifully read the documents that were set before you and recorded everything they wanted you to record. It's not your fault it's all a lie."

That did it. Even if he asked for my autograph, he wasn't going to get it.

"Give me one example of a lie," I demanded.

Shepherd gazed at something in the distance as though he hadn't heard me. "Actually," he said, "we're quite pleased with the finished product, and with you. You've done exactly what we've expected of you."

I was on the edge of my seat, spoiling for a fight, if only Shepherd would settle on a topic long enough for me to take a swing. "That's the second time you've implied you had something to do with the publication of my book."

Shepherd smiled.

His smile had a history, one that jangled my giblets. It wasn't your garden-variety grin, more like the smile of a gladiator looking down on his vanquished opponent as he is about to deliver the *coup de grace*.

I associate his smile with our sophomore year. The school was going through a chess craze. Guys carried miniature boards with magnetic pieces around in their pockets. We'd play chess before school, after school, and at lunch. When we thought we could get away with it, we played during class, passing the game back and forth across the aisle like lovesick girls passing notes. I remember one time seeing two guys standing in the showers after gym finishing a game.

On three occasions I sat across a chessboard from Myles Shepherd. The thing I remember most about our games—other than the fact that I lost all three—was the moment I knew I was going to lose. I'd taken my hand from a piece after making a move. Myles would lean over the board and say, "Maybe you see something I don't . . ."

Then, he would smile that smile.

That smile was a torpedo with my name on it. Had I been a ship, rats would have been jumping overboard.

But things were different now, I told myself. We were no longer sophomores, and this wasn't a chess game. And maybe Myles thought he knew something I didn't, but I wasn't about to concede anything.

"Nice try, Myles," I said. "I suppose you're also going to take credit for my Pulitzer Prize."

His grin widened. "More than you know," he replied.

"Sorry, old boy, but that dog won't hunt. You can sit behind your desk and cast all the aspersions you want—"

"However, we're not finished with you," he said, talking over me. "We need you to write one final chapter."

". . . and maybe you can convince some of your less intelligent students that you're the man behind the author, but we both know—"

"We need you to write the chapter of R. Lloyd Douglas's assassination."

". . . that you had nothing to do with—what did you say?"

Reclining in his chair, Shepherd did the steeple thing with his fingers. "Your task will be to secure R. Lloyd Douglas's legacy alongside that of Lincoln and Kennedy."

"Myles . . . if this is a joke, it's not funny."

"Have you read William Manchester's *Death of a President*? Of course you have. We want something similar."

With difficulty I climbed out of my chair. "Look, Myles," I said. "Joke or not, I have to report this conversation. You know that, don't you?"

Shepherd stared at me long and hard, and I could have sworn that at that moment the lights dimmed. "I'd be disappointed if you didn't try," he said.

"Whatever game you're playing, Myles, this time you've over-played your hand. All I have to do is grab my smartphone and—"

"He won't take your call. Ingraham, that is. That's who you were going to call, isn't it? Chief of Staff Ingraham? He won't take your call."

His comment knocked me off balance. How did he know I was thinking of Chief of Staff Ingraham?

"I'm . . . I'm sure you won't mind if I don't take your word for it," I stammered.

"And that cell phone number the president gave you at Camp David? Disconnected."

"How . . . how . . . do you know about that? No one knows about that, not even Ingraham."

"The president knows."

Pushing back his chair, Shepherd rose to full height. He looked every inch the self-satisfied prig I'd loathed for years.

"And that cute little number," he continued, "what's her name? Chrissy? No, Christina. Ingraham's aide. Despite your little dalli-ance, she won't take your calls either. You're cut off, Grant."

Shepherd's matter-of-factness unnerved me. At this point I had but a single thought—get away from him. Alarms were going off inside of me, warning me to get out now. I took a step backward toward the door.

"Besides," Shepherd said, easing around his desk, "informing the president about an attempt on his life would be a waste of time."

I took another step.

"Do you want to know why?" He smiled his gladiator smile. "Because he already knows about it. In fact, he's the one who's planning it. Ingenious, no? A president who plots his own assassination."

A cold chill poured over me like ice water. Shepherd's little bombshell was one of those statements that are so outrageous, so unbelievable, so farfetched that you want to dismiss them as frivolous, but in your gut you know they're true.

Shepherd rubbed his hands together in a that-settles-that manner. "Now, let's talk about the literary style of the assassination chapter. You'll want to avoid the tedious tone you used in the first five chapters."

My knees went weak. Only with effort did I take another step back.

"Don't go, Grant. We're not finished."

My feet stopped moving. I didn't stop them.

"Poor Grant," Shepherd said. "You've been in over your head from the beginning."

I tried to move. Couldn't. "Oh yeah?" My voice quivered as I tried to break free. "Well, I'll find a way to stop you . . . somehow. Count on it."

I began to panic. Maybe I was overreacting, but losing control of the ability to move my legs has that effect on me. "I . . . I . . . don't . . . know what you've gotten yourself mixed up with, Shepherd . . . but I'll expose you. . . . I'll alert the Secret Service . . . phone the media . . . I'll . . . I'll . . . I'll tell the principal!"

I've never been good at trash-talking. It always comes out sounding like a two-year-old's tantrum.

Shepherd chuckled. It was a deep, throaty rumble that made the cinder-block walls shudder and the picture frames rattle. "You can't stop us," he said. "We've been doing this for millennia."

About now I was wishing I'd taken the high road and left immediately following the assembly. I didn't know how Myles Shepherd was doing this, but I was obviously no match for it. I kept throwing verbal jabs, hoping one of them would land.

"We . . . you keep saying *we*," I said. "I suppose now you're going to tell me you're part of some ancient brotherhood, like the Knights Templar, or the Illuminati, or some other puerile organization of losers with secret handshakes, blood-drinking initiations, and decoder rings. Do you know how perverted that is, Myles? Most of us grew out of that stuff in junior high."

Shepherd's smile faded. As it did, the room grew darker, which was odd because it was nearly noon. Behind me, the sun streamed into the classroom, but it stopped at the office threshold, as though it was afraid to come in.

A movement caught my eye. High in the corner, above the file cabinet, wedged between ceiling and wall, grotesque figures took shape. Three-dimensional shadows with sunken eyes leered at me like medieval castle gargoyles. One of them dropped silently onto the top of the cabinet and clutched the tennis trophy like it was a doll.

I blinked and they were gone.

"Something wrong, Grant?" Shepherd asked. "Where's that smug superiority you brought with you into the room?"

I swallowed hard. Every instinct within me screamed for me to run. My heart banged against my chest, desperate to get out of the room, with or without me.

"I suppose you should feel honored, Grant," Shepherd said. "We've been grooming you for this task most of your miserable, pathetic life. You've been the perfect pawn. Predictable to a fault."

The shadow gargoyles reappeared. There were more of them this time, clustered in the corner, shoulders pressed against greasy shoulders. They glared at me with intense, hungry eyes, straining to get at me like hounds on a leash.

Clouds of darkness billowed across the ceiling while the fluorescents continued humming happily. Standing beside his desk, Myles Shepherd appeared to have grown a foot taller and twice as handsome—with a radiant glow.

I found it increasingly difficult to concentrate. I stood transfixed, my eyes locked on Shepherd. I couldn't turn my head aside, nor could I close my eyes. Myles Shepherd wanted me to see something, and I wasn't sure I wanted to see it.

"What's happening to me?" I cried.

Shepherd laughed. It was a laugh not of this world, sounding like a thousand wind chimes of such clarity and tone it brought tears to my eyes; a laugh that spawned laughter, bubbling in my gut, rushing to the surface in an explosion of guffaws. I couldn't stop it. I laughed like a madman. I laughed so hard I thought my belly would burst.

My ability to speak—the only weapon I had left—was being swallowed by convulsive spasms of mirth. I had to fight it. Somehow, I had to force myself to speak.

"This . . . is . . . about . . . the tennis . . . trophy . . . isn't it?" I managed to say.

"What?" Shepherd snapped.

I'd landed a blow. The satisfaction was exhilarating. It spurred me on. Two can play the taunting game, Mr. Shepherd.

"The trophy," I stammered. "We all . . . knew . . . you cheated . . . to win . . . it. We laughed . . . at . . . you . . . behind . . . your back . . . for . . . selling . . . your soul . . . for a cheap . . . plastic . . . trophy."

Shepherd's jaw clenched.

The floor trembled. The desk shook. Towers of papers and notebooks toppled over. From the corner, the shadow creatures screamed silently at me.

Scared out of my skin, if I'd had any sense I would have stopped goading him. "And the . . . chess . . . matches?" I continued. "We . . . let . . . you . . . win. . . . Everyone . . . knew . . . you were . . . a sucker . . . for the . . . Sicilian . . . defense."

The quaking intensified. Books rained down from shelves. My feet still firmly fixed to the floor, I couldn't move to avoid them.

Shepherd roared. "You insignificant worm! You cannot begin to know the nauseating torment I endure simply by being in your presence!"

"Whining, Myles? How unattractive."

The floor undulated like the sea.

I pressed on. "As . . . for . . . Jana? It's . . . a . . . shame . . . you . . . weren't . . . man enough . . . to . . . keep . . . her. After . . . she dumped . . . you, she . . . told . . . me . . . kissing . . . you . . . was like . . . kissing . . . a . . . trashcan. Ever . . . hear of . . . breath mints, Myles?"

The lights went out. The room was pitch-black while behind me the classroom remained flooded with sunlight. I could hear books falling all around me.

A ray of light shot past me.

Then another.

And another.

They came from Shepherd. Originating from inside him, they shot through his clothing, which took fire but wasn't consumed. The fabric transformed to . . . to what? The folds and seams remained intact, but it looked like no cloth I'd ever seen. They appeared to be folds of pure color. We're talking laundry-detergent-commercial special effects here—the reddest reds and bluest blues I'd ever seen.

The intensity of the colors vied for supremacy, growing ever brighter until something had to give. They began to chase each other, swirling around the shape that had once been Myles Shepherd, slowly at first, then faster, and faster, blending with each other until they became a dazzling white, a hurricane of radiance.

What was happening here? Was I hallucinating? I hoped I was, because the alternative was that Myles Shepherd, my constant rival, was not of this world. The idea that I'd gone to high school for four years with ET and never knew it was hard to admit to myself.

Overhead, the gargoyle shadow creatures—now looking mossy green and solid—stared at Shepherd with expressions of awe and adoration and painful longing.

I knew exactly how they felt. I felt the same way. Whoever, whatever stood before me was mesmerizing.

Think of a perfect starlit night when you're lost in your lover's eyes, a moment suspended in time and bliss. Multiply that euphoria ten thousand times and only then will you begin to grasp the beauty that lay just beyond my reach.

The attraction was so intense I had to grab a bookshelf to keep from dropping to my knees and worshipping it.

Here was an elegance that was wondrously strange. All-consuming, I wanted it to go on forever. Tears tracked my cheeks. I mumbled incoherently. I dared not blink lest I lose a moment of this marvel.

But then the light reversed itself. Blasts shot past me a second time as the glorious hurricane became a swirling accretion that began feeding on the colors in the room. Instead of giving off light, it was swallowing it, gulping it greedily.

How do I describe what I saw?

It was a vortex. A black hole. All at once wondrous and comical.

The red slashes on the graded exams lifted off the paper and, like snakes, slithered their way toward the vortex and were swallowed up. So, too, rivers of Times Roman font lifted from the papers, streamed to the vortex, and disappeared. Titles from books followed, peeled from the spines of the volumes on the shelves.

The file cabinet was stripped of its yellow color, reduced to a pale ghostly white. Even the blue of my tie was sucked off, and the color lifted from my class ring, leaving the ruby crystal clear.

The colors made the vortex—formerly Myles Shepherd, though he no longer bore any resemblance to a man—pulse with nightmarish power.

For not only was the room stripped of all color, it was stripped of every pleasure, every good feeling, leaving me bereft, emotionally bankrupt, despairing of hope and life. I was abhorrent to myself. Spasms of depression racked me. I craved annihilation, nonexistence, confident that my death would make the world a better place. I sobbed uncontrollably.

That's when he loosed the hounds.

The shadow gargoyles fell upon me with a vengeance, tearing through my clothing, penetrating my flesh, plunging into the inner depths of my being. They fed on me, occupied me with contentious voices.

My mouth contorted into a scream, but whatever sound I produced was instantly swallowed by the vortex.

I reached out to what had once been Myles Shepherd, begging him to make quick work of me. To unborn me, if that were possible. All I knew was that I was desperate to no longer be.

The last thing I remember were his words filling the room, sounding like a chorus of a thousand voices.

"I AM SEMYAZA. TREMBLE BEFORE ME."

My awaking sensation was cold tile against my cheek and the pungent odor of industrial floor detergent. It took several painful blinks before my eyes focused. I heard a moan. I think it came from me.

Memories like lost hitchhikers came straggling back. The high school assembly. The classroom. Myles Shepherd seated behind his desk, then morphing into a whirlwind. The shadow creatures, straining to get at me, clawing onto me.

I cried out and raised an arm to defend myself. But there was nothing in the corner. My hand flew to my chest. They weren't there either. I was alone in the room.

Moving slowly, I worked my way into a sitting position. My head swam with the effort. I glanced around. Everything was in its place. The towers of books. Stacks of papers. The trophy. The file cabinet was yellow. All the books had their titles.

I turned toward the doorway. The classroom was as dark as the office. It was night.

Somehow I managed to get to my knees, then to my feet. I had to steady myself on the edge of the desk.

When I felt I could trust my legs again, I navigated the short distance to the office door. My hand brushed my coat and tie. It hit something unexpected. I looked down.

Pinned to my tie was a square piece of pink notepad paper. I removed the pin. There wasn't enough light to read it, so I found the light switch and flipped it on. Fluorescents flickered, then burst to life. Light poked me rudely in the eyes. After several moments I gave the note another try—

Grant,
> *Let yourself out. Don't forget to lock up.*
> > *M.S.*

Staggering between rows of chairs, I made my way out and stumbled into the night air.

The world smelled disgusting. Rancid. Like a pair of dirty gym socks. Wrinkling my nose, I glanced around. The spring grass was muddy green. The stars were depressingly dim. The air tasted greasy. It was all I could do to keep from retching.

An annoying *squeak, squeak, squeak* pricked my ears as a pot-bellied janitor appeared pushing a mop pail. When he saw me, he started.

"Hey! What's goin' on here?" he cried.

He looked repulsive. Flesh hung from his jowls and arms like algae on a shipwreck. His voice was a parrot's squawk.

"It's all right," I croaked, my throat as dry as parchment. "I was here earlier. Just came back for my car." I motioned feebly toward the parking lot.

"Are you drunk?"

Without answering him, I started toward the parking lot.

The janitor watched my unsteady progress with a suspicious squint.

I was relieved to find my rental car still in the lot. As I unlocked the door I pacified myself with the thought that while Myles Shepherd may have won the battle, I had landed the last blow.

I didn't lock up.

CHAPTER

2

THE GRASS CRUNCHED LIKE SOUR MILK CARTONS BENEATH MY feet. Imagine traversing a landfill where everything you touch is filthy with a slimy film to it, and you have an idea of what it was like for me to get to my car.

Climbing into the rental—a luxury-edition sedan with barely thirty-seven miles on the odometer—was like crawling into a garbage dumpster. Windows up. Windows down. It didn't matter. The odors were suffocating.

I contributed to the stench. My flesh reeked. Not from lack of hygiene, mind you. I shower daily. My body had the odor of a carnivore. My skin was permeated with the stench of the dead flesh I'd consumed earlier—prime rib the night before, sausage for breakfast. Every time my hands came close to my face I winced. Each nauseating waft of decayed meat reminded me how pure, clear, and clean was the radiant presence in Shepherd's office.

But I couldn't think of that now. I had to warn the president about whatever or whoever attacked me in that office. Though I still hadn't figured out what I was going to say, I felt an urgency to warn him. Whatever that was in the office, the power was incredible.

Another word to describe it came to mind. I didn't want to use it. It wasn't a word you used around educated folk, the kind who walked the halls of Washington, DC. But something *supernatural* had taken place in that office. Whether I wanted to admit it or not.

2:00 a.m. Sitting in the car I made my first call to Chief of Staff Harold Ingraham's direct line. With the three-hour time difference, it was five o'clock in Washington. Ingraham should have answered. He didn't.

It didn't make sense. I knew he was there. The man was always in his office at five. He was proverbially punctual. The joke on the Hill was that the Naval Observatory set their atomic clocks by him.

3:00 a.m. After an hour of failed attempts to reach Ingraham, I called Christina. As I waited for her to answer, I could see her in my mind's eye, frantically pulling on clothes and shoes while juggling her cell phone and working her way to the front door of her apartment.

Frantic. It's the only mode Christina knows. Here is a woman who was born multitasking. She places phone calls between bites of breakfast, lunch, and dinner. She doesn't sleep, she catnaps. And if rapid eye movement beneath closed lids is any clue, even then she's planning, arranging, prioritizing.

Christina's leave-a-message recording kicked in. I left a voicemail.

At 3:10 a.m. I initiated a second round of calls with identical results. Ingraham, no answer. Christina, left another voicemail and a text. This cycle continued every ten minutes.

At 4:00 a.m. I decided it was time for the big gun.

I scrolled down FAVORITES looking for the number the president gave me at Camp David. He told me it was his family cell phone number. Fewer than a dozen people in the world had it. I was the only nonrelative.

How does one store the personal cell phone number of the President of the United States? I'd been hesitant to add it to my list of contacts. Smartphones get lost and misplaced. I had visions of an insurance salesman finding my phone on an airplane and trying to sell the president a whole life policy. I needed a code name.

My first thought was HH, for Head Honcho, but I'd settled on Doogie. It had been the president's nickname in elementary school. There were only a handful of people who knew that.

My thumb paused over the name on the touch pad.

What was I going to say when he answered?

I gave it a practice run.

"Ummm . . . Mr. President? Grant Austin here. Sorry to bother you, but I'm out in California, and I was chatting with a former high school buddy . . . well, he's not exactly a buddy, more like a rival . . . but anyway, he happened to mention that there was going to be an attempt to assassinate you and . . . well . . . sir . . . he says you know about it. Do you?"

For several indecisive moments I stared at Doogie on the touch-pad, trying desperately to think of nonlunatic phrases.

A moment of clarity dawned. This wasn't about me. Coming across as a lunatic wasn't a concern. At least it shouldn't be. The issue here was national security, alerting the president to a threat on his life.

Immersed in a wave of patriotic duty, I pressed the touchpad. The connection was made. I heard ringing at the other end of the line without knowing where the other end of the line was. The residence? The Oval Office? Air Force One? Poolside for the president's morning swim?

Keep it simple and straightforward, I told myself. Alert the president to the facts. Save the details—the X-Files details—for the Secret Service to laugh at.

Three sharp tones sounded. An automated message kicked in informing me that the number had been disconnected or was no longer in service.

Myles Shepherd's voice haunted me. "And that cell phone number the president gave you at Camp David? Disconnected."

How had he known?

7:00 a.m. The first students began arriving at the high school. Through tired eyes I watched as they drove into the senior parking lot. I recognized their kind. Overachievers. I could see it in their stride. School couldn't start early enough for them. A new day was another chance to shine, another day to add more flowery kudos to their already burgeoning bouquet. They were the student government leaders, the newspaper editors, the club presidents. The elite.

I never counted myself among them, though I associated with them. Even now I continue to work with them. Washington, DC is populated by a national roll call of valedictorians, every one of them determined to prove themselves.

Christina is one of them. Graduated top of her class at Midland High in Odessa, Texas, with a repeat performance at the University of Texas as a political science major.

Why hadn't she returned my calls or texts?

I tried again, having lost track of the number of voicemails and texts I'd left her.

"You've reached the desk of Christina Kraft, aide to Chief of Staff Ingraham. Leave a brief message and a number where you can be reached. I'll return your call at the earliest opportunity."

Straining to keep the frustration from my voice I left another message. "Christina . . . Grant. What's going on? I can't stress how urgent it is I talk to you. This isn't a personal call. Call me back . . . please."

A motorcycle blasted past me with an earsplitting roar, drowning out the last of my message. I repeated it.

As the sun broke over the mountains, I squinted against its glare. The flow of arriving students was increasing. I watched as broods of them—looking like Eloi marching blandly to their doom—filtered between rows of cars heading for their homerooms. That is, if they still had homerooms.

A breeze swept through the car. It didn't stink. I was acclimating to the odor of this world. In exchange, the memory of my brush with glory was dimming.

What hadn't dimmed was the terror I felt when I was curled up on the floor.

I am Semyaza. Tremble before me.

Reaching for the door latch, I got out of the car. Like it or not, I had to face the fear. I had to go back to that classroom. I had to know if what I'd experienced was real.

I waited ten minutes after the buzzer for the hallways to clear, wanting to avoid a repeat performance from the previous day. There was also the matter of enhanced odors with that many bodies bunched together. I didn't want to risk retching in front of the entire student body. The close encounter of a painful kind with the pole was enough embarrassment for one visit.

Passing open classroom doors, I heard the familiar sounds of another school day—attendance-taking, calls for reports and homework assignments to be passed to the front of the room, chatter across the aisles.

The door to Myles Shepherd's classroom was closed. I risked peeking inside the window.

At the front of the class, a middle-aged woman with premature streaks of gray clutched her hands and attempted to get the students' attention. She looked like someone's mother.

"Class? Class?"

Her voice had a cartoon quality to it, not quite Marge Simpson, but similar. It was obvious she didn't make her living teaching high school students.

"Class? If I could have your attention, please . . . please, your attention. . . . Your teacher, Mr. Shepherd, has been delayed. Due to an accident on the freeway, traffic is backed up. Many teachers have called in. They'll get here as soon as they can. In the meantime, I've been instructed to tell you that you are to read the next chapter in your—"

None of the students was listening to her. As soon as they heard Shepherd was delayed, the room exploded with conversation.

High school classrooms are jungles. Survival depends on strength, cunning, speed, and wit. This poor woman had none of these qualities. They were eating her alive.

Leaving her to her fate, I made my way toward the administration building. The backed-up line out the door resembled a morning commute. Most of the kids clutched blue slips of paper, but not all of them.

"You don't have a blue slip?" I heard one of them say. "You have to have a blue slip to get back into class, dude. They won't let you back into class without a blue slip."

Cutting through the line, I stepped inside.

A squat man in gray slacks, a white short-sleeved shirt, and with close-cropped salt-and-pepper hair spied an unauthorized movement out of the corner of his eye. His head snapped up to challenge me.

I remembered him from yesterday. Vice Principal Benton, or Benson. It took him a moment to recognize me. When he did, his scowl transformed into a public relations grin.

"Austin! Didn't expect to see you again so soon! To what do we owe the honor of this encore appearance?"

"Actually, I was just in Myles Shepherd's room and—"

"Ah yes! Come in! Come in!"

He took me by the arm and led me through a swinging gate into the restricted area of administration central, presumably so the students in line wouldn't overhear our conversation.

My long-dormant student senses tingled wildly. I'd seen students taken by the arm by the vice principal into the administration inner sanctum. Some of them were never heard from again.

"Several of our teachers are running late," Benton or Benson said in a hushed tone. "Big accident on I-8. Traffic is backed up for miles."

As though I needed proof, he led me to a portable TV sitting on top of a row of file cabinets. A square-jawed reporter wearing headphones was describing the situation from high overhead in a news helicopter. At the bottom of the screen a banner announced this was BREAKING NEWS.

The reporter was shouting into his microphone in order to be heard over the noise of the chopper, "*. . . backed up all the way to the Grossmont Summit. As you can see, all four lanes are blocked. Eastbound traffic is at a complete standstill.*"

While the reporter described every commuter's worst nightmare, the camera panned, providing a jittery view of three long lines of cars. At the front of the line, a lone vehicle was engulfed in flames. The inferno generated a column of black smoke that stretched to the heavens.

"*. . . battling the fire. The flames have been so intense, the firefighters have had to back away. All they can do now is let it burn itself out. As you can see, a second crew is just arriving . . .*"

A fire truck's flashing red lights could be seen inching up the emergency lane, slowed by onlookers who had gotten out of their cars to get a glimpse of the cause of the delay.

"*When we first arrived at the scene, we witnessed several bystanders attempting to fight the flames with handheld fire extinguishers in a valiant attempt to rescue the driver. The intense heat drove them back. (Ronny, see if you can zoom in on the men standing beside the black truck.)*"

The picture on the screen bounced crazily, then zoomed toward three men staring helplessly at the inferno. Their shoulders were hunched.

"As you can see, they're still holding the spent extinguishers in their hands."

Zooming in closer, the camera swung toward the vehicle. Flames feasted hungrily on the car's interior.

"Poor devil . . . never had a chance," Benton or Benson commented beside me.

Behind us a large woman in a floral print blouse gasped loudly, then again, as though she was trying to catch her breath. Her hand flew to her mouth as she stared with disbelief at the television.

"Oh . . . oh . . . oh!"

A coworker rushed to her side. "Roberta, what is it?"

Like a fish out of water the distraught woman gasped repeatedly. "The . . . the . . . plates!" she cried. "Look . . . look . . . at the . . . license plates!"

All eyes in the room squinted at the television screen, trying to see what Roberta saw. Gasps and wounded cries exploded across the room.

"One of your teachers?" I asked Benton or Benson.

The vice principal stood motionless. Tears ran down his cheeks, which was just downright scary. Vice principals don't cry, they make people cry.

The woman who had assisted Roberta now turned her attention to him. "Mr. Benson? Maybe you'd better sit down."

Stone monuments aren't easily moved. It appeared Benson hadn't heard her. He stood with his jaw slightly askew as though its hinge was broken.

I glanced again at the television to see what would have this kind of effect on him. Centered on the screen was the blackened license plate of the burning car. Even though it was charred, the raised letters were readable.

CA TCHR

Benson was weeping openly now, and it was painful to watch. "The Kiwanis gave him that license plate when he was voted teacher of the year," he said to me.

I felt a chill.

"Who?" I asked.

I already knew, but I had to hear it.

"Shepherd," Benson said. "Myles Shepherd."

CHAPTER
3

THE PILLAR OF SMOKE FROM THE BURNING CAR COULD BE SEEN from the high school parking lot. Myles Shepherd dead. I couldn't believe it.

Usually when people say that, they haven't yet come to terms with reality. I really couldn't believe it. Not after what I'd seen yesterday in his office. I had to see for myself.

I started the car with one hand while the other checked my messages.

No texts. No missed calls. No voicemail.

I hit the steering wheel with the palm of my hand. Why wasn't anyone returning my calls? It was as though Washington, DC, had been wiped off the face of the planet.

Heading west on Madison Avenue, I was in sight of the freeway overpass at Second Street within a few minutes.

I pulled into a gas station convenience store opposite the off-ramp. Throwing the gearshift lever into park, I took off across the street at a dead run.

On any other day crossing Second Street this way would be

suicide, but with no cars exiting the freeway, the road was so clear of traffic it was spooky.

I sprinted up the deserted off-ramp, drawn by the black column of smoke. The smell of burned rubber stung my nostrils. I crested the ridge and entered the scene I'd viewed on the television minutes before.

No one paid attention to me. Crowd control focused on the road side of the accident with all the cars.

I watched as firemen encircled the burning car frame, hoses shut off, but at the ready. The three would-be heroes stood off to one side holding spent fire extinguishers, their slumped postures unchanged.

Moving in as close as I dared, I did what I came to do. I peered inside the burning car, the driver's side. It took me a moment to sort out all the black-on-black shapes amid the smoke and flames, but eventually I made out the head of a driver. It was featureless and slumped to one side, as though he had nodded off. There was nothing to suggest a desperate attempt to get out of the car.

But was it Shepherd?

The body was burned beyond recognition.

The uncertainty of not knowing gnawed at me. I found it impossible to believe that the blackened corpse in the car was the same man who less than twenty-four hours earlier had burst into Technicolor.

Then again, as the effect of yesterday's fireworks dimmed, I was finding it increasingly difficult to believe it had happened.

I stared again at the blackened human form, almost daring it to prove me wrong, to do something unexpected, unexplainable, something supernatural, like turning into a raven and flying away.

The blast of a horn nearly brought me out of my skin.

Behind me a white news van was rumbling up the ramp. As I stepped aside, bold letters scrolled in front of me—KTSD Channel 2 *Today's News When You Need It Most*. It rocked to a stop. The front cab doors flew wide, and the side door slid open as the van disgorged its human contents.

A thin man in khaki shorts scurried up a ladder to the roof where he began preparing a satellite dish for transmission.

A husky, red-bearded lumberjack of a man tumbled out swinging a video camera onto his shoulder like it was some sort of weapon. He began shooting as he advanced on the burning wreck.

From inside the van a foot appeared, wearing stylish leather sling-back pumps. It was an attractive foot attached to an attractive leg. And then another.

I recognized them both. I used to date them.

Microphone in hand, Jana Torres stepped from the van. She hit the ground running, her luscious brown curls cascading over the padded shoulders of a tan suit coat. Like the cameraman before her, the instant she emerged from the van, her attention was on the burning vehicle. She didn't see me.

I watched with swelling pride as she took control of the broadcast, pointing and directing her team. She approached a fireman who directed her to the chief in a white helmet. When the chief saw Jana coming, his eyes lit with recognition. He smiled and met her halfway.

With a pair of news helicopters circling overhead and the constant roar of pumper trucks, I couldn't hear what Jana said to the chief, but in short order she motioned to the cameraman and the fireman squared his shoulders for an interview. The stalled lines of traffic formed a backdrop.

Jana donned an earpiece, looked into the camera's eye, and composed herself. She stood motionless for a few moments, presumably waiting for a signal from the studio. The delay was long enough for me to be conquered once again by her stunning good looks.

Gone was the girlish cheerleader I remembered from high school.

This Jana was comfortable with her womanhood. Her brown eyes flashed intelligence and personality and confidence.

She came to life and the interview began. The fire chief was stiff next to her. The only thing animated about him was a bottle-brush gray mustache that did a little dance when he talked.

A horrifying thought struck me. Jana didn't know the burning car belonged to Myles Shepherd! She didn't know the corpse a short distance from where she was standing might be that of a high school classmate and college boyfriend. How horrible it would be for her if she found out while on camera.

My first thought was the license plate. That's how the administration staff learned it was Shepherd's car. It was curled and completely blacked out now. Unreadable.

But what about the chief? What if he said something in the interview? He wouldn't do that, would he? Weren't they always withholding information pending notification of relatives?

I watched the interview with increasing nervousness. I readied myself to . . . to what? Swoop in and rescue her?

Mercifully the interview concluded with Jana showing no sign of shock or surprise. I breathed easier.

After thanking the chief on camera, she proceeded to do her wrap-up. The chief didn't wander far. He took a single step back and watched her. He clearly had eyes for her.

That didn't sit well with me. Old feelings stirred, poked alive like embers buried in ashes.

For some reason Jana chose that moment to glance my direction. Though she was still on camera, our gazes met and held, long enough to distract her. She stumbled in her delivery.

I wish I was secure enough to tell you that I was sorry to have messed up her broadcast. But I'm not, and I wasn't. It gave me pleasure. The chief noticed the stumble too. He scowled at me for causing it. That made me feel even better.

Jana recovered, regaining her focus even though she was no longer talking. It took me a moment to realize the station must be asking her a follow-up question. She gave a brief answer and then it was over. The cameraman lowered the camera. Jana pulled the earpiece free, handing it and her microphone to the cameraman.

She gave the chief's hand a single pump of thanks. He tried to engage her in further conversation. She excused herself.

With a flip of her hair, Jana strode confidently toward me, her eyes and smile sparkling in glorious harmony. She had such an over-powering sense of femininity about her. It stunned me.

The whoop of a police siren startled me. They were opening a single lane of traffic. I stepped aside.

Jana greeted me with a hug.

She smelled . . . she smelled great. Her breath was warm against my neck as she said, "Oh Grant . . . the Pulitzer! I'm so proud of you!"

Sense of duty wrung my heart like a dishrag. I hated that what I had to say next would spoil our reunion.

"Jana . . . I'm afraid I have some bad news."

She took it hard. She turned to look at the car. By now the blaze was extinguished. Three streams of water hit it from three different angles. All that was left was the frame.

I told Jana how the high school staff had recognized the license plates. The next thing I knew, she was pressed against my chest sobbing.

We held each other in the number three lane of eastbound Interstate 8 while a long line of rubbernecking commuters stared first at the burned car, then at us. I didn't care. I was content to hold Jana for as long as she needed me. It felt right. I began to wonder why we had ever split up in the first place. Then I remembered. Myles.

I rested my chin against her head. It was hot with emotion. Neither of us spoke.

Firemen mopped up. The three would-be heroes climbed into trucks and drove away. The camera crew loaded the van. A man in a stylish pin-striped suit stood beside the fire truck, his arms folded. Ignoring all the other activity, he watched Jana and me.

It was Myles Shepherd.

I must have started, or gasped, or flinched, or all three because Jana looked at me with alarm.

"What's wrong?"

"Myles . . ." I muttered.

I glanced down at her, and when I looked up again he was gone.

"I know," she said, comforting me. "I can't bring myself to believe he's dead either."

"No, you don't understand—"

My smartphone went off. *Hail to the Chief,* my text tone. Probably Christina. I reached to answer it, then stopped myself.

"That isn't the—" Jana said.

"President?" I smiled. "No."

Looking up at me with wet eyes, she said, "Do you need to get that?"

I couldn't. You don't check your texts when you're holding a crying woman. That's one of those unwritten man/woman laws, isn't it? But this wasn't an ordinary text.

The tone persisted.

I imagined Christina on the other end, exasperated, waiting for me to text back after I had dogged her all morning with messages about the urgency of reaching her.

Jana tried to pull away. "Read the text," she said.

I couldn't. It felt wrong to let her go.

"I can read it later," I said, trying to sound gallant. I held her tight.

Jana nestled against my chest.

My mind alternated between how I was going to explain this to Christina and scanning the area for signs of an increasingly spooky former classmate.

The arrival of a tow truck and an ambulance forced us to relocate. We decided to go somewhere where we could talk. Jana told her news crew to return without her.

I couldn't help taking one last look at the scene, one last look around for Myles, and one last look at the car. The burned remains sat in the center of a charred starburst.

CHAPTER
4

"It was Myles's body in the car. I'm certain of it." Jana spoke with conviction. "He would sooner share his toothbrush with a stranger than let anyone drive his Lexus."

I hadn't asked her if there was any chance Myles may not have been the driver. She offered the observation, her way of dealing with the unexpected loss.

Jana removed her sunglasses and placed them between us on the table. I hadn't told her I'd seen Myles standing beside the fire truck. I didn't know if I would.

It was Jana who suggested we go to Bruno's—a questionable little coffee shop we used to frequent on Friday nights after football games. The place was showing its age. The orange vinyl booths were patched. The tabletops worn. The clientele was mostly elderly men nursing cups of coffee and reading the newspaper.

While we waited for a waitress, Jana played absentmindedly with her sunglasses. The other patrons began to recognize her. They whispered and pointed.

Pulling a tissue from her purse, Jana dabbed red, swollen eyes.

The other patrons took note. From their expressions they seemed to conclude I was the cause of her tears.

"Grant, isn't that the same shirt and suit you were wearing yesterday?"

Before I could answer, our waitress appeared holding a pot of coffee. She was a full-figured brunette with the face and body of a woman in her late forties wearing the clothing of a twenty-year-old—tight, black jeans with a clingy, white blouse—with mixed success. It did not flatter her bulging midriff. "What can I get you folks?" She set down the coffeepot and pulled out a pad. She looked to Jana first.

"Hey! Aren't you that reporter? Yeah! The one on Channel 2. Umm . . . Torres!"

"Jana," Jana said with her on-camera smile. She offered her hand. "And you are?"

"Alida," the waitress said, flattered to be asked. "It's not often we get a real celebrity in this dump."

"And this," Jana said, motioning to me, "is a world-famous author."

The waitress's brow furrowed as she looked at me, trying her best to recognize someone famous.

"Grant Austin just won the Pulitzer Prize for his biography of the president."

"The president? I didn't vote for him," the waitress said. "Is the prize a big deal?"

"The biggest," Jana said.

Waitress Alida offered me a half-smile and limp handshake. "Well then, congratulations." Turning back to Jana, she said, "Tell me, is your weatherman as loony tunes as he appears on television? I mean, what's with that 'Woooooeeeeeeeeeee!' he always does?"

The waitress noticed the tissue in Jana's hand and her swollen eyes. The woman turned motherly.

"Are you all right, dear?" she asked.

Like the others, the waitress suspected I was the source of Jana's tears. Her attitude toward me went from indifferent to hostile. Jana assured her she was fine.

"What can I get you, dear?" she asked Jana.

"A cup of hot tea," Jana replied. "With lemon."

"Coming right up." Reaching down, she patted Jana's hand, then snatched up the coffeepot and turned to leave.

"Um . . . Miss—" I called after her. "If I could have some coffee, please."

The waitress swung around with tight lips forming the thinnest line I've ever seen on a face. I turned over a mug that was already on the table, making it impossible for her to ignore my request. She held a pot of coffee. I had the mug. We were in a restaurant. How could she say no?

She thought about it. Then, with a grunt, she returned to the table. I met her halfway by extending the mug.

The streaming coffee cascaded down one side, picked up momentum at the bottom, and slid easy as you please up the other side cresting like an ocean wave onto my hand. The waitress continued pouring. Luckily gravity came to my aid, turning the black wave around and into the mug. Swallowing the pain, I held it steady until it was full. The waitress stomped away without apologizing.

Jana didn't see the assault. She was staring absently out the window.

I looked for napkins. There were none. So I dried my hand with my handkerchief.

"Did you get to see Myles yesterday?" Jana asked.

The understatement of the century.

"Jana, about yesterday," I said. "I'm glad you brought it up. I didn't know you were back in San Diego. Besides, the White House press corps handles all access to media events, and you know how they can be. Believe me, had I known—"

Jana dismissed my apology with a flip of her hand. "No worries, Grant It's all part of the job. You can make it up to me by giving me an exclusive interview before you head back to Washington."

"That would be something, wouldn't it? I look forward to it."

"Did you get to see Myles?"

"I went to his classroom following the assembly."

Jana leaned across the table and took my hands. "How was he?"

There was a spark in her eyes that went beyond concern. My jaw tensed. She still had feelings for him.

"He was . . . he was Myles," I hedged. "Only more so."

Still holding my hands, Jana looked away, lost for a moment in memories.

"This morning I went to see him again. That's when I learned of the accident."

"So the two of you remained friends over the years? That's nice."

Before I could correct her, the waitress arrived with Jana's tea. For self-protection I put my hands under the table.

Jana performed a tea ritual that had not changed since high school. Two packets of sugar in an empty cup. A long squeeze of lemon. Stir. Add the tea bag. Pour the water. Let it steep to the count of seven. Stir again. She'd told me once the origin of the ritual, but over the years I'd forgotten it. I think it had something to do with her grandmother.

"How about you?" I asked. "When was the last time you saw Myles?"

She stirred her tea for a long moment before answering. Not part of the ritual. "Oh, I don't know . . . it's been so long . . . years, really . . . I guess, not since college."

"That long?" Pleased to hear it, my reply came out more

enthusiastic than I'd intended. "Did you keep in touch? Emails? Phone calls?"

"Not so much. Not until he emailed me about you coming back. He sent it to my station address. It was all business, you know? He wanted to know if I'd be covering your speech at the high school. Which reminds me—"

She squeezed my hands and smiled one of her patented Jana smiles—an array of white pearls set between parentheses of adorable dimples. It was the kind of smile that could stop a battalion of marines.

"I haven't congratulated you properly for your achievement! I'm so proud of you, I could bust! I've told everyone I know I went to school with a Pulitzer Prize–winning author!"

She was more gorgeous than I'd remembered. Had her praise been a drug, I'd be an addict. The only thing that could have possibly made the moment sweeter would be if Myles Shepherd had been here to hear it.

"Was Myles excited about your achievement?" she asked.

"You know Myles. He congratulated me in his own way."

Jana laughed. "He was a man of few compliments, wasn't he? Sometimes you never knew if he was praising you or mocking you."

"Yeah, Myles could be strange at times." Here was the opening I'd been waiting for. "Speaking of which, when you were going out with him, did you notice anything . . . you know, out of the ordinary? Weird? Strange?"

Jana's smile melted faster than butter on a hot skillet. She pulled her hands away. "Please don't do that, Grant. Not now." She sat back and stared sullenly at her tea, then took a long sip as though she could swallow the uncomfortable moment and it would be gone.

But I couldn't let it go that easily. I had to know what she knew about Myles Shepherd while they were dating.

"In college, did Myles ever do anything that was . . . well, off the deep end? Possibly involve himself with a radical fringe group? Did he experiment with drugs?"

Her teacup clanked angrily against the saucer. "Why do you do that?"

"Do what?"

"That thing you do with Myles. Everything has to be a competition between you." Fresh tears filled her eyes. "Well, it can stop now, Grant. Myles is no longer a threat to you. He's dead."

"Jana, it's not what you think." I reached across the table with open hands. They remained empty. "Something happened yesterday with Myles that I can't explain. That's why I was going to see him this morning. I was hoping to clear it up. It's not personal. . . . Well, that's not exactly true . . . there is a personal element involved . . . but it's not what you think."

My eloquent argument failed to convince her.

"Exactly what happened yesterday?" she asked.

Of all the words in the English language, why did she have to choose those four? What was I supposed to tell her? That Myles glued my feet to the floor? That I saw him magically strip colors and titles from things in his office? That he had malevolent gargoyles living on his ceiling?

A warning alarm sounded in my mind. Neither could I tell her about Myles's possible involvement in an assassination plot against the president. She might be a friend, but she was also a news reporter for a television station.

"Well? Are you going to tell me?"

My internal waffling had raised her suspicions. "I can't," I said.

She took it personally. Gone were her happy reunion eyes. She was hurt.

"Jana, I want to tell you," I insisted. "It's just that—"

My phone rang. *I'm Too Sexy for My Shirt.* The ringtone for Christina.

I made no attempt to answer it.

Arched eyebrows waited for an explanation.

My face reddened. I forced a laugh. "Funny story about that ringtone . . . um, private joke."

Jana wasn't laughing. "Answer your phone," she said.

I didn't want to, but "I'm Too Sexy for My Shirt" was attracting the attention of patrons in nearby booths.

"I'll make it quick," I said, digging for the phone.

She turned her head and stared out the window so I wouldn't see how upset she was. She couldn't hide her reflection in the window.

I answered my phone. "Christina—" I said.

"Grant Austin, where have you been? First, you broadcast emergency messages all over Capitol Hill, then you go into hiding! What's going on?" She spoke in hushed tones, as though she was afraid someone might overhear her.

"Christina, we have to talk."

Jana shook her head.

There was a long pause on the other end of the line.

"All right. But make it quick." I heard panic in her voice. Christina never panicked. I've seen her stand in front of a roomful of heads of state and show no fear.

"I can't talk now," I said, glancing at Jana.

Jana's brow furrowed. She began gathering her things. "Don't let me stop you," she huffed.

She slid out of the booth.

"Who's there with you?"

"Jana . . . please don't go," I begged. "This isn't what you think it is."

"Who's Jana?"

I reached for Jana as she passed. She dodged my hand. "Jana, please! Christina, can you hold on just a second?"

Jana's heels clicked across the tile floor as she pulled out her smartphone. A few thumb-touches and she was giving an Uber driver her location.

"Christina, I need to call you back," I said, climbing out of the booth.

"Grant, no! You don't know what's going on here! Don't call me back. Do you understand? Under no circumstances are you to call me!"

I've never heard Christina so shaken. "What's going on there?" I asked.

Silence. The display indicated the call had ended. Shoving the cell phone into my pocket, I went after Jana.

"Hold on there, buddy," Alida said, blocking my path. "Somebody's got to pay the tab."

"I'll be right back. Just let me. . . ." I pointed at the door.

I tried to step around her. She moved to block me, shouting toward the kitchen. "Jorge! We got a deadbeat out here trying to skip out on his bill!"

The kitchen door swung open. A mean-looking, heavily tattooed cook strode out wiping his hands on a towel. If it was Jorge, I knew I didn't want to tangle with him.

"All right . . . how much?" I cried.

Through the plate-glass window I could see Jana standing in the parking lot, her arms folded.

Alida pulled out her pad. "Let's see . . . the lady had a tea with lemon. The gentleman . . ." She spoke the word like it was an obscenity. ". . . had a coffee." She looked up. "Was that one cup or two?"

"Here," I said, slapping a ten-dollar bill on top of her pad. "That should cover it."

I don't know how the Uber driver got there so quickly. Through the window I could see Jana climbing into the backseat. By the time I was out the door, the car was pulling out of the parking lot. The last I saw of Jana was the back of her head in the rear window.

The door to Bruno's opened behind me. Waitress Alida watched Jana's departure with an expression of mission accomplished. "Hey, prize winner," she said. "Do you want your change?"

I knew she didn't mean it.

CHAPTER
5

Weariness wrapped itself around my shoulders like a shawl as I drove west on Interstate 8 toward my hotel. I hadn't slept in over twenty-four hours.

In that time I'd delivered a speech to an assembly of high school students who didn't want to hear it, endured the usual badgering of reporters at a press conference, been assaulted by an old classmate with some kind of voodoo or psychedelic drug, learned of a possible plot to assassinate the President of the United States, spent the night in a parking lot chatting with East Coast automated answering recordings, witnessed a fiery death on a freeway, thought I saw a ghost, and managed to infuriate a former girlfriend.

"Not a bad day's work," I muttered.

Before leaving the restaurant parking lot, I'd tried to reconnect with Christina. She wasn't answering, neither was there a voicemail message. She must have turned her phone off.

I also tried Chief of Staff Ingraham's office and got his secretary, Margaret. Finally, I thought, I was getting somewhere! Margaret liked me. She'd told me I reminded her of her little brother.

Apparently her little brother had ticked her off recently, because the voice on the other end of the line was very cold and very professional. Biting off the end of each word, Margaret informed me that Mr. Ingraham would not be available for the rest of the day, nor was it likely he'd be available to take my calls anytime soon.

Desperate now, I tried the president's private cell phone again. Even the service provider's computerized voice sounded miffed that I was calling again.

Lack of sleep was catching up with me. Like a horse at the end of a long journey, I headed mindlessly for the barn—the barn being the Red Lion Inn at Hotel Circle in Mission Valley.

I was functioning in three-word sentences. Take a shower. Order room service. Grab some sleep.

After my batteries were recharged I figured I'd fire up the laptop, jump online, and see if I could find some answers about Myles Shepherd and exactly what happened in his office.

I didn't have much to work with—a name and an experience I'm not sure I could put into words—but I'd started projects with less and researching was what I was good at.

With a game plan established I settled back and enjoyed the ride on rented genuine leather seats. In Washington my car was a rusting Ford Taurus that felt like it was kicking you in the pants every time it shifted into third gear.

Familiar landmarks whizzed past me. Grossmont Shopping Center. The community hospital. Freeway exit signs—Jackson Drive, Fletcher Parkway, College Avenue.

"Of course!"

I sat up so fast I nearly changed lanes, coming close to hitting a pest patrol truck beside me. Shrugging an apology, I filtered through the traffic toward the exit. Within moments I was swallowed up by the campus of San Diego State University with parking structures on one side and hillside classrooms on the other.

Despite the advances the Internet had made over the last few years, for anyone doing serious research, cyberspace still couldn't hold a candle to a determined, old-fashioned research librarian. My shower, nap, and room service would have to wait.

I descended the curved stairway into the subterranean atrium of San Diego State University library. Sunlight through the dome cast geometric shadows on the steps.

Approaching the circulation counter, I interrupted a coed in pigtails for directions to the research library. She glanced up from a copy of Schopenhauer's *The World as Will and Representation*, cracked her gum, and pointed down a wide passageway.

The underground hallway led to the heart of the facility, several stories of books and periodicals. To get there, I passed a row of glass cases featuring Indian artifacts from archaeological digs in Old Town, early San Diego.

The displays might as well have been mermaid sirens calling to me. There was no way I could walk by them without stopping to read the information cards.

I loved this stuff.

I breathed in the surroundings—the displays, the carpets, the photos, the books, the air-conditioning. This was my turf. This was where I felt at home.

Most people don't understand what a library does for me and I've given up trying to explain it to them. All I know is that I feel energized when I'm in one. My pulse quickens when I walk through the stacks. I feel like an explorer surveying an uncharted shore. Lost worlds are here waiting to be discovered. Ancient worlds; once glorious, now crumbled. Future worlds; no more substantial than the numbers or ideas or words of those who dream them. Mythical worlds. Worlds of limitless dimensions.

Libraries are medieval forests masking opportunity and danger;

every aisle is a path, every catalog reference a clue to the location of the Holy Grail. It is here that I become privy to the sacred songs of kings and the ballads of rogues. Here are tales of life-and-death struggles of other wayfarers as they battle personal dragons and woo fair maidens.

Walking down this hallway, I am a knight entering the forest in search of truth—the truth about Myles Shepherd and that carnival ride of sensations in his office; the truth about his involvement in the plot to assassinate the president; the truth about his death.

Having reached the research library, I went in.

"Grant Austin!"

My name echoed through the cavernous room. Every head in the library turned and looked at me.

The surprising thing about the outburst was that it prompted no immediate shushing from the library staff. For good reason. It was the reference librarian who was making all the noise.

She was a short, middle-aged woman wearing a long-sleeved white blouse and a man's black tie. Like a teenybopper catching sight of a rock star, she rounded the end of the counter and came toward me, her eyes electrified. "I can't believe it's actually you!" she gushed. "This is such an honor, Mr. Austin! Such an honor!" She teetered up and down on her tiptoes as she spoke, her interlaced fingers punctuating every syllable.

A pleated black skirt, white socks, and black patent-leather shoes completed her retro fashion statement. She didn't have the knees for it.

Before I could reply to her boisterous greeting, her expression clouded over. "Oh . . . please tell me you're not here for a signing!" she cried. "Please, please, please don't tell me that! Because if you are . . . well, they're not going to hang this one on me! You have to believe me, Mr. Austin, there is no way on God's green earth that I would miss a memo announcing a signing if your name was on it!"

"I'm not here for a signing," I assured her.

The woman's shoulders slumped in exaggerated relief. "Thank goodness! I can't tell you how glad I am to hear you say that!"

"Actually, I'm here to do a little research. Is there someone available who could assist me?"

Pressing one hand against her bosom as though she was taking a solemn vow, she touched my arm with the other hand. "Oh, Mr. Austin . . . it would be an honor . . . an honor, sir . . . to assist you," she gushed.

"Thank you, Ms—"

"Corbett," she said. "Please call me Kathy."

With a snappy about-face, Kathy returned to her post behind the reference desk, folded her hands on top, smiled, and said, "Name your poison!"

Behind her, a girl with straight, shoulder-length hair and large round glasses sat at a computer terminal entering data from a stack of cards. She glanced up at me and did a classic double take. Her eyes then darted to the end of the counter, and I understood how I'd been so readily recognized.

Propped up in a wire book holder was a copy of my book with the back-cover publicity photo prominently displayed to anyone working behind the counter.

"Would you mind?" the reference librarian said, reaching for the book.

She opened it to the title page. Dutifully, I smiled and autographed it. As I did, I noticed no one had checked it out.

"I suppose this is the noncirculating reference copy," I said. "If you'd like, I'd be willing to sign any circulating copies you have in the stacks as well."

Kathy corrected me with a smile. "Oh no," she said, "this is our circulation copy."

Circulation copy. Singular. Never checked out. Being an author can be a humbling experience.

She closed the book, patted it, and set it aside. "Now . . . how may I help you, Mr. Austin?"

"Yes, well . . . I'm researching a name," I said.

"Surname?"

"Um . . . no, I don't think so."

"Given name, then."

"Possibly . . . but I'm not—"

"Historical or contemporary?"

"Um . . ."

"Foreign or domestic?"

"Probably foreign, but not in the sense that . . . that makes sense."

She pursed her lips and cocked her head and looked at me as only research librarians can do. She was good at it. It was probably an expression she used at least a dozen times a day on freshmen.

Loud and clear was the unspoken question behind her expression: *How do you expect me to help you if you don't know what you're talking about?*

"Look, Kathy, I'm not certain, but the name may be rooted in mythology. It may be New Age. It may be the name of a fictional character. Or it may not be a name at all, it may be a title. I just don't know."

She nodded, encouraged to hear lucid sentences coming from my mouth. "All right," she said. "Let's approach this from another direction. Why don't you tell me the name, and we'll go from there."

"Semyaza."

"Semyaza," she repeated. Reaching for a slip of paper, she wrote the name down. "Semyaza. S-E-M-Y-A-Z-A?"

"That would be my guess."

Her eyebrows arched.

"I've only heard it spoken once," I explained. "I've never seen it written."

Putting on her researcher's face, Kathy turned to a computer monitor. She tapped in a few commands and waited. When the desired screen appeared, she typed in the name. Her eyes remained fixed on the monitor while the computer did its magic. "Hmm. Interesting," she said.

"What?" I leaned over the counter to see the screen, but she had it angled to prevent prying eyes. "What?" I asked again.

She punched a key and a printer jumped to life. It spat out a single sheet of paper which she grabbed and handed to me. "Why don't you start with these books," she said, "and I'll follow up on some leads on the computer."

The sheet contained a short list of call numbers.

Thanking her, I entered the stacks with printout in hand looking for the BT section. There were three books on the list. All of them with the reference call number BT966.2.

I found the BTs against the back wall and understood what the reference librarian had found interesting. I wasn't in the mythology section, as I had suspected; nor was I in the history, anthropology, or fiction sections. Section BT was reserved for books on New Testament theology.

Finding the three books on the list, I carried them to a table and dug in.

Moments later Kathy came walking up. "Somehow you don't strike me as the type," she mused.

"What do you mean?"

She set an open book in front of me. It was a collector's edition with full-color photographs of angel figurines. Displayed was a ceramic angel with a lute, a hand-painted angel with a trumpet made of resin, a guardian angel table clock, and a girl angel snuggling up with a polyester blanket. Prices ranged from $12.95 to $74.95.

Kathy the librarian held out for as long as she could, which wasn't long. She burst into laughter. "I'm sorry," she cried. "I couldn't help myself. Not after what I found. Here's the real scoop."

She set two printout pages from web sites she'd found on the Internet on top of the book. I glanced at them, then at her.

A reference librarian with a sense of humor. Go figure.

"There were more references, but they say pretty much the same thing," she said of the printouts.

SEMYAZA—Angel; of the rank of Seraphim. A leader of the angels who rebelled in heaven and cohabited with women. The two hundred angels under his command are divided into groups of ten, each with a prince.

The second printout was similar to the first:

Semyaza (Aramaic; Shemyahzah), which means "my name has seen" or "he sees the name." Possibly an indication that had the rebellion in heaven succeeded, he would have been granted the Archangel Gabriel's position, which he coveted. Semyaza was cast out of heaven with Lucifer. On earth, he is legendary for his corruption of humanity.

"Semyaza is the name of an angel," I muttered. "Which explains. . . ." I pointed to the book of figurines. "Very funny."

"You look like a man who enjoys a joke," she replied.

I stared at the printouts, not knowing what to think. What did any of this have to do with Myles Shepherd?

"You say you heard the name," Kathy said. "Do you mind if I ask where?"

"Um . . . from a high school teacher."

She shuffled through some other printouts she'd kept in her hand, placing one on top. "Is this him?"

The printout was from one of those web sites where people post their picture and personal information and invite friends to leave messages. The man in the picture had a large, oval face with straight jet-black hair down to his collar. He wore a goatee. His lips were black. And he wore round, wire-rim glasses. From his expression he appeared to have an upset stomach.

According to the bio, he was thirty-two years old and lived in Midwest City, OK. Under turn-ons he listed creative piercing; his favorite music was Black Sabbath, Kiss (the early albums), and Marilyn Manson. At the top of the page, next to his picture, there was a place for his name: Semyaza.

To me, this was funnier than the figurines. I laughed.

"Not him, I take it," Kathy said.

"No offense to Mr. Semyaza of Midwest City, but if a nationwide search were conducted to find the polar opposite of the man I know"—I tapped the printout—"this guy would win, hands down."

Kathy crumpled the printout and chuckled. "Would you like me to search some more, or have you found what you needed?"

"Give me a few moments to thumb through these books and I'll let you know."

"It's no problem, really! I'd be more than happy to search some more." Her eyes were eager, if not pleading.

"Thank you. Just give me a few minutes."

She stood there, staring at me with a silly grin on her face. I smiled at her, not knowing what she was waiting for.

She shivered pleasurably and cried, "I'm assisting a Pulitzer Prize–winning author!" With a squeal she did a little dance back to the reference counter.

The three books from the stacks were of little help. Using the index in the back of each one, I located the references to Semyaza. Without exception they were located in chapters on angelic beings and provided little additional information. Semyaza, as indicated by the printouts, was the name of an angel who aligned himself with Lucifer and was cast out of heaven.

Next, I noted the authors of the books. All three were professors of New Testament at conservative seminaries. One other thing had caught my attention. All three of the works were heavily footnoted, with one name appearing prominently in the citations: J. P. Forsythe.

Stacking the open books one on top of the other, I carried them to the reference desk. Kathy stood at the end of the counter, her head in an oversized volume. Opposite her was a young man, a student by the looks of him.

When she saw me coming, she swiveled the book around so that it faced the student and pointed to where he could continue searching. "Yes, Mr. Austin," she said, turning her attention to me.

I set the books on the counter. "All three of these authors reference the work of J. P. Forsythe," I said. "But they cite lectures or unpublished papers. I'd like to know who Forsythe is and if he's published anything."

She checked the footnotes. "Very good, Mr. Austin," she said. "Straight to the original source."

"This isn't my first time researching," I said good-naturedly. She laughed louder than was necessary.

A check of *Books in Print* revealed J. P. Forsythe had no published works.

"That's odd," Kathy said. "He's obviously a recognized authority. Well, if we can't find anything about a man's work, let's see if we can find something about the man."

I leaned on the counter as she pecked on the keyboard, paused, pursed her lips, and pecked some more.

"Ms. Corbett—" the student with the oversized volume interrupted.

Without taking her eyes off the monitor, the librarian waved a hand at him. "Just leave it on the counter."

The boy closed the book. He appeared to have another question. After a moment he walked away.

"Well! Look at this!" the librarian said, stepping back. "Your mystery source? He's local!"

"Forsythe is local? How local?"

"El Cajon. I found a reference listing him as a consulting editor for the *Evangelical Quarterly*, which says he's a professor of theology and the New Testament at Heritage College in El Cajon. Um . . . that was two years ago. Hold on . . . let me double-check."

Fingers flew over the keyboard. Her right hand moved to the computer mouse. "Let's see . . . Heritage College web site . . . faculty . . . Department of Theology . . . there you go!" She turned to me with a smile. With the satisfied grin of someone who had just solved a riddle, she said, "Your boy's still teaching at the college if you want to talk to him!"

CHAPTER
6

Convinced that some of the answers might be found in El Cajon, I retraced my steps, despite a growling stomach and a much-anticipated nap.

There comes a time in the course of every research project when relationships begin to appear between pieces of information and you get your first hint of the total picture. That moment came for me as I was leaving the library.

Walking back through the underground passage, past the Native American displays, I remembered some indigenous tribes used peyote while undertaking spiritual quests. A hallucinogenic plant, the peyote altered their state of perception.

The one thing of which I was certain was that while I was in Myles Shepherd's office, my state of perception had most definitely been altered. Semyaza was the name of a spirit entity. The pieces fit.

I began to formulate a theory. I had been fine when I arrived at the high school and throughout the assembly. It was in Myles's office that reality took a vacation. Somehow, he'd drugged me. If I knew what substance he'd used, I could probably figure out the delivery method.

We chatted while the drug took effect. I began to hallucinate and, before I passed out, Myles performed some kind of victory ritual in Semyaza's name. It was the only conclusion that made sense. Myles Shepherd was a member of some New Age cult that worshiped the angel Semyaza. Did Jana know about this? She'd gotten upset when I asked her about his activities in college.

The parking lot fit the theory too. The drug wore off and by morning all that remained were a few lingering aftereffects.

What about seeing Myles at the scene of the accident? Hallucinogenic flashback.

It all added up. The remaining question was, Why? I had a theory for that too.

Two pieces of the puzzle formed the basis of my motivation theory. First, the assassination threat. Somehow all of this was tied in to a plot to assassinate the president. I had to assume the threat was real and that Myles was not working alone. Second, Myles Shepherd's ego figured in. When he learned I had been invited to give a speech at our alma mater, that I would be returning as the conquering hero complete with press corps, he couldn't stop himself from boasting about the plot. He was aching to tell me he knew the final, unwritten chapter of my book.

This was vintage Myles Shepherd. He was forever predicting his victories. At the end of our junior year, he boasted he would be senior class president. He was. He boasted he would be valedictorian. He was. He boasted he would be the tennis team's Most Valuable Player. He had the trophy to prove it.

Of course he knew there was a risk in revealing the plot. He knew I'd try to stop him. So he devised a way to discredit me. If I notified the Secret Service, when they questioned me about the details of the plot it would also come out that I saw the alphabet dance across the room. So much for my credibility.

I had to give Myles credit. He might have gotten away with it. His plan was solid. The only thing he hadn't counted on was dying.

The irony of his death intrigued me. It had a Twilight Zone twist to it. An elaborate plot to assassinate the President of the United States thwarted by a common freeway accident.

But it wasn't over. I had to assume Shepherd's partners would continue with the plan to kill the president, even without him.

I was hoping the name *Semyaza* would help me figure out how to stop them. Myles had selected the name for a reason. If I could learn its significance, it might lead me to the conspirators. Professor J. P. Forsythe was the man holding the key to Semyaza.

It was nearly noon and eastbound freeway traffic was still sluggish. It had yet to recover from the accident.

My plan was to take care of business at Heritage College, then head back to the hotel for a nap. I'd call Jana and try to talk her into a late dinner. I wanted to patch things up with her before returning to Washington, DC. Then I'd grab a red-eye flight home. Come morning, I'd start knocking on White House doors until I got someone to listen to me.

Small colleges attract prospective students with their small teacher-to-student ratios. Large universities advertise programs, facilities, and faculty credentials. The moment I stepped into Heritage College's library, I was reminded why I chose to attend a major university.

The entire library could have fit inside the domed atrium at San Diego State University. There was no circular descending staircase and no subterranean passageway. It had a front door, a circulation desk, and rows of closely spaced metal bookshelves in what appeared to be a converted elementary-school classroom.

Upon arriving at the college, I'd begun my search for Professor Forsythe in the faculty building. He wasn't in his office. A student who was scanning the Employment Opportunities bulletin board suggested I try the library. Which I did. Another student at the circulation desk directed me to the study area in the far corner.

I found two men seated at a table beside a wall of windows that overlooked a distinctively Southwestern garden with a variety of cacti and rocks.

One of the men had his back to me. He was lecturing. He spoke in a hushed tone, but it was definitely a lecture. The other man, seated in a wheelchair, hung on every word as though it was gospel truth.

The lecturer had the shoulders of an all-American lineman. It amused me to think that a professor of theology had at one time played football. Most of the college linemen I'd met would have defined eschatology as the study of Eskimos.

The man seated at the end of the table was older. He had a full head of white hair and intense, blue eyes. I recognized the type.

His kind were retirees or widowers, or both, who hated golf. To pass time, they reenrolled in college. They took a single class per semester, devoted their entire life to it, treated the professor as their best friend, and inevitably succeeded in blowing the top off the class grade-point average, causing serious damage to all the other students who were taking a full load, working, and trying to have some semblance of a social life.

In this case, instead of being retired, the man was disabled. He sat with his chin cupped in one hand and showed all the signs of hero worship.

On behalf of all the students whose grade-point averages he was undermining, I felt no pangs of remorse interrupting this one-course wonder.

"Excuse me, Professor Forsythe?"

The lecture came to an abrupt halt. His shoulders tensed at the interruption.

"Professor, I apologize, but I must speak to you. It's important."

He refused to turn and acknowledge me.

I recognized the power-play tactic. Politicians in Washington are masters at playing power games. Here, if the professor let me interrupt, he would lose control. By not acknowledging me, the professor retained control by forcing me to return at a different time, thus admitting his schedule was more important than mine.

I refused to be intimidated. This wasn't Capitol Hill—it was a small college in east El Cajon. The least he could do was have the decency to turn around, even if it was to tell me to go away.

"Professor, I'm sorry if this is a bad time, but it's imperative I talk to you today."

The man in the wheelchair checked his watch. "It's later than I thought," he said. "You're right, I'm afraid this is a bad time. I have a class starting in a few minutes. If you'll check with my assistant, maybe we can find some time for you." He turned in the direction of the book stacks. "Miss Ling!"

An attractive young Asian woman stepped from between the rows of metal shelves. Brilliant black hair fell to her shoulders and swayed with each step. Her attire separated her from the other female students, whose standard uniform seemed to be jeans and a sweatshirt. She wore stylish, black slacks and a silky, red-and-white blouse with splashes of color that suggested flowers. She moved to the professor's side and looked as though she belonged there.

"Miss Ling," the professor said, "this young man would like to make an appointment with me for today."

She glanced at me and shook her head. "I'm sorry, Professor," she said. "You have no time available today."

"You're Professor Forsythe?" I asked.

The man with the broad shoulders still hadn't moved. He sat hunched over. His head down. He acted as though we weren't there.

"Professor, I apologize," I said, this time to the man in the wheelchair, "but it's urgent I speak to you. I'm flying to Washington, DC, tonight."

"DC? Do you live there?"

"I have an apartment there. Don't use it much." I stretched out my hand to him. "Grant Austin."

Some men feel at a disadvantage shaking a man's hand from a seated position. Not this man. Seated, he was a presence to be reckoned with. He had a prominent nose, intelligent, sky-blue eyes, and an easy smile. He spoke with the slightest hint of a Scottish brogue. "You're a lobbyist?" he asked.

"He's a writer," Miss Ling said.

Our heads turned toward her in tandem.

"You know Mr. Austin?" the professor asked.

"Of him," she said.

"Are you acquainted with his work?" the professor asked.

"You've read my book?"

She spoke to the professor. "He's written a biography of the president. It won the Pulitzer."

The professor was delighted. "The sitting president? Do we have it?"

Without so much as a glance at me, Miss Ling went to find the book.

Leaning toward the man hunched at the table, Professor Forsythe said softly, "I suppose we can continue this tomorrow?"

The man said not a word. He shoved back his chair and rose to impressive height. His broad shoulders seemed to unfold even broader. His bearing was powerful, knocking me back a step.

To the professor, he confirmed, "Tomorrow."

Turning to leave, he looked at me for the first time. His face registered surprise, then anger and distaste. He paused. His eyes turned hard as marble, like those of a Greek statue. His mouth twisted with such deep loathing I felt a strong compulsion to apologize, though I didn't know for what.

The moment passed and he strode away.

His reaction to me hadn't gone unnoticed. The professor was intrigued. "Who did you say you are?" he asked.

Miss Ling returned with my book. She handed it to the professor who examined the cover, front and back. He compared me to my publicity photo with a chuckle. He scanned the copy on the dust-cover flaps, the table of contents, and the first few pages. After that, he began thumbing.

"Have you read it?" he asked without looking up.

"Yes," Miss Ling replied.

"And?"

Miss Ling shot a nervous glance in my direction. "It won the Pulitzer."

The professor lowered the book "That's not what I asked."

I sensed a bad review coming. If she liked the book she wouldn't have hesitated to say so.

"Pedantic," she replied. "Contrived. A public relations piece."

"What?" I cried. That was the second time in as many days someone called my writing pedantic. I liked it even less the second time around. I rose to my book's defense. "Miss Ling, I'll have you know—"

My book hit the table, cutting short my rebuttal. "Miss Ling," the professor said.

On cue she began gathering up papers and books from the table in preparation to leave.

The professor placed a hand on her arm. "Miss Ling. I'm going to stay here and talk to Mr. Austin. Please start my class for me."

Miss Ling scowled. She directed her displeasure at me.

The professor gave her instructions. "They're supposed to have read the chapter on General Revelation," he said. "Discuss the material with them. If it becomes apparent they are ill-equipped for the discussion, give them a pop quiz. There's a list of questions in the front of my book."

Her gaze was dark and cold and unwavering. She didn't like me. "Miss Ling?"

She gathered up her things and was gone.

The professor folded his arms. "Two for two, Mr. Austin. Do you always have this effect on people?"

I was as perplexed as he was amused. "Honestly, Professor, I'm a very likable guy."

The professor motioned toward a chair. "How about if you have a seat and explain to me what's so important it's keeping me from my class."

"Yes . . . well. . . ." Now that I'd gained a hearing, I wasn't sure how to begin. I took the chair vacated by the brooding giant. "All right, I'm going to mention a name and I want you to tell me if you recognize it."

"Are you testing me, Mr. Austin?"

"Believe me, Professor, that's not my intention. If you'll indulge me."

I took his silence as consent. I let a significant pause cleanse the air, and I readied myself to judge his reaction. "Semyaza." He didn't blink.

"Do you recognize the name?" I asked.

"I do."

"Can you tell me in what context?"

Tilting back his head, he studied me a moment. "No," he said.

"No?"

"I prefer you to set the context, Mr. Austin."

His reluctance indicated he was leery of my intentions. Fair enough. He didn't know me. "What if I told you I might have met someone who is using the name Semyaza for reasons unknown. What would you say to that?"

"I'd say the phrasing of your question indicates you've been hanging around too many politicians."

I grinned. "All right. Let me rephrase."

"Now you sound like a lawyer." The man had a quick wit and wasn't afraid to use it. I like that in a professor.

I tried again. "What would you say if I told you I met someone who called himself Semyaza?"

"I'd say someone was playing a practical joke on you. Now, if you'll excuse me, I have a class to teach."

"Professor, wait! Please, this is important. Have you heard the name Semyaza used in any other context than . . . than . . ."

"Than what, Mr. Austin?"

I swallowed hard. "Than angels," I said.

He leaned back. "First, you tell me you've met someone named Semyaza. Then, you ask me if Semyaza can be anything other than an angel. Mr. Austin, are you telling me you've seen an angel?"

"No! An angel? Of course not! It's just that . . ." I sighed heavily. "Frankly, Professor, I don't know what I saw, or if I really saw it."

For a long time, the professor said nothing. "What is it you want from me, Mr. Austin? You're an intelligent man. I find it hard to believe you came all this way to ask me something you could have looked up in an encyclopedia."

I leaned forward, forearms on knees, and stared at my hands. Why was I so reluctant to tell him what I saw? What's the worst he could say to me? Taking a deep breath, I said, "I had an experience I can't explain. An unusual encounter. Highly unusual. And during that encounter, I heard the name Semyaza."

"You heard the name?"

"Yes."

"Spoken aloud, or in your head?"

I had to stop and think. I closed my eyes and tried to hear the voice again. I remembered it being unmistakably strong. Thunderous. I not only heard it, I felt it. It shook the room.

"It was audible," I said with conviction.

"Tell me exactly what you heard."

"Well, it didn't sound like a single voice, but more like a chorus of voices. It said, 'I am Semyaza. Tremble before me.'"

The professor cupped his chin in his hand and thought. When he looked up, he reached for my book. "Tell me, Mr. Austin," he said. "What exactly is your relationship to the President of the United States?"

The sudden change of topic caught me off guard.

"Um . . . I hold no official position in the White House, if that's what you're asking, though I have access to it. I have a desk at my disposal for the next six months while we publicize the book. I'm a freelance writer. But what does this have to do with—"

"What brings you to California?"

"I'm an alumnus of Singing Hills High School. I came back to speak at an assembly."

"That explains all the news trucks on Madison Avenue yesterday. It made me late for class." He set my book in his lap and folded his hands on top of it. "So, Mr. Austin, describe this encounter you had. When did it happen?"

"You believe me?"

"Let's just say I'm being polite. I don't know what you're up to, but you don't strike me as a man of guile. And, quite frankly, Mr. Austin, you intrigue me. I've never seen people take such an instant dislike to anyone like they do you."

"Do you know of any good Dale Carnegie courses?" I deadpanned.

"The encounter. When did it take place?"

"Yesterday. Following the assembly."

"Where?"

"At the high school."

The professor's eyebrows arched.

"In a teacher's office."

He laughed. "That's where you heard the chorus of voices, in a high school teacher's office? Are you acquainted with the teacher?"

"We were high school rivals."

"And did he or she also hear the voice?"

I hesitated. "Not exactly."

How far was I willing to go with this? If word got out the president's biographer was hallucinating in California or consorting with gargoyle spirits, it was all over for me. The tabloids would eat it up.

To his credit, the professor respected my hesitation. He didn't press me.

"I went to his office to gloat," I said.

As concisely as possible I narrated my history with Myles Shepherd and described how he tried to claim credit for my book's success, which prompted the professor to examine it for a third time.

"Is that when he told you to tremble before him?" the professor asked.

He sensed there was more. I could see it in his eyes. Somehow knowing that made the telling easier.

I told him how the light from the classroom stopped at the office threshold; how I was rendered immobile; about the gargoyle things in the corner; how the room trembled and Myles Shepherd changed into a being of incredible light, all at once wondrous, then painfully draining; how the gargoyle things plunged into me; and how it all climaxed with the thunderous command to tremble before Semyaza.

Throughout the narration, the professor remained solemn. Stoic.

I described what it was like sitting in the parking lot, the muddy colors and nauseating odors. It surprised me how easily it all came out once I started, and how relieved I was to be able to tell someone. I told him everything. Everything except the part about the plot to kill the president. I left that out. I'm not sure why—it just seemed the right thing to do.

With a toss of my hands I signaled the end of my tale. He said nothing at first, just stared thoughtfully out the window at the desert garden. When he spoke, it was as though he dredged up his voice from a deep pit.

"A hideous beauty," he said.

His response was so unexpected, I didn't catch it the first time. He repeated it for me.

"A hideous beauty. Wondrously alluring. Incredibly evil."

"That's it!" I cried. "That's it exactly!" A sense of relief washed over me. He not only believed me, he understood!

"Where is he now?" the professor asked.

"Myles? Well, actually, he's dead. Killed this morning in an accident on the freeway."

The professor's jaw clenched. His hands balled into fists. "No," he said. "He's not dead."

"I saw the car, professor. The charred body. It was him. You have to know Myles. He's not the sort of guy who would loan his car to—"

"That wasn't him," the professor snapped. "Believe me, he was not killed in that car." Anger flashed in his eyes. So strong was his reaction, it took him a moment to fight it back.

My book hit the table with a thud.

"Why you?" he said.

"I beg your pardon?"

"Why you? What aren't you telling me?"

The question hit me hard. How did he know I was holding something back?

The book lay between us.

He was an intelligent man. He could see that this wasn't about a freelance writer. This was about the president. It was a logical conclusion.

But matters of national security were not something to be taken lightly. Telling a theology professor about an assassination plot against the President of the United States before warning the president himself didn't seem wise. Then again, I'd come this far. Maybe he could help me understand how Semyaza fit into the plot.

I decided to take a chance on him. "He told me my work wasn't finished. That I was to write one final chapter. A chapter that would record the president's assassination."

The professor nodded an emotionless nod. Did nothing alarm this man?

He released the brakes on his wheelchair. "Mr. Austin, I suggest you find yourself a very big hole and hide in it."

He wheeled himself toward the exit.

"Wait! That's it?" I ran after him. "Find a hole and hide in it? We're talking about the President of the United States!"

The professor wheeled around to face me. He was all business. "A man doesn't write an officially sanctioned biography of the president," he said, "without having contacts in the White House. I assume you've contacted them and warned them about the plot."

"I've made several calls."

"And I further assume they have alerted the president and the Secret Service?"

My face flushed. "No one will take my calls. It doesn't make sense. There must be some kind of—"

"Uh-huh." Having made his point, the professor wheeled around and headed for the door. He called over his shoulder, "A big hole, Mr. Austin."

"I can't do that!" I shouted, library or no library.

He wheeled out the door. I was right behind him.

"I've got to stop them . . . whoever they are."

This time when the professor turned to face me, he did it so suddenly I almost ended up in his lap. "There is nothing you can do," he said. "You can't stop them. They've been doing this sort of thing for millennia."

His words hit with paralyzing force. Those were the exact words Myles Shepherd used.

CHAPTER
7

I STOOD IN FRONT OF THE LIBRARY AND WATCHED PROFESSOR J. P. Forsythe coast expertly down the handicapped ramp. I'd come all this way for nothing. When a man doesn't want to talk to you, you can't make him, right?

Wrong. Something in my gut wouldn't let it end like this.

"What aren't you telling me?" I called after him.

He acted like he hadn't heard me.

I hurried after him. Didn't run. With classes in session the campus wasn't exactly busy, but there was something about chasing after a man in a wheelchair that didn't feel cool. I closed the distance between us.

"What aren't you telling me?" I said to the back of his head.

"You don't want to know," he replied.

"At least tell me what you know about Semyaza. The basics. A thumbnail sketch. Is he bigger than a breadbox?"

"Use an encyclopedia," he snapped. "If you look it up yourself, you'll remember it longer."

He wheeled up a walkway toward double glass doors that opened to a wing of classrooms. I knew once he got inside I'd lose him to his class.

"Professor—" I pleaded.

"A big hole, Mr. Austin. Find a big hole."

He reached for the door.

I stepped past him and blocked the door from opening with the flat of my hand.

"That's it!" I cried.

"Step aside, Mr. Austin," the professor said icily. "I have a class to teach."

"I get it now—you're running, aren't you? You're scared and you're running. That's it, isn't it? All this talk about finding a big hole. You're advising me to follow your example, to hide under the covers and pray for morning. Heritage College is your hole, isn't it, Professor? Your hideout from the scary things of the world."

The professor yanked at the door. I held it closed. I was right. I knew I was right.

"You're hiding in the footnotes, down at the bottom of the page in six-point type, wanting to be the authority, but not wanting to be the target. You hand other authors the ammunition, content to let them fight on the front lines while you dwell safely in the obscurity of a little college nobody's ever heard of."

He yanked hard at the door with surprising strength.

"What is it you're afraid of, professor? What is it that scares you so much? What aren't you telling me?"

He released the door, backed away, and took off—I presume toward another door into the classrooms. Maybe he was heading for the security office. At this point, I didn't care. I wasn't going to let him go. I grabbed the grips on the back of his chair. There must be at least a half-dozen laws both civil and moral about restraining a handicapped man against his will, but I held on. His forearms bulged as he strained to break free.

"Is it Semyaza? What is it about that name that frightens you?"

"You don't know what you're talking about," he said, his head down, straining like a dog on a leash. "Semyaza isn't someone you dismiss lightly."

"Someone. You said, someone. So Semyaza is a person. You've had dealings with him?"

"Not directly."

His arms went limp. The grips no longer fought me. I stepped around the chair and faced him.

"But you know of him, Semyaza," I said. "He's not just a name or a legend. He exists. And he scares you."

The professor's head snapped up suddenly, his eyes wide and glistening with tears. "OF COURSE HE SCARES ME!" he screamed.

The ferocity of his response startled me back a step.

"Tell me . . . tell me what you know."

"You don't want to know what I know."

A moment of silence passed between us.

"Is he an angel?"

The professor looked around. At first I thought he was going to make another run for it, but then he said, "Over there."

His arms limp and defeated inside the chair, he made no effort to wheel himself, so I pushed him to a cozy circular landing overlooking the parking lot. A round cement table was ringed by three matching benches. The view of the valley was a modest one. A familiar breeze which reminded me of my tennis days on courts less than a mile from here kept the porch comfortable.

"You don't know what you're getting into," the professor said. His words were measured. He gazed absently at the hazy view, but it seemed to me he was seeing not the valley, but scenes from his past.

I chuckled. "That's obvious," I said.

I do that. Laugh at inappropriate times. It's how I face fear. I sat on one of the concrete benches.

"But I don't see I have a choice," I added. "I didn't go looking for this. It came to me."

"That's the puzzle, isn't it?" The professor's eyes squinted at me. "Why you?"

I avoided his gaze. "That's the second time you've asked that question. I'm trying not to take it personally."

"What do you want to know?" he asked.

"I want you to tell me everything."

He laughed. "That would take months, if not years."

"Then tell me about Semyaza."

He took a sharp intake of breath. "I'll make you a deal," he said. "Question for question. I answer one of yours. You answer one of mine."

"Fair enough. Who's Semyaza?"

"He's an angel. My turn. When you said—"

"Wait, wait, wait . . ." I protested. "I want more than a three-word answer."

"To what end? You've already demonstrated a familiarity with sources that identify Semyaza. Do you want me to repeat what you already know? All right, he's a Seraph angel who is in league with Lucifer in the war against God. He has two hundred angels under his command, divided into groups of ten."

"But he's a myth, right? Like Zeus and Hermes and all the other residents of Olympus. You speak of him as though he's real."

"Of course he's real. My turn."

"Why does he scare you?" I blurted.

The professor shook his head. "That's an entirely different question. You'll have to wait your turn. How long have you known this man Shepherd you were telling me about?"

"Myles Shepherd? Since we were freshmen in high school."

"He attended school with you, the entire four years? What about after that? Have you had regular contact with him since high school?"

I started to object. The professor anticipated my objection. "It's not a second question. I'm asking for a clarification. The original question remains, How long have you known him?"

"All right. Yes, he attended high school with me the entire four years. Until yesterday, I hadn't seen him since graduation, but I did follow his career. Newspaper articles, things like that. He was California Teacher of the Year."

"Amazing," the professor mused. His brow furrowed. My answer apparently perplexed him.

"My turn," I said. "Why does Semyaza scare you?"

One of the professor's hands sought the other one out, as though to comfort it. "Among angels there is a hierarchy of power," he said. "Semyaza ranks near the top, though it's unclear how near, possibly second only to Lucifer. If indeed he is anywhere close to this region, it's not good. Not good at all. It would mean something truly horrific is about to happen."

A sense of foreboding came over me, an unsettled feeling that a dark cloud was parking over my life.

"My turn," the professor said. "Tell me about your parents. Do they still live in the area?"

I frowned, wishing I'd had the foresight to restrict the questions to nonpersonal subjects. I didn't want to tell him about my parents. But a deal was a deal. "My mother does. We're not close. My father died when I was three years old." I fell silent. I answered his question, or so I thought. He apparently didn't agree.

"And?" he prompted.

"Professor, what does this have to do with—"

"Answer the question. Tell me about your parents. How did your father die?"

"Suicide."

"Oh. I'm sorry."

His apology wasn't your standard gift-store variety apology, the kind you accept and discard. Heartfelt compassion filled his eyes. For some reason it surprised me. I didn't know exactly what to do with it.

"Um . . . thanks . . . yeah, well, my mother blamed me for his death. I don't know why. All I know is she never forgave him, and she took it out on me."

"What did your father do for a living?"

I shrugged. "Don't really know. I think he tried to produce some films. None of them ever made it to the screen. He inherited money. His mother, my grandmother, was Gigi Beaumont."

Whenever I speak of my grandmother, I always pause at this point to see if anyone recognizes her. She was big in her day, but now only old people remember her, and even then they need a little prompting.

The professor didn't appear to recognize her, so I told him about her. "She was an actress. She made several films in the late forties, early fifties, with Ricardo Montalbán, Fernando Lamas, Cyd Charisse."

Now the professor's eyes lit with recognition. He recognized those names. Everybody did.

"She began as a swimmer. Swam with Esther Williams." I named some of her better-known films. "*On an Island with You. Neptune's Daughter. Dangerous When Wet.*"

The professor had not seen any of them. I should have known. When those films were made he probably had his nose buried in a systematic theology text.

"My turn to ask a question," I said. "You're obviously an intelligent man, well-schooled, articulate, respected."

The professor laughed. "With a lead-up like this, you must have one doozy of a question."

"Do you believe in angels?"

"You obviously don't," he replied.

"I'm willing to admit there's a lot we don't know about this universe, that there might be life on other planets, and that they may have at some time in the past visited earth, giving rise to stories of supernatural visitations from heaven, but really, professor—angels?"

"They obviously believe in you," he replied.

I must have rolled my eyes or given some other sign of exasperation because the professor's teaching finger appeared.

"Hear me out," he said. "I have a point to make. Do you believe in the terrorist threat ISIS presents?"

"It's not your turn to ask—"

"Just answer my question. Do you believe ISIS presents a credible threat to you as a United States citizen?"

"I'd be a fool not to."

"Have you ever met a member of ISIS?"

"Personally? No."

"Neither have I. What if I were to tell you I don't believe ISIS exists. That I'm convinced ISIS is a myth, fabricated by our current administration to distract us from problem issues at home."

"All right, I'll play," I said. After a moment or two of thought, I answered. "I'd say that's exactly what ISIS would want you to believe. If they can get enough people to believe they are not a credible threat, better yet, that they don't even exist, it gives them greater freedom to carry out their attacks. But professor, surely you're not saying angels are—"

The professor leaned forward and spoke in earnest. "The real battle is spiritual, Mr. Austin. Everyday forces we cannot see influence our thoughts, our lives, our world." He paused to judge my reaction before continuing. "This isn't the world you think it is, Mr. Austin. Our borders are being breached by a hostile unseen force. There are no government funds to stop them. Homeland Security doesn't acknowledge they exist. Metal detectors are useless against them. Yet hundreds, possibly thousands, of enemy agents cross our borders every day.

"They're dedicated, insidious soldiers of destruction from a supernatural realm. They move among us virtually undetected. For millennia they have acted as sleeper agents, living among us, influencing human history."

You can't stop us. We've been doing this for millennia.

"The original war between good and evil never ended, Mr. Austin, and in these last days the battle is gaining momentum, and you can believe our friend Semyaza will play a key role. We can expect fresh assaults. Whether you choose to recognize the threat is irrelevant. Believing they don't exist doesn't make the threat any less real."

I had to give him this: He believed what he was saying. But I wasn't buying it. "Professor, I attended Sunday school. I've seen the pictures of angels and Joseph and Mary—"

He cut me off. "You asked me if I believe in angels, Mr. Austin. I do. I've seen them. Conversed with them."

I scoffed. "You've talked to angels?"

"Do you want to know what I believe, Mr. Austin? I believe something big is about to go down, and that for some reason you have been selected to play a crucial part in it."

CHAPTER

8

ANGELS. I DON'T THINK I'VE MET A GROWN PERSON WHO BELIEVES in angels since the fourth grade, when I played Joseph in a Christmas pageant.

Classes had let out at Heritage College. The professor and I sat in silence on the porch overlooking the parking lot. Clusters of students passed by, blowing off pent-up energy. Below us, for every car that vacated a parking space, two cars vied to replace it.

The professor and I retreated to our thoughts. He was probably hoping I was pondering what he'd just told me. I wasn't. My mind had wandered back to Sunday school and the fourth grade.

My mother never took me to church. When I learned other children went to church on Sundays, I asked her why we didn't attend. She said she didn't believe in church, then laughed. She thought that was funny.

Mother had her own ideas of worship. First, it was never done before noon because she never got up before then.

Second, when she did worship, she worshipped at the flat screen cathedral of television, mostly old black-and-white movies. Her version of responsive reading was saying lines in unison with the actors. Communion was taken with wine, usually two glasses per show.

Not long after I started the fourth grade, Mrs. Lipton, our next-door neighbor, invited me to her church which was having some kind of high-attendance contest, and she happened to be the fourth-grade teacher. As it turned out, her class won, and we were treated to a pizza party at ten o'clock one Sunday morning. The pizza tasted like pepperoni-flavored cardboard, but eating cardboard pizza was better than Mrs. Lipton having us take turns reciting the names of the apostles.

I've always wondered if Mrs. Lipton would have invited me to Sunday school had she been the teacher of the fifth grade.

The highlight of my Sunday school stint was the Christmas pageant. A stage production, I saw it as the possible debut of an acting career. After all, I came from good Hollywood stock. And I'd be lying if I didn't admit that the thought of my mother attending the performance and being proud of her actor son had crossed my mind.

When I informed Mrs. Lipton I wanted to audition for the lead role, she laughed. She said I was too big for the manger, which I learned was nothing more than a barnyard baby crib.

I asked her what the second-best role was. She laughed again and told me if I wanted that role I'd have to wear a wig and hold a doll in my arms. Even then the part had already been promised to Louise Stouffer, the daughter of one of the church's elders. I knew Louise from school. She was a pretty blond sixth-grader, meaner than a snake, with a poisonous tongue to match. Rumor had it she once outcussed a high school football player.

Mrs. Lipton cast me as Joseph because I was the tallest boy in the class. At first, I thought it was a choice role until I learned Joseph had no lines. All he did was stand next to Mary. The manger had a bigger part than Joseph.

When we started rehearsals, I requested a new assignment.

I wanted to be an angel. At least they sang. But you had to be a fifth- or sixth-grader to be an angel. Mrs. Lipton misinterpreted my request for a different role as stage fright.

"There's no reason to be nervous," she counseled me. "Nobody will be looking at you. They'll all be looking at Mary and baby Jesus."

As a prophet, Mrs. Lipton was uncannily accurate. On the night of the performance, I commanded as much attention as the cardboard scenery. During the manger scene, even though I was standing right next to her, when the spotlight focused on Mary, it missed me entirely.

Louise Stouffer sat there looking beatific, cradling a plastic doll in her arms. She was the only person with a solo. To a lullaby tune, the mouth that spewed curses at school sang with rapture about being the handmaiden of the Lord.

The doll that was used for baby Jesus was one of those dolls that closed its eyes when it was reclined. However, its left eye was broken, and the entire time Louise Stouffer sang her song, the thing stared up at me with one eye.

When the shepherds and wise men did their bit, my crepe beard started to itch something horrible. At first I resisted scratching it. But why? Nobody looked at Joseph.

No sooner had I lifted my hand than I heard a hissing sound coming from Louise Stouffer. Murderous eyes glared up at me.

"Your hand!" she hissed.

I looked at it, wondering what was wrong with it. Nothing I could see.

"It's in the light!" she hissed. "You're casting shadows on baby Jesus, you moron!"

The shepherds, who were third-graders, tittered.

She was right, of course. My hand was casting shadows on the baby Jesus and everyone in the auditorium seemed to notice, aided no doubt by the consternation of the production's leading lady.

I could have turned crimson with embarrassment and pulled my hand out of the spotlight, but for some reason I saw this as an opportunity for a little theatrical improvisation.

Directing the shadow of my finger to the tip of the baby Jesus's nose, I did what any father would do—"Gootchie, gootchie, gooo!"

That was my last Sunday at church. Mrs. Lipton came down sick and missed a couple of Sundays in a row. Soon after she quit teaching the fourth-grade class.

My mother didn't come to see me in the Christmas production, which was just as well considering how it turned out.

All this talk of angels reminded me of the fourth grade and the Christmas production and not being old enough to be an angel, and I wondered if the professor believed in the Christmas angels too. A couple of times I almost asked, but just couldn't bring myself to do it. Sitting around talking about angels. It's just not something grown men do.

"You've seen one," the professor said, breaking the reverie.

"You're still talking about angels, right?"

"In the library, a short time ago," he replied.

I grinned. He was pulling my leg. Big joke. I take him seriously and he retorts with, "I thought you didn't believe in angels?"

He stared at me deadpan serious.

"I've seen an angel?" I repeated.

He nodded.

I thought back. She certainly looked heavenly. Miss Ling had an aura about her that was striking, especially the way the tips of her hair brushed her shoulders as she walked. Her skin was pale and flawless, almost radiant.

But I wasn't biting.

"Do you really expect me to believe she's an angel?"

"She?"

Humiliation torpedoes come in all sizes. Some are as small as a single word.

The professor's guffaw was so loud he attracted the attention not only of those on the sidewalk, but several people in the parking lot below us. "You thought I was talking about Miss Ling?" he said through tears.

"No, of course not!" My protest had no legs, but I felt compelled to make it. "You were talking about the guy with the broad shoulders, right? I knew that."

"This is rich!" the professor said, wiping his eyes. "Miss Ling's going to get a kick out of this."

"Only if you tell her," I said with growing alarm. "You don't have to tell her."

"Tell me what?"

Miss Ling's timing couldn't have been worse.

"Tell me what?" she said again.

"Did the students give you any problems?" the professor asked her, giving me a momentary reprieve.

She handed his textbook to him. "We covered the material in the chapter," she reported. "I gave them their assignment for Wednesday."

An involuntary chuckle escaped the professor as he received the book and the report. He glanced at me, his eyes sparkling with mischief. I implored him silently not to say anything. "Thank you, Miss Ling," he said. Unable to resist, he added, "You're an angel."

We both burst out with laughter. Miss Ling didn't know what to make of us.

"You have an academic review meeting with Dean Atkinson in five minutes," she said. "You've already postponed it twice. This morning he cornered me and asked if you were going to be there. I promised him you would be."

The professor nodded. Placing the textbook in his lap, he started the wheelchair in motion. "Oh, Grant. Come to the library tomorrow

HIDEOUS BEAUTY

morning at ten o'clock. I'll introduce you to Abdiel. You can judge for yourself."

"Abdiel?" Miss Ling said, shocked. "You told him about Abdiel?"

"I'll fill you in later," the professor said. He disappeared around a corner.

I didn't know what to do with the invitation. I'd never been invited to meet an angel.

Miss Ling's heels clicked on the cement as she walked away.

"Miss Ling. A moment of your time?"

She turned around, polite but chilly. "Don't you have a job or something? Or are you so famous now that you no longer have to work?" She stood with attitude, one hip thrust out.

"How long have you known the professor?" I asked her.

Miss Ling gave me one of those "I don't see how that's any of your business" looks.

I explained. "It's just that he has some rather unusual concepts of reality."

"You could learn a lot from Professor Forsythe," she said.

"Are you one of his students?"

"Former student. Now I'm at the University of California, San Diego."

"Really? Do you mind if I inquire as to your major?"

"Yes, I mind," she said. She didn't appear to be joking.

I shrugged. "I didn't mean to—"

"Yes you did. Physics, to answer your question. I'm writing my doctoral dissertation in quantum physics."

"Impressive. But it surprises me. You strike me more as the comparative lit type."

She sneered at me. "Is that supposed to be some kind of clever quip, Mr. Austin? Or is it a lame attempt at a pickup line?"

Her persistent antagonism was wearing thin.

"I didn't mean anything by it," I said. "It's just that where I

–93–

attended school, the quantum physics students were geeky types who played *Dungeons & Dragons* and attended *Star Trek* conventions."

She turned and walked away.

I called after her. "Angels, Miss Ling? A woman of your obvious intelligence, doesn't it bother you that the professor believes in angels?"

She swung around with fire in her eyes. "I'll have you know," she said, "Professor Forsythe is the most brilliant, dedicated, compassionate man I know. If you were given two lifetimes, Grant Austin, you would never be half the man he is!"

"What's with the attitude? Ever since I arrived you've treated me with contempt. You've been rude and just plain mean. Are you taking it out on me because I look like some guy who dumped you? You don't even know me."

Her eyes squinted disdainfully. "Oh, I know you," she said. "I know all about you."

"We just met!" I argued. "What is it about me that ticked you off? The rumpled suit? Is that it? You took one look at my rumpled suit and concluded I was a slob, right? Well, I'll have you know, beneath this rumpled suit beats the heart of a nice guy."

"I suppose you think you're charming, don't you?" she shot back.

"Wait a minute, you can't say that wasn't charming. Admit it. You found me charming right then."

"Apparently, you never learned the difference between charming and childish. You think you can scuff your foot on the ground and say, 'Aw, shucks,' and you're being adorable. Well, let me tell you, Grant Austin, you're not the least bit adorable. You're disgusting, insecure, and needy."

"Needy? I'm not needy! I'm so far from being needy, needy is extinct in my world."

"Get a clue, Grant. When a woman looks for a man she wants a mature relationship, not a babysitting job."

I was definitely at a disadvantage. It was obvious Miss Ling was drawing on background material and I didn't know the source. "Just who have you been talking to?"

She grinned with sarcasm. "So, you recognize the description of yourself, do you?"

"You've obviously been talking to someone who knows . . . who *thinks* she knows me."

She mulled for a moment. I hadn't stopped her, but I had slowed her down a bit.

"Before attending UCSD," she said, "I earned a master's degree at State. Lived on campus. University Towers. Roomed with an incredibly talented woman who majored in broadcast journalism."

"Jana," I said. It was all coming together now.

"Between you and that reptile Shepherd, when I wasn't attending classes, I was helping her pick up the pieces of her life. For both being 'nice guys,' the two of you really did a job on her."

"Hold on just a second," I protested. "Jana and I split up . . . what? Ten years ago? We were a couple of kids back then. And she left me! How would you like to be called to account for something you did ten years ago?"

Miss Ling played her trump card coolly. "Jana called me this morning from a cab."

"Oh."

"That's it? That's your defense?"

"I can explain what happened this morning."

"And does the explanation have anything to do with the fact you obviously haven't grown up in the last ten years?"

"I was going to call her . . . I *am* going to call her after I leave here. Invite her to dinner. I want to work things out."

"And will Christina be joining you?" Miss Ling asked.

She walked away. This time I didn't stop her.

CHAPTER
9

FATIGUE STALKED ME FROM EL CAJON TO MY HOTEL ROOM IN Mission Valley, and I was ready to surrender to it. This time yesterday I was passed out on Myles Shepherd's office floor. I wouldn't call it a nap, but it was the last time I'd closed my eyes for any length of time.

I took a much-needed shower, left a voicemail for Jana, listened to Christina's phone ring a couple dozen times, grabbed a jar of peanuts and a soda from the honor bar, and crashed onto the bed.

Three hours later I awoke holding an empty jar. Peanuts lay scattered on the bed, the floor, and plastered to the side of my face. It could have been worse. I could have fallen asleep holding the soda can.

From my balcony I watched the sun expand until it was a huge orange ball. It dipped itself into the Pacific Ocean. I tried Jana's cell phone a second time, then tried calling her at the television station. They took a message.

The six o'clock evening news broadcast Jana's story of the freeway accident during the morning commute and the resulting traffic jam. I knelt inches from the screen and searched the crowd behind her, hoping to get a glimpse of Myles. I didn't, of course.

7:00 p.m. How much longer should I wait for Jana? Should I order room service?

Reaching for the remote, I sat at the foot of the bed and clicked on the television. The Los Angeles Angels were dominating the Devil Rays. I wasn't familiar with either team, and after a few innings my interest waned. I changed channels.

Click.

The Angels were still playing, only this time it was a movie, and heavenly angel Christopher Lloyd was lifting the baseball outfielder off his feet to make a miracle catch.

"It could happen!" I quoted the line with little J.P.

Click.

Redheaded angel Roma Downey was revealing her true identity to a suicidal artist. "I'm an angel, sent from God," she said with her soft Irish brogue. Special-effects lighting simulated a halo.

"It's nothing like that!" I shouted at the screen. "Trust me, I know."

I couldn't believe I'd said that. I knew nothing of the kind. This whole angel scenario was Professor Forsythe's theory, not mine. What I saw in Shepherd's office was a hallucination, not an angel.

But three angel programs in a row? What a coincidence, especially considering all the talk about angels today.

My thumb paused over the channel changer. I grinned. What were the odds of four programs in a row about angels?

Click.

John Travolta was the Archangel Michael. His wings were molting.

I stared dumbly at the television. This was beyond coincidence. It was downright spooky.

Click.

Angel Cary Grant swooped his arms and a Christmas tree was miraculously dressed.

Click.

Probationary angel Michael Landon adjusted his ball cap and climbed into a car driven by Victor French.

Scared now, I turned the television off. It came back on by itself.

Angel Clarence explained to Jimmy Stewart that every time a bell rings an angel gets his wings.

Click.

I didn't change the channel. It changed by itself.

Pluto the dog was torn between two opinions, with an angel on one shoulder and a devil on the other shoulder.

Click. Click. Click.

I pushed the Off button repeatedly.

Angel Nicholas Cage stood on a beach with a whole city of angels wearing trench coats and listening to the sun rise.

Click. Click. Click. Click. Click.

Feminine hands displayed a ceramic angel figurine on the shopping channel.

I dropped the remote. Reaching behind the set, I pulled the plug. The screen blinked out.

My hands were shaking.

"Now that was weird," I said.

I paced the room.

"Coincidence. Malfunction. Had to be."

I stared at the television's electrical plug.

I ordered room service. Feeling the unmistakable need to distance myself from anything even remotely related to heaven, I ordered a burger and fries and a dessert, Chocolate Sin.

---

10 p.m. Jana obviously wasn't going to call.

"Why am I still here? I should be thirty thousand feet over Kansas by now, halfway home."

I kept telling myself I'd stayed because of Jana, that I wasn't staying because I'd been invited to meet an angel. "I'd be a fool to go out there in the morning."

Big joke on Grant. I knew what would happen. I'd show up and the professor would give me some lame excuse about the angel being called away suddenly to deliver an emergency scroll, or administer a plague in Kazakhstan, or transport a holy man in Tibet to heaven on a fiery prayer rug.

"It would have to be a Tibetan holy man," I said. "Who'd believe an angel could even find a holy man in Washington, DC?"

I chuckled at my own humor and crammed a cold fry into my mouth.

"Now if the angel looked like Roma Downey, that would be a meeting worth going to," I said.

———

10:30 p.m. I climbed into bed and turned out the lights. I was tired, but not sleepy. My eyes were closed, my mind active.

Why Semyaza? I asked myself.

It had to be a code name. The other participants in the assassination plot no doubt had similar names.

The thing that disturbed me about the name Semyaza was that historically it was the name of a subordinate, an angel lieutenant. Semyaza answered to Lucifer, and Myles Shepherd wasn't the kind of person who answered to anyone. It was a matter of ego.

But, as unlikely as it seemed, I had to allow for the fact that given the scope of the plot, Myles might be someone's subordinate. Did that mean the code name of the top guy was Lucifer? Or better yet, Satan?

"This is ridiculous. What am I doing here?" I said to the darkness.

Throwing off the bedcovers and chastising myself for letting a small-college professor pull me into his religious fantasy about supernatural beings, I got dressed, threw my stuff into my travel bag, and ordered a cab to take me to the airport.

I booked a flight that would get me to Reagan National Airport in Washington, DC, by 9:40 the next morning.

At thirty thousand feet over Omaha, Nebraska, my eyes were too tired to read but not tired enough to sleep. I've never been able to sleep on planes. My legs are too long, and the headrest hits me in the back of the neck. The best I can do is doze.

The cabin was dark. I had an aisle seat four rows from the back galley. Flight attendants floated up and down the aisles like night fairies. A dozen or so reading lights were on, but mostly people slept. Some wore earbuds or headphones.

My back hurt, and my right leg had fallen asleep. I shifted positions for the hundredth time. My eyes were closed, and I was dozing when I heard a skittering sound in the overhead luggage bin across the aisle.

Awake now, I focused on the bin and listened. Nothing. Just the constant drone of the engines.

A man with heavy jowls, seated next to the window across the aisle, squirmed, folded his arms, and laid his head against the window, his eyes closed. His cheek twitched nervously as he slept.

I tried folding my arms to see if it would help. My eyes drooped closed.

Scritch. Scritch. Scritch.

There it was again! Something was in the overhead bin. Something alive.

Scritch. Scritch. Scritch.

It sounded like some kind of rodent.

Scritch. Scritch. Scritch.

I pushed the Call button. A flight attendant responded immediately. She turned off the call light. "Can I get you something?" she asked.

Thick was the best way to describe her—thick middle, thick legs, thick neck. She appeared to be Scandinavian, with a slight accent and a motherly demeanor.

"I think there's something in the overhead bin," I said, keeping my voice low. "Something alive."

She turned and looked at the bin. "Alive?"

"An animal. Maybe a rodent. I heard scratching."

We both listened.

Nothing.

"I don't hear anything," she said.

To my chagrin, neither did I.

"I'm sure I heard something," I said.

She assessed me and apparently concluded I wasn't drunk or the practical-joker type. She pushed the Call button.

Another flight attendant appeared. Younger. Black hair. No-nonsense eyes. Before inquiring, she sized me up, the man with the problem that required a consultation of attendants.

"He says he heard a rat in the luggage bin," the first attendant reported.

"A rat?"

"I didn't say a rat," I protested. "I said I heard something. Something scratching."

People three rows in front and behind me were awake and looking at us. The word *rat* skittered from row to row.

"What do you think we should do?" the first attendant asked.

"Open the bin," the second attendant replied.

"What if there's a rat in there like he says?"

The first attendant took another assessment of me. "You're certain you heard it?"

"I'm sure I heard something."

She put her hand on the bin, not to open it, but to keep it from opening. Then she put her ear close to it.

"I don't hear anything," she said.

"Neither did I," the first attendant said.

Without taking her hand off the bin, the black-haired flight attendant asked if anybody else had heard scratching noises. If they had, nobody admitted it.

She thought a moment. "All right. Here's what we'll do."

She sent the first attendant to get a large trash bag. Then, she had everyone sitting within three rows of the bin get out of their seats and move a safe distance away. To protests the length of the plane, she had the lights turned on. Then she informed the pilot they might have a rat in a luggage bin. Within minutes the copilot was present to oversee the plan.

"Ready?" the second attendant asked.

With the first attendant holding the trash bag, the plan was to open the bin and brush anything that moved into the bag. Taking a linebacker stance, the copilot stood at one end of the bin. The second attendant would open the bin and man the opposite side.

"On three."

The copilot and bag-holding attendant indicated they were ready.

"One . . . two . . . three!"

The door to the bin flew open.

A gray streak fairly flew out of the bin and into the trash bag. People jumped. Gasped. Muffled screams.

"I got it!" the first attendant shouted, closing the bag with a stranglehold.

Something definitely was in the bag. But it wasn't moving. The attendant held up the bag to get a better look at it.

"Let me see," the copilot said.

She handed him the bag.

The copilot instructed people to step back. He looked inside the bag. His face registered disgust. He reached into the bag. A woman passenger squealed in protest. Ignoring her, the copilot pulled the rat out of the bag by its tail.

A gray, plush toy rat with big eyes and a silly grin.

"It appears we do indeed have a rat on board," he said. "Only it's a passenger."

He tossed the toy at me. I caught it.

For the next hour I stood in a corner of the back galley and endured the scorn of passengers, flight attendants, the copilot, and the pilot, who left the cockpit to lecture me on why there was no place for practical jokes on commercial flights.

I heard most of it. When I wasn't listening, I was thinking about what else was in the overhead bin with the plush toy rat—a Los Angeles Angels sports bag and ball cap, and a child's backpack decorated with angel wings.

When I was finally allowed to return to my seat, I avoided eye contact with the other passengers, buckled into my seat, folded my arms, and closed my eyes, though sleep was the farthest thing from my mind.

It wasn't five minutes later when I heard it again.

Scritch. Scritch. Scritch.

Same sound coming from the same bin.

Scritch. Scritch. Scritch.

I ignored it. I didn't care if the whole plane was crawling with rats.

Scritch. Scritch. Scritch.

Through half-opened eyes I saw a demon fall out of the bottom of the bin and plop onto the back of a seat. It was the same kind of creature I'd seen in Myles Shepherd's office, a three-dimensional spirit resembling a gargoyle.

It looked at me, then jumped onto the chest of the man with heavy jowls next to the window. He appeared to be asleep. The demon clung to the man's shirt, looked at me again, then clawed its way into the man's chest.

I looked around me, hoping someone else had seen what I'd just seen. No one had. Those who weren't sleeping were glaring at me and shaking their heads with disgust.

The man next to the window moaned and squirmed with a pained expression, but he didn't wake up.

In the front of the plane, a man was excusing himself as he stepped over the aisle-seat passenger in his row.

It was Myles Shepherd.

He looked at me. Nodded. Smiled.

Turning his back, he made his way to the front lavatory.

I bolted from my seat but was held in place by the seat belt. Clutching frantically at the latch, I freed myself and charged up the aisle.

A few rows in front of me a woman got up, blocking the aisle. She just stood there.

I tried to slip by her. "Excuse me," I said.

She refused to let me by. "Wait your turn," she said. Belligerent eyes glared at me from a well-wrinkled face.

"I'm going to the lavatory," I said.

"So am I, joker. Whatever happened to ladies first?" Mumbling something about the sad state of the world due to an absence of gentlemen, she made her way forward with a modified crawl, hand over hand clutching the backs of seats.

At first I danced anxiously behind her until I realized that in order to get back to his seat Myles would have to pass us.

Following the woman through the forward galley, when she reached for the lavatory door I said, "I believe it's occupied."

She swung the door open. "It is now, sonny."

I craned my neck to look past her. The lavatory was vacant. The woman pulled the door shut in my face. "Pervert," she said.

Bewildered, I glanced around. There was no place for Myles to have gone. No place to hide.

I asked the flight attendant if she'd seen a man of Myles Shepherd's description. She said no one had walked by recently.

It didn't make sense, but then nothing about Myles Shepherd had made sense lately. I retraced my steps to the row where I'd seen him exit.

In the window seat a young woman wearing earphones slept with her head against the pane. A curly-headed man occupied the aisle seat. He was hunched over a book of word puzzles.

"Excuse me, I'm looking for the man who was sitting in the middle seat. He's a friend. Do you know where he went?"

The curly-headed man looked at me, then at the middle seat as though he expected to find someone sitting there. "There's no one in that seat," he said.

"I know there's no one sitting in it now," I said. "He was sitting there earlier."

"No one has been in that seat all flight."

The puzzles must have done a number on this guy's brain. How could he sit next to someone for two hours and not notice him? "He just climbed over you to use the restroom!" I said. "No one has sat in that seat—"

Despite his protests, I reached over him and shook the shoulder of the girl in the window seat. From beneath bangs, sleepy eyes tried to focus on me.

"The man who was sitting in the middle seat, do you know where he went?"

She shook her head. "No one's been sitting there, dude."

Someone behind me took my arm. The black-haired flight attendant. "Is there a problem, sir?" she asked testily.

"I'm just trying to find my friend," I explained. "He was sitting in the middle seat and he's not there now."

"He's crazy," the puzzle guy said. "There's no one sitting there."

The attendant looked to the row's other occupant. "Is someone sitting in the middle seat?" she asked.

The girl shook her head.

"I just saw him!" I protested. "He climbed over this guy and went to the forward lavatory."

The attendant looked to the front of the plane. The forward attendant shook her head. "He asked me. I told him no one had walked by."

Having finished her business in the lavatory, the woman I'd followed up the aisle was making her way, hand over hand, back to her seat. She pushed her way past us, but not without comment. "If you ask me, he's a pervert," she said.

I have to give the airline personnel credit. To satisfy me, they politely checked the manifest and showed me the computer printout that indicated the seat in question was open. No one had occupied the seat the entire flight.

I was positive I had the right row. All the other rows around it were full.

My request—all right, it was more of an insistence—to check inside the pilot's cabin was met with an introduction to an air marshal who escorted me back to my seat.

For the remainder of the flight I pretended I was asleep, although in reality I spent the hours cursing Myles Shepherd. He'd haunted me with his success all my adult life; it was just like him to haunt me in death.

I knew one thing, though. If Myles Shepherd didn't want me going to Washington, DC, I was on the right track.

CHAPTER
10

Professor J. P. Forsythe stared out the library window. He did some of his best thinking here. It was quiet, and he was sandwiched between two things he loved: books on one side, a blue sky on the other.

Familiar footsteps interrupted him.

"It's ten o'clock. Do you think he'll come?" Sue Ling asked.

"Grant? No."

Setting an armload of books on the table, Sue Ling sat down. The professor studied her for a moment with an amused expression. "You were pretty hard on him yesterday," he said.

"I had my reasons." She looked away. It was her way of saying she didn't want to talk about it.

"He's on his way back to DC," the professor said.

"He called you?"

"Abdiel told me."

Sue Ling showed no surprise that the professor would get word of Grant's no-show from an angel.

"He visited me last night," the professor said. "Abdiel, not Grant."

Sue Ling's eyebrows rose. "That's unusual, isn't it?"

"He had news. It has to do with our Mr. Austin."

"Oh?" She made a poor attempt to feign indifference.

"Abdiel knows why Semyaza is interested in him."

"Why do I think that's not a good thing?"

"Because you know enough to be cautious."

"But not enough to be scared out of my wits?" she asked.

"Are you?"

"Yes. Shouldn't I be?"

The professor grinned. It had taken a little more than a year of working together for Sue Ling to treat him as an equal rather than a professor. He was comfortable with her familiarity. More than comfortable.

"Are you going to tell me?" she asked impatiently.

"It's not my news to tell. Mr. Austin will have to tell you himself."

She let out an exasperated gasp. "Why bring it up if you aren't going to tell me?"

"Abdiel brought other news."

"More news? Oh my. . . ." She rubbed her bare arms as though she'd suddenly felt a chill. It didn't go unnoticed.

"You know the account he's been narrating to me?" the professor asked.

"The history of angels."

"Yes, but more accurately, history from an angelic point of view."

"Always the professor." Sue Ling sighed.

"He wants me to write it down."

It took a moment for her to assimilate the news. She stared at him blankly, then said, "He's changed his mind."

"I think it was changed for him."

"I see. Is this because of Grant?"

"He didn't say directly, but I think so."

"Are you going to do it?" she asked. "You know the risk. Of course you know the risk. You know it better than anyone."

She was babbling. It wasn't like Sue Ling to babble.

"Yes, I know," he said. "It's not me I'm worried about. I want you to move back on campus. Work on your dissertation full-time."

Sue Ling's chair screeched loudly as she pushed it back abruptly and stood. "I don't see that that's your decision to make," she said. "And it hurts me that you'd even suggest it."

"If you won't do it for yourself, do it for me. How can I concentrate on the project if I'm worried out of my mind about you?"

She gathered up her books. "You'll just have to find a way, because I'm not going anywhere. In case you missed the memo, this isn't your personal battle. You're not the one who determines who fights and who doesn't."

The professor stared at her with sad eyes.

Sue Ling grew angrier. "Don't sit there with that hangdog expression of yours as though you have a say in this. You don't."

She whirled around to leave.

"I want you to reread Mr. Austin's biography," the professor said to her back. "Study it. Dissect it. Read between the lines. Grant told me Semyaza claimed credit for its publication. I want to know why."

Sue Ling turned back. Their eyes met in silent understanding. He was conceding. She accepted with a nod. "Don't ever question my loyalty again," she said, close to tears.

"I won't."

Sue Ling moved to his side. "This is really happening, isn't it?" she said.

"To quote Dante: 'Whatever plot these fiends may lay against us, we will go on. This insolence of theirs is nothing new.'"

Sue Ling sighed. "The world is crashing down around us and you're quoting Dante."

"It's who I am."

CHAPTER
11

WITH MY IDENTITY BADGE CLIPPED TO MY LAPEL, I APPROACHED the metal detectors at the White House. A queue of staff and personnel formed a line in front of me, routinely opening bags, purses, and briefcases for inspection. The chatter was the usual going-to-work banter but restrained. There's something about men with guns that puts a damper on things.

I'd taken a cab straight from the airport, after spending a couple of hours chatting with security over plush-toy pranks and false alarms. Seeing Myles's ghost onboard set off an alarm in my gut that had no Snooze button. Time was short. The president was in danger. I had to get someone to listen to me.

"Good morning, Mr. Austin."

"Jeffrey. You're looking well."

The security guard was a large black man with a sweet grin. A man doesn't usually say that sort of thing about another man, but it was true. Jeffrey's grin was powdered sugar on strawberries, the perfect start to the day.

Our usual banter involved an exchange of quips about football. I try to sound optimistic about the Redskins, while Jeffrey's a Raiders fan. But football season was months away, so instead we exchanged pleasantries.

I placed my bag onto the table next to the metal detector. There was nothing of consequence in it. It had already been through airport security at San Diego. As I moved to the threshold of the metal detector, Jeffrey glanced down at his clipboard. He frowned, then looked up at me with an expression I'd never seen on his face before. I didn't like it. He blocked my passage. "Please step out of line, Mr. Austin," he said.

I grinned, thinking it was a joke.

"I hope you're not going to call for one of your drug-sniffing dogs," I quipped. "You could be charged with cruelty to animals. I didn't take a shower this morning."

Hands like vise-grips grabbed my arms from behind while two of Jeffrey's buddies flanked me. Nobody was smiling. Jeffrey's hand rested on the butt of his gun.

"Please step out of line, Mr. Austin," he said again.

"Jeffrey, it's me!"

Everyone in the vicinity had stopped talking. They were all looking at me, backing away as though I might go off any moment.

Jeffrey snatched my bag from the table as his buddies escorted me to the door. He dropped my bag at my feet and ripped the identity badge from my lapel.

"Go ahead, Jeffrey, do your worst," I cried. "But I want you to know that no matter how much you torture me, I will never become a Raiders fan."

"Mr. Austin, I must ask you to leave the premises."

Not a trace of humor was in his eyes.

"Is something wrong with my badge?"

"Your credentials have been revoked."

"Not possible," I said. "The badge worked fine three days ago when I had lunch in the cafeteria with half of the West Wing staff.

I have clearance for the rest of the year while we promote the book. Call Chief of Staff Ingraham, I'm sure this can all be worked out."

"Mr. Austin, please leave."

"Jeffrey, cut me some slack here, will you? You know I'd never—"

He gripped his weapon but didn't draw it. "If you do not leave willingly, Mr. Austin, I am authorized to consider you a credible threat and use whatever force is necessary to neutralize you."

"This is insane!" I shouted.

The grip on my arms tightened to the point of real pain. Any hint of resistance and I'd be kissing tile with a knee in my back.

"Fine," I said. "I'll leave. But it's a bureaucratic mix-up, that's all. And it's not like this is the first time a bureaucratic mix-up has ever been made at the White House, is it?"

That last part was to save face with the people standing in line. I didn't know any of them. They didn't know me. All the same, I had to say something.

Jeffrey's buddies shoved me out the door.

So it had come to this.

Bag in hand, I stood at 1600 Pennsylvania Avenue outside the White House fence with the tourists and their cameras. In the course of writing my book I'd been in nearly every room of the White House. I could give tours. Now, I couldn't even take a tour.

The idea had crossed my mind—the tour—and I would have tried it had I thought it had a chance of succeeding. But with security alerted to my presence, I wouldn't get ten steps inside the entrance.

I reached for my smartphone, giving the airwaves one last chance. I called the chief of staff's office and got . . . . I don't know who I got, but as soon as I identified myself, I got cut off. I tried Christina's cell phone. No luck.

"Can't be accused of not trying," I said to no one in particular.

I took one last lingering gaze at the White House.

"If only I had wings," I muttered.

A lack of wings didn't stop my bag from flying over the fence. I jumped to follow it and had one leg over the top when I felt something pulling me back.

A Japanese man with a camera around his neck had grabbed hold of my coat. His eyes frantic, he let loose with a torrent of words, none of which I understood. What I did understand were the expressions of horror on the faces of his wife and children.

"It's okay! It's okay!" I shouted at them. "I work here."

You had to admire the man. For all he knew I had a knife or a gun which I could easily have turned on him. Yet despite the potential danger, he did what he thought was right, and this probably wasn't even his country.

Our struggle caught the attention of other tourists. Some of them came running toward us to help the Japanese man. My grip was giving way.

"I have a bomb!" I shouted. "A bomb! I have a bomb!" It was the only thing I could think of that would make them back off.

The Japanese man didn't understand me. The other tourists did. They reversed course, slowly backing away.

The man's daughter understood. She shouted something at her father in Japanese, repeating it over and over. If she wasn't saying bomb, she was saying something equally effective, because the man let go of me.

I scaled the fence, dropped onto the grass, and offered a reassuring wave to the Japanese man, his family, and a growing audience. "Everything will be okay," I said to them.

No sooner had I turned and picked up my bag than I heard them coming. Barking, actually.

Dogs. I hadn't counted on dogs.

I heard snarls fast approaching and in stereo. They came at me from the left and from the right, so I ran forward.

Didn't get far.

The next thing I knew my face was in the grass and my keister was a dog's chew toy.

"Can I have a pillow, or a chair with a cushion?"

My plan had worked, though with unforeseen, painful complications. I was talking to the Secret Service.

"It's him, all right."

A copy of my book thumped onto the table, bio-picture-side up.

The three of us were squeezed into a room barely big enough for the table—which was metal, dinged, and bolted to the floor. There were three matching dinged chairs. Mine was broken. The seat tipped forward right. It took constant effort to keep from slipping off it.

The walls and ceiling and floors were painted sickening green, giving it all the hominess of a sensory deprivation tank. No air circulated in the room, and both agents had a sheen of sweat. I was literally dripping after my little romp with the dogs on the grass.

To get here I was dragged down so many windowless corridors and passageways, for all I knew we were in Philadelphia.

My bag lay open on the table, its contents scrutinized. The deadliest item in it was a tube of toothpaste.

The younger of the two agents was the one who went to get the book. A copy from his office. He had a rogue hair curl on his forehead that reminded me of Christopher Reeve in *Superman*. He and Reeve also had the same build. His name was Agent Phillips.

"A good read," he said of the book. "Austin did the president proud."

The other agent, who could have made a living as a model for

Marine Corps posters, flipped through the book, not wanting to take the other agent's word for it. His name was Agent Cunningham. "So, Mr. Austin," Agent Cunningham said, "why do you want to kill the president?"

"I don't!" I said. "I'm trying to warn him of a possible threat, only for some reason, nobody will listen to me."

"So you violated the perimeter of the White House just to get our attention."

"I had no other choice."

"Have you ever heard of a phone, Mr. Austin?"

I can sling sarcasm with the best of them, and I was tempted to engage him in the verbal equivalent of a food fight, but given the circumstances it might prove counterproductive, so I just answered the question. "Nobody would take my calls."

"And why is that, Mr. Austin?"

"You'll have to ask them."

Agent Cunningham's unflinching gaze hardened. "Earlier today you attempted to enter the White House with an invalid pass."

"It smelled fresh this morning when I sniffed it." Inwardly I cringed as soon as I said it. Hadn't I just told myself I wasn't going to do this?

Agent Cunningham was not amused.

I modified my answer. "I didn't know it was invalid. I was under the impression it was good for the rest of the year."

Agent Phillips inched forward, signaling it was his turn to ask a question. "All right, Mr. Austin. You have our attention. Tell us about the alleged threat against the president."

Finally we were getting somewhere. I knew Agent Phillips liked me.

"Can I have a pillow or something?" I asked.

Two pairs of uncaring eyes answered in the negative.

Given my discomfort, it was easy to be brief. I explained my trip to California, the speech, and my meeting with Myles Shepherd, leaving out the Twilight Zone special effects.

Midway through my discourse Agent Phillips extracted a pad and pen from his inside suit pocket. He took notes and requested a spelling of Myles Shepherd's name. "So, you sought out Shepherd. He didn't invite you to his office."

"That's correct."

"Given your history of antagonism, why did you want to see him?"

"To gloat."

"To gloat. You sought him out to gloat."

"Look, I'm not proud of it, okay? But yeah, I went there to throw my success in his face. Didn't you guys have someone in high school that just . . . I don't know, got under your skin?"Apparently not.

"So you threw your success in his face, and in return he told you he was going to assassinate the president."

"If you knew Myles Shepherd, it makes sense. You see, my success is because of the book. By attacking the subject of the book, Shepherd undermines my success."

Agent Cunningham wasn't following. "So you're saying Shepherd wants to kill the president because you wrote a book?"

"Not exactly, but something like that."

"And that was the last time you saw Shepherd?" Agent Phillip's asked.

"Not exactly."

What else could I say? I'm a terrible liar and the men across the table from me are trained at spotting liars. They waited, wanting me to elaborate.

"I saw him on my flight here."

That got their attention.

"You're certain it was him?"

"Positive."

"Did he see you?"

"Yes."

"Did you confront him?"

"I attempted to confront him, but he got away."

"Got away? During a layover?"

"Not exactly." Again, they waited for me to elaborate. "The flight was nonstop."

"Where did you attempt to confront him?"

"In flight."

Agent Cunningham was shaking his head. "You attempted to confront him in flight, but he got away? Where did he go?"

"I don't know."

"Did you alert flight personnel?"

"I did."

"And how did they respond?"

Clearing my throat, I said, "According to the flight attendants, Myles Shepherd was never on the flight."

Agent Cunningham sat back with a groan.

Agent Phillips rolled his eyes.

A chair scraped.

Agent Phillips left the room.

Agent Cunningham continued the interrogation. "In your opinion, is Shepherd capable of assassinating the president? Does he have the means? Access?"

"Yes, he's definitely capable of it. Most definitely. He's boastful, competitive, highly intelligent, opinionated, and Machiavellian."

"Machiavellian?"

"Scheming. Immorally ruthless. While I was in his office, he drugged me."

Agent Cunningham showed surprise for the first time. "Drugged you? With what drug?"

Before I could answer, Agent Phillips returned. His lips were pursed. His jaw set. He slapped a manila folder down on the table and took a seat. "I made some preliminary calls," he said, not bothering to ask if he was interrupting. "I spoke to—" He looked inside the folder for the name. "Fred Benson. Do you recognize that name, Mr. Austin?"

"He's the vice principal at Singing Hills High School."

"According to Mr. Benson, Myles Shepherd is dead. Are you aware of this, Mr. Austin?"

"Dead?" Agent Cunningham blurted.

Agent Phillips didn't wait for me to reply. "Mr. Benson says you were standing next to him when he learned of Shepherd's death. That the car accident in which he was killed was broadcast live on local television."

Two pairs of experience-hardened Secret Service eyes bored into me, waiting for an answer.

"That wasn't his body in the car!" I said, defending myself. "Besides, that doesn't change anything, does it? There are others involved in the plot, and they're still out there. They use code names."

Agent Cunningham said in all seriousness, "These coconspirators. Are they dead too?"

Agent Phillips's pad and pen appeared again. "Do you have the names of these coconspirators?" he asked.

"I have possible code names."

"Go ahead."

"Shepherd's code name was Semyaza." I spelled it for him. "As for the others, well, it's conjecture based on research."

Agent Phillips sighed.

"You see, Semyaza is the name of a lieutenant in an ancient organization, and from that I have deduced the name of the mastermind."

"Which is?"

Hesitation. Again with the hesitation.

The agents waited. Expressionless.

"Most likely," I said, "the code name of the head of the organization is . . . is Lucifer. . . . Satan."

Agent Phillips's pen dropped onto the table. He didn't write the name down.

After an uncomfortable silence, which to me was doubly painful because the place where the dog bit me was burning, Agent Phillips asked, "Did Shepherd give you any indication as to the identity of Satan?"

I smiled. The question sounded funny. "Actually, yes," I said, fidgeting, which hurt like crazy, "he told me it was a waste of time to inform the president of the assassination plot because . . ." This is the part I hadn't told anyone. But I had to tell the Secret Service, didn't I? While I didn't believe it was true for a moment, the information might provide a clue that could lead to the conspirators. "Because the president already knew about it."

The agents exchanged glances.

Phillips said, "Okay, I'll bite."

I laughed at the unintended joke despite the pain.

They didn't laugh with me.

"Exactly how would this information have reached the president?"

"Before answering that," I said, "you have to remember I'm just reporting what I heard."

"Noted."

"According to Myles Shepherd, the president knows about the assassination plot because he's the mastermind behind it."

Neither man blinked. It was amazing.

"President Douglas is plotting his own assassination?" Agent Cunningham said.

"You're saying President Douglas is Satan?" Agent Phillips added.

"I know how this sounds," I said.

"Tell us about how Shepherd drugged you," Agent Cunningham said.

"Drugs?" Agent Phillips shouted. He was out of the room when I'd mentioned drugs.

I told them how I suspected Shepherd might have used peyote, which has hallucinatory qualities. Then I described everything that happened in Shepherd's office.

Their response was to give me a ride home. They suggested I sleep it off.

And they told me not to come anywhere near the president or the White House again.

Ever.

CHAPTER
12

A NOTE WAS PINNED TO MY FRONT DOOR.

Stop trying to contact me!—C

I tore it down and unlocked the door, wondering how long the note had been up there, how many times the mailman had seen it.

With a mail slot on the front door, whenever I'm gone even for a few days the accumulation of mail on the other side makes opening the door an experience. Glossy magazines are slipperier than ice.

Steering around the pile of mail on the floor, I tossed my bag onto the sofa and opened windows to air out the place. Then I returned for the mail. I bent over and felt like I'd been bit all over again.

The bite that keeps on biting, I lamented.

Through trial and error, I found that bending over didn't hurt as much if I was on my knees. Just as I was reaching for the electric bill, my smartphone rang. The display said it was Jana.

"Hi, it's me," she said softly.

"Hi. I'm glad you called."

"I apologize for not returning your calls last night," she ventured.

"No, not at all."

"It's just that—"

"We both had a rough day," I said. "I just wanted to take you to dinner and apologize."

"Well . . . how about today? Are you free for lunch?"

I groaned.

"I understand," she said.

"No! No, it's not that . . . it's . . . well, I'm on my knees here."

"Grant, you don't have to beg. After all we've been through together?"

I laughed. "It's not that, I'm on my knees in my apartment, picking up the mail."

"Your apartment?"

"In DC."

"Oh! Now I feel foolish. With cell phones you never—"

"Yeah, you never know where you're calling."

"I don't know why I assumed you would be staying in San Diego longer," she said.

"It was important I get back here."

"I guess I keep forgetting what an important man you are now," she said.

"Not so important."

"Is San Diego on your itinerary anytime soon?"

I sighed. "At the moment I don't have an itinerary. Everything's sort of up in the air. I don't know when I'll be out West again."

"Okay. I understand. I was just hoping to clear the air a little, to talk with you when I wasn't so emotional."

She paused. "And to tell you I overreacted about Christy—"

"Christina."

"I really don't know why I acted like I did, it's not like we've been seeing each other or anything, I mean, it's been years! But the way you held me on the freeway . . . it brought back a lot of old feelings and they surprised me."

"About Christina. We're not—"

"Really, Grant, it's none of my business. Oh! And I hear you met Sue Ling! Small world, huh? Isn't she special?"

"Yeah, special. She thinks the world of you."

"It's mutual. She's the smartest person I've ever met! Well, I'm sure you have a thousand things to do. Oh, are you going to come to Myles's funeral? It's next Tuesday."

A dozen quips leaped to mind regarding Myles, none of them kind or appropriate. I went for the simple answer, "I don't think that will be possible."

"Well, if things change, you know? I know he would have wanted you there. It looks like the whole city is going to be there. The mayor. Chief of Police. You know, honoring the former teacher of the year. The station tried to get me to cover it, but I don't think I'll be in any shape to do a broadcast."

"My thoughts will be with you."

"Keep in touch, Grant, okay? And the next time you're going to be in San Diego, try giving a girl a little advance notice." I slipped the phone into my pocket. There are no feelings like old romantic feelings. I gathered my mail in an emotional fog.

———

I stood in the shadows of Christina's three-story, brick apartment building in Adams Morgan. My usual place to wait for her was parked on the street within sight of her parking space in the rear of the building. Circumstances suggested a change of tactics. I was afraid if she saw me while she was still behind the wheel, she'd rabbit. So I parked two blocks away on Mint Wood and waited in the shadows beside the steps.

Actually, the shadows weren't necessary. I stood there because I couldn't sit. The side of the steps gave me something to lean against. I had no idea how long I'd be waiting.

People who work in the West Wing live in the West Wing. Their apartments are little more than walk-in closets and staging areas for the next meeting, party, or event.

As it turned out, I got lucky. Christina came home before midnight. I had to wait only three hours.

She walked with her head down, preoccupied. As she started up the steps, I moved out of the shadows. "Hello, Christina."

Startled, her hand flew into her purse rummaging for a container of Mace.

"Christina, it's me."

Her hand continued its search.

"Christina?"

"Grant! It's you! You scared me!" She glanced up and down the street. "Didn't you get my note?" she said. "I told you not to contact me!"

I approached her, keeping a wary eye on the hand in the purse. It had slowed but was still groping.

"We need to—"

She pushed me back into the shadows. Her voice low, her eyes menacing, she said, "Go away!" She started up the stairs, her keys dangling.

I followed her.

Mid-step, she swung around. "What are you doing?"

I thought she was just peeved at me for leaving all those messages, but this was beyond peeved. She was scared.

"Christina, can't we—"

She pushed me back a step. "Go away!"

"Not until you tell me what's going on!"

"Not now!" She stepped into me, grabbed my shirt, and yanked me close. "Not now!" she hissed.

Again, she was looking up and down the street.

"Okay, if not now, when?"

She pushed me down another step. "I'll call you," she whispered, inserting the key into the hallway door.

"Okay. When?" I took a step up.

She opened the door, but didn't go in. "I told you, I'd call you!" she said. Reaching down, she pulled me up the steps to the landing. "Go!" she cried. "I can't be seen with you!" She shoved me back.

Christina has always been good at keeping me off balance—that's one of the things that attracted me to her—but this little pushing-and-shoving routine had me thoroughly confused.

Her apartment was the first door on the left. She jabbed repeatedly at the lock with her key.

"Christina, what do you want?"

"I want you to leave!" she said, forcing the key into the lock.

"All right, I'll go. Can you just tell me who—"

She lunged toward me, grabbed my shirt, and pulled me into the hallway.

"Christina, what are you—"

"Shush!"

"But this is crazy!" I whispered.

"Shush! Shush! Shush!"

Her apartment door swung open.

"For the last time, go away!" she shouted, shoving me inside her apartment.

She double-checked the hallway, then slammed the door and fell back against it, her chest rising and falling as though she had just done a wild sprint across the White House lawn with dogs chasing her.

Frenzy doesn't look good on Christina. Frantic, but in control, is her style. This temporary madness didn't suit her. I gave her the time she needed to collect herself.

Her blond hair, parted over her left eye, fell in parenthetical curves framing a face with intelligent eyes and a sensuous mouth.

The necklace she was wearing brought a smile to my face. I'd picked it up in France for her during the economic summit. It was a gold collar with a single dangling pendant. I'm not usually good with gifts, but I thought I'd done a good job with this one. The necklace was simple and elegant. Simple for me; elegant for her.

"You can't stay," she said.

"Will you at least tell me what's going on? Nobody will take my calls. My White House credentials have been revoked. What have I done?"

"That's what I want to know! What have you done?"

She pushed past me, dropped her purse at the base of a hat rack, and kicked off her shoes. "On Sunday I drop you off at the airport. You tell me you're giving a speech at a high school."

"My alma mater."

"And the next thing I know memos are flocking like pigeons telling everyone we're not to have any contact with you for any reason; that if you attempt to contact us we're to notify the chief of staff immediately."

"Did you?" I asked. "Notify Ingraham?"

"Are you kidding? Even before you started your phone-solicitor routine, he pulled me into his office and grilled me."

"Grilled you?"

"He wanted to know if I'd heard from you, when I spoke to you last, when I saw you last, dated you last. He asked me if I ever knew you to be part of a subversive, anti-American organization, or participating in any subversive activities."

"What?" I couldn't believe this.

"He wanted to know if you've ever spoken in a subversive fashion or taken me to any anti-American rallies."

"This is crazy!"

"Then, he made me hand him my smartphone and ordered me to

tell him my PIN so he could listen to my voicemail. I felt like I was a teenager at home all over again."

"He can't do that!"

"You're kidding, right? You don't tell Chief of Staff Harold Ingraham what he can and can't do."

"Christina, you have to believe me, had I known . . . I had no idea . . . I never would have. . . . How many messages were on there?"

"Luckily, only one. The blitzkrieg came later. When it did, I checked my messages every fifteen minutes and immediately deleted them. Finally, I turned it off."

"That was smart."

"You don't work your way into the West Wing without learning how to watch your back."

"I had no idea it was this bad," I said by way of apology.

"Grant, what have you gotten yourself involved in? Everyone is paranoid. They've all taken your book off their shelves. They avoid me and whisper behind my back."

"I'm as stumped as you are."

I meandered into the alcove. The windows faced the street. Christina had turned it into a book nook. Beneath the windows were bench bookshelves stocked with her favorite titles. In preparation for my trip to Europe, she had taught me key French phrases here.

Headlights flashed against the windows, and the next thing I knew, Christina dove to the hardwood floor and, grabbing my back pocket, pulled me down with her.

Yeah, the side the dog bit.

A stab of pain from my back forty nearly made me pass out. I was definitely going to have to tell her about the injury.

While I tried to keep from passing out, Christina crawled to the windows and pulled the draperies closed.

"Was that really necessary?" I cried.

I started to get up. She pushed me back down and joined me. We lay on our sides facing each other.

"Grant, I'm really scared," she said.

She was. I felt guilty. It was time to give her a few pieces of the puzzle.

"While I was in California, I learned of a threat against the president's life. An assassination plot."

"Grant! This is huge! Why didn't you tell me?"

If I weren't hurting so badly I would have laughed.

Realizing the ridiculousness of the protest, she waved it off. "I mean, I thought you were going to a high school. Where did you hear—"

My cell phone rang. The anonymous-caller ringtone. It was in my floor-side pocket. I started to roll over on my back to get it, remembered my injury, then rolled over onto my stomach and retrieved the phone. The display had a number I didn't recognize. I did, however, recognize the area code. Six one nine. San Diego. "I need to take this," I said.

"Who is it?"

"I don't know." I hit the green Answer button. "Hello?"

"Grant?"

I'd only heard an afternoon's worth of her voice, and then mostly angry tones, but I'd heard enough to recognize it. "Miss Ling," I said.

"Is this a bad time?"

I took stock of the moment. I was lying on the floor of my former girlfriend's apartment hiding from anonymous headlights while trying to explain to her that an old high school rival, who was possibly dead, was trying to kill the President of the United States and, for reasons unknown, implicate me in the plot.

"Not at all, Miss Ling," I said.

Her head propped in her hand, Christina watched me with interest.

"Maybe you should call me Sue," Miss Ling said.

"All right, Sue."

Christina rolled her eyes in exasperation.

"You didn't show up at the library this morning," Sue said.

"Um . . . no, I didn't. I had to return to Washington. Urgent business. Unexpected."

"More urgent than meeting an angel from heaven?"

I tried to sit up. It hurt too much, so I returned to my side, squirming to get comfortable. "Did he show up?" I asked.

"No. Not in the library."

I knew it! I grinned victoriously. "Somehow, I'm not surprised," I said.

"He visited the professor earlier, though."

"Earlier. Convenient. When no one else was around."

"I assume the professor was alone. I didn't ask. Abdiel didn't come to the library because he knew you'd returned to Washington."

She knew I was in Washington. When Jana called, she thought I was still in San Diego. I grinned. Miss Ling had talked to Jana. That's how she knew I'd returned home.

I played along. "It makes sense he'd know I'd returned to Washington," I said. "Angels are pretty well connected."

Christina frowned. "Angels?" she mouthed.

I shrugged.

Getting up in a huff, she went to the kitchen. The light came on and cabinet doors opened and closed.

It was awkward talking on the phone on my side. I tried to sit up. A yelp of pain erupted from my lips.

"Are you all right?" Sue asked.

I did my best to sound fine. "A little stiffness from the flight, that's all," I said.

Sue Ling already had a low opinion of me. I didn't want to justify it by telling her about the dog bite.

Christina's voice came from the kitchen. "Do you want some coffee?"

I covered the phone. "That would be great," I shouted back.

"Is that Christina?" Sue Ling asked.

I cringed, hoping she hadn't heard the exchange.

"Um . . . exactly why are you calling, Miss . . . um, Sue?"

The voice on the other end of the line cooled. "The professor asked me to take another look at your book. To dissect it."

"Dissect it." This conversation was going downhill fast. "Okay, so you called to give me a review?"

"I found something. Something disturbing."

"Disturbing. Factually or grammatically?"

"Does Christina have a copy of your book in her apartment?"

I frowned. "How did you know I was in Christina's apartment?"

"I didn't, until now."

I cringed. She had set me up and, just like a guy, I walked right into it.

"Um . . . let me check," I said.

In order to get up I had to crawl on my hands and knees to the padded benches that rimmed the alcove and use them to push myself to my feet. I poked my head in the kitchen.

"Christina, do you have a copy of my book?"

Her hand was atop the coffee grinder. "Who's on the line? Your editor?"

"I'll tell you later. Do you have a copy?"

Christina didn't appreciate being dismissed. When she walked by me it felt as though someone had left the refrigerator door open. She went to the alcove and pulled a book from the very shelf I'd used to push myself up.

"Thanks," I said sheepishly. To Sue on the phone, "All right, I have a copy."

"You'll need a paper and pen."

Christina had just placed her hand atop the coffee grinder again when I said, "Do you have a scratch pad, or something I can write on?"

She yanked open a drawer, rattling its insides, and rummaged around until she found a scratch pad, which she flung at me.

I mouthed the words *thank you* to her. I was definitely going to have to do some damage control when this call was over.

Pulling out a chair from a small tea table, I sat down slowly on half of it, placing the book and scratch pad in front of me. At the top of the pad was a female cartoon mouse, her gloved hands clasped against her chest as she gazed amorously at her counterpart male on the far side of the pad. Little hearts floated between them.

Beneath the graphic, Christina had written: "Call Dr. about birth control pills."

Tearing off the top sheet of the scratch pad, I turned it facedown and placed it at the far side of the table.

"I'm ready," I said to Sue, my mind on Christina.

Birth control pills?

The coffee grinder buzzed to life. I had to wait for the grinding to stop before I could hear what Sue had said.

"You'll need to repeat that," I told her.

"Go to chapter 1," Sue said.

I opened the cover and saw my autograph and inscription to Christina: "My light . . . my inspiration . . . my ever-present help. With love, Grant."

"Are you at chapter 1?"

"Almost. All right. There."

"First word."

"First word? Don't tell me you're going to review my book word by word?"

"Just write it down."

I wrote it down. "All right, now what?"

"Chapter 2. Second word. Write it down."

I flipped the pages to chapter 2. "None of this is making any sense," I said.

"You'll see. Chapter—"

"3," I said. "Third word."

"Correct."

"I'm sensing a pattern here."

"Smart boy. Keep working your way through the book."

"How far?"

"You'll know."

As I turned from chapter to chapter, a growing sense of horror came over me.

"I don't believe this!" I cried.

Coffeepot in hand, Christina looked over at me.

"Are you saying you didn't write it?" Sue asked.

I stared at the words on the scratch pad. My words.

"Of course I wrote it," I said. "But I didn't mean it. I mean, not like this. I'm going to have to check my manuscript."

"It's hard to believe the wording is mere coincidence," Sue said.

"You took the words right out of the prosecuting attorney's mouth," I replied.

Christina set the coffeepot down, her fear having been resuscitated.

"What do you want me to tell the professor?" Sue asked.

"What do you mean?"

"He's the one who instructed me to review the book. He's going to want to know your response."

"My response? Tell him I didn't write it! That I wrote it, but didn't know I'd written it, because I never would have written this. Tell him I'm going to check my original manuscript."

My emotions were getting the best of me. I fought for control. I told myself not to panic, to attack the problem. "How did you find this?" I asked her.

"I'm good at recognizing patterns," she said.

I sighed. "I wonder how many other people who are good at recognizing patterns will recognize this one?"

"I have to go," Sue said. "Someone else is calling me. It's Jana. Is her call going to make me angry?"

"You mean you haven't talked with her today?"

"Did you make her cry?"

"No! Everything's fine. We talked earlier, it's fine. But you haven't talked with Jana already today?"

She hung up.

"Who's Jana?" Christina asked. "And Sue? My, you were a busy little boy while you were in California, weren't you?"

"Not now, Christina."

"Not now? Not now? You stalk me for two days, then force your way into my house—"

"I didn't force my way into your house!" I protested.

"That's exactly what the police report is going to say unless you start talking. And here's a news flash for you, buster: I know we agreed to cool things off for a while, but taking calls from your girlfriends while you're with me in my apartment is beyond rude—it's mean."

I handed her the piece of paper. It was the only way I could think to shut her up.

Her eyes grew wide. "Grant, this isn't funny."

"Tell me about it."

"You shouldn't write things like this, not even on a notepad . . . *my* notepad!"

"How would you feel if I told you I not only wrote it, I published it?"

"Grant!"

I patted the open book. "A sequential pattern. One word per chapter."

"Why would you—"

"I didn't! Someone is messing with me!"

She stared in disbelief at the note. "Well, whoever they are, they're doing an outstanding job."

CHAPTER
13

ON MOST NIGHTS IT TAKES ME TEN MINUTES TO DRIVE HOME from Christina's apartment. Tonight it took longer because I had to walk the first two blocks to get to my car.

My apartment is a cozy one-bedroom on Thirty-fourth Street within walking distance of Georgetown University. Call me nerdy, but I like the atmosphere of a university neighborhood, and it's only ten minutes to the White House and fifteen minutes to the Library of Congress.

Christina was waiting for me when I arrived at my apartment. She insisted on taking separate cars. She said that if an army of Feds jumped out of the trees and bushes she wanted to be able to put her Toyota into gear and drive away as though she didn't know me.

When no army appeared, she sprang out of her car and shoved me into the apartment faster than I could unlock the door, which resulted in collision.

While my laptop booted up, I searched for the printed copies of the manuscript. There were two: an early first draft and the final draft. They were somewhere in the back of my bedroom closet buried beneath empty printer boxes, worn-out pairs of shoes, and stacks of clothes that no longer fit.

While I was rummaging, my computer played the Hallelujah Chorus, signaling it had booted up. I used to have Robin Williams shout, "Good morning, Vietnam!" but after a while, that got annoying.

"It's ready," Christina said, in case I hadn't heard Mr. Handel. She hovered in front of the computer, nervously working the page from the scratch pad between her thumb and forefinger. The hearts floating between the cartoon mice were taking a beating.

I fell into the chair in front of my corner desk. Most of the biography had been written on the road or at a desk at the White House. But a good number of late-night hours were spent here in this corner polishing the manuscript.

I put the cursor through its paces, opening folders to get to the master manuscript file.

"I can't believe you wrote this," Christina reiterated.

"No matter what we find in the file," I replied, "I didn't write that sentence intentionally."

"Are you saying your subconscious wrote it?"

Is that your defense, Mr. Austin? That your subconscious wrote the sentence?

"I'm saying I didn't write it," I said to the prosecuting attorney in my head, loud enough for Christina to hear.

"Maybe you did it as a joke or a dare and forgot to fix it before it went to press."

"I think I'd remember something like that."

"Maybe it's a prank and only a limited number of copies are printed with these words—have you thought of that? Do you know anyone in the White House or at the publishers who would play a prank on you?"

"It's not a prank, Christina."

I clicked on the manuscript file.

Christina bent over my shoulder, her cheek close to my cheek. It seemed to take the file forever to open.

The title page appeared.

I clicked an icon at the top of the window, and a list of chapter headings appeared to the left of the text. By clicking on each heading, I could navigate from chapter to chapter.

"Here we go," I said, the mouse hovering over the link that would take me to chapter 1. "The first word of the first chapter in the published book is *when*, correct?"

Christina consulted the scratch paper. "Correct."

"We don't want to see the word *when*."

"That's right," she said.

I took a deep breath.

Click.

Chapter 1 appeared on the screen.

"Yes!" I shouted, thrusting my fists into the air.

The first word of chapter 1 was *it*.

Christina's voice trembled. "Chapter 2, try chapter 2! We don't want the word to be *he*."

I positioned the cursor on the chapter 2 link.

Click.

My heart fell to my stomach.

"What?" Christina cried. "Does it say *he*?"

All the exuberance had drained from me. "Second word *he*," I said.

A new fear was born. What if most of the words of the condemning sentence were present in my text?

Christina motioned me to continue. "That could be just a coincidence. Go to chapter 3. Chapter 3."

I positioned the cursor on chapter 3. "What is the word we don't want?"

"*Is.*"

My hopes sank. Such a common verb.

Click.

"Yes! Third chapter, third word . . . *Senate!*" My hopes revived.

Momentum picked up from there. We found no matches in chapters 4–13.

Christina stepped back and dropped onto the edge of the bed. "Oh Grant, I'm so glad you didn't write this!"

"I'm not out of the woods yet," I said.

Inserting the backup CD into the computer, I checked it against the file on the hard drive. They were identical. Then I unearthed the two hard-copy printouts from the bottom of my closet. Neither of them condemned me. "Which means the text was changed during editing," I concluded.

"So you're in the clear!" Christina said.

"Not completely. I could have made the changes during editing."

"But you didn't."

"And then there's the proofs, the typeset printout I get from the publisher after it's gone through editorial. It's my last look at the manuscript, my last chance to make any corrections. I could have altered it then."

"But you have your copy of the proofs to prove you didn't do that, don't you?"

I winced.

"Tell me you made copies."

"I'd like to tell you that. But I didn't make copies."

"Why not?"

"Christina, it's over five hundred pages. It would cost me a small fortune, and for what? A changed phrase here, a sentence there. During the proofing stage changes are largely cosmetic."

She shoved the mice and hearts in my face. "This is not a cosmetic change," she said.

"But it is, that's the beauty of the deception. Editors, copy editors make word changes here and there all the time without affecting the meaning of the sentence."

"You're the author!" she cried. "You didn't notice the changes when the book was released?"

"I haven't read it."

"Haven't read it? Your own book?"

I shook my head. "Why would I? I already know what's in it, or at least I thought I did."

"That's why!" she replied.

In retrospect, she had a point.

"Which leaves us where?" Christina said. "First thing in the morning you contact the publisher?"

"First thing we do is get our hands on a copy of the proofs."

"But you just said—"

"I'm not the only one who approved the proofs."

"Yes! Yes!" Christina shouted. "No! Oh no!"

"What?"

"Margaret. She threw them away! I remember now. Ms. Irwin—"

"Ms. Irwin, the president's personal secretary?"

"Yes. She sent a memo to Margaret saying she was making a copy of the proofs for the president and wanted to know if the chief of staff wanted a copy, since he'd made comments on it. Margaret told her it wasn't necessary. The next day, a runner delivered a copy of the proofs to Margaret's desk anyway. I remember Margaret sniping that Ms. Irwin was the most annoying, pushy busybody she'd ever worked with, always telling people how to do their jobs."

"What did Margaret do with the copy?"

"She put it in the shredder bin."

"All right, disappointing, but that means Ms. Irwin still has a copy. If we can get our hands on it, we can find out who made the corrections before it was sent to the publisher."

"You suspect someone in the White House? Who?"

"Ingraham."

"Oh Grant, do you really think so? You don't want Ingraham as an enemy."

"A man can't always choose his enemies. I have a feeling he's behind all this, which means it's imperative we get a look at those proofs."

"But how? Are you just going to walk in and ask her?"

"I wasn't thinking of asking her."

Christina laughed derisively. "I suppose you're going to waltz into her office while nobody is looking and search through her files."

"Not me. I can't even get in the door."

"Then who?"

I folded my arms and stared at her.

"Oh no . . . oh no . . . Margaret is keeping close tabs on everyone. She knows exactly how long it takes to perform every task, and if you take a minute longer, she demands an explanation."

"Only when she's there. How about when she's not there? How about . . . oh, I don't know . . . now?"

"No, Grant. Absolutely not. Out of the question."

"People work through the night in the West Wing all the time. It's not that unusual. No one will suspect you."

"But if someone asks, what do I tell them?"

"The truth. Tell them it's imperative you find some papers by morning."

Christina backed away from me. She shook her head emphatically. "No, Grant. No. I can't do it. Rummage around Ms. Irwin's office? What if I get caught?"

"You're my only hope."

"I don't care what you say, Grant. It's too much to ask. I'm not going to do it."

As Christina made her way through the empty halls of the West Wing she couldn't get Watergate out of her mind—the second-rate office burglary that culminated in the first presidential resignation in history. It was the ripple effect that intrigued her. A small pebble tossed into political waters creating an ever-expanding ripple that led to the downfall of a President of the United States.

Tonight, she was the pebble. For all she knew, the proofs she was after would reveal nothing of consequence, and tomorrow morning Grant would begin making inquiries at the publisher's office to determine who there had implicated him. But Christina's political instincts argued that the answers were in Washington, not New York. Intrigue of this nature was the heart and soul of DC.

Christina was certain the White House copy of the proofs would be the smoking gun. The question that remained was, Who fired the shot? In whose handwriting were the changes made?

There were three primary suspects: the president, Chief of Staff Ingraham, and Ms. Irwin, acting on the president's behalf. There were other possibilities; other aides or writers could have been hired to review the proofs, but until she eliminated the primary suspects, they were inconsequential.

Getting into Ms. Irwin's office would be no problem; her office was rarely locked, the door rarely closed. Restricted access to the heart of the White House made it unnecessary. The hard part would come once she was inside the office. The cabinets were undoubtedly locked. But there were a few places she knew to look, and she hoped that old publishing proofs would not be a matter of tight security.

Christina strode into her own office and flipped the light switch.

Overhead fluorescents sputtered to life as though she'd awakened them.

What surprised her was that she was enjoying this.

At first, when Grant suggested she do this she thought he was out of his mind. Finally caving to his pleas, she formulated a plan while driving to the White House, and not only did she realize she could do this, she had to admit she was good at the planning phase.

Getting past security was no trouble. West Wing staff was frequently called to work in the middle of the night.

"If I don't have that environmental report on Ms. Irwin's desk by morning, it'll be my head," she quipped to the guard at the security checkpoint.

He was a new guy. She hadn't seen him before. Average size. Crooked teeth.

She noticed his teeth in particular because of the way he grinned at her. It was more of a leer. Either manning security at the White House was lonelier than she thought, or the guy was hitting on her. It was hard to tell because if he was making a pass at her, he wasn't very good at it.

The security guard laughed a little too loud at her quip, and when she glanced back while turning a corner, he was still looking at her, still leering.

Now that she was in her office, she focused on the task at hand. She searched her desk for her copy of the environmental report. It was the key to her plan. Earlier in the day Margaret had instructed her to deliver a copy of the report—which outlined the long-range impact of offshore oil drilling on California's coastline—to Ms. Irwin for the president. Just as she was walking out the door, Margaret had called her back. Chief of Staff Ingraham was screaming for follow-up calls to the Hill regarding a vote on an upcoming minimum wage bill. Working the phones was Christina's strength.

She didn't know who Margaret had sent to deliver the report, but if anyone were to ask her, Christina could say in all good conscience that she'd been instructed to deliver the report and at the last minute got sidetracked, so it was either come early to work in the morning and deliver the report or do it tonight.

"There you are," she said, spying the report buried under a landslide of fiscal graphs.

"Found it, did you?"

The voice startled her, nearly sending her heart through the ceiling. She swung around to see the guard with crooked teeth. He leaned casually against the doorjamb, his thumbs hooked in his belt. "Would hate to see you lose that pretty head," he said, making a guttural sound while dragging a thumb across his neck execution style.

Charming, Christina thought.

"I'll walk you down," he said.

Smiling as sweetly as she could, Christina said, "Oh, that won't be necessary. I'm sure you have more important things to do."

"Not at all. I'm making my rounds. It's on the way."

"Oh. Well, in that case."

She clutched the report to her chest with both arms and exited the room. He barely gave her room to get by him. He smelled her hair as she passed under his nose.

They strolled casually down the hallway. She had to figure out a way to get rid of him.

He began narrating his life story without asking if she wanted to hear it. He'd been raised in the Bronx, his first job out of high school was as a New York cop. After taking a bullet to the leg during a grocery store holdup, he landed a job in security at the governor's office. Then, when a buddy got hired at the White House, he thought, "Why not? It'll impress the ladies."

He'd been divorced two years following a four-year marriage to a Georgia Peach—his words. Their marriage didn't last, "because Southern girls are stuck on themselves and don't get city boys."

Christina wondered what the Georgia Peach would say to her ex's version of their breakup.

"You're not a Southern girl, are you?" he asked.

"As a matter of fact I am," she said brightly.

His face fell.

Christina was delighted. "Born and raised in Texas," she boasted.

"Texas?" he cried. "Texas? That's not Southern!"

"It most certainly is!" Christina said, thickening her Southern accent.

"Nah. Texas is Texas, and from what I've heard, Texas girls— mmmm doggie—are in a class all by themselves. They're nothing like them prissy Georgia or Alabama girls. Texas girls know how to keep their cowboys smilin', if you know what I mean."

They were fast approaching Ms. Irwin's office. Christina was running out of time. After his last remark, she could think of nothing she'd rather do than slap him, call him a pig, and report him for sexual harassment, but if she did it would involve reports and Margaret would find out she'd been here. This was supposed to be a covert operation.

The problem remained, how to get rid of him? If he stood in the doorway and waited while she dropped off the report, she wouldn't be able to snoop around.

They reached the doorway to Ms. Irwin's office. She turned to him. "Thank you for walking me, Officer—"

"Kowalski," the security officer said. "Didn't I tell you that already? Claude Kowalski."

"Claude. Of course," she said.

"Actually, it's Eugene. Claude's my middle name. I don't tell just anyone my real name, you know. Only special people. You have to promise you won't spread it around."

"Your secret is safe with me, Officer Kowalski."

"Claude."

"Yes . . . Claude."

He flashed his crooked teeth. "Don't mention it, Christine." His grin widened. "Surprised I knew your first name? I didn't need to look at your badge. I memorized it when you came through security. I don't always memorize pretty girls' names, but something told me you were special and I just might want to use it again sometime soon. Guess I was right, right?"

Christina did her best to keep smiling. "Well . . . again . . . thank you, Claude. It was nice meeting you." She extended her hand.

Take the hint, take the hint, please take the hint, Christina pleaded silently.

"Oh, I don't mind waitin' for you," Kowalski said. "I'll wait right here, and when you're done, I'll walk you back."

His radio crackled.

"Kowalski, are you still in the john?"

With surprising speed, Kowalski snapped up the radio. Lowering the volume, he turned his back on her and spoke in a hushed tone, but not so low Christina couldn't hear.

"I'm making my rounds," he said.

"Your rounds aren't for another half hour! You told me you were going to the john. Get back here ASAP!"

"But, Sarge—"

"ASAP, Kowalski!"

"They need me back at check-in," he said to Christina. "Seems like I have to do everything around here. Stop by on your way out. Maybe we can arrange our own personal hoedown at a bar. I get off work in a couple of hours." He winked at her and made a checking sound that, if Christina were a horse, was the equivalent of *giddyup*.

As Officer Kowalski sauntered back down the hallway alone, Christina checked her watch, noting she had thirty minutes to fill before exiting the building, while Officer Kowalski was making his rounds.

When the hallway was clear, Christina stepped tentatively inside the outer office, known by everyone in the building as Ms. Irwin's office.

She was relieved not to find anyone—she might not be the only one working late. Without turning on the lights, she took a quick look around.

Just inside the door to the right was an aide's desk. The person who sat here was the keeper of the office gate. At any given time, up to five secretaries worked in this office. To get to any of them, you had to get past Stewart, Ms. Irwin's aide.

Farther inside the room, five desks sat at right angles along the far wall, evenly spaced. Behind them, the wall was lined with metal cabinets of various sizes: some file cabinets, others drawer cabinets for large, flat items, such as maps. The desk closest to the door to the Oval Office was the desk of Ms. Irwin.

"Might as well start at the top and work my way down," Christina mumbled to herself.

She rounded Stewart's desk. She jumped back with a gasp when she saw a pair of bare feet sticking out from behind Ms. Irwin's desk.

This was a problem. Christina's well-thought-out plan had not factored bare feet into them.

Bare feet. In a dark office. Late at night outside the Oval Office. No matter how you spun it, that couldn't be good.

They were male feet, from the size and shape of them. Whoever they belonged to was reclined on the floor behind Ms. Irwin's desk. Whether the feet were attached to a living person or a dead person, she couldn't tell. They hadn't moved.

Should she call out for help?

The thought of Claude running to her rescue was enough to

make her think twice about that course of action. So far she wasn't in any danger, was she?

She could use a phone on the desk and dial security. But that might wake the feet up, if that were possible. If she was going to call for help, what would she say? She knew nothing of the condition of the person who belonged to these feet. She should at least look first, shouldn't she? What if the person needed medical attention?

Her curiosity got the best of her. She took a tentative step forward. Then another. And another. As she drew closer, feet gave way to legs. The legs were wearing pale blue pajama bottoms.

Christina wished she'd turned on the lights, but if she went to do that now, she knew she'd keep going out the door and down the hallway. Since she was already this close, she'd look first, then run.

Two more steps and she saw hands, lying lifeless on each side of the body. Another step and instead of seeing a chest she saw a stack of papers bundled with rubber bands sitting on a chest.

Two more steps and she saw—

"Mr. President!"

At the sound of her voice, the president stirred. His eyes blinked open. With effort they focused on her. "Miss Kraft," he said. "I've been expecting you."

Christina knelt beside him. He lay slumped against the wall in his pajamas. No robe. In this position, and in this wardrobe, there was nothing presidential about him. He looked old, vulnerable, human. His hair was mussed. His face drawn. But the thing that seemed strangest to Christina, the thing that bothered her most, was that he was barefoot. It just seemed obscene to her to see the most powerful man in the world in bare feet.

"Are you hurt, sir? Can I call someone?"

The president took a deep breath and pulled himself up into a sitting position, his back against the wall. The stack of papers tumbled onto his legs. He appeared groggy, disoriented. He looked around and seemed surprised to find himself on the floor. Grinning sheepishly, he said, "I was aiming for Ms. Irwin's chair. Guess my aim was a bit off."

"Mr. President, stay right there. I'm going to call—"

"Miss Kraft, wait," he said. He patted the bundle on his legs. "This is what you're looking for. The proofs to Grant's manuscript."

Christina stared at him dumbly. How could the president know what she was looking for? How could he be expecting her when less than an hour ago she didn't even know she would be here?

He took another deep breath and blinked his eyes. They were clearer, but he still looked at her as though he was trying to look through the haze of a migraine the size of Texas. "My question to you, Miss Kraft, is why? Why do you want the proofs to a book that has already been published?"

For a moment, the briefest of moments, Christina considered lying to him, using her cover story, telling him she wasn't here for Grant's proofs, she was here to deliver the environmental report he needed in the morning.

"We think there may be something in them that falsely implicates Grant in a plot, sir. We're attempting to determine who's behind it."

"We. You and Grant?"

"Yes, sir."

"What kind of plot?" the president asked.

Christina couldn't bring herself to tell him. Instead, she fished in her pocket and produced the scratch-pad page with the cartoon mice linked by a smudged trail of hearts. She handed it to him.

The president pulled a pair of eyeglasses from the front pocket of his pajamas and wrestled them on. He read the note aloud. "'When he is suspended between earth and heaven I will kill the president.'"

He removed his glasses. "Grant wrote this?"

"No, sir," Christina said with conviction. "The message is comprised of thirteen words that appear code-like in your biography. One word in each chapter."

"The published book?"

"Yes, sir."

The president cursed. "But these words are not found in Grant's original manuscript?"

"No, sir."

He looked to the stack of pages on his legs. "Of course, the proofs. The changes were made in the proofs."

The president seemed in complete control of his faculties now and content to continue with this matter on the floor. He handed the scratch-pad page back to Christina.

She explained to him the sequence.

"One word at a time," he said to her, unbundling the proof pages.

He flipped pages. Christina was unclear as to whether she was to read the words one at a time to him, or if he would—

"Chapter 1. *When*," he said.

"Yes, sir."

"Chapter two. Second word . . . *he*."

The president continued through all thirteen chapters.

". . . is . . . suspended . . . between . . . earth . . . and . . . heaven . . . I . . . will . . . kill . . . the . . . president."

When he was finished he cursed again.

Whose handwriting is he reading? Christina wondered. He's obviously surprised by the changes. And what happens now? Do I ask him? Or will he take care of it?

"Where do we go from here, Miss Kraft?" the president asked. Before she could answer, he erupted, "But why Grant? That's what doesn't make sense. Why Grant? Doc Palmer, maybe. But Grant?"

Christina said, "Sir, if I may ask—"

With a suddenness that startled her, the president grabbed her by the arm. He pulled her close, nearly yanking her on top of him. "I like your Mr. Austin," he said in a whisper. "And I want you to assure him I had nothing to do with this. Nothing! Do you understand?"

"Yes, sir."

"It is only because of Ms. Irwin's thoroughness that these proofs even exist. All the other copies have been . . . well, let's just say they're missing . . . the chief of staff's and Ms. Irwin's. And I'd be willing to bet all the copies at the publishing house have been conveniently lost. This is the only copy they didn't get, because they didn't know about it."

"They, sir? Who are they?"

"That doesn't matter," the president said gruffly, still gripping her arm. He spoke like a man possessed. "Listen carefully, Miss Kraft. Get a message to Grant. Tell him that under no circumstances is he to go to San Diego. Is that clear? Hog-tie him if you have to, but keep him away from San Diego."

"Yes, sir. But sir, if I may ask—"

The lights overhead flickered and came to life.

"There you are!" The president's wife, wearing a robe, rushed into the room. "We've all been worried! Are you all right?" she cried.

Two Secret Service agents were close on her heels. They flanked Christina and pulled her to her feet as though she was a threat. At that moment Christina was very much aware of the piece of paper in her hand that threatened the life of the President of the United States.

"I'm fine! I'm fine!" The president waved off the attention as he would a pesky fly. "I just wandered off for a stroll and got a little woozy, that's all. Probably the new medication. . . ."

As his wife helped him to his feet, he zeroed in on the two Secret Service agents. "Back off, you pit bulls. Miss Kraft found me and was kind enough to come to my aid. She's working late, one of Ingraham's overworked subordinates."

The president's wife bent down and picked up the proofs.

"Those belong to Miss Kraft," the president said, directing his wife to hand the proofs to her.

Christina took them gratefully. "Thank you, Mr. President."

The president stood erect now, dignified, looking very presidential, even in his pajamas and bare feet.

CHAPTER
14

THE LAST THING I EXPECTED TO BE DOING THE DAY AFTER CHRIStina's espionage mission at the White House was driving the long I-15 stretch in Montana. But then, I never expected I'd be accused of plotting to assassinate the President of the United States either. I guess it just goes to show, you never know what you're going to step in on any given day.

After a hasty trip to the airport, I hopped my way to Great Falls by way of Charlotte and Minneapolis in just under eleven hours, the last leg of the journey in one of those small-plane commuter flights where every seat is a window seat. The first thing I did after bouncing around at a high altitude hour after hour was to invest in one of those inflatable doughnuts for my sore backside.

It was my first trip to Montana, and it didn't take long to learn one fact about the state. Its roads stretch to forever and beyond. The people who live here must be the deepest thinkers in the world. What else is there to do while traveling mile after endless mile?

The drive gave me plenty of time to mull the improbable scene of Christina holding an impromptu meeting on the White House floor with a pajama-clad president. That's an image I'll not forget anytime soon.

The weird part about the scene was that the scene itself wasn't the weird part. Not only did the president know Christina was coming, he knew what she was looking for. How was that possible? Christina and I were the only two people who knew about our plan, and I'd spoken to no one.

Then, when she returned to my apartment with the proofs, we lined up all thirteen chapter heading pages on my bed and studied the handwriting to see if we could discover who was framing me.

We ruled out the president, Ingraham, and Ms. Irwin. We also ruled out Margaret, Ingraham's secretary. Christina would have recognized her handwriting instantly.

Who did that leave?

Every White House staff member who worked for the president, Chief of Staff Ingraham, Ms. Irwin, or Margaret. In other words, anybody could have recorded the changes on the pages, but at whose instruction?

We were back to square one. Whoever *they* were remained a mystery. My only consolation was that the president wasn't behind it. From what Christina told me, he was surprised and upset when he learned what they'd done.

Personally, my money was on Ingraham. While I had no hard proof and I didn't have a motive, he was in the position not only to make the changes but also to revoke my access privileges to the White House and cut me off from everyone in the West Wing. The fact that he played the role of a Nazi when he demanded to listen to Christina's voicemail messages was, for me, proof enough of his guilt.

In all the time I spent at the White House, I had never warmed to Ingraham, nor he to me. But then, I don't think anybody did. The man was pure political power in a three-piece suit. Working with him was like working with nuclear fusion. He could produce a lot of energy to forward a career, or he could burn you to a crisp. You had to respect the man, but you never felt comfortable around him.

That Ingraham was part of the *they*, if not their leader, I had no doubt.

But it was a comment the president made that sent me winging to Montana. I asked Christina to repeat it several times to make certain she'd heard correctly.

"Why Grant? Doc Palmer, maybe. But Grant?"

First off, it was the musings of an—at times—semi-incoherent president on the floor in his pajamas. But what made the thing so odd was that Doc Palmer was dead. He had been for over a year. Why would anyone want to frame a dead man for a future assassination attempt?

On the car seat next to me was a research folder from the book project. I'd taken out the obituary from the *Shelby Reporter*.

Ricky "Doc" Palmer

Ricky Michael Palmer, 65, a Shelby resident and former Lewistown physician, died late Friday afternoon, October 26, in the Marias Care Center from injuries sustained in a single vehicle accident. Graveside services will be held Tuesday, October 30, at Mount Calvary Cemetery. Visitation is Monday, October 29, in Twin Oaks Chapel. The Twin Oaks Funeral Home is in charge of arrangements.

The obituary had been handed to me just as I was making reservations to fly to Montana to interview Doc Palmer for the book. Palmer and the president had served in the same platoon in Vietnam. And, after the war, Palmer was the president's personal physician, retiring at the end of the first term.

On the one hand, not having to travel to Montana came as a relief. The deadline for the book was fast approaching, and I really didn't have time to squeeze in a trip to Montana. Besides, I'd interviewed plenty of other members of the platoon and had more than enough quotes to write the chapter that culminated in the president receiving the Distinguished Service Cross.

But even back then Palmer's sudden death had been unsettling. Ingraham didn't want me to interview him. Summoned me to his office and told me I was wasting my time. Well, I don't like people telling me how to do my job. And—truth be told—I didn't want to be some moldy old history professor's anecdote at Yale or Harvard of a historian who took shortcuts in his research. So I told Ingraham the chapter needed a quote from Doc, and I was going to Montana despite his objection.Two days later Ingraham slapped Doc Palmer's obituary on my desk. He didn't send it by messenger. It was important enough to him to deliver the *coup de grace* himself.

That pretty much settled it. I mean, what kind of person would I be to suspect the president's chief of staff of such duplicity that he would manufacture a phony obituary just to win an argument with a freelance writer?

So I didn't call to confirm Palmer's death.

At least for an hour.

Both the *Shelby Reporter* and Twin Oaks Funeral Home confirmed the obituary notice. Apparently Palmer flipped his truck on Interstate 15. They estimated he was traveling over a hundred miles per hour. Alcohol—Palmer's lifelong personal demon—contributed to the accident.

Which brings me back to the president's pajama party. Why would he think Doc Palmer would be a better frame than me if Palmer was dead?

With more than an hour to drive, I shifted the inflatable doughnut to a more comfortable position. Maybe all that would come of this trip would be a visit to Doc Palmer's grave. But I had to see for myself. I still had Palmer's home address. I figured I'd start there and work my way to the grave.

———

I climbed out of the car into a dust cloud of my own making. If my directions were correct, this was the Palmer place. If I'd taken a wrong turn, this was probably Idaho, because there weren't many turns and the roads were long.

The house and barn had seen better days. Both showed evidence of being punished by strong winds and extreme temperatures. The barn had once been red. Now, it was weathered gray with red streaks.

"Hello?" I shouted.

The double barn doors gaped open. There was no sign of life. Same with the house. While the front door was closed, it looked like it had been dead for over a year.

"Just like its owner," I muttered.

I decided to try the house first. All three porch steps groaned when I stepped on them. Or was that me groaning? It had been a long trip. The paint on the screen door, what was left of it, was peeling. The screen was torn at the corner.

I knocked.

"Hello?" I called. "Anyone home?"

With no answer I turned to the barn, but my chances of finding anyone there looked remote. This place was deserted. I'd made the trip for nothing.

Halfway to the barn a voice stopped me. "Hold it right there!"

I turned to see a man with a shotgun rounding the house. A faded red ball cap was pulled down tight, trimmed around the edges with ragged gray hair. His flannel shirt was wrinkled, and his overalls were worn and dirty. He advanced until he was close enough to kill me without aiming.

I displayed empty hands. "I mean you no harm."

"That's the difference between us, then," he spat. "I mean you plenty of harm unless you jump in that car and go back to wherever you came from."

A huge black hole at the business end of the shotgun punctuated his point. For reasons unknown—other than that I have a tendency to see the ridiculous side of danger—I imagined myself getting a load of buckshot in the backside. My only hope was that it would hit the left cheek to balance the dog bite on the right and my limp would then be even.

Offering my friendliest smile to the man, I said, "There's no need to—"

BLAM!

Shotgun thunder rent the air. With a practiced motion he pumped the next round into the chamber and leveled the barrel at my chest.

"All right!" I shouted. "All right! I'm going!"

I began working my way around the front of the car.

"It's just that I came all the way from Washington, DC, to—"

BLAM!

Another round scattered the air. He reloaded and took two threatening steps toward me.

"I'm going! I'm going!"

Only for some reason I seemed to have forgotten how to open a car door. I clawed repeatedly at the latch, but for some reason the combination of what to push and what to pull had suddenly become a mystery to me.

"What's your name?" the man barked.

Great. Not only couldn't I remember how to open a door, I couldn't remember my name. "Um . . . um . . . it's . . . um. . . .

Give me a second here, will you, buddy? Do you know how embar-rassing it would be to die because you couldn't remember your own name?

"I . . . um . . . ah . . . ah! Austin. Gr-Grrrant Austin."

"Who do you work for?"

"Actually, I don't work for—"

"WHO DO YOU WORK FOR?" he shouted.

"I'm a writer! Freelance! I wrote a book about the president."

His brow furrowed as he chewed on that.

"Step around the car," he said. He motioned in the direction he wanted me to go with the barrel of the shotgun.

I did as he instructed. I stepped around the front of the car until nothing was between me and the weapon.

"Take your shoes off," he ordered.

"My shoes? What do my shoes—"

BLAM!

Bending over, I pulled off my shoes without unlacing them.

"Socks too."

The socks flew off.

He blinked hard several times to focus on my feet with eyes so bloodshot I couldn't see any white in them. His tongue worked the inside of a cheek that was rough with salt-and-pepper whiskers. He tilted his head to get a better look at my feet. Then he leaned over even farther.

Do you know how hard it is not to wiggle your toes when someone is looking at your feet? He leaned so far it must have made him dizzy. He stumbled sideways but caught himself.

"Shuffle them in the dirt," he said.

I started to object, then figured the fewer times he pulled the trigger on the shotgun the better my chances of leaving here alive. I shuffled my feet in the dirt.

"Let me see the bottom of one," he said.

I lifted my right foot and showed him the bottom.

He nodded and seemed to relax a little, but he didn't lower the shotgun. "Austin, you say."

"Yes, sir."

"You're the idiot they paid to write all them lies about Douglas. Or maybe you were duped. You don't look like the mercenary type to me."

"I researched the book thoroughly," I insisted.

"Did you now? You wrote what they wanted you to write, and that makes you a liar—only worse—since you sugarcoat the lies so nice that people smile when they swallow them."

"Listen," I said, my ire rising, "just because you hold a weapon doesn't make you right. Who are you to pass judgment on what I wrote, or upon me for why I wrote it?"

He shook his head. "For being a high-priced writer, you're not too smart, are you? Just what did you expect to find out here?"

"The truth."

"And if you find the truth, will you be able to die happy?"

I never liked those Siamese-twin questions where it's assumed two queries are linked at the hip. Since I didn't have an answer for it, I kept my mouth shut.

"Just as well," he said. "You'll find no truth here, only more lies."

The only pictures I'd seen of Doc Palmer were of him when he was young and in the army. This man looked like he could be Doc Palmer's father, or the way a young Doc Palmer might look when he got old.

"Some very powerful men don't want me to find the truth about Doc Palmer," I said.

The old man sniffed. "Go back to where you came from, kid. Doc Palmer is dead."

"It's not that easy. The same men who don't want me learning the truth about Doc Palmer are attempting to frame me in an attempt to assassinate the president."

That got his attention. "What the blue blazes are you talking about?"

"Do you have a copy of my book?"

He scowled at me.

"It's easier to show you if you do," I explained.

I must have piqued his curiosity, for he marched me behind the barn to the lip of a garbage pit.

"I think it's in this end," he said.

The scent of rotten milk and meats and vegetables stirred in an unholy stew of odors. I waited for him to reach for a rake or a pole or something to aid the search.

"Jump in," he said.

"What?"

"You're the one with something to prove."

There was a three-foot drop into banana peels, eggshells, coffee grounds, and what looked like some kind of ledger paper saturated with salad oil.

He motioned with the gun for me to jump.

I picked my spot carefully. My feet hit a large piece of cardboard, then slid from under me. I went down hard, the corner of a milk carton jabbing me in the back. Scrambling to right myself, I stuck my foot in a mess of coffee grounds.

"Try over there," he said from above, oblivious to my situation.

Luckily, I managed to find the book in short order beneath a flattened Wheaties cereal box. The cover had cottage cheese on it. I brushed the curds off.

"Toss it up," he ordered.

I tossed him the book and began searching for a foothold to climb out.

"You stay down there," he said.

"I'm not staying down here! You'll have to shoot me."

He repositioned the shotgun so that it was pointed at my head. "Don't tempt me," he said. "This way I can look at what you want to show me and keep an eye on you at the same time."

I looked around and was tempted to pelt him with a fuzzy blue stalk of celery. Instead, I said, "First chapter, first word."

Tucking the shotgun under his arm, he pulled a pair of reading glasses from his shirt pocket, then opened the book to the first chapter. He began to read aloud.

"No, just the first word," I said, trying to find a place to stand where something wasn't squishing up between my toes. "Now . . . second chapter, second word."

With the third chapter he caught on to the scheme. I let him continue on his own for a while, offering only, "It ends at the thirteenth chapter."

After reading the thirteenth word, he closed the book and laughed. "If that don't beat all. And you had no idea they'd done this to you with your own book?"

"Go ahead, rub it in."

"What did you do to deserve this? Mess with someone's daughter? Oooeeee. They really did a job on you, didn't they?" He reached down, offering me a hand.

"Thank you," I said.

"Call me Doc."

CHAPTER
15

With the shotgun harmlessly at rest on his forearm, Doc Palmer walked me back to my car. I did a little jig as we walked, trying to shake the coffee grounds off my feet. "Doc, is there some place I can—"

He groaned loudly. "I'm getting too old for this. I gotta sit down."

I thought he was going to take me inside the house. Instead, he slumped onto the front bumper of my rental car. He propped the shotgun beside him, pulled out a handkerchief, doffed his cap, and proceeded to mop his forehead. As he did, he chuckled again, still amused at how I'd been set up with my own book.

"They're clever. Yessiree. You gotta give them their due."

The coffee grounds wouldn't come off. I tried wiping one foot clean with the other.

"Doc, is there a—"

"You know," he mused, "I've always wondered if things would be different had Noonan lived. What do you think? Can one man change history?"

Noonan. I recognized the name. "You're talking about Lieutenant

Roy Noonan. The man the president attempted to rescue in the Ho Bo Woods."

Doc Palmer looked at me with great sadness. It was clear he took no joy in what he said next. There was no righteous indignation, no satisfaction at setting the record straight, only sadness, the kind that comes when you're forced to peel back reality's skin and show someone how ugly life can be.

He said, "Lloyd Douglas may have pulled Noonan out of the Ho Bo Woods, but only after he killed him."

"No . . . I can't accept that."

My denial rang hollow. Even as I stood there with coffee grounds on my feet, the story I'd written, now a screenplay, was being filmed for a television special, and all of a sudden I sensed what I hadn't sensed before—that the reason it would make such a great movie was because it was no more real than any other movie made in Hollywood.

In the account I'd penned, Lieutenant Noonan was a likable fellow, dashing, handsome, but ambitious, and his ambitions often put his platoon in danger.

Living in the shadow of a famous father—all-American at Yale, World War II hero, congressman-turned-senator—Roy Noonan was in Vietnam for one reason only, as a springboard to political office. His father, inspired by Joseph Kennedy, had charted a path for him that would lead to the White House.

According to the account, fresh from personal leave, Noonan returned just as Alpha Company had come off a long, difficult mission. To curry favor with his superiors, he volunteered his platoon for a dangerous mission in the Ho Bo Woods, a notorious death trap. Alpha Company could expect to come up against fresh Vietcong forces, elite units of sappers, and a complex system of tunnels and speed trails. All of this under a triple-thick jungle canopy.

It was a suicide mission. That's how everyone in Alpha Company saw it. Everyone except their ambitious platoon leader. He saw it as a chance to impress a few generals.

The night before the mission, the men were unusually quiet. They drank heavily to numb their nerves and prepare themselves for certain death. Sensing their mood, indeed sharing it, nevertheless Douglas moved among the men, encouraging them, praying with them.

The next morning, with a whine of turbines, Alpha Company was airlifted to a savannah-like clearing where they were dropped into swirling smoke and chaos. With gunfire erupting from the trees, they maneuvered their way around stumps, termite mounds, and the carcasses of a hundred or more cattle. Fighting their way to the perimeter, they dug in.

The plan was to press the initiative, to keep the enemy off balance and not give them time to react. After establishing a defensive position, they were to set ambushes along the enemy's speed trails. The plan never had a chance.

Shaken by heavy resistance, Lieutenant Noonan fell apart. He curled up, hugging his knees and mumbling incoherently. The slightest sound set him off. The only way to calm him was for Douglas to promise to remain at his side.

Twilight came, and darkness engulfed the jungle with surprising speed. Everything they touched was wet and slimy and dripping. Traversing the forest to the extraction coordinates was like walking blindly through a tunnel of vines that entangled their weapons and arms and legs.The enemy struck without warning, lighting up the area with a barrage of mortars, grenades, and tracer bullets. Everyone scattered from the trail, diving into the woods. True to his word, Douglas stuck with Noonan, even when they started lagging behind.

That's when Noonan lost it. He fell to the ground in a fetal position, refusing to move. While Douglas returned fire, an enemy grenade landed between them.

In a frozen moment, the two men exchanged glances. Noonan's eyes crystallized with the realization of what he had to do. He threw himself on the grenade.

Wounded by shrapnel, Douglas cradled his wounded platoon leader in his arms. Just before Noonan died, he said to Douglas, "It's better this way, that you live and I die. Go home. Make your life count. Remember, from this moment on, you're living the hopes and dreams of two men."

Despite heavy fire and at great personal risk, Douglas carried his fallen comrade back to the medevac helicopter. When Vietnamese regulars, scared from fighting, swarmed the chopper and began pulling off American corpses so they could climb onboard, Douglas held them off at gunpoint.

For his heroic actions in the Ho Bo Woods, Lieutenant Lloyd Douglas was awarded the Distinguished Service Cross. And when his political party nominated him as their candidate for president, his campaign slogan was: "He carries the hopes and dreams of all Americans on his shoulders."

At Doc Palmer's farm, I shuffled my feet in the dirt and sat next to him on the front bumper.

"Enlighten me," I said. "If it didn't happen as I recorded it in my book, how did it happen?"

Doc sighed as though debating whether he should wade into these emotional waters.

"You have the basic timeline and events of the mission correct," he said. "We had just come off a long march and our tails were dragging. We were surprised when they told us we'd be going out again so soon. But Noonan had nothing to do with our unit being selected for the mission. We were notified of the mission before he returned from leave. Like the rest of us, he didn't like it, but when the orders came down, he obeyed them.

"As for Noonan falling apart under fire? Hogwash. Don't get

me wrong. Any of us woulda been nuts not to be afraid. But to the point of cowardice or incapacitation? Your characterization doesn't fit the man."

"You claim Douglas killed Noonan. How can you know that? They were separated from the rest of the platoon."

"Douglas was there," Doc said. "He told me."

"Now I know you're blowin' smoke. Douglas told you he fragged Noonan? You expect me to believe that?"

Doc stared sadly at the ground. In a low voice he said, "I didn't want to believe it either."

Having forgotten all about the coffee grounds on my feet, I waited for him to offer an alternative account. He repositioned himself on the bumper.

"Let me tell you something about Roy Noonan," he said.

His eyes took on an unfocused stare; behind them played images of the past. "We had holed up in a bombed-out pagoda at an intersection of sorts, little more than a cluster of dirt lanes that connected nearby farms and villages. We set up an ambush. Just before dawn we heard an ominous creaking sound. The way the sound ping-pongs among the trees we couldn't tell which direction it was coming from, only that it was getting louder. There was a curfew in effect, so we interpreted any sound as unfriendly. We figured it was a twenty-millimeter gun, or maybe one of those recoilless rifles on wheels. Anyway, the order came down to take it out as soon as it entered our kill zone.

"The next thing we know, there was a thunderous flash of claymores—antipersonnel mines—being set off, and in the middle of it all was an old man and a team of oxen pulling a heavy cart. The oxen were riddled with shrapnel and they began bellowing something awful and thrashing about. They blindly pulled the cart off the road and into a field where it got mired in the mud.

"In all the confusion our unit hit the road with mortars. It beats all reason, but even after all that, some of the oxen and the old man were still alive. That he had survived was a miracle itself. The only thing we can figure is that the thick sides of the cart protected him.

"As the sky grew lighter, the situation went from bad to worse. The bellowing of the injured oxen was getting on everyone's nerves. So was the old man's wailing over the loss of oxen and his crop—peanuts. Finally, one machine gunner couldn't take it anymore. He walked to the side of the field and opened up on the oxen until they were all dead.

"That's when Lieutenant Noonan arrived to assess the situation. Moments after that, the enemy opened fire. We all scattered, diving for the nearest hole we could find, while the farmer, caught between two armies, continued wailing.

"Noonan took out after him. Under heavy fire he sprinted across the road, grabbed the farmer by the shoulders, and dragged him into a ditch where he tended the man's wounds. Then he called for a medevac to airlift the farmer to the hospital. Under a hail of bullets, Lieutenant Noonan carried the farmer to the chopper.

"Does that sound to you like a man who would wimp out during an exchange of enemy fire in the Ho Bo Woods?" he asked.

I had to admit it didn't.

"A few days later," Doc continued, "I was at the hospital getting supplies when I saw Lieutenant Noonan visiting that same farmer. I overheard him apologize for the actions of his men and instruct the man where to submit the necessary forms to recover his loss.

"You don't hear stories like that on the news. You hear about the atrocities, the ugliness. But that day I witnessed a man acting like a man. Taking responsibility. Doing what he could to make things right. For what? A peasant farmer he didn't know. There were no cameras to record what he did. Noonan stood up for what was right and decent. To me, that's a true leader, and I knew I would follow that man anywhere."

Sometimes the way a man speaks of another man is more reveal-ing than the words themselves. I felt a respect for Lieutenant Noonan simply by the way Doc spoke of him.

But Doc still hadn't answered my question. "What reason did Douglas have for killing him?"

"What reason does any man have for killing another man?" Doc replied philosophically. His face became drawn and saddened again. "Douglas told me what happened shortly before he announced he was running for a second term. At the time he was depressed and in a lot of pain."

"Physical pain?"

The knowing smile reappeared. "Vietnam took its toll on Doug-las more than is generally known. Not only his combat wounds, but diseases he contracted while on leave, and a degenerative disc in his back. We managed to hold him together for the rigors of the first campaign, but in doing so he became addicted to pain medication."

"Addicted?" It was the first time I'd heard any of this.

"As his personal physician it was my role to make him present-able to the public and lucid during key meetings and speeches. Each year my job grew increasingly difficult. I'd signed on for one four-year term, and when Douglas decided to run again, I opted out. At the levels he's at, the medication is as much of a killer as the disease. Much of the time the man is so heavily medicated he isn't competent."

"Isn't competent! I don't believe this!" I cried.

"Naturally, it's kept secret. Only a few people know how serious his condition is. As for what you believe. . . . You came looking for the truth. Whether you believe it is not my concern."

When I was researching the book, my access to the president came in ten- and fifteen-minute chunks of time, and on more than one occasion was cancelled without warning. Pressing affairs of state was the standard excuse.

"You said he was depressed when he told you about Noonan," I prompted.

"He overreacted to my decision to leave him, threw a tantrum. He knew how I felt about Noonan and wanted to hurt me."

Doc fell silent. Digging up the memory uncovered old pain with it.

"He told me when they separated from the rest of the platoon in the Ho Bo Woods, he saw his chance to rid himself of Noonan, whom he saw as a threat. Not so much in Vietnam, but when they got back home and into politics. Douglas could see himself playing second fiddle to Noonan for the rest of his life."

Doc's gaze wandered off for a moment.

"I can't prove it," he continued, "but Thorson may have had something to do with it."

"Thorson," I said, reaching for a writing pad I keep in my shirt pocket. "I don't believe I came across that name in my research."

"First name, Gregory. Don't bother to look him up. Presumed MIA."

"And you think he influenced Douglas into killing Noonan?"

Doc shrugged. "A hunch. I just know I never liked the guy. Competitive. And he always acted like he was smarter than everyone else. Know the type?"

I laughed. "I could tell you stories."

"This guy, Thorson—Thor's son, he made a big deal of it—latched onto Douglas. The two of them became inseparable. And I'm telling you, the man was strange. One time in the middle of a firefight I happened to look up and there he was sitting at the top of a tree paying no attention to what was going on below. A VC spotted him and fired. The guy dropped out of the tree like a ripe piece of fruit. Then, when we went to get him—to pick up the pieces, we thought—he wasn't there. Later that night he came strolling into camp, pretty as you please. Said he'd gotten turned around."

Doc rubbed his stubbled chin, then turned deadly serious.

"In the Ho Bo Woods," he said, picking up the story, "when Douglas and Noonan were separated from the rest of the platoon, a grenade exploded near them. It stunned Noonan, knocked him out. Douglas said he saw an opportunity, the kind that can change a person's life.

"Noonan started to come around, so Douglas leveled him with the butt of his machine gun. Then he took one of Noonan's grenades—Douglas was very clear about this—pulled the pin, stuffed the grenade in Noonan's shirt, and rolled him over, face to the ground."

The huge Montana sky stretched over us in silence. The only sound on Doc Palmer's farm was a breath of wind that whipped into a whirlwind of dust.

Clearing his throat, Doc said, "He miscalculated, Douglas did. He got hit with shrapnel in his leg. Turns out, it worked to his advantage. When the soldiers saw him bloodied and limping and carrying Noonan's body, he was an instant hero."

We sat there. The two of us. Mourning Noonan's death. But also, at least for me, mourning a day that would be sadder when I went to bed than it was when I woke up.

Doc slapped, then rubbed both legs. "I don't know about you, but I could use a drink. I'll settle for a cup of coffee. Want a cup?"

"Thanks," I said, "but I still have a couple of hours on the road if I'm going to make my flight."

Truth was, I just wanted to be alone right now. My world had changed dramatically, and it would take me some time to adjust.

"Word of advice?" Doc offered. "Don't mess with them. A smart man knows not to fight if he has no chance of winning. Do what I did. Disappear, Mr. Austin. Plenty of land around here to do that. Once they see you're no threat to them, they'll leave you alone."

Find a big hole, Mr. Austin.

Ten minutes later I was driving south on Interstate 15 mulling over my encounter with a dead man. His story. His advice.

I was angry with myself. I drove away without asking him what all that business was about having me take off my shoes.

My head hurt from thinking. When you write a book, you create a world that has a sense of order to it. But since my book had come out, it seemed that every time I turned around someone was challenging that sense of order, and my grasp on reality. I kept hearing the same refrain over and over—

Things aren't the way you think they are.

The first thing I was going to do when I got back to Washington was slap Doc Palmer's obituary on Ingraham's desk and tell him that for a man who is supposed to be dead, Doc has some interesting opinions on life and presidents.

Then what? Rewrite the book? Do an exposé on the president's medication addiction for the *New York Times*? It wasn't in my nature to be a muckraker reporter, but then I hated the thought that I'd been played for a patsy.

For the moment though, out here under an endless sky, passing endless stretches of scrub brush, I was going to give it a rest. A brain can only take so much stirring up. After a while everything becomes murky, like an ocean bottom when the silt is fanned. It does no good to thrash around. You have to let the silt settle. And what better place to do that than on a Montana road?

I punched the radio On button.

For some reason I remembered a television commercial from my youth. The scene is of a cowboy herding cattle in the great open spaces. He is listening to music on a transistor radio, a live performance of a New York opera. Joining voices with the featured tenor, the cowboy belts out the signature aria from *Pagliacci*.

Classical music in cowboy country. That might be fun. I pushed the Search button and listened to the cascading lineup of stations, most of them country western or news.

". . . next week where President Douglas will attend several key fundraisers. San Diego party officials have pulled out all the stops on the president's trip, knowing that this may be . . ."

San Diego.

I muttered the words of the president's warning to Christina. "Under no circumstances is Grant to go to San Diego. Is that clear? Hog-tie him if you have to, but keep him away from San Diego."

Turning the radio off, I pressed the accelerator and recalculated my arrival at Great Falls airport at the increased speed. I tried using my smartphone to make an airline reservation. No bars showed on the display. I was still out of range.

I didn't know when the next flight was from Great Falls to San Diego, but I knew I was going to be on it.

After coffee and a nap, Doc Palmer nudged the screen door open with his elbow. His arms were full. One arm carried empty whiskey bottles—the other, his shotgun. Both had become a significant part of his daily routine. The whiskey helped him sleep better at night; and the shotgun . . . well, it helped him sleep better at night.

Maybe it was his Montana surroundings, but he felt like an old, retired gunslinger. He knew sooner or later they'd send someone to hunt him down. He knew they'd kill him. All he wanted was to get a shot or two off before he died, get a lick or two in, just so they'd say Doc Palmer didn't go down without a fight.

The empty bottles clanked in his arms as he walked into the barn and found his case of whiskey. He put the two bottles back in the carton and pulled out two fresh bottles.

When he turned around, someone was standing just inside the door of the barn. With the light behind him, the figure appeared as a flat silhouette. The figure was empty-handed, so Doc was startled, but not alarmed.

Doc took a couple of steps toward the stranger, ready to drop the whiskey bottles and raise the shotgun at the first sign of trouble.

The man made no move. He just stood there.

"Whoever you're looking for," Doc said, "he's not here."

Doc heard a rustling sound behind him. Holding his ground, he glanced over one shoulder, then the other. There were two more of them, black and featureless, standing in the shadows. The back of the barn was closed off. They must have already been in the barn waiting for him. Doc saw no weapons. That meant they were sneaks, and sneaks were never up to any good but were usually scared off with a gunshot blast or two.

"I don't have anything worth taking," Doc said. "Leave now and no one gets hurt. I'm going to give you only one chance."

They didn't move. The three of them just stood there, not making a sound. Doc dropped the whiskey bottles; one of them broke in half, spilling spirits in the dirt. He pointed the shotgun at the man standing in the barn door, figuring he was the leader.

"I'm telling you, you're wasting your time. There's nothing here for you." He could hear fear in his voice.

The figure in the doorway took a step back. With one foot, he stepped on the heel of the other foot and kicked off a shoe. Then he kicked off his other shoe.

Doc saw the man's feet. He gasped.

The figure said, "Douglas told you about us, did he?"

Doc had seen some strange things in his life, but nothing like this. The man's feet didn't reach the ground. He stood a good inch above the dirt.

He approached Doc. He made no footprints.

As he came closer, Doc was able to get a better look at him. "Thorson!" he cried.

Yet Thorson hadn't aged. He looked the same as he did in Vietnam, and he grinned the same insufferable grin that made Doc grit his teeth.

"Actually, it's Semyaza," he said.

Lightning fast, Doc lifted the shotgun at the man's chest and fired three quick rounds.

BLAM! BLAM! BLAM!

The man didn't flinch. The blast went right through him. His chest, his clothes were undisturbed.

Doc lowered the shotgun, resigned to his fate. "I knew if you really existed, someday you'd come for me," he said. "The boy. Austin. You wanted him to find me."

"He needed to hear what you had to say."

Doc nodded. The shotgun clattered to the ground. "Do me a favor? Make it quick."

The grin appeared again. "Oh, we will kill you, Doc. Make no mistake about that. But not for years. You're far more use to us alive than dead."

Movement in the rafters caught Doc's attention. He heard skittering sounds like rats in an attic. Only these rats were whimpering. And they had faces, the faces of medieval gargoyles, leering down at him with hungry eyes.

There were dozens of them—no, more—in the corners, in the shadows, the far reaches of the rafters. Hundreds of them.

They strained to come down, but something was stopping them. What?

In the next instant, Doc knew. They were waiting for a signal. With the slightest of nods, Semyaza granted their request.

The first one hit Doc in the back, clawing its way into him. An instant later, another hit his chest; another, his head. At each place, the first one to enter him met some form of natural barrier, but once that was broken through, the others streamed in effortlessly.

Doc's head filled with hundreds of voices.

He sank to his knees. He screamed, but he couldn't hear himself—the shouts in his head were louder than the shouts from his throat.

He could feel them moving inside of him, wrestling for room, elbowing their way deeper and deeper, tearing at his spirit, snapping at it like dogs fighting over a scrap of meat.

Doc remained aware of his surroundings. He could see Semyaza and the others. They oversaw the possession with compassion in their eyes, not unlike what he would expect to see on the faces of Red Cross workers handing out bowls of food to starving children.

Then, the three were gone. Vanished. Leaving Doc Palmer alone on the floor of his barn with the voices screaming in his head.

CHAPTER
16

IT FELT GOOD TO PULL ON A CLEAN PAIR OF SOCKS. I HAD COFFEE grounds between my toes from Shelby to Great Falls, then for four hours in the air with a layover in Salt Lake City, a shuttle to the rental car company, and even when I registered at the historic U.S. Grant Hotel in San Diego. Next time I tracked a dead man in Montana, I would be sure to use his garden hose to clean my feet before driving away.

Other than the gritty feeling in my shoes, the trip from Montana to California was uneventful, just the way I like my flights, and the final approach into Lindbergh Field was spectacular. Whenever I fly into San Diego I request a window seat on the port side. Starboard side passengers get a nice view of Balboa Park, but it's nothing compared to the picturesque panorama of the bay, the strand, and the Coronado Bridge.

The bridge is two majestic miles of blue, curved ribbon stretched across mission arches that rise two hundred feet above the bay, tall enough for naval ships to pass under, the exception being the humongous aircraft carriers that are docked on the Coronado side of the bay at North Island.

Nothing says San Diego to me like this bird's eye view of the bridge set against a deep blue, rippling bay that is dotted with dozens of white sails. To me, it says, "Welcome Home."

I think we were somewhere over Nevada when I decided that on this trip I was going to treat myself to a classy hotel for winning the Pulitzer Prize. What better way to do that than to stay at a hotel with history?

Originally built in 1910, the U.S. Grant had recently undergone a $52 million renovation. Thirteen presidents had lodged here, and the clerk was giddy when he informed me the fourteenth would soon be arriving and that if I'd be staying that long I might encounter a few minor inconveniences due to heightened security.

"I can imagine," I replied.

"But it'll be worth it, don't you think?" he said, bouncing on his feet. "To be able to tell your grandchildren you once stayed at the U.S. Grant at the same time as President Douglas?"

I didn't tell him I'd stayed at the White House and at Camp David with the president. I didn't tell him I'd slept on Air Force One on the way to Paris with the president. Neither did I tell him I hoped to do more than just stay in the same hotel with the president.

As I signed the register, I wondered what he'd say if he knew that in my biography I'd threatened to kill the president. This time anonymity worked in my favor.

My plan was simple. Gain an audience with the president. Achieving that goal . . . well, not so simple. The key was Jana.

No longer smelling like a stale cup of coffee, I tried her cell phone. As it rang I thought of places I could take her for dinner. "Jana?"

"Grant! Where are you?"

"San Diego. Listen, I need to see you—"

"You came back for the funeral? Grant, how sweet!"

I wanted to kick myself. I'd forgotten about Myles Shepherd's funeral.

"Where are you right now?" Jana asked. "Do you need directions?" She sounded very pleased with me.

"I'm . . . downtown."

"Downtown? Grant, the funeral's going to start in ten minutes. Well, get here as soon as you can. The important thing is that you came."

How do you tell someone you forgot a funeral? How do you tell someone the person in the casket isn't who they think it is?

"Jana, I just flew in from Montana and I didn't pack a suit."

"Montana? What were you . . . Never mind, it doesn't matter. Are you saying you're not coming to the funeral?" Her voice dripped with disappointment.

"I don't see how I can."

"I have to go now. The service for our friend is about to start."

"Wait! It's important that I see you. Can we meet later? Dinner, maybe?"

For a few moments I listened to Jana's angry breathing. Then she spoke to someone, telling them she'd be right there. "I have to go," she said.

"Meet me for dinner. Please."

"I'll call you after the funeral." She cut the connection.

Not a second passed before my phone rang. *I'm Too Sexy for My Shirt.*

"Christina."

"Did I wake you?" she asked. "What time did you get in?"

"You didn't wake me."

For the moment I offered no further explanation. When Christina learned I was in San Diego, she was going to go ballistic. "I have only a few minutes," she said. "Was the trip worth it?"

"I interviewed Doc Palmer."

"He's alive? Grant, why would they . . . we'll get into that later. What did he say?"

"To say his version of events bears little resemblance to what I wrote in the book is an understatement."

"Did you show him the chapters?"

I knew she was referring to the thirteen chapters that contained a coded threat to the president.

"I did."

"And?"

"He laughed. But it was a sympathetic laugh. Does that make sense? And he told me . . . Christina, when you were with the president, did he seem . . . did he appear to be . . . you know, sedated?"

"He was sitting on the floor in his pajamas, Grant."

"What about his speech?"

Christina gave it some thought before answering. "He was lucid. Maybe a little slow. His eyes looked tired. But then, when he stood up, he seemed to rally. I guess he could have been on medication."

I digested this. It could mean something. But then again, it could just mean the president was tired.

"Grant, what is this all about?"

"Doc told me some things that were disturbing."

I wanted to tell her more. To tell her all of it. I was aching to tell someone. I wanted to hear the words come from my own mouth to see if they sounded as crazy as they did in my head.

"Listen, Grant . . . I gotta go. I stepped outside to make this call. Let's get together for dinner. You can tell me all about it then. DeLugo's at eight. Gotta go. Bye."

She hung up before I could tell her I wasn't in Washington. I touched her contact number. A familiar automated voice told me her phone had been turned off. Smart girl. If Ingraham pulled his Gestapo act again, there wouldn't be any messages to listen to.

But tonight she would think I stood her up.

My phone rang. I didn't recognize the number. "Hello?"

"How long will you be in San Diego?"

The sound of Sue Ling's voice brought a smile to my face. Jana must have called her.

"Word gets around fast in this town," I said.

"The professor wants to talk to you."

"At the moment, I don't know for sure what my schedule is. I'm in the process of working it out."

"Work out a time to meet the professor. It's important."

"I don't know if I can promise anything. You of all people know what I'm up against. You're the one who found the coded message."

"The confession."

"It's not a confession!" I protested. "It's a setup and I still don't know who's behind it, and until I do I'm vulnerable. The Secret Service could shut me away for a long time."

"Talk to the professor. He can help you."

I doubted the professor's fixation on angels would serve any useful purpose, but I hesitated saying anything to Sue. She wasn't objective when it came to the professor. "Look, Sue, the professor's a good man, and I know he means well, but not everything is an angel conspiracy."

"You're right," she admitted. "But this is."

"Tell you what . . . let me see how my schedule works out. Give me a number where you can be reached and I'll—"

"Meet me."

I found myself smiling. It was the first friendly thing she'd ever said to me.

"When?"

"Right now."

She was going to try to talk me into meeting with the professor, that much was clear. It was a risk going. I'm not very good at saying no to attractive women.

Sensing my hesitation, she said, "Meet with me now, and Jana will join us after the funeral."

"You can guarantee that?"

"I can."

"Where do you want to meet?"

Abdiel paced as he dictated. He moved back and forth in front of the professor's desk. It was a tight space, barely enough room for him to turn around with his broad shoulders. Every so often he would knock a hat from the hat rack in the corner, or brush against the professor's collection of knickknacks that lined his bookshelves. Three paces was all it took for him to cover the distance. Each day when they began, it took several turns for him to adjust to the limited space, but once he got into the telling, he no longer seemed to be bothered by it.

Other teachers' offices, though this same size, didn't have this problem. It was an old building and the rooms didn't conform to modern codes of handicap accessibility. The professor made do.

Perched behind his laptop, head down, brow furrowed, the professor listened with two index fingers racing from key to key, recording every word Abdiel spoke. Every so often the professor smiled or shook his head or grunted with astonishment at what he was hearing.

Abdiel paused in his dictation to offer commentary. "The invasion caught Lucifer and his forces completely by surprise," he said. "The brilliance of the plan was its audacity, that the Son of God would lower himself to such a state, that he would clothe himself with the very material that formed the basis of Lucifer's complaint. However, once the shock of the invasion wore off, Lucifer spied his chance to turn it to his advantage."

He pivoted, took a breath, and prepared to continue his narration. The professor sat back, signaling he needed to take a break.

"Why do you type with only two fingers when God has given

you ten?" Abdiel asked. "This would go much faster if you used all your fingers."

The professor held up his two index fingers like they were smoking guns. "I'll have you know these babies got me through college and postgraduate school. The way I see it, if ever they break down, I have eight fresh fingers standing in the wings ready to take their place."

Abdiel wasn't amused. He rarely laughed at human humor. The professor's eyes fell back onto the laptop screen. "You make the Nativity sound like D-day," he said.

"Very good," Abdiel replied. "The comparison is accurate. The birth of the Christ was an invasion into Lucifer's territory. Everything that followed was a direct contest between Lucifer and the Son, culminating in the battle of the cross. That the two would meet in head-to-head combat had become inevitable." With a yawn, the professor stretched.

"I see you are tired," Abdiel said. "I will come back tomorrow."

Rubbing his eyes, the professor agreed. Then, when they focused again, he was surprised to see Abdiel still standing there. He appeared to have something on his mind.

"She is delivering the narrative?" Abdiel said.

The angel's interest intrigued the professor. He never showed much concern over what humans did.

"As we speak. The first chapter only."

Abdiel nodded. He stared at the floor with a sour expression.

"You should meet him," the professor said. "Talk to him. It may ease your concern."

"Or compound it."

"Once you get to know him—"

"No."

"He may surprise you."

"Not likely."

"Why? Why won't you meet him?"

Abdiel took to pacing again. "The memory of the Watchers is too painful for us."

From an earlier dictation the professor knew he was referring to preflood angels who had mingled with the human population in the pretense of guiding them spiritually. Semyaza, Azazel, and others had mated with the human women and produced offspring who, when they were killed in the flood, became nomad demons wandering the earth in torment.

Abdiel said, "The fate of the offspring troubles us. Does that surprise you? You have to understand, angels were once a united community. Those in rebellion were once our friends. To see their offspring subjected to . . ." He didn't finish. "The fact that they brought it upon themselves," he added, "doesn't lessen our pain."

"Neither did Grant bring this upon himself," the professor said.

The comment stopped Abdiel in his tracks. He didn't like it but made no reply.

"Just talk with him."

"I said no."

"Are all angels as stubborn as you?"

"Insulting me will not make me change my mind."

"What will change your mind? There are larger issues here, surely you of all beings can see that. Talk to him. You owe him that much."

"I SAID NO!"

Abdiel's shout shook the walls. A mounted picture behind the professor fell, shattering the pane of glass. He leaned over in his chair to pick it up. When he turned back, Abdiel was gone.

"Fine, be like that," the professor said to the empty room.

CHAPTER
17

HOWARD'S BAKERY ON BROADWAY IN EL CAJON ANCHORED THE
eastern corner of a typical California strip mall featuring everything
from art supplies to an exercise studio to flowers and a ninety-nine-
cent store, with the majority of the property consisting of parking lot.

When I pulled into a parking space I could see Sue Ling waiting
for me at a table on the other side of a panel window. She was dressed
in a simple black-and-white leaf-pattern dress that accentuated her
slight figure, and my initial thought was that she looked natural
in a store window. With her sitting there, the male clientele would
increase significantly.

She sat with her elbows on the table and hands folded. Her legs
were crossed at the ankles. A small, black portfolio-style carrying
case rested against the leg of her chair next to her feet.

Her smile was cordial when she saw me.

"Can I get you something?" I offered once inside.

She gave me her order and I returned moments later with two
coffees, a lemon bar for her, and an eclair for me.

When I sat down, I winced. The chair reminded me of my injury.

"Something wrong?" she asked.

I grinned sheepishly. "Just a minor disagreement between me and some White House guard dogs."

A comment like that begged the story. I told it briefly and with humor, downplaying the seriousness of it all.

"Why do you do that?" she asked. "Dismiss everything with humor?"

I shrugged. "I don't know. Defense mechanism, I guess. If the seriousness of this whole ordeal ever catches up with me, I'll probably end up on a remote farm in Montana with no trespassing signs posted all over the place."

"So that's why you came back," Sue said. "You're here because the president is coming to San Diego. And you think Jana can help you get close to him."

"Very good," I said, impressed.

"She won't help you."

I smiled rakishly. "I can be rather persuasive when I want to be."

She smirked. "You're not as charming as you think you are."

For several moments we concentrated on our pastries and coffee.

"Thank you for agreeing to meet with me," she said.

Since I knew her agenda, I decided a preemptive denial was the best approach. "My schedule is up in the air," I said. "I can't promise to meet with the professor."

Sue Ling smiled sweetly, sipped her coffee, and stared out the window. She took my statement as a challenge.

I changed the subject. "Do you mind if I ask you something?"

She set the cup down, folded her hands, and met my gaze, awaiting the question. Her brown eyes so mesmerized me, I almost forgot what I was going to ask her.

"You're a student of physics," I said. "How is it you've hooked up with a professor of theology? The disciplines are so far apart."

"Not as distant as you might think," she said. "I went to Heritage College after high school. I was a Bible studies major, and the professor was one of my teachers. I eventually became his teaching fellow.

"Actually, it was Professor Forsythe who encouraged me to pursue physics. My senior year I was having a hard time finding a suitable topic for a term paper, and he suggested I do a study of the spiritual side of the cosmos."

"I've always thought the spiritual and the physical were opposites, irreconcilable, in tension with each other."

"That's what most people think. You're wrong."

I laughed. "Simple as that."

"Simple as that."

"Unless I completely missed the boat in my college physics classes, I could probably find a few hundred noted scientists who would take my side."

"You could introduce me to a million scientists. It wouldn't make any difference. They're all wrong."

I admired her confidence, even though she was academically misguided. "It always comes back to the supernatural with you and the professor, doesn't it? Not everything is about angels."

"More so than you think."

I sipped my coffee. "Don't get me wrong. I deal with intangibles all the time. Speech. Ideas. But the difference between us is that my intangibles are verifiable. I deal with facts that can be checked and corroborated, facts so powerful they can change the world. I don't have time for fairy tales and myths."

"Then maybe it's time you double-checked your so-called facts. Real? You don't know what real is. I'll take what you so ignorantly refer to as fairy tales and myths over your biased collection of interpreted history any day, and over the political forces you naively claim shape the world. All this . . ." She patted the table. Lifted her coffee cup. Crumpled her napkin.

I got the message. All matter.

"This is the stuff of the cosmos. To you it's real, only it's temporary. And the supernatural, the stuff of the spirit? It existed before the cosmos was created and will continue to exist after the cosmos is burned up and gone. It's eternal. And let me tell you something else . . ."

She was on a roll and getting animated.

"All this matter? All this dirt and rock and territory and human flesh that is so important to your history? It's shaped by the supernatural more than you're aware. You want to know what's real?" Her jaw trembled. She was getting emotional.

She reached into her bag and pulled out a purse. From the purse she retrieved three photos in succession and slapped them on the table, side by side.

"This is real!" she said, tears coming now. "This is real history shaped by real supernatural forces."

I looked at the photos. The first was a studio shot of the professor, younger, though his hair was white. He smiled a carefree smile I had yet to see during my time with the man. A handsome woman embraced him from behind, her arms draped around his neck, clasped against his chest. Her head reclined against his. Her eyes, her smile, her demeanor, were that of a woman in love.

The two other pictures were also portraits, the kind taken once a year at school. Two girls, both strawberry blond. The older girl looked like she was a fifth- or sixth-grader. Her smile was strained because she was trying to hide the braces on her teeth, but her eyes were those of a happy girl. The younger girl, possibly third grade, was a little pixie with mischievous eyes.

"The professor's family," I surmised. Something told me there was a story attached to these pictures and it wasn't a happy one.

"The professor was in his second year at Heritage," Sue said. "His doctoral study had been on kingdom warfare as portrayed in the New Testament, chiefly the book of Ephesians. He taught a course on kingdom warfare at the college that became quite popular. As a result, speaking invitations began to pour in and he traveled frequently, preaching on Sundays and teaching during the week."

Sue took a ragged breath before continuing. "He was beginning to get national attention and had just signed a contract to write a book when they visited him the first time."

"They?"

"Beings you so easily dismiss as myths and fairy tales."

A shiver that stretched all the way back to Myles Shepherd's office chilled me.

"They tried to intimidate him, scare him. Shut him up."

"Why? If they're so threatening, you'd think they would want people to know about them."

"Myths and fairy tales manipulating and controlling people? How ridiculous, Grant."

I accepted her chastisement. My statement made it sound like I believed they existed. It was obvious she believed it. But I was confident the story wouldn't hold up under investigation.

"At the time," she continued, "the professor was serving as a volunteer chaplain for the police department. Once a week he would ride along in a squad car and basically make himself available to counsel victims. One day, while he was on duty, his unit was dispatched to an automobile accident with injuries."

Another ragged breath. She glanced down at the pictures on the table.

"The professor didn't know it was his family until he arrived at the scene."

Sue fished for a tissue. "A hit-and-run. Nora had just picked up the girls from school. She was turning left with the light. A red pickup truck ran the light. Nora and Jenny were dead when he got there."

She pushed the picture of the youngest girl closer to me. "Terri died in her father's arms."

From the table four smiling faces looked up at me.

"It wasn't an accident, Grant. It was a message. While the professor was holding Terri, he looked up and saw the same three EDs who had threatened him. He blinked and they were gone." Sue reclaimed the pictures one at a time and put them back in her purse.

"EDs?"

"A term I coined for my thesis. Extradimensionals. Angels. They have the ability to move between physical dimensions."

"The accident. How do you know—"

"That it wasn't just a common, everyday hit-and-run?"

"That's unfair, Sue. I wouldn't make light of the professor's pain."

"But that's their intention, isn't it? To make it appear as an accident. It wasn't. It was murder. If you stick around for long, you'll come to realize they like the convenience of car accidents to cover their tracks."

The image of Myles Shepherd's car burning on the Second Street off-ramp flashed in my mind.

"In the Middle Ages they used forests. A person wanders in and is never seen again. The ocean was popular for a time. Sailors get lost at sea. Their methods adapt with the times."

For one insane moment I found myself contemplating what she was saying as though it was true.

Her cell phone rang. She answered it. Looking at me, she said, "Yeah, he's here." She ended the call. "Jana's on her way."

We both sipped our coffee.

I said, "While I'm sympathetic to the professor's loss, and please believe me, I am. It's just that . . . well, here's the thing . . ." Clasping my hands together, I leaned forward. She met me halfway with intelligent, defensive eyes. "You see, when I write history, I interview people who witnessed an event. And from these eyewitness accounts

I'm able to piece together what most likely happened. If I were to interview the witnesses at the scene of the accident where the professor's family was killed, how many of them would tell me they saw or even suspected the accident had anything to do with angels?"

"All right," she said, playing along. "If you happened to come across an eyewitness account of angels, you're saying you'd believe it?"

I thought I knew where she was going with this. Admittedly, my grin was condescending.

"While the professor is an honorable man," I said, "given the circumstances, I wouldn't consider him a credible witness. You have to take into account his emotional state at the time of the accident."

"I'm not talking about the accident now," she replied. "If you were to come across a bona fide eyewitness account of angels, would you believe it?"

Why did I feel like I was being set up?

When I hesitated, she said, "Unless you prejudge the people you interview. You know, root out those who will give testimony contrary to your preconceived conclusions."

"That's bias. It's unprofessional."

"So then, as a professional, one who values eyewitness accounts, if you were to come across an eyewitness account about angels, you'd believe it?"

I sighed. She was relentless. I could think of only one way to find out what she was getting at, and that was to step into her trap. "If the source was credible. Yes."

Sue Ling reached into her bag and pulled out a manila file folder. Inside there was a slim manuscript. I recognized the formatting instantly. She turned the pages so they were facing me. "This is an eyewitness account of a war in heaven."

"Heaven."

"It's a narrative history of the events of a war that started before the creation of earth and time. You wanted an eyewitness account, here it is. Abdiel, a veteran of the war, has been recounting the events to the professor."

I picked up the papers and looked at them suspiciously. "White paper?" I said. "I would have expected golden tablets." She didn't laugh. I thought it was funny.

The professor had attached a note to the front page. I lifted it to look at the text. I scanned the first couple of paragraphs.

> *Before the clock of cosmic time was wound,*
> *In heaven, fresh made, there dwelt a holy race.*
> *Conceived in light for worship we were cast*
> *To walk in luster and eternal grace.*
> *Until a fatal wickedness was found . . .*

How do I, Abdiel, Seraph of the heavens, describe to humans clothed in flesh the horrors of celestial war?

How do I explain countless dimensions to beings entombed in time? How do I narrate the tales of eternity, of heaven's enduring villains, to a people who cannot conceive of life without a past, present, or future?

> *And what of war itself and angel death?*
> *Of battle's din and hills alive with celestial tribes. . . .*

I looked up. "The professor's not serious, is he?" I asked.

I saw what was happening. I'd accused him of hiding, of letting other men take the heat of publishing while he contented himself with doing research from the sidelines. I must have hit a sore spot and now the professor wanted me to help him get published.

I closed the manila folder and pushed it back across the table at her.

"This isn't history. It's fantasy fiction. Taking one's personal theological beliefs and attempting to bring them to life with fictional characters is fantasy. While I have to give the professor an A for creative writing, if I showed this to any credible historian, he'd laugh in my face."

"You haven't read it," Sue said testily.

"I've read enough."

Sue Ling snatched the folder off the table and stuffed it back in her bag just as Jana Torres was walking by. She wore a dress skirt that swished just above her knees and black high heels.

Before I could say anything, Sue was gone. She and Jana passed each other at the door. They exchanged words. Sue left, and a none-too-pleased Jana joined me.

"What did you say to her?" she cried. "I've never seen her so angry."

Jana sat down in Sue Ling's seat and began clearing Sue's things away, wadding up the napkin and corralling the crumbs into a neat pile.

"She wanted me to look at Professor Forsythe's manuscript," I told her.

"Is it bad?"

"It's not that it's bad. It's not my thing. It's fiction."

"You mean it's about angels."

For some reason the revelation that Jana knew of the professor's fascination with angels took me by surprise. To me, it's one of those things you don't talk about with other people. Like personal finances. A person's beliefs about angels and miracles and other biblical stuff is personal.

"Sue has told you about the professor's angels," I said.

"We're friends. We talk about everything."

The comment was made as a casual remark, but it sat uneasily with me. It shouldn't have surprised me. Sue Ling had already berated me based on Jana's version of our high school dating experience.

Jana was looking at the refrigerated display cases.

"Would you like something?"

I got her an orange juice and a low-cal oatmeal bar. As I set them in front of her, I continued our conversation.

"It doesn't bother you that Sue Ling believes in angels?" I asked. "She calls them EDs."

"So she told me. But she's a scientist. How can a scientist believe in all this supernatural stuff?"

Jana picked at her oatmeal bar, placing a piece of oatmeal about the size of a molecule onto her tongue. She chewed. Swallowed.

"Sue's the most brilliant woman I've ever met."

"So you believe her? You believe in angels?"

"Let's just say I keep an open mind. If Sue is convinced they exist, who am I to discount them? I mean, as a reporter I interview all kinds of people. I once interviewed this guy at Qualcomm who attempted to describe to me quantum entanglement, where two particles are joined in some weird way even though they're separated by as much as a million miles.

"Apparently, if you change one of them in some way, the other one instantly reflects that change. He said that scientists have done successful experiments on particles as far as sixty-two miles apart. He was all jazzed about it, saying that experiments would improve communications and make quantum computers possible. He claimed it may even make teleportation a reality. Did I understand everything he said? Of course not. Did I believe him? Why shouldn't I? The guy knew what he was talking about. And anything that will eliminate the dead zone in Rose Canyon for my smartphone, I'm all for."

She pinched off another molecule, looked at it, and popped it in her mouth. She was refusing to look at me, which meant she was still miffed for my not going to Myles Shepherd's funeral. But I wasn't going to bring it up, and I hoped she wouldn't either.

"Jana, I need your help," I said, getting down to business.

Still staring at her oatmeal bar as though it was the most fascinating oatmeal bar she'd ever seen, she said, "You flew all the way out here to ask for my help? Why didn't you just use your phone? Two days ago, you told me you had no plans to return to San Diego."

"Things changed," I said.

I hadn't told Jana about the coded confession in my book. Had Sue Ling? Even though Jana said they shared everything, I doubted Sue had told her. Jana's a reporter. If she knew about a threat to the president, she wouldn't be acting aloof. Which meant she didn't know about my access to the White House being cut off or my trip to Montana. So without revealing any of this to her, somehow, I had to convince her to help me get close to the president.

"Does this have anything to do with that silly death threat in your book?" Jana asked.

I stared at her dumbly.

She smiled. "I told you Sue and I tell each other everything."

My life suddenly got easier or more complicated depending on how she answered my next question.

"Have you told anyone else?"

Exasperated, she turned her attention away from her oatmeal bar to me.

"Do you mean will you hear about it on the evening news? Of course not. I know you. It's a prank. It's not newsworthy unless you write for the tabloids, which I don't."

Her news director might disagree with her, but I wasn't going to press the point.

"Thank you, but I fear it's more than just a prank."

As briefly as I could, and speaking in a low whisper, I caught her up to date, everything that had happened since I learned about the coded message, including my interview with Doc Palmer.

She wasn't aloof anymore.

"Grant! What have you gotten yourself involved with?" she cried.

"That's what I have to find out. And that's why I need your help."

She shook her head while brushing crumbs from her hands. She shook her head while taking a sip of orange juice.

"No . . . no . . . no . . . no, Grant. I will not help you assassinate the president."

"But you just said—"

"I didn't know the full story then."

"Jana! You know me. Do you really think I'm capable of assassinating the president?"

In my exuberance I let my voice carry. A pair of shocked faces stared at us from behind the refrigerated display cases.

"I'm a writer," I explained to them. "We're working on some dialogue for a novel."

The bakery employees nodded as though they believed me, but a spark of doubt remained in their eyes.

"See?" Jana said. "That's what I'm talking about. No, I don't think you're plotting to assassinate the president. But it doesn't matter what I think. If something happens, it'll appear you had something to do with it."

"What you think matters to me."

"Look at it from a reporter's perspective. One, you confess to the killing in print. Two, the president himself warns you to stay away from San Diego, yet here you are. Three, you tried to break into the White House, and even though the Secret Service has warned you to keep your distance, you are currently trying to find a way to get close to the president."

"Do you think you can get me a press pass?"

Jana raised her hands in exasperation.

"Look at it from my perspective," I pleaded. "Everything you said is true. Someone is setting me up. But I can't just sit back and do nothing, can I? I have to find out who's doing this to me and why, so I can clear myself."

"You could fly to Oakland," Jana said.

"Why Oakland?"

"It's not San Diego."

I reached across the table, across the oatmeal bar, and took Jana's hand.

"I need your help," I said. "The president will clear me, I know he will. All I have to do is get close enough to ask him."

"Close enough. How?"

"With a press pass."

"Out of the question."

She pulled her hand away, pushed back her chair to leave.

"At the fundraisers," I said. "Maybe I could get close to him there."

"Good luck," Jana said.

"Maybe I don't have to get close enough to talk to him," I said. "Just get his attention."

"How?"

"Four words," I said. "Doc Palmer is alive."

"Do you think it'll work?"

"If the president knows I know the truth about Vietnam and his drug problems, he'll talk to me."

"Or eliminate you."

"He wouldn't do that."

"A man doesn't rise to his level of power without having the means to protect himself."

She had a point. Though I still didn't want to admit it, Douglas wasn't the man I'd portrayed in my book.

"Are you going to help me?" I asked.

"No. And I don't know how long I can sit on this, Grant. I really don't. Just Doc Palmer being alive. This is . . . this is big."

She gathered her things and walked out of Howard's Bakery.

By ten o'clock that night I was in bed, exhausted from the trip and from arguing with three women. Christina had called just as I was settling into my hotel room. Not until I heard *I'm Too Sexy for My Shirt* did I remember she was expecting me to meet her for dinner at DeLugo's.

"Are you stuck in traffic?" she asked.

"Sorry. I tried to call you."

"No problem. I got us a table. How long will you be?"

"Christina, I'm not in Washington. I tried to tell you, but our conversation ended so quickly, and then you turned your phone off."

Silence.

"Christina?"

"Did you miss your connecting flight?"

From the tone in her voice, she was hoping my excuse was simple and explainable.

"No." I swallowed hard. "I'm in San Diego."

The silence was so silent I thought we'd lost our connection. Then I heard her sniff.

"I see," she said frostily.

"When I heard on the radio that the president was coming to San Diego, I had to come."

"Despite his warning."

"Yeah."

"Grant, the president was trying to warn you. Protect you."

"Christina, I had to come. Somehow I have to—"

"I can't deal with this right now, Grant. I just can't deal with it."

This time her silence was a severed connection.

As much as I wanted to make the most of my stay at the historic U.S. Grant Hotel, I didn't feel like going out again and chose a pizza from room service over dinner in the newly refurbished Grant's Grill. I turned on the TV and watched the Padres blow a four-run lead in the top of the ninth to the Dodgers at Petco Park just a few blocks away and went to bed early.

At 10:30 p.m. I was awakened by the sound of pounding. I opened the door to double trouble.

"Hi, Grant."

"Hi, Grant."

Jana and Sue stood shoulder to shoulder wearing conspiratorial grins. I greeted them in my bathrobe.

"You weren't in bed already, were you?" Sue asked.

The evidence was too overwhelming to deny it.

Jana pushed past me into the room. Sue followed.

"All right, here's the deal," Jana said.

My phone rang. *I'm Too Sexy for My Shirt.*

Jana and Sue looked at each other. "Christina," they said in unison.

"I've got to change that ringtone," I muttered as I crossed the room to my phone.

"I'm furious with you for going to San Diego, you know that, don't you?" Christina began.

"Hello, Christina!" Jana and Sue sang in unison.

"Grant?" Christina said. "Do you have girls in your room?"

"No," I said. "Just Jana and Sue."

Christina didn't share Jana's and Sue's playful spirits.

"Well, that's just . . . you're just full of surprises, aren't you? I called you because I may have news. I was going to tell you at dinner, but I got so angry . . . it's important . . . but I don't want to interrupt your party."

"It's not a party," I protested.

"It's late, Grant . . . and I'm tired. Good night."

"Christina?"

She'd hung up.

I signaled to Jana and Sue to give me a minute while I thumbed

Christina's Contact button. No surprise that she'd turned off her phone.

"Here's the deal," Jana said, as soon as I ended the call. "Sue—"

Sue Ling reached into her bag and pulled out the professor's manuscript. She set it on the table in the corner.

"You read the professor's manuscript," Jana said. "Then, you meet with the professor tomorrow morning. Once you do that, Sue will call me, and I will do what I can to help you contact the president. Within reason."

I looked at the manuscript on the table, then at the girls who were once again shoulder to shoulder in a united front against me.

"You'll get me a press pass?"

"I said within reason."

What could I say? I was better off than I was five minutes earlier.

"I still don't know what you want from me with the manuscript."

"Just read it," Sue said.

"All right. I agree to your terms."

The girls nodded their agreement. Business concluded, they turned toward the door.

"You're right. He does have nice legs," Sue said on the way out.

"Would I lie about something like that?" Jana said, pulling the door closed behind her.

With little chance of sleeping anytime soon, I pulled out a chair at the table. With the night skyline outside my window I read the professor's manuscript, beginning with a note in the professor's hand, paper-clipped to the front page.

CHAPTER
18

The Spectacle

A HISTORY OF ANGEL WAR

As told to J. P. Forsythe

This is the faithful narrative passed down to me by the seraph Abdiel, an eyewitness to the events contained herein. Having served under the Archangel Lucifer before the rebellion, Abdiel proved himself "faithful among the faithless—unmoved, unshaken, unseduced, unterrified." His loyalty, love, and zeal for the Almighty God are well documented in the annals of angels.

I would add a note about style. During the dictation I have observed that angels—beings who were created to exist outside of time—struggle with chronology. The phrasing in the narrative reflects this. At times Abdiel would slip into a rhythmic cadence. From this and other more subtle clues, I got the impression that the narrative itself is not solely of Abdiel's creation, but rather a telling that has been handed down, not unlike an oral history.

J.P. Forsythe

ὑπερνικῶμεν
(We are more than conquerors.)

You were the seal of perfection, full of wisdom and perfect in beauty . . . You were on the holy mount of God . . . till wickedness was found in you . . . and you sinned. So I drove you in disgrace from the mount of God . . . I threw you to the earth; I made a spectacle of you.

—EZEKIEL 28:12, 14–17

And having disarmed the powers and authorities, he made a public spectacle of them, triumphing over them by the cross.

—COLOSSIANS 2:15

How do I, Abdiel, Seraph of the heavens, describe to humans clothed in flesh the horrors of celestial war?

How do I explain countless dimensions to beings entombed in time? How do I narrate the tales of eternity, of heaven's enduring villains, to a people who cannot conceive of life without a past, present, or future?

And what of war itself and angel death?
Of battle's din and hills alive with celestial tribes,
Of angels clad in armor clear as crystal,
Their swords flashing with sacred light,
Of bugled advances and tattooed retreats,
Of chariots converging on heavenly plains?

These are but fantasies of a fallen race. War is never glorious. And spiritual warfare, which has none of these attractions, is most hideous of all.

Lucifer's weapons are largely unseen;
discounted by fools, they strike straight and true,
skewering the heart and piercing the soul.

Depression is his dagger, deceit his poison.
An efficient assassin, he slips in unnoticed,
Destroys a career with a well-timed lie.

With visions of grandeur he lays waste to nations,
With guilt and suspicion he undermines lives.

He understands the nature of mankind—
Spill a man's blood and he fights to live,
Wound a man's spirit and he prays to die.

Do angels die? As surely as light can be extinguished. Anything created can be uncreated. Where injury or loss or death are absent, there can be no war. This is the account of how a great Archangel seduced himself, then others, creating eternal enemies of eternal friends and turning paradise into a battlefield. For clarity, I will speak of time and space where there is no time or space, using terms you understand.

I speak from pain. For the time was when angel and honorable were one and the same, when the courts of heaven were free from sin and strife; when the bringer of light, the son of the morning, the chief of all angelic host, second only to the Father himself, was my mentor, my brother, my friend. Lucifer is his name.

He walked among the fiery stones in highest regard, his magnificence unequaled, his beauty flawless, and his wisdom unsurpassed. He had no equal. Not Michael. Not Gabriel. Not Uriel. He was our advocate to the Father, our captain, our counselor. Nothing he asked of us we wouldn't do . . . or so we thought.

How regally he ruled the angelic council, dispensing justice and mediating feuds between agents of free will. Unrivaled at peacemaking, Lucifer settled disputes with equity for all. His judgments went unchallenged. He charted the course of the will of the Father with boldness, imagination, and verve. With voice and example, he led us in worship, our hearts lifted in praise to God.

And thus, my narrative begins—

Summoned to the throne room,
A wonder we beheld,

A marvel mixed with mystery,
Such as angel eyes had never seen.
Two thrones where one alone had stood;
The second, a seat of favor.

Excitement crackled through the room
As Lucifer arrived.
We fixed our eyes on him.
He fixed his eyes upon the throne.
A single thought we shared.

With intent clear, the Father would,
Before the day was done,
Elevate the best of us
To this high honored throne.

As God the Father graced the room,
Divine decree He made;
A proclamation thunderclap,
But not our expectation.

He told us of a cosmos dancing,
Stars and worlds in pinwheel galaxies;
Immense and intricate it was
A companion universe.

Sculpted chaos, matter and time
becoming an ever-changing art.
Moment on moment in unbroken chain,
With colors and textures never the same.

A plan unimagined of force and space,
The crown of creation, humans would be.
Composed of matter with spark divine,
Endowing them with eternity.

The shepherd of man Lucifer would be,
According to the Father's plan.

A singular honor, a guardian grand,
Their teacher and mentor he.

Reward turned to snare as pride swelled his head,
When Lucifer accepted the post.
He fantasized how they would love him,
Revere him, praise and adore.
He'd take for himself the worship due God,
And dwell on the earth evermore.

Transparent as glass we are to be
Wherever mankind is concerned.
Looking at us, they should see God,
This from our lessons we learned.
Lucifer coveted what was not his,
First step of his downfall he made.

With plan under way,
Assignments doled out,
We waited creation's first light.
We nearly forgot the throne to God's right
As we labored with anticipation.

But soon came the day for a great convocation,
The birth of the earth was at hand.
Assembled we there, we opened with song
In the hall of the Almighty King.
High and lifted up was He,
Entering with power, moving with grace.
Foundations shook, incense rose,
As Seraphs, their voices raised.

All glory to the Father God,
Forever is His reign.
The King of Kings, the Lord of Lords,
And worthy of all praise.

Conspicuous in vacancy,
the throne beside Him stood.
Anticipation filled the room,
As we awaited word
Of announcement as to who would sit
Upon that holy chair.

Lucifer, the Morning Star,
stood serenely by.
A perfect pairing it would be,
to see him sitting there.

How could we that day foresee
That it was not to be?
Jehovah Father, God alone,
Is all that we had ever known.

The floor became fiery stones,
A rainbow encircled the room.
Bursts of light shot from the throne,
As thunder rumbled our heavenly home.
The Father stood, tall and proud, as He said,
"Behold, my Son."

A Being so pure it pained us to look
Appeared at the Father's right hand.
Surprised by joy,
Laughter welled.
Praises spilled from our lips.

Worthy is the Son of God,
Our love endures forever.
You fill our hearts with wondrous joy,
Our love endures forever.
With every breath we shout your name,
Our love endures forever.

We dance and weep in joyous song,
Our love endures forever.

It was a new day.
Everything changed with the coming of the Son.
Take all the pride, all the admiration,
All the love we held for Lucifer,
And it would be but a fleeting glimpse
Of the love we held for the Son.

God the Father presented His heir
And gave Him a name above all.
That at the name of Jesus
Every knee shall bow
In heaven, and soon on earth,
Every tongue shall confess
Exalted Lord is He,
No other Lord above Him stands,
His reign endures forever.

We shouted to our God and King
Until we could shout no more.
Every tongue confessed Him Lord,
Every knee before Him bowed.
Every knee but Lucifer's.

In one swift moment, snatched from him
was everything Lucifer dreamed.
That's how he saw it,
That's how he felt.
Jesus, not he, would sit on the throne.
Jesus, not he, was Lord of creation.
Jesus, not he, would be worshipped and praised.

The Father spoke,
"Lucifer? Why are you downcast?

Would you be God?"
No answer he offered,
The throne room he fled.

Conceived at that moment,
Spawned by disappointment,
An Antichrist was born.

CHAPTER
19

WHILE I DROVE TO HERITAGE COLLEGE THE NEXT MORNING, I was reminded of a conversation I'd had with a writer friend who was trying to break into Hollywood.

As in any industry, he told me, Hollywood has its own language. Apparently, producers are unable to grasp a concept unless it's couched in reference to a film that's already been produced. He said a pitch usually goes something like this: "It's a World War II story about a soldier and a German shepherd who is combat trained. Think *Band of Brothers* meets *Lassie*."

The key was that something always met something else.

We had fun with it.

"It's a blockbuster, I tell ya! Think Godzilla meets Scarlett O'Hara!"

The conversation came to mind as I tried to think of what I'd say to the professor about his manuscript. It's *Screwtape Letters* meets *Lord of the Rings*, I thought, referring to two popular books on college campuses. Think Screwtape and his nephew Wormwood in an adventure with a band of Hobbits. The emphasis, of course, was that both of these works were entertaining, but fictional.

The trick would be to tell him this without sounding derogatory.

On the other hand, some religious writers were finding success publishing their particular brand of theology as fiction. Some of the books were even bestsellers. If the professor was interested in having his manuscript published, I was prepared to offer to write a letter of introduction to my publisher's fiction editor.

It was still early when I arrived at Heritage College. Classes hadn't yet started. A few students milled about half asleep and carrying coffee cups as I made my way to the library. The sign in the library window indicated it wouldn't be open for another thirty minutes. I found the door ajar.

The scene that awaited me was reminiscent of my first meeting with Professor Forsythe. He was seated in the back at a table behind which was a wall of windows overlooking a desert garden. He sat at the end of the table in his wheelchair. He wasn't alone. A figure with broad shoulders sat with his back to me, just as he had that first day. The two men were hunched over the table, their heads together, speaking in whispers.

As I approached them, another figure off to the side caught my attention. Sue Ling stood alone between the bookshelves, her arms folded as though she was cold, or afraid. The room was warm.

Since neither of the men had paid any attention to me, I altered my course to greet her first. She shook her head, directing me toward the professor. The look in her eyes disturbed me. It was all business with a touch of fear, the same look you'd see on the face of a person called to a meeting with IRS auditors.

The professor noticed me. He looked up. Didn't smile.

Without turning to look at me, the man with the broad shoulders stiffened noticeably.

"You're expecting me?" I said.

The professor spoke to the other man. "Abdiel, I apologize for the deception, but I feel it's important that Grant meets you."

It was clear this wasn't the meeting I thought it would be. Was the manuscript just a ruse to get me to the library? I shot a glance at Sue Ling. It was she who insisted I read the manuscript. It was she who had set up this meeting.

Her eyes were wide with fear.

"I told you no!" the man thundered.

"Abdiel—"

"NO!"

His chair tumbled backward as he stood. His voice made the ground shiver, books fall from shelves, tables tremble.

"NO!"

A surge of energy rippled through me, like the force of an earthquake through solid rock, and he was gone. Not walking-out-the-door gone, but gone gone. One second he was there. The next, he wasn't.

The professor shrugged apologetically. "We need to talk," he said.

I didn't say anything. I couldn't say anything. All I could do was look at the empty space that moments before had been filled with a man the size of a professional football linebacker.

A hand touched my shoulder. Sue. She put her arms around me and laid her head against my chest and held me. I don't know which of us needed the hug more.

This wasn't the Sue Ling I knew yesterday. This was a different Sue. Something had happened to change her. She was trembling.

She stepped away and looked up at me, and that's when I really became frightened. She had the same look in her eyes that she had had earlier—the look of fear.

She was afraid of me. Or for me. But her fear was unmistakable.

"Students will be coming in soon," the professor said. "Walk with me."

On any other day I would have found humor in a man in a wheelchair saying, Walk with me. But at the moment, nothing was funny.

"Did you feel that?" I exclaimed. "That jolt of energy when he . . . when he—"

Two coeds passed us walking in the opposite direction. They greeted the professor. Their perfume billowed around them like a cloud—a nice scent, but definitely overdone.

With other students within earshot, I whispered, ". . . when he disappeared."

The professor led me on a circuitous route through campus hallways so that I had no idea where we were until we emerged in a spacious quad with a desert garden at one end. We had come complete circle and were on the outside of the library windows. "We can talk here," the professor said, pulling to a stop in front of a slatted wooden bench.

I sat facing him. In spite of the events in the library, the morning showed promise. Everything was fresh. The sky. Spring colors. The air. It was shaping up to be a nice day.

"Tell me you felt it," I said, "that surge of energy, wasn't that something?" I felt invigorated, like I could run a marathon and not be winded. And I hated jogging.

The professor looked at me with sad eyes.

"No, Grant, I didn't feel it." I must have looked at his paralyzed legs, because he added, "And neither did Sue Ling. Only you."

"What are you saying? How could you miss it? It's like saying you didn't feel an 8.0 earthquake."

It took him a moment to find the words. "Do you remember when you first came here, and you told me what you'd experienced in that teacher's office—"

"Myles Shepherd's office."

"Do you recall what I said then? I said, 'Why you?'"

I remembered, and I told him so.

"I know the answer to the question now," he said.

Why did I think this wasn't going to be a good thing? Possibly because good news is shouted. It isn't something shared in some out-of-the-way garden by someone with the expression of an undertaker.

"From the expression on your face, I wasn't selected because of my natural wit and charm."

Despite himself and the apparent weight of the news, the professor smiled. "Grant, you were selected because you're one of them."

I waited for the punch line.

There wasn't one.

I said, "Professor, I don't even believe in angels."

"Despite what you just saw? What you just felt?"

He had me there. I just saw a grown man vanish. I just felt the equivalent of a carton of energy drinks.

"To put it in understandable terms, you have angel blood in you. You're part angel. One quarter to be exact. Your grandfather was—"

I was on my feet but didn't remember standing up.

"I don't know what you're trying to do here, Professor, but you're not going to pull me into your fantasy world. What is this? Some kind of variation of *Dungeons & Dragons* where we each assume mystical powers? Or are we pretending this is Middle Earth? Let me guess. You're Gandalf, right? You look like you'd be a Gandalf."

I was rambling. I couldn't help myself. I was scared.

Sue Ling stood solemnly in the library window watching us.

"You told her, didn't you? That's why she acted like she did. You told her I was some sort of freak. Part human, part ED. Isn't that what she calls them? Extradimensionals? Well, you're wrong, Professor. I have trouble enough with three dimensions; I don't need more."

The professor persisted. "The extreme reaction you had to Semyaza when he revealed himself to you, the charge of energy you felt just now . . . Grant, a part of you vibrates in tune with heavenly—"

"Shut up!" I shouted. "Just . . . just . . . shut up, will you? I need to think."

Only I couldn't. This was so utterly ridiculous . . . so far out in left field . . . so crazy. . . . I should be laughing at the absurdity of it all. But I wasn't. Why wasn't I laughing?

"I'm outta here," I said.

I didn't want to hear any more. I didn't want to think about it. I didn't even want to look at him any longer. All I wanted was to get away from here, from him, from all this talk of supernatural beings, or extradimensionals, or whatever you wanted to call them.

I just wanted to be left alone.

I stopped running when I couldn't run any farther. It was either that or start swimming.

The shores at La Jolla have always been a place of solace for me. There's something seductive about the rhythm of the sea; it calms me and calls to me. The crashing of waves against the rocks, the colorful sea life in the tide pools, the ocean spray on my skin: these have always relaxed me, and they didn't fail me now.

As I drove out here over the Grossmont Summit, my phone rang. I turned it off without looking to see who was calling. I didn't want to know. I didn't want to talk to anyone. When you talk to people you hear things you don't want to hear, so I did the mature thing. I decided I would never talk to anyone ever again.

"Who is feeding him this stuff?" I shouted at the waves. "That vanishing linebacker? I don't know about you, but it's been my experience you can't believe a word a vanishing linebacker says."

The waves pummeled the rocky shoreline. Maybe that's why they were soothing. They took your anger and aggression and slammed them against the rocks.

Part angel. Big joke.

Well, I knew one person who could set the record straight. My mother. Mothers know where their children come from.

Thirty minutes later I was back in El Cajon on Mulgrew Street, where I grew up. The house looked uninhabited. The front yard was dead and parched—not even weeds were growing in it. The exterior paint was as weathered as Doc Palmer's barn. A half-dozen newspapers had yellowed in the sun. The bedroom window facing the street was lined with tinfoil. There was no car in the driveway, only oil spots.

I didn't know what kind of reception to expect. Mother and I weren't close. Her choice. We had barely spoken a dozen words to each other since I graduated from high school and moved out of the house. When I called to tell her I'd won the Pulitzer Prize, she hung up on me before I could say Pulitzer. When I was invited to speak at Singing Hills, I sent her an invitation. She didn't respond. Didn't attend.

Even as I was knocking on the door, I hadn't decided how I was going to broach the subject. How do you ask your mother if your grandfather was an angel?

As it turned out, it didn't matter.

I never got the chance.

The door opened just a crack, stopped by the security chain. Bleary eyes over sagging cheeks labored to focus. I almost didn't recognize her at first, my own mother. Her hair was disheveled. She was still in her housecoat. Musty odors of a house shut up too long combined with whiskey poured through the opening.

The first words out of my mother's mouth when she recognized me was a curse, followed by, "What are you doing here?"

"I need to talk to you," I said.

"Got nothing to say."

She started to close the door. I stopped it with my hand.

"It'll just take a moment. It's about Grandpa Tall."

At the sound of my grandfather's name her unfocused eyes quickened. She looked past me, as though she expected to see someone behind me.

Tall Mann was my grandfather's stage name. Born Ulysses William Austin, he made a living as an extra and stuntman. At six feet five he was an imposing figure and was often cast in the role of the Tall Man in the credits. It became a joke on the film lot, one he apparently didn't mind because he began using it as his stage name, adding an extra *n*. So if you're watching an old black-and-white western and you see in the credits, "'Tall Man' played by Tall Mann," that's my grandfather.

I never knew him. Shortly after I was born, he drank himself to death—six months before my father committed suicide.

"I need to talk to you about Grandpa," I repeated, since she hadn't answered me the first time.

Her eyes darted wildly, not only behind me, but above me, searching the sky.

"You brought them with you, didn't you?" she cried.

She was beginning to panic.

"I came alone, Mom," I assured her. "I just want to talk to you."

"Go away!" she shouted.

"Mom—"

"Go away! Go away! Go away!" She leaned her shoulder against the door and tried to force it shut. The lack of weight she was able to put behind the effort was alarming.

"Go away!" she sobbed.

"Grandpa Tall," I said. "Is there something I should know about him?"

"Go away! Please, go away!"

She was hysterical, pounding the door first with her fists to get it to close, then with her forehead, all the while weeping.

I've seen her stinking drunk. I've seen her passed out on the sofa in her own mess. But I had never seen her like this.

She slumped to the floor, her mouth twisted with grief.

"Go away," she pleaded.

"Can I get you anything?" I asked. "Can I call someone?"

"Go away. . . ."

"All right. I'm going."

I eased the door shut and heard her lock it with the dead bolt.

For several minutes I stood on the doorstep. I didn't want to leave her like this, but we didn't have any relatives in the area I could call, and I didn't know her neighbors or friends.

Making my way to the car, I determined I'd get the phone number of a local church and see if they had someone they could send to check up on her, possibly take her some food.

I was just about to climb into the car when her front door flew open. In her pink slippers, her housecoat flying open to reveal a white silk nightgown, she came running out the door with an armload of liquor bottles which she proceeded to heave at me as though they were Molotov cocktails.

The first bottle hit the top of the car, flew inches from my head, and shattered in the street. The second bottle came straight at my head. I ducked and heard it shatter as it hit the pavement.

"Demon blood!" she shouted. "Demon blood!"

I slipped into the car for my own protection. A bottle hit the passenger side window with more force than I thought she was capable of in her condition. The window spidered.

My mother's yelling brought neighbors out of their houses. She threw the last bottle. It skipped across the hood of the car.

The woman directly across the street, seeing my mother standing in her front yard screaming at me, shouted for someone inside to call the police, then ran to my mother and took her by the shoulders. But it was clear my mother wouldn't be consoled until she could no longer see me.

With the words *demon blood* ringing in my ears, I drove away.

CHAPTER
20

MEMO TO SELF: DON'T ASK QUESTIONS IF YOU DON'T WANT TO know the answers. My mother's voice shouting two words—demon blood—echoed in my head.

Navigating the late morning, downtown traffic, I returned to the hotel thinking I'd wallow in self-pity until lunch, then call Jana and hold her to her end of the agreement. I had read the professor's manuscript and had kept the meeting. Now I had a president to save.

With the professor's manuscript tucked under my arm, I slipped the key card into my hotel door and stepped into my room to find it occupied.

"What are you doing here?" I said. "I guess I don't have to ask how you got in."

Seated comfortably at the table in the corner was the professor's friend, Abdiel.

"I thought you didn't want to talk to me."

"I don't." He didn't get up.

"Then why are you here?"

"Orders."

"Orders? Someone ordered you to talk to me?"

"My superiors."

For some reason that struck me as funny. I laughed.

I laughed alone. Whoever or whatever he was, Abdiel sat on the room side of the round table within arm's reach of my unmade bed. He'd turned the chair toward the door waiting for me. How long was anyone's guess. If he really was a member of some sort of supernatural extradimensional alien race, he'd probably appeared the moment I slipped the key card into the slot.

"Is Abdiel your last name?" I said. "What's your first? Ed? Ed Abdiel. Has a ring to it, don't you think?"

My sarcasm generator had switched into overdrive, which meant I was afraid.

He sat there straight-backed, in tan pants with the sharpest crease I'd ever seen, and a pale yellow, short-sleeved dress shirt. A massive neck bulged from the collar, and muscular arms stretched down to the largest hands I'd ever seen, which rested on the tops of his legs. His eyes were pale blue and his complexion nicely tanned.

Apparently he was waiting for me to run out of sarcastic comments. He'd have to wait a long time. I was blessed with a lifetime supply.

I tossed the professor's manuscript at his feet. "Is that your handiwork? Did you dictate that to the professor?"

He bent down and picked it up. He examined it, then placed it on the table behind him.

"Yes," he said.

"And you expect me to believe that the events you described actually happened? That you are a veteran of a war in heaven?"

"I don't expect you to believe anything, nor am I here to convince you."

Folding my arms, I remained standing. I felt looking down on him gave me an advantage. To put it in Washington terms, I was in the power position.

"Then why are you here?" I asked. "Exactly what are your orders?"

"You have questions."

"The understatement of the century. How long do you have?"

"An eternity."

I laughed. He had a sense of humor after all, you had to give him that.

"All right," I said. "Let's start with a simple one. Is the professor correct? Am I part angel?"

"Yes."

The bluntness of his answer hit me harder than I wanted to admit, hard enough to knock me out of the power position. I sat on the bed.

They were all in agreement. The professor. My mother. Now Mr. Eternity here. The whole universe seemed to know I was part angel. But I knew that wasn't true; surely some of the back-water planets hadn't gotten the news yet.

"All right . . ." I said. I nodded. Then nodded again. I was sucking air. "All right . . . all right. . . ."

This was going to take a while to sink in.

"All right. Um, next question—"

The door latch rattled. The door opened.

"Housekeeping."

A maid entered, her arms full of bedding. She was barely five feet tall with a face that had seen a hard life. She hadn't expected anyone to be in the room, because when she looked up and saw us . . . saw me—

Abdiel had disappeared.

"Sorry, *senor*," she said. "I will . . ." She motioned to the hallway.

"Give us . . . um, me . . ." I glanced at the empty table. " . . . about an hour."

Looking at the floor and backing out, she said, "I come back in an hour."

The door closed.

Abdiel was back in the chair as though he'd been there the entire time. His little disappearing trick was unnerving.

"Isn't that always the way?" I said. "Every time you're interviewing an angel, the maid interrupts."

"Calynda is a good woman," Abdiel said. "She works two jobs. Here and at a diner on Fifth Avenue. Did you notice her eyes? She's worried about her two-year-old daughter, Nuria, who woke up last night with a fever. Calynda didn't want to leave her, but she needs the money."

I cut him off with an upraised hand. "I get it," I said. "No need to flash your credentials."

Abdiel looked at me with the expression of a disapproving schoolmaster.

"Believe me, if I flashed anything, you'd know it."

A dozen quips like puppies in a box wanted to spill out from my lips. I regret it now, but I swallowed them and returned to the subject at hand.

"Question," I said. "My grandfather, Grandpa Tall. Was he an angel?"

"Yes and no."

"That's it? Yes and no? Would you care to elaborate?"

"I don't care to do any of this. As I informed you, I am here only because—"

"I know . . . I know . . . you were ordered to talk to me. So talk. Tell me about my grandfather."

"Yes, your grandfather is an angel. No, Ulysses William Austin was not an angel, nor was he your paternal grandfather. Reality is not what you think it is."

"That's what everyone keeps telling me. So what is the reality of my birthright?"

"It was born of scandal."

"Makes sense. Hollywood is the scandal capital of the world."

"Not even close," Abdiel said. He didn't elaborate. "You know about the fame of your grandmother."

I nodded. "Gigi Beaumont. Real name, Denise Garrett. Movie star. Gorgeous, if her publicity photos are to be believed. Witty. Talented. Would have eclipsed Esther Williams had she not died tragically soon after giving birth to my father."

"Do you know the details of her death?"

"She died in an—" The next words caught in my throat. "An automobile accident."

"They like the convenience of car accidents to cover their tracks."

I narrated the incident by rote just as it had been handed down to me. "She attended a Hollywood party. Got tipsy. On her way home, she lost control of the car and drove off a cliff into a Hollywood ravine."

"That part is correct."

Abdiel sounded like a schoolmaster evaluating an assigned lesson. Didn't he realize this was my life we were talking about?

I continued. "The way I heard it, Grandpa Tall took her death hard. He isolated himself in a cabin, got drunk, and blew his head off with a shotgun."

"That part is only partially correct."

"Enlighten me," I snapped, irritated by his attitude.

"Ulysses Austin did indeed take his own life, but only after learning he was not the father of his wife's child. The father was Azazel."

"Azazel. Sounds like an angel name."

"It is. However, the world knew him as Jerry Thoms."

"Never heard of him."

"He was the insurance commissioner for the state of California."

"Insurance commissioner? You're kidding, right? An angel was the state's insurance commissioner."

"Powerful position, low profile. Perfect for their purposes."

"Okay. So how did he and my grandmother . . . you know, hook up?"

Was I mistaken, or did Abdiel pause and take a deep breath?

"During the rebellion, Azazel sided with Lucifer and was driven from his place in the heavenlies. On earth, he became a Watcher and, like many of them, developed a lust for human women. His lust, dormant for centuries, was rekindled when Lucifer's forces infiltrated California. Azazel rose to the position of insurance commissioner and, as such, mingled with California's elite. At a Hollywood party he seduced a rising young starlet. Gigi Beaumont. When that seduction produced a male child, the news was kept secret from all but a select few. For decades, not even Lucifer knew."

"Lucifer's minions keep secrets from him? I didn't know that was possible."

"You have much to learn of the angelic order."

"I understand this much: You're saying my father was the love child of an insurance commissioner and a starlet?"

"That is correct."

"Did he know?"

"Yes. Azazel revealed himself to your father."

"He didn't take it well, did he?"

"No. Your mother took the news even worse. She did not know she had married a Nephilim, nor did she know—"

"Nephilim?"

"The offspring of a son of God and a daughter of man."

"So I'm a Nephilim?"

"In a manner of speaking. You are only one-quarter angel."

My head was spinning. I wanted to walk out the door, take a flight to Washington, DC, do a book signing, take Christina to dinner, and revel in my Pulitzer Prize achievement. I wanted a normal, everyday, boy-makes-good ending to the story of my life. All this was giving me a headache.

"Your father didn't tell your mother the truth until after you were born," Abdiel said.

"And then he killed himself. Seems to be the standard reaction to the news, doesn't it?"

"Are you going to kill yourself, Grant Austin?"

"Would you miss me?"

Abdiel didn't answer.

"No wonder my mother hated me," I mused. "Explains why she acts like she does. And it certainly explains why my whole family is whacko."

"The circumstances behind your family's life are only a partial explanation as to why your family is whacko," Abdiel said.

I grabbed my head to try to stop the spinning. "How do I know any of this is true?"

"You know. You can feel it."

"You mean like back at the library when you threw a tantrum and disappeared. Neither the professor nor Sue Ling felt the force of your leaving. I did."

"And you felt it with Semyaza."

The sudden mention of that name stunned me for a moment. "You mean Myles Shepherd."

"His name is Semyaza."

For a moment I was there, back in Myles Shepherd's office, reliving the experience. "But with you in the library, it was just a ripple. It wasn't like—"

Abdiel stood to imposing height. A ray of light erupted from the center of his chest.

"Oh no," I heard myself saying, "here we go again."

Abdiel's clothing transformed to folds of pure color that curled, then swirled around him, until he became a dazzling white hurricane of radiance. I heard the sound of a thousand wind chimes, with harmony so clear it brought tears to my eyes. My entire body vibrated in harmony with the sound while ripples of pleasure swept through me repeatedly, of such magnitude that I giggled and laughed like a fool. So overwhelmed was I by the sensation that I dropped to my knees.

"No," Abdiel said. "Do not bow."

That was the difference between them. Abdiel reflected the glory. Semyaza sparked it, only to feed off it.

Abdiel returned to normal . . . or to human . . . or to . . . I don't know. I was beginning to think I didn't know anything anymore.

"Do not bow," Abdiel repeated most solemnly.

"Sorry to disappoint you," I said, "but I wasn't bowing. I thought I dropped a penny."

Abdiel chuckled. I finally got a laugh out of him.

It took me a few moments to catch my breath. Even then, when I opened my eyes a riot of color assaulted me. Whenever I inhaled, I inhaled an explosion of odors. The tips of my fingers tingled with everything I touched.

"Question," I said.

Abdiel took his seat.

"Do Semyaza and . . . well, the forces of Lucifer. Do they intend to kill the president?"

"It appears so."

I nodded. "All right. Now for the million-dollar question. Will I be the one to do it?"

Abdiel studied me for a long moment. "Only you know the answer to that question, Grant Austin."

"What do you mean?"

"You are a creature of free will. You choose what you do."

"Part of my human side."

Abdiel started, surprised by the comment. He said, "Like humans, angels have been created by the Father with free will. How else would you explain the rebellion?"

I was thinking out loud now. "So they can't force me to kill the president."

"But they can persuade you, or trick you. Do not underestimate their powers of deception."

He spoke as someone who was speaking from experience. "Can I stop them?"

"You can try. You will fail. In fact, I would estimate your chances of success as infinitesimal. After all, they have been doing this sort of thing—"

"Yeah, I know. For millennia."

"That is correct."

"What about you?"

"What about me?"

"You and your side. The good guys. You could stop them, couldn't you?"

"Why would we want to?"

Today had been a day of being stunned, but this comment was the capper.

"What do you mean, 'Why would we want to?' We're talking about the President of the United States!"

"A weak and feeble man who has given in to his lusts and sold his soul to Lucifer."

"What about the fate of America? We're talking about changing history, altering the course of America!"

Abdiel's lack of concern was infuriating. He looked like he was about to yawn. I wanted to grab him and shake him until he came to his senses.

"The events of the next few days will unfold as they are meant to unfold. They will not alter the outcome of the larger conflict. All is in the Father's hands."

I was on my feet again. "Well, excuse me if I don't share your optimism! This is my president and my nation, and I don't take kindly to the fact that a bunch of rogue angels are messing with it! I'm going to stop them!"

"As you should. Each of us must fight our own battles."

Behind me, the door latch rattled. The door opened. The maid walked in, surprised again that we were still . . . that I was still here.

Abdiel was gone.

"I come back?" she asked.

"No. We're . . . I'm on my way out."

Her gaze fixed on the floor, she stepped back to allow me to exit.

As I passed her, I said, "I hope Nuria's fever breaks soon. The best medicine for a sick child is a mother who loves her."

"Señor?" the maid said, astonished.

The maid's arrival was a blessing. I needed to get out, to walk. With nowhere in particular to go, I stepped out the hotel's front door onto Broadway. Horton Plaza, an open-air shopping center with colorful and interesting multilevel passageways, lay directly across the street. Some people can get lost in a crowd. I prefer open space and plenty of it.

That gave me an idea. I turned west. A few blocks later I walked into Emerald Plaza, a hotel and business center. At night its neon-green lights circling the tops of the towers are a distinctive landmark in the San Diego skyline.

I crossed the highly polished tile floors to the elevators in the tallest tower and pushed the highest button. Minutes later I stood at the top of one of the tallest buildings in San Diego overlooking the bay, and beyond that, the Pacific Ocean.

The view was similar to the view from the airplane as we were coming in for a landing—the bridge, Coronado Island, the bay with sailboats.

Wind whipped through my hair and brushed my cheeks. With

my heightened senses it felt positively exhilarating. If I had any sense at all, I'd find an upscale restaurant and order the biggest steak on the menu.

Leaning against the guardrail, I breathed in the ocean air and tried to clear my mind. I closed my eyes.

When I awoke this morning, my thoughts had focused on ways to tell the professor I didn't think much of his fantasy world of angels. Now I was one.

I still wasn't convinced. It was easy for Alice. Tumble down a hole and you're in Wonderland having tea with the Mad Hatter. I was still in the world . . .

. . . *that isn't what you think it is.*

I looked over the edge of the building. Maybe this was Wonderland.

Standing over Broadway Avenue from on high reminded me of another scene. This one from the Bible.

The way I remembered it, the devil took Jesus to the highest point of the temple with the wind blowing through their hair like mine was now.

The devil taunted Jesus. Prove yourself. Throw yourself down from here. If you are who you say you are, surely your angels will catch you so that you do not hurt yourself.

I leaned over the edge and looked at the street below. Why had I remembered that story right now? Was someone trying to tell me something?

I guess one way of proving I had angel blood in me would be to throw myself over the guardrail. Would one of my relatives swoop down to save me?

Cars backed up at the lighted intersection. Pedestrians crossed the street in front of them.

Who would most likely come to my rescue? Surly Uncle Abdiel? Or evil Uncle Semyaza?

CHAPTER
21

INSTEAD OF THROWING MYSELF OFF THE EMERALD PLAZA TOWER, I took the elevator down. Returning to the U.S. Grant Hotel, I entered the lobby and headed for my room.

The concierge hailed me.

Then, looking past me, he hailed two security guards. In quick order they flanked me.

"Is something wrong?" I asked them.

Now the concierge made a phone call and within seconds two Secret Service agents appeared. It's easy to spot Secret Service agents, they all look alike. It's easier still to spot them when you've spent an afternoon with them in a tiny interrogation room. My hand moved involuntarily to my backside.

"Agent Cunningham. Agent Phillips," I said.

Phillips, the one with the rogue curl that made him look like Superman, smoothed it back. It instantly fell to his forehead again.

A bellboy appeared with my luggage. He was instructed to set the bags down in front of me.

"Am I checking out?" I asked.

"I'm sure you'll have no difficulty finding alternative lodging, Mr. Austin," Agent Cunningham said.

There was a seating area off to my right. A television was tuned to a live news report from North Island Naval Air Station. The picture showed Air Force One landing.

The president was in San Diego.

Agent Phillips said, "The concierge has been kind enough to call a taxi, and these two fine gentlemen will escort you to it."

One security guard grabbed my bags. The other grabbed my arm.

"Wait!" the helpful and efficient concierge called from behind the counter. He turned to some files behind him and retrieved an oversized white envelope. "This was delivered to Mr. Austin a short time ago."

He rounded the end of the counter and on long spindly legs danced his way toward us. He held out the envelope to me. Agent Cunningham intercepted it and opened it.

"That's my mail!" I cried. "That's a federal offense!"

"No stamp," Agent Cunningham said.

He pulled out a half-inch-thick stack of letter-sized pages. The pages flopped over, and I could see they were additional pages of the professor's manuscript. A note was attached to the first page with a paper clip.

Agent Cunningham read it aloud.

"Honestly, Grant, I don't know if this will hurt or help you right now. I just felt compelled to send it to you."

Agent Cunningham looked up. "Who's Professor Forsythe?" he asked.

"A colleague."

"And this?" he asked, flipping through the pages, scanning the paragraphs.

"My family genealogy," I said.

CHAPTER
22

AFTER RELOCATING TO THE RED LION IN MISSION VALLEY, I called Jana. Now more than ever I wanted to talk with the president. I'd spent over a year orbiting his world, conducting interviews that resulted in a portrayal of a life that now appeared to be all smoke and mirrors—and I was angry. My professional pride had been bruised, and I felt like a patsy.

The questions kept stacking up:

Exactly who was behind the changes in my book and why?

What was the president's response to Doc's version of events in Vietnam and the medications while in the White House?

Why didn't the president want me here in San Diego?

"It's because there's going to be an assassination attempt, isn't it?" I said, practicing my anticipated interview. "But you know that, don't you? Why? Why would you, the President of the United States, consent to your own assassination?"

Even before I asked, I could hear his reply: *This world isn't what you think it is, Grant.*

I was beginning to believe it.

Before my bags hit the bed in my second hotel room, Jana's phone was ringing and ringing and ringing. Just when I thought I was going to get a voicemail recording, Jana answered.

"Grant?"

Her voice was shaky. I knew why.

"You talked to Sue Ling," I said.

"Yeah," she said quietly.

Was this how it was going to be for me from now on? Grant, the cosmic freak.

"Jana, I'm not a monster," I said. "I'm not going to reach through the phone and rip your face off."

"You're angry."

"You bet I'm angry! I'm angry, confused, hurt. And right now I could use a sympathetic ear. I'd expect as much from someone who has known me as long as you have."

A stretch of silence was her reply.

I switched topics.

"The reason I called is that I need to get the information you have on the president's itinerary. Would it be possible for us to—"

"Grant, I can't talk about this right now. I . . . I—"

"Jana, I need that information. Could you at least send me a press packet or—"

"Grant, I really have to go."

She hung up.

Frustrated, I tossed my phone onto the bed. It landed next to the professor's envelope, the one with the additional manuscript pages.

Setting the manuscript on the table, I stared vacantly out the hotel window. I couldn't read right now.

A trio of boys splashed and screamed in the hotel pool. On the golf course a foursome was teeing off at the tenth hole. A man with a large belly and plaid pants took a healthy swing, tracked his ball, leaned to his right, leaned farther, said something I couldn't hear and probably didn't want to hear, slammed his club into his bag, then took off in a golf cart in search of his ball.

Not one of these people was thinking about angels. A few days ago I was just like them. I missed those days.

Pushing myself out of the chair, I turned back into the room. My heart catapulted into my throat when I saw Myles Shepherd standing there.

CHAPTER
23

Myles Shepherd. Looking very much alive.

It took several hard swallows for me to get my heart back where it belonged, and a couple more before I was able to form words.

"Aren't you dead?"

"You're not that lucky, Grant."

Two men appeared from nowhere behind him. Since they hadn't entered through the door I felt it was a safe assumption they were angels, too, and the fact that they weren't attacking Myles meant they were probably on his side.

All of these appearings and disappearings were starting to get on my nerves.

"Reinforcements, Myles?" I said. "Are you afraid to face me alone?"

"Semyaza," he said, sneering. "My name is Semyaza. That should be clear even to you by now."

We faced off as we always had, whether it was across a tennis net or over a chessboard or sparring over Jana.

"A lot has changed over the last few days, Grant," Semyaza said. "This world isn't what you thought it was, is it?"

"That's what everybody keeps telling me."

"As a concerned friend, I thought I'd drop in and check up on you. See how you're doing."

"Your concern is touching." The fact he'd brought reinforcements troubled me. Unless they weren't reinforcements.

"Is one of them—"

"Your grandfather?"

Semyaza exchanged grins with his buddies.

"No, Grant. I'm afraid Azazel couldn't make our little meeting today. He's rather busy at the moment, what with the assassination extravaganza. There are so many details to consider in a presidential assassination, and Azazel wants to make sure everything is perfect. He likes to put on a good show."

"I can imagine," I quipped. "Deciding on a design for the cocktail napkins must have kept him up nights."

Semyaza bristled. It annoyed him when I didn't take him seriously. He'd always been that way, and I always got a kick out of annoying him. And then he'd smash me at whatever it was we were competing over, and he'd get the last laugh.

With more conviction than I felt, I said, "I'll stop the assassination. You know that, don't you? But then, that's why you're here, isn't it? What do you plan to do, Myles? Get your buddies to tie me up and stick me in a closet until it's over?"

Semyaza sniffed indifferently. "You know they hate you, don't you?"

I glanced at the two angels behind him.

"They don't even know me."

"Not them. Abdiel and the others. They despise you because you're one of us."

"I'll never be one of you."

Semyaza chuckled wickedly. "Oh, I beg to differ, Grant. I do beg to differ."

The room grew dark and the ceiling began to stir. I glanced up to see it populated with demons, just as the ceiling in Myles Shepherd's office had filled with hideous gargoyle things. They clustered in the corners, straining as though on a leash.

"You don't choose family," Semyaza said. "That's what they are. Your family. Think of this as a family reunion."

The flesh on my arms and neck began to tingle.

"This is your destiny, Grant. Because of who you are, you have no hope of a blissful afterlife. Your future is with them, elbowing for ceiling space, in constant torment, aching for a moment of peace, pleading with the God who has turned his back on you for annihilation so the pain will stop."

Above him the activity increased like a beehive disturbed. Gargoyle mouths twisted in silent cries.

The thought of being one of them . . . of writhing among them on the ceiling . . . chained . . .

"So that's the plan, is it, Myles? Because I learned the truth, now you're going to kill me?"

"The truth?" He laughed hard. "The truth? You've read the ramblings of an ancient fool and you think you know the truth? I'll show you the truth."

When would I learn not to goad Myles?

At his signal a lone demon dropped from the ceiling onto the bureau. I recognized him from Myles Shepherd's office. It was the same demon that had dropped onto the file cabinet and clutched the tennis trophy.

"Call me sentimental," Myles said, "but I just love family reunions, don't you?"

I was too horrified to reply. My eyes were locked on the tortured soul on the bureau. It stared at me and drooled like I was a T-bone steak.

Semyaza said, "Grant Austin. Meet your father."

Before I had time to blink, the demon hit me in the chest and clawed its way inside. I clutched at my clothing, tearing open my shirt, as though I could go after it and pull it out. My fingers ripped away the shirt and began clawing at the flesh, digging deep red channels. But I made no progress. My own flesh, my own rib cage, kept me from getting at him.

I could feel him inside me. Restless. Stirring. Gnawing. I could hear him in my head, whimpering and moaning. He babbled words I couldn't understand, but I understood his anguish . . . oh, how I understood his anguish . . . an anguish so thick, so heavy, it dripped inside me and coated my soul with an oppressive, oily depression.

I dropped to my knees, my hands clenched helplessly in fists as I fought the torment and the mounting anxiety.

Semyaza stood over me, grinning that insufferable grin he'd perfected as Myles Shepherd. His cohorts flanked him. Above them, on the ceiling, gargoyle demons danced with glee at the thought of one of their number finding a measure of satisfaction at my expense.

"Let's leave Grant and his father to get better acquainted," Semyaza said. "I'm sure they have a lot of catching up to do." The three rogue angels disappeared. The ceiling cleared. I fell onto my back, clutching at my head, writhing on the floor.

CHAPTER
24

IT WAS NIGHT WHEN MY DEMON FATHER VACATED ME. THE HOTEL drapes were open and, from the floor, I could see stars. I don't know why he left when he did. Maybe he had dinner plans. All I know is that he left me completely exhausted. I felt like I'd spent the afternoon wrestling a grizzly bear.

I lay on the floor, my arms and legs splayed, my chest rising and falling as if I'd run a marathon. Not until the ache of lying on the floor was greater than the ache of moving did I get up.

Crawling to the bedside table, I reached for my phone and scrolled through the list of recent calls that had been made to my number. I found the listing I was looking for, the call that had reached me at Christina's apartment.

"Sue, this is Grant."

"Grant." Her voice was hesitant.

"I need to reach the professor. Do you have a contact number I could . . . oh, hello, Professor."

I don't know why I was surprised. Sue Ling was never far from the professor. I told him I needed to speak to him, tonight if possible. He gave me an address in North Park.

A small corner house, 3198 Landis Street appeared to have been built in the late thirties. It had a front porch with wooden pillars on each corner that looked like thin Egyptian pyramids. A long, wooden ramp for handicapped access indicated I was at the right house.

My knock was answered by an invitation to let myself in. The screen door creaked as I opened it. The door had been left open a crack. I stepped into a cozy living room lined with bookshelves. Two floor lamps with shades provided soft light. The absence of a television, or the sound of one, made me feel like I was stepping back in time.

"Come in, Grant!" the professor said cheerily, wheeling himself into the room from the more brightly lit kitchen.

Behind him I could see Sue Ling wiping a dish towel around an appliance. Shoving the appliance into place, she continued wiping down the counter and putting dishes away in the cupboards. Her movements were automatic. She didn't have to think, let alone ask, where anything went.

The professor offered me a seat on a soft sofa—blue cornflowers on a maroon background. He wheeled to a position facing me and gave me a good long look.

"Rough day," he said.

It wasn't a question. I guess I looked even worse than I felt.

"Still wrestling with the news?" he asked.

I laughed.

"Something I said?"

"The news is wrestling back."

I described what had happened in my hotel room. As I spoke, the professor closed his eyes. He listened as though he was in pain.

Sue Ling's voice preceded her entrance.

"Coffee will be ready in a—Grant, you look horrible!"

"Thanks. I'd hate to feel this lousy and nobody notice."

It took half an instant for Sue to put the pieces together. She's quick. I was impressed not only with the speed of her deductive reasoning, but with the fact that she hadn't been listening to our conversation from the kitchen.

What she deduced scared her, and the expression of horror on her face reminded me I had demon blood racing through my veins. All of a sudden she couldn't look at me.

Her gaze laboriously avoiding me, she inched closer to the professor and placed a hand on his arm. The professor didn't acknowledge it. He seemed comfortable with it.

"Anyway," Sue said to the floor, "the coffee will be ready in a minute. I set out sugar and spoons. If you want creamer, it's in the refrigerator. Oh, and there are some cookies on the shelf beneath the toaster oven. The shortbread kind. They're the professor's favorite."

She gave his arm a pat.

"Thank you, Sue," the professor said, reaching for her hand. Squeezing it.

"It's been a long day," she said. "I'm going to go to bed."

Her next move was of great interest to me. Which direction would she go from here? To the back of the house? Or the front door?

She bent over and kissed the professor on the forehead.

"Good night," she said.

"Sleep well, Sue," the professor replied.

Sue Ling then reached behind a chair, retrieved her purse, and let herself out the front door. I smiled. I think it was the first smile I'd smiled all day.

Now that we were alone, I said, "How do I fight angels, Professor?"

Hands clasped in his lap, he thought a moment.

"Have you read the narrative accounts I sent you? The ones Abdiel dictated to me?"

"One of them."

"How many do you have?"

"Two. Are there more?"

The professor's eyes lit up.

"Oh my, yes! Accounts of Lucifer's attempt to corrupt the kingly Davidic line from which the Messiah was promised; heaven's major offensive through the incarnation of the Son; the three years of head-to-head combat between Lucifer and Jesus; the battle of the cross; the raid on Sheol with the release of the captives. All of it. It's fascinating."

"Will it help me fight them?"

"Those narrations are for you."

"Me? I thought Abdiel didn't like me."

"He doesn't. That's why he's dictating the narrative to me. Heaven has taken an interest in you, Grant."

"I guess I should be flattered."

"If you had any sense, you'd be scared."

The comment reminded me how scared I was. I got up and paced.

"So how do I fight them?" I asked again. "I'm tired of being Myles Shepherd's . . ." It was going to take a while to adjust to his new name. "Of being Semyaza's pawn. How do I fight him?"

I was eager to get my hands on something I could use to pummel Semyaza.

"Listen carefully, Grant. Reality is comprised of two parts: that which is seen and that which is unseen. Don't think of them as separate worlds, but as a unified cosmos. The world in which we live is comprised of the natural and the supernatural. Actually, even the term *supernatural* is misleading. It implies it's not natural, when in reality it's just as much a part of the natural world as—"

"Excuse me, Professor."

"Yes?"

"You're sounding like a professor."

"Are you saying you don't understand?"

I slumped back on the sofa. "Don't take this the wrong way, but right now I don't need a lecture. What I need are weapons."

"I see."

"Semyaza has all the weapons. I can't stop him. I don't even know where to begin."

"Weapons."

"Yeah. Something I can use to defend myself. Something that will hurt him, or at least threaten him and make him back off."

"Like a sword."

"Exactly!"

"And maybe a shield."

I was getting through to him.

"Yes! Or if you have something more modern, maybe an automatic weapon or nuclear device."

"A spiritual machine gun."

"Now we're talking!"

The image of me leveling one of those babies at Semyaza and pulling the trigger played in widescreen format in my head, complete with surround sound.

The professor was nodding. He understood now.

"Here it is," he said.

He leaned forward. I leaned forward, as though we were huddling under a super-secret confidential security bubble.

"Truth," he said.

I waited for more. Blinked.

"Truth," I repeated.

"An upright heart."

"Professor, maybe you didn't understand me—"

"Faith."

"I need something I can use to—"

"The Word of God."

He nodded and grinned knowingly as though he'd just handed over an arsenal of weapons.

"Professor, what I need is—"

"You just don't get it, do you?" he snapped, his voice rising. "After all you've been through and you still don't grasp the concept."

"What I understand is—"

"Your enemy is not human!" the professor shouted. "He is a supernatural being with cosmic power of evil proportions which you cannot begin to comprehend! And for reasons unknown to us, he is stalking you, and he will annihilate you unless you find a way to fight him off!"

"But that's what I'm trying to do!"

"No you're not! You're searching for an enchanted supernatural sword that will intimidate and possibly kill him, a weapon forged by someone else that will swing the balance of power in your favor."

I couldn't argue with that. That's exactly what I wanted.

"Well, I have news for you. It doesn't work that way. You'll have to look elsewhere, Grant. I'm all out of magic swords. I'm sorry you wasted your time coming here tonight."

He wheeled himself back to give me room to stand.

At the front door I turned back.

"You can teach me how to fight him?"

"Yes."

I closed the door and took my seat on the sofa.

"I believe you were telling me about the true nature of this universe," I said.

"If you don't understand the nature of the cosmos, you understand nothing," the professor said.

He gestured with a book containing a collection of ancient texts that was old and worn with use. As he spoke he sometimes patted it for emphasis, but rarely did he open it. He gave every indication of having memorized it.

"The Bible unashamedly portrays a world that is at once natural and supernatural, a cosmos that is inhabited by both natural and supernatural beings. The spiritual realm is not something that is far away, it is here and now. It is part of the very fabric of the universe.

"Jacob is a wonderful example. The Bible describes how one day he took a journey, and on his way stumbled into an encampment of angels. He called the place Mahanaim, which means 'two encampments.' The next day, he got up, and continued his journey."

"What was the encampment of angels doing on earth?"

"The Bible doesn't say."

"Does it say where the angels went after Jacob left them?"

"No."

"Did they deliver a message of some sort, something useful Jacob recorded that has been passed down to us?"

"Nothing."

I was stumped. "So the angels were just vacationing on earth?"

The professor laughed. "We don't know what they were doing. That isn't the point of the story."

"What is the point?"

"That they're here. It's that simple."

"If that's true, why don't more people know about them or act like they're here?"

The professor sat back in his wheelchair and mulled a moment.

"The level of awareness of the supernatural has varied throughout history, by design largely, whatever suits the purposes of Lucifer. God has always been up-front about its existence. Maybe it would help to think of Lucifer and his bunch as the Mafia."

"That's easy to do," I said.

"A person can drive through downtown New York and never see the Mafia. That doesn't mean they're not there. People can live all their lives in New York and never knowingly encounter the Mafia, though they have probably been affected one way or another by the

Mafia's presence. Just because they don't operate out in the open, or people don't talk about them often, doesn't mean the Mafia doesn't exist. But when it is in the Mafia's best interests to make themselves visible, they are more than capable of making their presence known in dramatic and powerful ways. Does that help?"

"So the cosmos consists of natural and spiritual. One is as real as the other. Both are present. Got it. Now what?"

The professor sighed. "The hard part."

"How come there's never an easy part?"

"If I was talking with anyone else at this point, Grant, I would tell you the good news."

"Which is?"

"For a person in Christ, the good news is, 'He who is in you is greater than he who is in the world,' meaning that, for the Christian, God has placed His Spirit within him to protect and guard him against the devil's evil schemes."

"You're talking about salvation, right? And because I'm Nephilim, I can't be saved."

"Correct. If God's Spirit was inside of you, Semyaza's demons would not be able to possess you."

"So God's Spirit is unavailable to me."

"I have nothing that says otherwise."

"Which means?"

"You're on your own."

Before I realized it, I was on my feet, pacing and fuming.

"I didn't ask for this," I said. "And I didn't do anything to deserve it either. At least, I don't think I did anything to deserve it. There was that time with Karen in the backseat of her father's Buick, but. . . . No! I may not be perfect, but at least I deserve a chance, don't I? It seems like I don't stand a chance here."

"Grant, your anger is understandable."

"Is it? Is it? Well, that'll be helpful the next time Semyaza sics his demon hounds on me! Or the next time he turns himself into a supernova and levels me. It's not fair, Professor! I'm not an angel, so I can't disappear or walk through walls and whatever else they do. And I'm not a human, so I'm not protected by God. And then, for good measure, when I die I go straight to the ceiling with a mess of slimy green gargoyle demons, and I have done nothing to deserve any of this!"

I had lost the professor halfway through my rant. He stroked his chin in thought.

"What?" I asked him, hoping he'd remembered he had a magic sword in the back of his closet.

"You are part angel. Is it possible that you may have some of their powers?"

"I like this line of thinking. How do we find out?"

"I have no idea."

"But you're the man with all the answers."

"I've never encountered a Nephilim before."

Falling onto the couch, I said, "Well, I have. Trust me, you're not missing anything."

It was late. The professor rubbed his eyes. "The only thing we can do right now is to continue with what we know."

"Which is?"

"Weapons."

It was late and I was tired—too tired to get excited over the weapons the professor mentioned earlier—but at this point, I was willing to try anything that might give me an advantage over Semyaza.

"Truth is a powerful defensive weapon," the professor said, "especially when you're dealing with an enemy whose chief offensive weapon is deception. Stay alert. Don't let Semyaza trick you. And whatever you do, don't help him by deceiving yourself. It's more common than you might think. See things for what they are. Be honest with yourself. Face your challenges head-on, and make your choices with your eyes open."

For the next hour the professor gave me a primer of the spiritual weapons that were available to me.

"Be constant in prayer," he said.

"Prayer? What good will praying do if I'm praying to a God who has made it clear He is not my Savior?"

"Pray to the Father. The Creator. You may be unique, but you are still part of His creation."

"What do I pray for?"

"The ability to stand."

"Bloodied, but unbowed?"

"The legacy of the faithful," the professor said.

It was well after midnight when the professor showed me to the front door.

"Read the Gospels," he said. "You know what the Gospels are, don't you?"

"The first five books of the New Testament."

"Four."

"I thought it was five. Aren't they called the Pentateuch?"

"That's the first five books of the Old Testament."

I sighed. It was late. "I guess I'll stop showing my ignorance and go home."

He handed me his Bible.

"Thanks, but I can check one out of the library," I said.

"I want you to have it."

His offer touched me. I took it, not knowing what to say. I opened the front cover and saw an inscription.

PhD!!!

 *Congratulations, sweetheart! I'm so proud of you. I couldn't
have chosen a more gentle man to be the father of my children—
yes, you read that correctly, Daddy.*

Yours forever,
Nora

I handed the Bible back to him. "Professor, I can't . . . really. . . ."

"You're right," he said, taking the Bible back.

Angling it so that light fell on the pages, he located a specific page
and marked it with the ribbon bookmark. He handed the Bible back
to me.

"Now, you can," he said. "Start there. Read that passage several
times a day, plus the Gospels. Study Jesus, how he recognized and
moved in the spiritual world while on earth. Study his tactics. Practice them."

"But professor, your wife gave you this Bible."

He smiled. "Nora would have liked you. She was a lot of fun."

Back in my hotel room, I opened the Bible to the page the professor
had marked.

*For our struggle is not against flesh and blood, but against the rulers,
against the authorities, against the powers of this dark world and
against the spiritual forces of evil in the heavenly realms. Therefore,
put on the full armor of God, so that when the day of evil comes,
you may be able to stand your ground, and after you have done
everything, to stand.*

I placed the book on the nightstand. For me, the day of evil was
fast approaching, and while I may have had a classroom session on
spiritual weapons, I had no experience.

CHAPTER
25

GROGGILY I RAISED MY HEAD OFF THE PILLOW. THE KNOCKING wasn't in my dream. Someone was at my hotel door. The room was dark, though it was morning. A sliver of sunlight sliced across the floor through a crack in the blackout curtains. Disoriented still, I swung my legs over the side of the bed and felt the carpet with my toes.

The knocking continued.

I'd been awakened out of a dream in which my father came to me in demon form and apologized for possessing me the way he had. We sat on a park bench and chatted.

"It's not so bad, son," he assured me, "being a demon. Sure, it has its downside, but we get to travel, meet interesting people. Last year, for example. We went to Cannes." He winked at me. "You'll like possessing French women."

The knocking at the hotel door persisted. Caught in no man's land between dream and being awake, without thinking, I opened the hotel door in my boxer shorts.

"Grant!"

It was a duet. Jana and Sue Ling reacted identically and in harmony, staring at my shorts, covering their surprised mouths.

Still in a fog, I misinterpreted their reaction for fear.

"Look, I know you're frightened of me," I said, "but I'm scared of me too."

"At least last time he wore a robe," Sue said to Jana.

"Grant, honey, it's hard to be scared of a man standing in nothing but his boxer shorts," Jana said, amused.

Of course, it was at that moment I woke up, or came to my senses, or however you want to describe the feeling you get when you realize you're not dressed for the occasion, or hardly at all.

"How about if we—" Sue said.

"Yeah. Get dressed, Grant. We'll wait for you downstairs."

To say I felt exposed is an understatement. My chest and legs were chilled while my face burned. And just when I thought it was almost over, it got worse.

"Grant!"

"Christina?"

She came up the hallway behind Jana and Sue. Her expression clearly registered her emotions—shock, followed by anger which bordered on nuclear meltdown.

"Christina?"

"Christina?"

The duet again. Jana and Sue in harmony.

Before Christina had a chance to storm away, Jana had her by the arm.

"Girlfriend," she said, "we have got to talk."

She led Christina down the hallway.

"We'll be downstairs," Sue said, following them and grinning at me over her shoulder.

For a long moment I stood there, wallowing in my humiliation.

The door to the room across from mine opened. A middle-aged woman in a pink jogging suit holding a poodle with a pink bow scrunched up her face in disgust.

"Put some clothes on!" she snapped.

I sat on the edge of the bed mechanically pulling on my socks. Twin thoughts occupied my mind. The first thought was to climb back under the covers, pull them over my head, and never answer the door again. Its twin suggested I get dressed and sneak down the back stairway, fly to Morocco, change my name, and become a used camel salesman.

As I pulled on pants and shirt and shoes, all I could think of was how Christina and Jana and Sue were sitting together downstairs with one common denominator among them—me.

I dragged a razor across my chin, brushed my hair and teeth, and stepped into the hallway. Decision time. Turn right to the elevator, which led to two former girlfriends and a woman who mystified me, or left to Morocco and the camels.

I found the three of them in a restaurant off the lobby. They hadn't spotted me yet. All three of them were laughing like they'd been best friends all their lives.

Taking a deep breath, I entered the lion's cage.

When they saw me coming, boiling laughter simmered down to grins and snickering.

"Good morning, Grant."

"Good morning, Grant."

"Good morning, Grant."

Was it too late for Morocco?

They were seated in a booth, the half-circle kind set against a wall, with Christina sandwiched in the middle. I started to squeeze next to Jana.

"No, no, no, no, no," she said. "You sit there."

She pointed to the front of the table, where the waiter usually stands to take orders.

The two others nodded their agreement. Apparently they'd discussed the seating arrangements before I'd arrived. On cue, a waiter arrived with a chair. I sat in front of the three women feeling very much like a convict at a parole hearing.

Each woman had a silver teapot with a wedge of lemon perched on the saucer. The table was littered with empty packets of sugar and sugar substitute.

It became evident the challenge before me was to look at them without looking at them. It had been my experience women don't appreciate a man who looks at another woman when he's out with her. And while you might think this law would be null and void given the fact that I wasn't technically out with any of them, when it comes to former girlfriends, there is only one rule: Whatever you do is wrong. And I knew that if I looked at any one of them for any length of time, the other two would take offense.

So I tried not to look at any of them.

But I wanted to look at them—Jana with her dark, full hair cascading to her shoulders, her charismatic smile and radiating sensuality; Christina with her East Coast professionalism and sparkling, energetic blue eyes; and Sue Ling, quiet, sweet, and brilliant.

I was a dead man.

"Isn't this great, Grant?" Christina exclaimed. "We've all heard each other in the background of your phone conversations, and now we have a chance to get to know each other."

"Um . . . yeah . . . great," I said. "Listen, Christina, about what you saw upstairs in the hallway. I had a late night and Jana and Sue had just stopped by when you—"

Christina waved off my explanation. "Oh, we've already been through all that," she said cheerily. "However, they did inform me that the previous time they were with you in your hotel room, you at least had the decency to wear a robe."

A gray-haired woman in the booth next to us glared at me with disgust.

Jana, Christina, and Sue laughed.

"We are all in agreement on one thing, though," Sue added. "You have nice legs."

They fell against each other laughing.

I tried to be a good sport, to laugh with them, but all I could manage was a half-smile. I craned my neck to see if I could find a waiter. I could really use a cup of coffee.

"There it is," Jana said, leveling an index finger at me.

"You're right," Christina agreed.

"What?" I asked.

"A few moments ago, I was asking Christina if she noticed how quick you are to find the humor in someone else's discomfort, but when it's you who is uncomfortable, for some reason it's not funny."

"I don't know what you're talking about," I said, fidgeting in my seat.

"For me," Jana said. "It was a run in my stocking at the senior prom. I tried to get Grant to take me home so I could put on a new pair. He refused."

"You monster!" Sue Ling cried.

"Instead, he took it upon himself to do an informal survey of every guy who walked by our table. He even had me stand up and show them the run. His conclusion? Nine out of ten guys didn't think the run made me any less attractive. He honestly thought that would make me feel better."

"Well, I did . . . at the time," I said defensively.

My only hope now was to get a last-minute reprieve from the governor.

"He did a similar thing to me," Christina said. "We were sitting in a restaurant, just a few blocks from the Capitol, for an important lunch meeting with the senator from Massachusetts. The waiter spilled coffee on the sleeve of my two-piece suit."

Jana and Sue gasped.

"It was too late to do anything about it. I had no choice but to remove the jacket and proceed with the meeting. Do you know what Grant did during the entire lunch? He kept commenting about how cold it was in the restaurant and asked me if I wanted help putting my jacket on."

"Grant!" Jana and Sue chimed in.

I felt like a worm. Like the underbelly of a worm. Like a parasite crawling on the underbelly of a worm.

"And have you noticed how Grant gets moody when he doesn't get his way?" Sue Ling said.

"He does!" Christina said, surprised. "How long have you known Grant?"

"Just a few days."

"You're absolutely right, though. He does," Christina said.

"I do not," I objected moodily.

"Yes, you do," Jana said, making it unanimous.

With cup in hand, I turned to look for the waiter, needing coffee desperately now.

"All right, ladies," Jana said. "Let's get down to business."

"Business?" I said.

"Grant, we're here to help you," Sue Ling assured me.

"Help me?"

"You are one lucky guy, Grant Austin," Jana said. "Three gorgeous and talented women show up on your doorstep with a single thought. To help you."

"Lucky me."

"Christina, you've come the farthest," Jana said. "You go first." To me, she added, "Christina flew all the way across the United States to bring you some news, and she took personal time off from work to do it. I hope you appreciate what a good girlfriend she is."

"Ex-girlfriend," Christina and I said in unison.

"But I do have good news," Christina continued, smiling at me. "I discovered who doctored the manuscript."

"You're kidding!" I cried. "Who?"

"Sylvia Jakes."

The name clunked onto the table meaninglessly. Who was Sylvia Jakes?

"It may have been her handwriting," I said, "but someone else orchestrated the changes, right?"

Christina nodded, still smiling.

"Ingraham?"

She shook her head. "Margaret."

"Margaret!"

"Who's Margaret?" Sue Ling asked.

"Chief of Staff Ingraham's personal secretary," I explained. "Are you sure this Sylvia person wasn't working under Ingraham's orders?"

"Positive," Christina said. "And if needed, Sylvia has agreed to testify you had nothing to do with it. You're off the hook."

"Thank you, Christina," I said with emotion, because indeed a weight had been lifted from my shoulders. "What does Margaret have to say about it?"

Christina hooked her hair behind an ear. It was an endearing gesture, the equivalent of a man rolling up his sleeves to work.

"We don't know," she replied.

"What do you mean, you don't know?"

"Margaret has disappeared. I mean, literally, Grant. I followed her into the supply closet, and when I got there, she was gone. I couldn't have been more than a second behind her. It's the supply closet at the end of the hall where you had your desk."

I was familiar with it. There is only one way in or out of that closet.

"The mystery deepened when we went that night hoping to find her at her town house. The place was so proper and neat, it looked like a model house or a showroom of some kind. But no Margaret. I wanted to tell you the other night when I called."

"Why didn't you?"

Even as I asked the question, I knew why. She hung up when she heard Jana's and Sue's voices in my hotel room.

"You flew out here to check up on me!" I cried.

"I did not!" Christina objected. "I had a message to deliver and needed to get away for a while. What better place than San Diego?"

"I believe her," Jana said.

"So do I," Sue said.

I pondered the realization that Christina still cared for me. I wasn't sure how I felt about that.

Jana reassumed control. "Sue, you're up next."

"Mine's not a big thing like Christina's and Jana's," Sue began, "but I've been thinking about the coded phrase in your book. Even though you can prove you didn't write it, its placement and the phrase itself was meant to implicate you, which means it's still a clue as to what's in store for the president. Do you still want to talk to him?"

"I do," I said. "I may be off the hook, but I still have questions for him. And if there will be an assassination attempt—and I'm confident there will be—I want to stop it."

"If you ask me, it'll take place in San Diego," Christina said. "You wouldn't believe how crazy it's been around the White House. Something big is happening. Besides, the president warned Grant away from San Diego to protect him. The attempt will be made here; you can count on it."

"And Myles Shepherd told me the president himself was in on the plot," I added.

"What?" Jana cried. "When did he tell you that?"

"The day of my speech."

"And you've been sitting on that information all this time?"

"I didn't want to believe it," I said, which was true. I only hoped Jana wouldn't press any further.

"You didn't tell me because I'm a reporter, isn't that right?" Jana said. "You didn't trust me."

Three angry faces glared at me.

I was without defense.

Mercifully, Sue Ling continued with her contribution. "To remind everyone of the sentence, it read: 'When he is suspended between earth and heaven I will kill the president.' The timing of the assassination is dictated by the place, 'suspended between earth and heaven.'"

"We considered places like the Skytower at Sea World—it's two hundred and sixty feet high," Jana said. "But the president's itinerary doesn't place him anywhere near Sea World."

"What about a high-rise?" I suggested. "He's staying at the U.S. Grant Hotel, which has a rooftop terrace."

"We considered that as a possibility," Sue said.

"But not likely," Christina added. "The president doesn't usually wander outside his hotel when he travels unless it's to go someplace specific."

"He did some wandering the night you found him with the

manuscript copy," I said, "and if he really is planning it himself, he would have to take the Secret Service by surprise."

"Remembering that the plan was to implicate you, Grant," Sue said, "it would mean you would have to be on a rooftop or in a helicopter to get some kind of shot at him on the terrace. Do you have any plans to be on a rooftop?"

"No."

I didn't tell her that I had recently been on the roof of the Emerald Plaza towers.

"Given the president's itinerary," Sue said, "we think the phrase 'between earth and heaven' most likely refers to Air Force One."

"That certainly fits the description," I said, "but how would I—"

"Before we go there," Jana interrupted, "let me show you the itinerary." She shoved a piece of paper in front of me and proceeded to go down the list. "There are two scheduled fundraisers," she said. "The first, a private reception at the home of Gerald Keneally in La Costa."

"The computer-chip millionaire," I said, recognizing the name.

"It's a single-story residence, and Del Mar Road is the only access into and out of the neighborhood."

"There is an adjoining polo field," Christina added, "which means the president will most likely arrive by helicopter."

"Which flies between earth and heaven—" I said.

"But the chances of you getting anywhere close to that polo field are remote," Christina replied.

Jana continued, "Then, there's a dinner at the convention center, which will be preceded by the president throwing the first pitch at Petco Park. The Padres are playing the Nationals that night."

"The ballpark is at sea level," I mused.

"There will be a designated area for protesters," Christina said.

"The president's third and final appearance is not a fundraiser, but a huge send-off on Coronado Island. The president will visit the

USS *Ronald Reagan* aircraft carrier, and there will be a public rally with plenty of bands and balloons and choirs."

"The place where you will most likely be able to get close to the president," Sue said.

"And Air Force One takes off right there from North Island Naval Air Station," I said.

"That's right," Jana replied.

"But how would I kill the president while Air Force One is taking off?" I asked.

Sue sighed. "We didn't say we had it all figured out," she said. "Only that by putting one and one together—you in proximity to the president and him suspended between earth and heaven—the most likely scenario is the closing rally."

"Which means I have three days in which to reach him and talk him out of it," I said. "Thank you," I said to all three of them. "Thank you all. At least now I know what I'm up against."

Jana wasn't listening. "Christina, have you ever been shopping at Fashion Valley?" she said. "I have an hour before I have to get back to the station."

"Wait . . . Jana. . . ." My mind was still on the president's schedule. "This itinerary. It isn't much for a three-day visit. Are there any meetings or conferences between these events?"

Jana shook her head. "Just these. People at the news station made the same observation. Usually these whirlwind tours are packed with meetings. Everybody wants five minutes with the president."

I think I knew why the schedule was so sparse. In my mind's eye I could see Doc Palmer working feverishly to patch together a drug-addicted president so that he would present a suitable public image for a few hours.

The girls were sliding out of the booth.

"Take care of the tab, will you, Grant?" Christina said as she passed me.

"You're welcome," Jana said, referring to the itinerary.

"You have good taste in women, Grant," Sue said. "I like them. They're fun."

I remained behind and paid the check, but not before I got my cup of coffee.

CHAPTER
26

A SENATOR ONCE TOLD ME THAT PROTESTORS WERE LIKE MACAWS. Colorful, loud, and demanding, but harmless. "Who takes macaws seriously?" he said.

Standing at the polo field in Del Mar, I had to agree with him. Most of the protestors seemed to operate under the assumption that if you waved a sign and shouted loud enough, the president would change any domestic or foreign policy. It was all in the volume.

I stood in the midst of a whole flock of macaws holding my sign: DOC PALMER IS ALIVE. I was surrounded by protestors of offshore oil drilling, the president's handling of the wars in Lebanon and Venezuela, the Save Our Penguins brigade, and a man who wanted the president to investigate irregularities in the handling of his son's Little League candy sales.

In every other attempt to reach the president, I'd struck out. A man who is hesitant about revealing his true identity has few options when contacting a head of state. This was my last-gasp effort, futile as it was. I felt ridiculous standing here.

"Nice sign, Grant," Semyaza said.

He'd popped in from nowhere. "I have to admit, you have proven to be a formidable adversary. A protest sign. We never saw it coming. Stunning tactic. Lucifer and his generals are huddling in a desperate attempt to come up with a strategy to stop you."

I lowered my sign. "Does your presence mean it's going to happen tonight?" I asked.

The president's helicopter was approaching, stirring the macaws. The squawking jacked up to deafening decibels.

The helicopter was so far distant it looked the size of a sparrow. It hovered, suspended between earth and heaven, without incident. After it landed, there was a seamless transition as the president climbed into a limo and was whisked away.

Semyaza vanished without further comment.

Somewhere—wherever journalists were flocking—Jana was doing her part. She was not only covering events but was trying to get word to the president on my behalf through the press corps. I watched her reports each evening on the nightly news.

Christina reinserted herself into the White House staff during the Del Mar visit after one of the event coordinators became sick from shellfish she ate in Tijuana. While Ingraham proved an insurmountable obstacle between her and the president, at least she was able to give us inside updates, on average, thirty minutes before the press got them.

The president left Del Mar the same way he came. In a helicopter and without incident.

A mad dash to the convention center fundraiser was an even worse waste of time. The designated protest area was conveniently tucked away and well out of sight.

That night Jana reported on the news that the convention center fundraiser had been a huge success. Douglas was nothing if not charismatic. To party officials he was the golden goose.

In the mornings, as the professor suggested, I read the call-to-arms verse every day and portions of the Gospel accounts. While I was familiar with some of the more recognizable accounts of Christ's life, I had never studied the Gospels in-depth. And while I couldn't share in the world's salvation, I saw in Jesus a heroic figure. While he couldn't be my Savior, I determined he could be my hero.

According to the professor, Abdiel and many of the other angels refer to the historical Jesus as the Divine Warrior. I could see it.

On the third day I awoke early with a sense of quiet desperation. This would be my last chance to get the president's attention.

According to the itinerary that had been given to the press, the president's motorcade would travel south on Harbor Boulevard past the county courthouse that had been dedicated by President Franklin Delano Roosevelt, and then over to Coronado for a farewell rally, after which he would board Air Force One at North Island Naval Air Station.

The way I saw it, I had two chances. The motorcade route and the rally. Once the president was onboard Air Force One, it was all over.

The rally would be a last-ditch effort. I'd promised Jana, Sue Ling, and Christina that under no circumstances would I go over to the Coronado side of the bay. They were afraid that, once events were set in motion, there would be no stopping them and I would be swept up in history.

I intended to keep my promise, if possible. But I could think of at least one scenario that could land me on Coronado Island—by invitation of the president. If he saw my sign, it was conceivable he could ask me to accompany him to the rally where we could talk, or to join him on Air Force One.

And if he didn't see my sign?

I'd cross that bridge—pun intended, would you expect any less? —when I got to it.

I parked at Horton Plaza and walked to the bay. Finding a parking place on Pacific Coast Highway was a hit-and-miss proposition on a normal day, wishful thinking on a day like today.

When I reached Harbor Boulevard, I groaned with frustration at what I saw. A mistake from the night before had germinated and bloomed.

At the convention center a goofy-looking, bald-headed guy had struck up a conversation with me. He asked me about my sign. I made the mistake of telling him the sign wasn't so much a protest, but a step toward getting an invitation to a private meeting with the president.

"You know something, don't you?" he said.

"Something like that."

"You really think it will work?"

"I wouldn't be standing here if I didn't think so."

Now, as I crossed the street to the bay side of Harbor Boulevard, I saw five signs identical to mine—DOC PALMER IS ALIVE—held by the goofy-looking bald guy and what looked like his wife and three children. When he saw me, he waved at me with a gap-toothed smile.

Trying to make the best of a messed-up situation, I distanced myself from my competition by moving farther down the motorcade line. While their signs had the same message, I was the exclamation point. The fact that I knew Doc Palmer was alive put teeth in the message.

I know. I was grasping at straws. But when life gives you straws, the lemonade's going to taste lousy.

Positioning myself at Navy Pier, I settled in for the wait. This was my last chance. One way or the other, I was going to get the president's attention. I could think of one sure way. By stepping in front of the presidential limo.

Brake lights lit on a school bus as it negotiated the curve on the ramp from Interstate 5 North to the Coronado Bridge. Jana Torres hoped they were just slowing for the curve. The last thing she needed right now was for traffic to back up.

Six months ago, she'd committed herself to a breakfast speaking engagement in Chula Vista. Being a successful, articulate, and attractive Latina career woman made her popular with women's groups. Normally she enjoyed giving motivational speeches, and the station encouraged her since it was good public relations. However, six months ago she hadn't known that the president would be in town and that there would be an attempt on his life.

She hadn't told anybody at the station about what she knew. She treated the knowledge as any other tip. She'd follow it up and if it played out, she'd be in the right place at the right time. If it didn't . . . it was just another tip that didn't pan out. At least that's what she told herself to calm her racing heart.

Officially, she hadn't been assigned to the story, though she had fought for it. The station wanted her to keep her speaking commitment. Assigned to cover the story were two news crews; one was on Harbor Boulevard for the motorcade and the other on Coronado for the festivities and departure.

After a morning of smiling, shaking hands, and thanking people for watching her report the news, Jana drove toward Coronado. She believed Sue Ling was correct in thinking that "between earth and heaven" referred to Air Force One, and she wanted to be there. If something dramatic happened, she could always grab an extra cameraman or, if nothing else was available, she could use her cell phone.

On the ramp ahead of her, the single pair of brake lights became two, then six, then a dozen. She applied her brakes and slapped the steering wheel in frustration. Within seconds the entire ramp was at a standstill backing up onto the freeway.

She set her car radio to scan the channels in search of a news report. Reaching for her mounted smartphone, she tapped the selection to call her station to see if there was an update on the president's itinerary. Over the car's speakers, the news desk told her the itinerary hadn't changed. Neither had Christina, her inside source, left any messages.

She looked at her watch. There was still plenty of time. A couple hundred feet ahead of her, the ramp curved sharply to the left, so she couldn't see what traffic on the bridge was like. It was probably backed up into Coronado like it was every morning, when military personnel reported for duty.

Jana drummed her fingers on the steering wheel. She was not going to sit here stuck in traffic while the biggest news story of the century unfolded just a few miles away.

Broken bones and casts awaited me. Men had sacrificed far more for their country. I took a deep breath, ready to do my duty and step in front of the president's limo.

At the moment the street was empty of traffic. It had been rerouted for the motorcade.

I gripped my sign.

"What's the big deal about Doc Palmer?" the guy next to me asked.

My cell phone rang. *I'm Too Sexy for My Shirt.*

"Excuse me, I have to take this," I told him. "The president."

The guy's eyebrows shot up.

"Well . . . not the president himself . . . one of his staffers . . . *senior* staffers."

I answered the phone.

"Grant?" Christina said on the other end of the line. "Change of plans."

My heart sank.

"We're leaving the hotel right now and taking the freeway to Coronado. We're not going down Harbor Boulevard."

"Really? Why?"

"They didn't say. Sorry."

So that was it. The only other possibility was Coronado.

"Grant? You're not thinking of going to Coronado, are you? You promised."

"Sorry, Christina. I can't talk now."

Lowering the phone, I dropped my sign.

"He's not coming," I said to the man next to me.

"Yeah, like you were really talking to the president."

"Suit yourself, but I'm telling you his itinerary has changed. He's taking the freeway. He's not coming down Harbor Boulevard."

The woman next to him, chewing gum and wearing an orange ball cap, pulled earphones out of her ears. "Radio says he's not coming," she told her husband. "He's taking the freeway to Coronado."

The man stared at me in disbelief.

I shrugged.

The professor and Sue Ling heard the news about the change in the president's route to Coronado from a news update on the television. She sat on the sofa and the professor sat next to her with the sofa arm separating them. They watched a small thirteen-inch screen from a combination television/DVD player that was kept in a closet when not in use.

It was unusual that the television was turned on during the day. Its use was normally restricted to Friday nights. Sue insisted the professor take Friday nights off. It was their movie night. Their routine alternated between action/adventure movies and romantic comedies. The adventures for her, the romantic comedies for him.

"Poor Grant," Sue said when she heard the news.

The professor said nothing. He stared intently at the screen as though he was trying to see things that weren't there.

Jana's cell phone rang. She smiled when she saw Christina on the display, the newest addition to her FAVORITES list. The two women had hit it off famously from the moment they met in the hotel hallway.

"I hope you have good news," Jana answered.

"Where are you?"

"Stuck on the on-ramp to the bridge. Traffic's backed up."

"It's not traffic. The bridge is closed."

"Closed? Already?"

"The time schedule has been moved up. We're on the freeway," Christina said. "Is there another way for you to get to Coronado?"

Jana looked around her. She was boxed in. "I'd have to hop a freeway divider, hitch a ride south down to Imperial Beach and come up the strand."

"Hop the freeway divider? Do you do that here in California?"

"If I remember my high school civics lessons, I think there's a law against hopping freeway barriers while wearing high heels."

"You've been spending too much time with Grant," Christina said. "You're beginning to sound like him."

"Sorry. I'm frustrated that I'm stuck here."

"What's ahead of you?"

"It's hard to tell. The road curves onto the bridge. There are probably twenty cars between me and where it merges with the southbound ramp."

"The one the motorcade is taking?"

"Yes."

"Jana, get up there. I'll . . . try to think of something. Just be ready to jump into a black limo if the opportunity presents itself."

"You got it, girlfriend. Just remember I'm in heels."

Abandoning her car, Jana Torres took two steps, stopped, slipped off her shoes, and ran past a traffic sign that indicated she was on the road that would take her across the Coronado Bridge into Coronado.

Standing on the wharf, I gazed dejectedly across the bay to Coronado Island and the profile of the aircraft carrier USS *Ronald Reagan*, where the farewell rally would take place. The president's final farewell rally in all probability.

There were two ways to get over there. The bridge, or drive all the way down to Imperial Beach, then come up from the south by way of the strand. The bridge was closed to traffic and the longer route was, well, longer. On normal days there was a ferry service, but the Coast Guard had shut it down until the president was away.

All I could do now was wait for the bridge to reopen.

Staring across the bay, I wondered what the next hour would hold. Douglas always had a flair for the dramatic. It would be just like him to throw his own farewell party as a kickoff to his assassination.

With the water lapping the pilings several feet below me, I'd never felt more helpless. Telling myself I'd done all I could was hollow comfort. How could I have not seen what was really happening at the Douglas White House? And how could I have allowed myself to be spoon-fed the research that resulted in a glamorized account of Douglas's war record? I should have trusted less and dug deeper.

Despite the damage it would do to my career as a writer, when this was all over I was going to return to Montana and convince Doc Palmer to come forward and set the record straight.

"I'll tell you one thing," I muttered. "If I do write a final chapter to the biography, it won't be the one Myles Shepherd or Semyaza or whoever he is wants me to write. It'll be the truth."

I glanced across the bay again and wondered how much of the final chapter I'd be able to see from here.

That's when I saw him.

Semyaza.

It was as though I'd summoned him by speaking his name.

He stood just a couple of hundred yards away from me on the flight deck of the USS *Midway*, which was now a floating museum docked at Navy Pier. He just stood there looking across the water at me, his pants legs flapping in the breeze.

Eyes fixed on him, I made my way along the wharf to the pier, walking, then jogging, then running. I sprinted down the pier and up the gangplank, past a startled ticket-taker.

"Hey! You need a ticket to get in!" he shouted at my back. "You need a ticket!"

I burst onto the hangar deck looking for stairs or a ladder up to the flight deck. I found myself in an enormous metal cavern with several different aircraft on display.

At the far end, to my right, I saw a man in a Hawaiian T-shirt heading up some stairs. By the time he huffed and puffed his way to the top, I was right behind him.

The deck was a display area for nearly two dozen jets and helicopters. I started jogging in the direction where I saw Myles last, looking around fuselages and wings and rotors as I ran. Passing the island superstructure, I found him standing at the far end of the deck.

I stopped running a hundred yards before reaching him, reminding myself of who he really was. Even now, without a ceiling overhead, I glanced up to see if there were any gargoyle demons close by.

His back was to me. He stood casually as though he was admiring the bay.

"Glad you could make it," he said. "You're right on schedule. Predictable to a fault."

He was just trying to goad me, and I wasn't going to give him the satisfaction. I'd boasted that I would stop him and had failed. Just like in high school, he'd bested me. But I wasn't going to give him the satisfaction of getting my goat.

I followed the line of his gaze.

A chill sliced through me and not from the breeze.

Semyaza wasn't looking at Coronado.

"Beautiful, isn't she?" he said. "I've always liked her graceful lines."

He was looking south at the bridge spanning the bay, a blue ribbon stretched over a series of arches, suspended between earth and heaven.

CHAPTER
27

HER LUNGS WERE FEELING THE BURN. WITH SHOES IN HAND, Jana rounded the bend of the on-ramp, which looked more like a parking lot than a freeway. Bored drivers whistled, honked, or shouted suggestive comments as she ran by them. At the top of the ramp, a pair of California Highway Patrol motorcycles blocked access to the bridge. Beyond them the upward slope of the roadway was empty of traffic in both directions.

Jana slowed to a walk as she passed a school bus of screaming children, first- or second-graders from the looks of them. They were unattended. The door to the bus was open. The engine was turned off. The driver's seat was empty.

Between the front line of cars and the roadblock, a drama with five actors was taking place, featuring two CHP officers and three women. The hoods of cars served as front row seats for bystanders who had nothing else to do while waiting for the motorcade.

Of the actors, the most animated was a woman with close-cropped, black hair, barely five feet tall and shaped like a fire hydrant. She stood toe to toe with the officers, waving a piece of paper under their noses. Two taller women who were dressed like elementary-school teachers—conservative style, comfortable shoes—backed her up. From the brunette's trucker vocabulary, Jana concluded she was the bus driver.

"Look at it!" she screamed. "Look at it! This is my pass! An invitation . . . on White House stationery!"

The CHP officers stood shoulder-to-shoulder presenting a united front. With their helmets, reflective sunglasses, and headset microphones, they looked like Stormtroopers from Star Wars.

The taller of the officers said, "Lady, I don't care if you have a letter signed by Abraham Lincoln. We're not letting you through."

The brunette's solo became a trio as the women behind her added their voices to the argument. The CHP officers remained unfazed and unmoved by the barrage of arguments.

"But we have an invitation!"

"Explain that to a busload of kids!"

"They've been practicing for more than a month!"

"I want to speak to your supervisor."

"A once-in-a-lifetime experience."

Reclining on the hood of a blue Ford Mustang, a young couple looked on with amusement. Other drivers from the line of cars behind them had filtered forward and were standing around with arms folded, some shielding their eyes from the sun.

Jana moved among them, doing her best to blend in. She glanced in the direction of the motorcade route, a crazy scenario playing in her head of a black limousine slowing, the back door flying open, and Christina yelling from inside for her to jump in. It was a ridiculous idea, she knew, but nevertheless she positioned herself near the front, hoping that one or two of the bystanders would unintentionally run interference for her.

"Here he comes!" the man on the Mustang shouted.

All eyes turned toward the motorcade route as an assortment of limousines and oversized SUVs snaked up the freeway toward them.

Six CHP motorcycle officers led the motorcade, their emergency lights flashing.

To Jana it looked like a funeral procession. She spotted the presidential limousine, marked with furiously fluttering flags that bore the presidential seal.

She tightened the grip on her shoes. Her heart hammered as she readied herself for whatever would happen next.

To cheers from the northbound ramp audience, the lead motorcycles zoomed by them impressively.

Then, to everyone's surprise, the motorcade slowed and stopped. Doors to three limos flew open, disgorging big men in dark suits with dark sunglasses and one attractive blonde in a red skirt and matching jacket.

Christina.

"You go, girlfriend!" Jana muttered, impressed.

All but two of the Secret Service detail surrounded the presidential limousine, looking outward, vigilant, their heads in constant motion. The other two agents approached the roadblock. While they were still a good distance away, the brunette bus driver began making her appeal to them directly.

"Tell these Nazi thugs to let us through! We have an invitation," she shouted, waving the letter as though it was a historic proclamation backing a noble cause.

While everyone else was watching the drama unfold, Christina caught Jana's eye. With a tilt of her head she motioned Jana toward the school bus. Jana signaled she understood with a nod. Turning, she wove her way through the crowd toward the bus.

She could hear Christina's voice behind her. "Officers, we need those children at the rally."

A deep male voice said, "Ma'am, we'll take care of this. Please get back in the car."

The now-familiar protest of the bus driver started up again, prompting a response from the CHP officers. The Secret Service agent played referee.

With everyone engrossed in the Jerry Springer–type drama, Jana was able to wander unnoticed to the school bus. Slipping on her shoes, she casually climbed aboard as though she belonged with the children. Only when she was inside did she risk a glance back at the motorcade through the windshield.

She saw Christina climbing into the limo as the stout brunette thrust her fists skyward to a smattering of cheers and applause. The CHP officers mounted their motorcycles to move them out of the way. And the Secret Service agents returned to the motorcade, one of them bending down to give a thumbs-up sign to the back window of the presidential limo.

Maybe this wasn't Christina's doing after all, Jana concluded. *The president wants this bus at the rally. Why?*

The driver and two teachers were making their way back to the bus. Jana turned and made her way down the aisle toward the back. Curious eyes watched her. Some of the children smiled and waved. She smiled and waved back.

"We're going to sing for the President of the United States!" one girl told her proudly.

"I know!" Jana replied. "Sing pretty for him, okay?"

"Teacher! Manuel hit me!"

Next to the window a boy with innocent brown eyes was sitting on his hands.

"Stop hitting her!" Jana scolded him. Manuel didn't fool her for a second.

Jana made it to the back row just as the trio of adults was boarding the bus. She slid down low, displacing a skinny little boy from the back corner.

She whispered to him, "Thank you for sharing your seat with me."

"We're going to sing for the President of the United States!" he told her.

"I know."

"My daddy said that he didn't vote for the president, but that I could sing for him anyway."

"Can you keep a secret?" Jana said. "I didn't vote for the president either."

The boy grinned.

"Can you keep another secret?"

The boy nodded.

"Pretend like I'm not here, okay?"

He agreed. She won him over with her smile. Little boys, grown men, Jana knew her smile could get them to do whatever she wanted them to do.

From the front of the bus, adult voices issued orders for the children to sit down and be quiet. The motor roared to life. With a series of starts and jerks, the bus inched forward, backed up, then inched forward again as the driver maneuvered around the cars in front of them.

Hunkered down in the backseat, Jana congratulated herself. With Christina's help she was in the motorcade. Whatever happened from here, she would be there to report it.

With time to kill, she mulled over the Secret Service agent's thumbs-up sign. News copy for tonight's broadcast formed in her head.

Moments before the assassination, the president stopped his motorcade to assist a busload of children who were scheduled to sing for him. Ironically, their song would be the last song he ever heard.

As the bus picked up speed Jana risked a peek out the rear window. With the city skyline behind them and the bay below them, they were about a quarter of the way across the bridge.

"Don't do this, Myles."

"Myles is dead. My name is Semyaza."

From the flight deck of the USS *Midway*, I scanned the Coronado Bridge and surrounding area for anything that could be a threat to the motorcade. Coast Guard patrol boats plied the waters beneath the bridge, duplicating my effort.

I felt as useless as the museum aircraft on the deck beside me. The president's motorcade came into view, a long line of black vehicles followed by a yellow school bus.

"No!" I cried.

Semyaza grinned. "Nice touch, don't you think? The school bus was the president's idea."

The motorcade sailed smoothly across the bridge under clear blue skies. It was a perfect San Diego Chamber of Commerce day.

I had to find the threat and reveal it. What were the possibilities?

Sniper. No. There were no buildings close enough to the bridge for a sniper. Besides, the bridge was too high, the angles were all wrong.

Portable rocket launcher. But from where? Again, distance and angles were a problem.

Explosives. The pilings beneath the water surface could be rigged. But that was so obvious. It was the Secret Service's job to secure the bridge. But then, it was their job to secure buildings and they had missed the school-book depository in Dallas in 1963, hadn't they?

Of course, if the president was part of the plot, any of the vehicles in the motorcade could be rigged to . . .

The school bus!

No! It was unthinkable.

I shot a glance at the nonhuman being beside me. Was human life so cheap to them that they would kill a busload of schoolchildren for show? What was I saying? Since when did Satan or demons have any regard for human life?

I have to warn them. I have to warn the people on the bus. Or maybe . . . maybe I don't have to warn them. Maybe the answer to putting a stop to this whole thing is standing beside me.

"You have the power to stop this, don't you? If not the power, the authority."

Semyaza sneered. "You cannot begin to comprehend the power I have," he said.

"Then stop this!"

Without answering me, Semyaza turned northward. "Ah! Right on time," he said.

I followed his gaze. In the distant sky I saw a speck that at first glance appeared to be a blackbird. But it wasn't a bird. Its flight was mechanically straight. And it was coming directly toward us.

Jana turned toward the front of the bus just as the driver glanced up into the oversized mirror. Her eyes locked on Jana.

Busted! Jana thought.

But the driver resumed driving and said nothing.

Before Jana had time to breathe a sigh of relief, one of the teachers sitting in the front seat checked the mirror for herself. The way she popped out of her seat, you would have thought it was spring-loaded. She charged down the aisle.

"What are you doing on this bus?" she shouted.

On both sides of the aisle, the kids watched with wide-eyed fear, the expression they get whenever someone is in trouble and they're glad it isn't them.

Reaching the back row, the teacher snatched up the skinny boy, Jana's coconspirator, as though Jana was a child molester. The woman's cheap salt-and-pepper wig was knocked askew by the effort.

"Who are you?" she screamed.

The second teacher, shorter and with Chihuahua-like protruding eyes, leaned at a crazy angle from behind to punctuate the question with an angry glare.

Jana smiled her smile, even though she knew it didn't have the same effect on women as it had on men. She decided now would be a good time to play the celebrity newscaster card.

"Maybe you don't recognize me," she said. "My name is Jana Torres, a reporter with the—"

Something out the window caught the second teacher's attention. She used it to distract the kids from the backseat stowaway.

"Hey, kids! Look! On this side. Up in the sky. A fighter jet!"

Children poured across the aisle like water sloshing in a tube, plastering their faces against the windows.

"It looks mean," one girl said.

The teacher chuckled at the girl's innocence. "I suppose it does," she said. "But that's only to frighten away our enemies. He's friendly to us."

"Cool! He's coming right at us!" a boy shouted.

"He's probably doing a flyover," the teacher explained. "You know, like they do at parades and football games."

"Why?"

"It's the military's way of saluting the president."

Jana lifted herself up onto the seat and looked out the window. She agreed with the little girl. The fighter looked mean.

"He's the lead pilot enforcing the no-fly zone," Semyaza said, introducing the approaching aircraft. "Thirty seconds ago, he broke from his designated flight path. His name is Danny Noonan."

"Noonan!"

"I thought you'd recognize the name. After your little jaunt to Montana, you can probably piece together his motive."

The jet was targeting the bridge. I'd found the threat, but there was no alarm for me to sound. It seemed every time I turned around lately I felt helpless. It was getting tiresome.

"He knows, doesn't he?" I said, swallowing hard. "He knows Lloyd Douglas killed his . . ." I had to do a little generational math. Noonan's son would be too old to be a fighter pilot. That meant that Douglas had killed the pilot's—

"Grandfather!" I said.

"Very good, Grant. In case you haven't noticed this about us already, you'll soon learn that angels love irony. When Danny was a little boy, Lloyd Douglas was his hero. Douglas used to parade the boy and his father around the country to political rallies and fund-raisers. It was a great spectacle, the survivors of the Vietnam hero Douglas tried so valiantly to save."

"You told Danny the truth."

"Imagine his disappointment. A patriotic young man, the product of a proud military family. Imagine how he felt when he learned it was all a lie, that the man he worshipped was in reality his grandfather's killer. For a warrior like Danny, there is only one way to right such a grievous wrong. Blood vengeance."

The blackbird-sized speck in the sky had transformed into an F/A-18 Hornet, bristling with armament. Its nose dipped, taking an attack posture.

Semyaza rubbed his hands together. "This is going to be good!" he said.

Two additional F/A-18s appeared from nowhere on an intercept course.

"Don't get your hopes up," Semyaza said. "They won't catch him. Danny has superior skills. Besides, he has an edge. He's their trainer.

He knows the tactics. He knows their weaknesses as pilots. He'll exploit them."

Noonan's jet streaked in front of us with such ferocity it looked and sounded like it was ripping open the sky. A rocket flared beneath one wing, then the other. Twin smoke trails looking like white serpents struck the bridge.

I held my breath, unable to comprehend what was happening.

When he is suspended between earth and heaven . . .

Two explosions less than a second apart created a single ball of smoke and fire. The one-two punch took out the section of bridge immediately in front of the motorcade.

Noonan pulled up. An instant later the pursuing F/A-18s screamed past us.

On the bridge, the line of vehicles bowed forward with simultaneous clouds of white smoke rising from the tires. Some fishtailed. Others rear-ended the vehicles in front of them. The bus swung sideways, the front slamming against the bridge railing, and for a moment it appeared as though it might go over. But it didn't. It came to a stop.

None of the vehicles plunged over the bridge's severed end. From what I could see, some limos were crumpled, but nothing serious. There was no serious damage.

"Ha! He missed!" I shouted.

Jana, along with everything and everyone inside the bus, was thrown forward when the driver hit the brakes. She hit her head on the seat in front of her. Already a knot was forming.

It took a moment for her eyes to focus on the aftermath. Children lay scattered everywhere and in every conceivable position: in the aisle, on the seats, under the seats. It looked like a doll factory had exploded.

The teachers had been thrown backward on top of children. Now they were groggily trying to disentangle themselves, sorting out whose limbs were whose.

When the brakes locked, the driver had lost control of the bus. She'd swerved to the right in an attempt to miss the back of the SUV in front of them. She clipped the SUV and slammed into the side railing. For one nerve-rattling instant it appeared the bus would climb the railing and go over the side. But then it slumped back and came to a halt.

"Is anyone hurt?" Jana shouted.

Without exception every child was crying, making it impossible to tell who was hurt and who was just scared. Starting with her row, Jana began checking when a pounding on the back window startled her.

She turned to see the black suit and dark glasses of a Secret Service agent. His hand moved in a circular motion, as though he was winding yarn.

"Back it up! Back it up!" he shouted. "We'll retreat the same way we came in."

Retreat. The word sounded ominous.

Shouting over the din of crying children, Jana relayed the information to the driver, who sat stiff-armed at the wheel. Jana could see the woman's face in the mirror. She looked petrified. She was crying.

"I . . . I can't," the driver shouted back. "If I put it in gear, we'll go over the edge."

Her prediction of doom was a stick and the interior of the bus a beehive. The children became agitated.

"We're not going over the edge," Jana cried. "Ease the gearshift into reverse. We have a guardian angel behind us guiding us."

Jana thought that sounded more comforting than Secret Service agent, and it seemed to work. At least with the children.

"I . . . I don't think I can do it!" the driver wailed.

"Yes you can!"

Jana was beginning to wonder if she was going to have to go up there and drive the bus. But the driver managed to calm herself enough to put the gearshift in reverse.

The bus lurched. Children screamed.

Jana looked out the back window. The agent was looking at the tires and the length of the bus. He seemed unconcerned about any danger. Jana took her cue from him.

"You're doing great!" Jana shouted. "Keep going."

The bus moved away from the side railing. And just when Jana was convinced they were going to be fine, she saw a black speck in the sky.

"Oh no!" she cried.

———

"Oh no!" I cried.

Danny Noonan was coming back for another run.

Moments earlier I had watched as Noonan pulled up sharply, doing that slam-on-the-brakes maneuver Tom Cruise pulled in *Top Gun*. The two pursuit planes flew beneath him. What was wrong with them? Hadn't they seen the movie? Once again, the bridge was in Danny Noonan's sights.

Semyaza observed the maneuver stoically, as though presidential assassinations were daily events.

"Did I tell you Danny Noonan is eager to meet you?" he droned. "Let me see if I can recall his exact words. I believe he said he wanted to meet the 'lowlife scum who immortalized the lie' surrounding his grandfather's death."

He'd have to get in line, I thought. When the truth about Lloyd Douglas came out, there would be a lot of people eager to take a swing at me.

I focused on the attacking F/A-18's approach. The pursuit aircraft had circled back, but they were too far away to do anything. The vehicles on the bridge were sitting ducks.

"One more thing," Semyaza said, "the school bus driver? One of us."

"You mean, an angel."

"She took physical form to ensure that the bus's arrival was delayed long enough to get caught behind the traffic barrier. How else does one get a bus in a presidential motorcade except by invitation?"

"Why children?" I cried. "Why kill innocents?"

"It looks good in the history books. Murdering innocents solidified Herod's legacy, didn't it?"

Words exploded from my mouth. "You vicious, cruel, barbarous, diabolical monster!"

Semyaza smiled as though I'd complimented him. "I'm partial to Old Scratch, myself. Azazel likes Mephistopheles. But then, he was fond of Goethe. You have to remember, Grant, we're the ones who inspired those names." As an afterthought, he said, "Oh yeah . . . Jana's on the bus."

"What!"

I took a swing at him. My fist passed through him.

"Act two," Semyaza said, turning his attention to the approaching F/A-18.

Twin flashes lit the underside of the wings, spawning white serpents identical to the previous strikes. This time they hit the east end of the bridge. The explosive force lifted huge chunks of concrete into the air. Gravity reversed their course. They splashed into the bay.

As before, the rockets missed the vehicles.

"Another miss!" I shouted. "Looks like your hotshot pilot isn't so—"

A blast of machine-gun fire from Noonan's F/A-18 strafed the bay in front of me so close I could hear the bullets sizzle as they knifed into the water. The backwash of the jet knocked me onto my backside, reopening old dog bite wounds.

Semyaza stood unaffected.

"I think he recognized you," he said.

Great. Now someone recognizes me.

I started to get up. The pursuit aircraft knocked me back down.

Danny Noonan's F/A-18 shot up perpendicular to the ground. This time the pursuit pilots were ready for him, and Noonan was forced to bank sharply left. He hightailed it out to sea.

Semyaza stood over me. "So, Grant," he said, cheerfully, "enjoying yourself?"

"This is it!" the wigged teacher shouted when she saw the rockets.

Jana braced herself.

The explosion lifted the bus off the bridge, and for a moment everything and everyone was suspended in midair. It was one of those heart-in-the-throat moments when you don't know what's going to happen next, but you know it's going to be bad and may even be fatal. It felt as though the proverbial rug had been pulled out from beneath them, leaving nothing but two hundred feet of air separating them from death.

A moment later the bus found the bridge again, hard, slamming everyone against the seats and floor. The long, bulky vehicle rocked, then settled. Inside it was battlefield quiet, when the shooting stops and the moans begin.

With the help of the seat in front of her Jana pulled herself up and looked out the side window. She saw a ragged concrete edge and then nothing but distant bay. They were sitting literally inches from where the bridge ended.

"It's . . . it's . . . gone!" the driver cried. "One second it was there and now it's gone!"

The bridge wasn't the only thing that was gone. So was the Secret Service agent. When Jana looked out the back window to see if he was all right, all she saw were sunglasses lying broken on the pavement.

"We have to get out of here before the bridge collapses!" the driver shouted. She pulled the lever that opened the door and screamed.

There were three bus steps then . . . nothing.

"How are we going to get out?" she wailed. "We're trapped! The bridge is going to collapse, and we're trapped!"

By now the children were gathering enough of their senses to be scared again, and the driver's panic was whipping them into a frenzy.

"We're going to die!" the driver shouted.

Screaming erupted the length of the bus.

"We're not going to die!" Jana shouted over them.

But they weren't listening. Neither were the two teachers. One had curled up into a ball, with a small boy pulled against her chest like he was a teddy bear. The teacher with the bad wig sat on the edge of a seat whimpering.

"If you get me out of this," she prayed, "I'll tell him . . . I promise . . . I'll make it right."

"Listen to me!" Jana shouted. "We're not going to die! The bridge is not going to collapse! You've seen pictures of it, haven't you? It must have twenty supports holding it up."

"Thirty mission-shaped arches," a girl with braces said, her cheeks wet with tears. "We learned about it in class."

Jana smiled at her, grateful for the assistance. "Then you all know how strong it is! It was built to survive earthquakes. If it hasn't been knocked down by now, it's not going to be knocked down!"

"What if he comes back?" the driver cried from the front of the bus. "What if he fires more rockets?"

Jana scowled at the woman, who seemed to be deliberately trying to upset the children.

"What do you do when you're in bad trouble and need help?" Jana shouted. "Who can tell me?"

Several kids replied.

"Stop, drop, and roll!"

"Call 911!"

"Hug a tree!"

"Those are all good," Jana said, "but actually, I was thinking of dialing 911."

She reached into her purse for her cell phone. She spoke loudly to the children.

"Now you all have to be quiet so the police dispatcher can hear me. Can you do that? Can you be quiet?"

She had their attention. Not only the children, but the two teachers. The driver smirked sarcastically. "What good will it do to call 911 when—"

Jana cut her off. "Shush!"

The children came to Jana's aid, placing forefingers to their lips and shushing the driver into silence.

The call was a ruse. Of course it was a ruse. What were the police going to do? Send a gap-leaping patrol car to investigate? But it was the only way Jana could think of getting the children's minds off being frightened.

"Hello, police?" Jana said loudly when the dispatcher answered.

The children let out a cheer.

Signaling with her hand, Jana urged them to be quiet.

To the dispatcher she said, "This is Jana Torres. I'm on the Coronado Bridge with a busload of schoolchildren, and we need help."

Jana talked for several minutes with the dispatcher, knowing that dozens of young ears were hanging on every word. At first the dispatcher thought it was a crank call. Then, she became suddenly serious. "We're watching it on television. What exactly do you want us to do?"

At the same time she was talking to the dispatcher, Jana was looking out the bus windows assessing the situation. The span of the bridge was littered with vehicles. Nearly every door was open. Wherever she looked there was confusion and chaos.

Jana lowered her phone. Small faces waited eagerly for her report.

"The police said it's very important that we sit tight, be quiet, and wait for help to arrive. Do you think we can do that? I think we can."

She deliberately looked at the bus driver, who appeared angry.

"Everybody find a seat," Jana instructed them. "Don't look out the window at the water. If you're scared, hold the hand of the person sitting next to you. If you can't find a seat, raise your hand and one of the teachers will help you."

Order had been restored. The children moved methodically, some of them still sniffing and crying softly, but finding a seat nonetheless. The teachers, too, had regained a measure of composure. Jana checked on the bus driver . . . who had vanished.

One moment she was there, the next she was gone. In less than a blink of an eye, the driver had disappeared.

One of the teachers saw the expression on Jana's face. Turning to see what had caused it, she screamed, "The driver . . . the driver . . . she fell out the door!"

Panic swept through the bus, threatening the order Jana had just restored.

"Stay in your seats!" she shouted repeatedly. "The police told you to stay in your seats!"

She worked her way up the aisle, ordering, pointing, physically assisting when necessary, until all the children were back in their seats. Reaching the front of the bus, she swung around.

"There's nothing we can do to help her!" she shouted, even though she didn't believe the driver had fallen. "But we can help each other and make sure everyone else is safe. Sit quietly in your seats. Look, help is on its way."

She directed their attention to bridge-side windows. Four men in suits were running in their direction.

The wind from the open bus door whipped Jana's pants legs. Maybe it was her imagination, but she could have sworn she felt the bridge shudder.

CHAPTER
28

FOR ALL THE FIRE AND SMOKE AND DRAMA, MIRACULOUSLY, THE central portion of the bridge remained intact. The school bus with Jana was perched precariously on a concrete cliff, but all the bus's tires were on the road and the children were being assisted out the rear emergency door.

And while the president's motorcade was stranded on a newly made island, there appeared to be no real damage. From what I could see no one had been hurt and, most important, the sky was clear of threatening black specks.

"Well, what do you think?" Semyaza said.

My heart was doing a drum roll and my knees felt like jelly. But relief is a tonic, and I was feeling better by the second.

"You failed." It felt good to say it. "A lot of fireworks, a lot of ooohs and ahhhs, but in the end everyone is going home safe. The president is still alive."

A roar in the sky startled me, and for one frightening moment I thought Noonan had brought company. But it was a news helicopter charging onto the scene.

The sleek chopper was immediately intercepted by a Coast Guard helicopter with several surface craft speeding to its aid, guns at the ready. A bullhorn voice warned the chopper away. The voice was loud, no-nonsense, but youthful and unsteady.

The news chopper wisely backed off but didn't go away. There is a time to test the limits of free speech and the press, but this was not it, not when a trembling finger is on the trigger of a big gun aimed at you.

A pounding of boots and heavy, labored breathing approached us from behind, announcing the arrival of a three-man news crew. They'd parked their van on the pier and run to the end of the flight deck. Paying no attention to us, they proceeded to set up camera and sound equipment with a speed that comes from experience.

One of them, a man with a steel chin and large forearms, hefted a camera to his shoulders and aimed it at the bridge. A second man plugged patch cords into equipment and donned a pair of headphones, while the third man uncoiled the cord of a handheld microphone. Of the three, he was the only one wearing a suit and tie. I assumed he was the reporter, though I didn't remember ever seeing him on the evening news.

"Hey, guys!" the cameraman shouted. "Jana's on the bridge!"

Just then a monitor flickered and came to life. The camera zoomed in on a woman running from the bus to the motorcade.

"How did she get on the bridge?" the tie shouted with a voice that made no attempt at hiding his professional envy.

"She's good," the cameraman said, keeping his eye glued to the eyepiece. "I've worked with her before."

"This is great!" the wiry-haired technician shouted. From his expression and quick movements, it was evident he was the excitable type. "We have a reporter on the bridge! No other station has a reporter on the bridge, not even the networks! We're gonna scoop the networks, boys! We're gonna scoop the networks!"

"How?" the tie countered. "With hand signals? We have picture, but no sound."

"Cell phone!" the technician cried. "We'll call her cell phone. I can patch it in."

"Does anybody have her number?" the cameraman asked.

"They'll have it at the station. Adrian, call the station and get her number."

The tie tapped his phone without enthusiasm. "What if she doesn't have her phone with her?"

"She does," the cameraman said.

"How do you know?"

"Look at the monitor."

A close-up image of Jana showed her answering her smartphone.

"What are you doing on the bridge?" I asked her.

The three newsmen did a double take. They stared at me like I was Merlin performing a bit of magic. I don't know why I didn't think of calling her sooner.

"Grant? Where are you?" Jana said. She continued toward the motorcade. I followed her progress on the monitor. "Hold on just a second, Grant."

Jana lowered her phone. I watched as Christina and Jana met and embraced. I could hear them asking each other if they were hurt. They assured each other they were fine.

"Grant, Christina's here with me."

"I know. I can see you."

That surprised her. "Grant says he can see us," she told Christina. Now both women were looking for me.

"I'm on the deck of the *Midway*."

Jana pointed for Christina's benefit.

The wiry-haired tech appeared in front of me. "Hey, buddy, we need to use your phone," he said. Not waiting for an answer, he tried to take the phone from me. I blocked his arm.

"Jana, one of your news crews is here," I told her.

"It's me, Jana. Craig!" the tech shouted loud enough for her to hear. "We have a crew here. We can have you live in—"

I turned my back to him and walked away.

"First," I said to Jana, "are you and Christina really all right?"

She assured me they were. Shaken, but not hurt.

"What do you want me to do about this news crew?" I asked her.

Adrian, the tie, approached us with his phone pressed to his ear. To the tech, he said, "I have Burns on the line. He says if Jana is really on the bridge and doesn't go live, she's fired."

I began to relay the order. "They say if you don't go live—"

"I heard," Jana said.

"It's your call," I told her. "Right now, your first responsibility is to get off the bridge to safety. You can always tell the world later."

"No!" the tech shouted, grabbing for the phone.

To my surprise Semyaza stepped between me and the tech. He was a formidable presence. It wasn't just posturing; he radiated power and authority. I could feel it. So could the tech. He backed off.

"It's your call," I repeated to Jana. "Give the word, and I'll toss my cell phone into the bay."

"No!" the tech shouted. He had a mind to reach for the phone again but thought better of it.

"Give him your phone, Grant," Jana said. "That's why I'm here."

"You're sure?"

On the monitor I could see her look to the sky. I did the same. It was clear.

"Let's do it," she said.

I handed my phone to Craig, the tech, who let out a whoop and ran with it back to his equipment. "Two minutes," he cried, "and I can have her patched in. Jana, do you hear me? We'll go live in two minutes."

Semyaza took up position beside me. "She's too good for you," he said. "I've always thought so. That's why I stole her away from you. I knew I couldn't have her, but I didn't want you to have her."

The cameraman zoomed in on Jana. Her face filled the monitor. As she prepared to broadcast a live report from the bridge, she looked confident, professional, and alluring.

A thumping sound came from across the bay as a pair of Navy helicopters lifted off the deck of the USS *Ronald Reagan*. They set course toward what was still standing of the bay bridge.

From atop the Coronado Bridge Jana faced the USS *Midway* and, talking into her smartphone, reported the news:

"This is Jana Torres reporting live from the Coronado Bridge, where moments ago an F/A-18 Hornet fired four missiles at the president's motorcade in an apparent assassination attempt. The president is unharmed. However, the missiles severed both ends of the bridge, effectively cutting the motorcade off from land. As you can see behind me, a rescue effort is under way."

The view on the monitor focused on one of the transport helicopters as it landed on the southern lanes. The second helicopter hovered a short distance away beside the bridge, awaiting its turn.

"About a dozen vehicles are stranded," Jana reported, "including a school bus of children who were scheduled to sing for the president at a farewell rally. A last-minute addition to the motorcade, all the children on the bus are safe, thanks to the heroic effort of one Secret Service agent who fell to his death during the attack on the east end of the bridge."

It was difficult to hear her. The noise of the helicopter was almost drowning her out.

"Just a few moments ago," she shouted over it, "I spoke with an aide to the president and was informed that while the Secret Service has made every attempt to get the president to safety, the president refuses to leave the bridge until all the children are safe."

Again the camera transitioned from Jana to a line of schoolchildren being led by an attractive woman in a matching red skirt and jacket to the rescue helicopters. Christina carried a girl in one arm, while holding the hand of another girl.

The Secret Service and staff had formed a line, lifting the children over a cement divider and into the waiting helicopter. The last man in the line, the one handing the children to the helicopter crew, was President Douglas.

When the helicopter reached capacity, the president stepped back and gave the pilot a thumbs-up. As soon as the first helicopter cleared the bridge, the second helicopter landed. The rescue effort proceeded in orderly fashion.

Semyaza sighed as he watched. "Frightening the natives was so much easier in the Dark Ages. A little lightning, a little thunder—"

"I'm glad you're amusing yourself," I said, alternately checking the monitor and the bridge as the rescue effort unfolded.

Everything was proceeding smoothly. Too smoothly in my opinion.

"And why shouldn't I be amused?" Semyaza said. "This is like opening night at the theater for me. The curtain has gone up after years of preparation. The staging. Casting of characters. Watching it all come together gives me goose bumps. Well, if I had flesh, it would give me goose bumps."

I ground my teeth and said nothing. He was toying with me. Cat and mouse. I was mouse enough to know that when he tired of playing with me he was going to hurt me.

My gaze fastened on the bridge.

Me, or someone I care about.

Semyaza said, "More importantly, Grant, are you enjoying our little production? Our boy on the bridge is looking pretty good, isn't he?"

The image of R. Lloyd Douglas filled the television monitor. His coat was off. His shirtsleeves rolled up. His hair was in his eyes and he was sweating. He looked every inch a military hero, the most powerful man on earth endangering his own life to save the lives of children.

Only they were children he'd put in harm's way for the occasion. And his hero strength had been injected by his physician.

"He's still alive," I said.

"For the moment," Semyaza conceded. "But let's talk about you."

"I'm not going to do what you want me to do," I said.

"And what is it you think we want you to do?"

"You said it in your office. You want me to write a final chapter . . . a final lie . . . for Douglas's biography."

"Did I say that?" Semyaza asked.

"That's exactly what you said."

"I lied."

I glared at him.

He was unapologetic. "I said what needed to be said at the time."

"Regardless, when this is all over, I'm going to write a book exposing everything. All the lies and cover-ups. Vietnam. Douglas's addiction. And I'm going to clear my name."

"Clear your name? What are you talking about?"

"I know about Sylvia Jakes," I said.

"Who?"

He scrunched up his face as though he didn't know. Not surprising. I imagine you can get quite good at it when you're a follower of the Father of Lies, a being who has lied for millennia.

"Sylvia Jakes. The White House intern who doctored the manuscript to make it appear as though I had confessed to assassinating the president."

Semyaza burst out laughing. "That's good. That's rich! I'd forgotten all about that!"

"You have a habit of forgetting your failures. I'll help you remember this one."

Semyaza was still laughing. "Mastema has a knack for this sort of
thing. She's the practical joker of our team. You know her as Margaret. I believe she was—"

"Secretary to the chief of staff."

"Her task was to keep an eye on you while you were at the White
House."

"You expect me to believe that you had nothing to do with impli-
cating me in the assassination attempt?"

Semyaza guffawed. "Heavens, no! Who in his right mind would
believe you were capable of pulling off an event this grand? It was a
lark."

"A lark."

"If I remember correctly, it was Mastema's idea, but she wasn't
going to do it. Then someone dared her. The whole thing was a
diversion, an amusement. We made wagers as to whether you'd find
it. I bet you wouldn't. But then, you didn't find it, did you? You had
help. That meddlesome Ling girl is the one who found it. I wonder
how Mastema is going to settle the bets."

A diversion. An amusement. A prank. I felt like a chump.

"Don't take it hard, Grant. It got you here, didn't it? That's the
important thing."

"I'm still going to tell the truth once this is all over."

"Are you? And what is the truth, Grant?"

"That unscrupulous angelic beings have infiltrated world govern-
ments to manipulate leaders and alter the course of history to benefit
their own evil designs. If it takes the rest of my life, Semyaza, somehow I'm going to get the message out. I'm going to expose you. You

keep telling me you've been doing this for millennia. Well, maybe if enough people get wise to you, this millennium will be your last."

I felt like the mouse that roared, but I was tired of being toyed with.

Semyaza became serious. "Is that what you see, or are you guessing?" he replied.

"That's my conclusion based on research and personal observation."

"Look at the bridge and tell me what you see."

What was he up to? I looked. "I see vanity and deceit. I see the future of a nation in the balance."

"Yes, yes, yes. What else do you see?"

Lifting the last of the children into the helicopter, the president gave a thumbs-up signal to the pilot.

"I don't understand," I said.

Semyaza became exasperated. "You're stating the obvious," he said. "Yes, the President of the United States will die today. No, he will not be immortalized with Lincoln and JFK as is his plan. The whole thing will blow up when the designated medical examiner will be delayed at the Los Angeles airport. The local medical examiner is a gung-ho type, a straight arrow. When he discovers the drugs in the president's body, his report will launch an investigation and the whole thing will unravel."

"You speak as though you know the future."

"We've been creating the future for—"

"Yeah . . . yeah . . . I know. For millennia."

"Vice President Rossi will serve as president for six months, then we'll leak reports of his gambling addiction and his ties to the New York Mafia. He'll resign to avoid impeachment and David Lamott, Speaker of the House, will become president. He's our candidate. We've been moving him into position under the radar. Just when your nation needs strong leadership, you'll have Lamott, a man driven by his insecurities, a man who is so desperate for approval he refuses to make a decision. In the absence of real leadership, special interest groups will tear the nation apart."

He paused to let the scenario sink in.

"Now, I ask you again," he said, "when you look at the bridge, what do you see?"

The scene on the bridge hadn't changed. "I don't know what to say," I replied.

Semyaza cursed. He seemed to think I was being obstinate, but I really didn't know what he expected of me.

Then, he rippled. I don't know how else to explain it. Waves of energy passed over him, through him. It radiated outward. The deck trembled beneath my feet.

The news crew felt it too but didn't realize Semyaza was causing it. The tech turned to the tie and said, "Feel that? Tremor."

The tie laughed nervously. He said, "Now all we need is for the sun to turn blood red and the day will be complete."

The ripple expanded beyond the edge of the *Midway*, across the bay and toward the bridge, climbing the arch-shaped pillars, spreading across the span and beyond, to the horizon, until the entire canopy of sky had been engulfed. As the ripple spread, it revealed an extra layer to the universe, a layer inhabited by spirit beings.

I swallowed hard at what I saw. A universe atop a universe. And while the beings in my universe were unaware of it, the beings in the spirit world acted and moved as though the two were one.

I saw a sky that was still blue, yet overlaying it was a menacing, swirling dark cloud. It looked as though a terrible storm was brewing, only it wasn't a storm. It had a presence. There were legions of them. I could feel their ferocity and my skin prickled and the hairs on my arms and neck quivered. I heard voices. Millions of voices. And I knew who they were.

"Lucifer's army," I mumbled.

Semyaza looked on with pride.

I felt an ancient dread as they swirled over the bridge, a band of rebel angels who had warred against God before time began, fighting a conflict that had never ended, at least in their minds, now using earth as their battlefield. Their primordial grudge sent a shiver through me.

On the bridge, the second helicopter lifted off with the last load of children and Christina. A blond woman in a red suit stood out in a military aircraft. She was seated next to an open door.

On the news monitor, Jana continued her report. "With the children safely off the bridge, now the White House staff and Secret Service—Oh my! Oh my!"

Just as the helicopter cleared the bridge railing, something shot out of the dark cloud, a streak like a missile's tail fire but without the missile, and hit the engine. The engine coughed, the chopper lurched. Children screamed as a crew member spilled out the door and fell to his death.

A boy instinctively reached for the crew member when he fell, lost his balance, and would have taken the same path to his demise had Christina not grabbed him. The boy's legs dangled helplessly over the water as she clutched his arm.

"Are you getting that? Are you getting that?" the tech shouted at the cameraman.

The monitor showed that the cameraman was getting it. He'd abandoned Jana for the crippled aircraft the moment it lurched. He captured the crewman's deadly plunge for viewing audiences around the world.

I took an involuntary step toward the bridge as the top of Christina's blond head appeared on the monitor, leaning out the door fighting to keep a grip on the boy.

I was not alone in wanting to help her.

Two beams of light broke through the swirling dark army. Different from the jagged weapon that had struck the helicopter, these lights were larger and softer, and they had intelligence that emanated emotions in stark contrast to the cloud of evil.

"Meddlesome fools," Semyaza spat.

I found myself praying aloud. "Help her, help her, please, help her," I cried, urging the angels on.

Streaks of jagged light shot past them. Then one found its mark, hitting one of the angels.

I staggered backward, feeling the blow. How was that possible? In my head I heard the angel cry. My heart felt his pain. Sharp, then lingering. I moaned.

Semyaza winced.

"You felt it too!" I said. "You feel each other's pain? You feel the very blows you inflict!"

"It is our nature," he said without emotion. "We choose to ignore it."

Rubbing my chest, I watched as the injured angel retreated while his partner reached the boy and, cradling him in his arms, lifted him onboard.

"Did you see that?" the tech shouted, watching the monitor. "Did you see the way she pulled him up? That chick must work out."

"They didn't see him," I muttered.

Semyaza didn't hear me. He watched with the grim expression of a field general.

With the boy inside, the helicopter limped toward the USS *Ronald Reagan*. The angel hovered beside them.

There was a bolt of light and he was gone, blindsided by a dark force.

The cry of the rescuing angel's sudden death exploded inside of me. I felt diminished, as though a part of me had been ripped out.

Twin jagged bolts shot from the swirling cloud and hit the

helicopter engine a second time. It shuddered, belched smoke, then tipped at a crazy angle. Christina tumbled out.

"No!" I shouted.

Jana's voice could be heard on the monitor. "Christina! Oh God . . . oh God . . . oh God . . ."

Somehow Christina had managed to grab hold of a safety harness. She dangled over the water as the crippled helicopter jerked and rattled as though it was trying to shake her off. Somehow she managed to hold on, but it didn't appear to matter. The aircraft was losing altitude.

A dark band of rebel angels encircled it. Their maneuver appeared to be twofold: to discourage any further rescue attempts, and to keep the helicopter from landing. Despite the pilot's best effort, they prevented him from making any progress toward the carrier.

"They're doomed," the tie concluded.

The tech agreed.

"Call them off!" I shouted at Semyaza. "Do you hear me? Let it land!"

The tech and tie stared at me like I was crazy. I didn't care. They didn't understand. They couldn't see what I was seeing.

"Semyaza, I'm begging you. Let it land!"

With a stony expression, he said, "Every war has its casualties."

The helicopter coughed again. This time the black smoke from the engines flowed with a steady stream. It was going down.

Then, above it, a hundred streaks of light looking like righteous comets broke through the dark ceiling and engaged the devilish perimeter. A burst of light signaled every blow with explosions popping all around the crippled helicopter. I felt them. Every thrust, every wound, every death. It was as though the battle I was watching had a twin inside me.

I shielded my eyes from the intensity so bright I could barely see the helicopter. But I could see enough.

A dark spirit took shape and attached itself to Christina, pulling her down, prying her fingers from the strap.

My chest inflated with rage. My hands clenched so hard they hurt. My feet danced for a chance to launch into the fray. All I wanted was to be able to fly to Christina's rescue, sword in hand, if possible, but if not, barehanded. I wanted to get a good grip on just one of them, to rip his—

Semyaza stood beside me, smiling. "You would strike, even if you felt the blow?"

I didn't answer. We both knew I would.

The tempest surrounding the helicopter dimmed as it emerged from the turmoil as though it was flying out of a cloud, and as it did, I saw angels.

Supporting the fuselage.

Cradling Christina.

Carrying the crippled aircraft to safety.

Christina dropped into the waiting arms of sailors on the deck of the USS *Ronald Reagan*. A moment later the angels gently set the helicopter down.

The tech and tie let out a whoop of joy.

I swiped at tears.

"That was unfortunate," Semyaza said.

CHAPTER
29

"GIVE THAT PILOT A DISTINGUISHED FLYING CROSS!" THE NEWS crew tech shouted, thrusting his fist into the air.

"He made it! He made it! I can't believe he made it!" the tie shouted with him. "There's no way he could have made it, but he did!"

The tech and the tie were jumping up and down like little boys. The cameraman celebrated in his own way by keeping a tight focus on Jana.

On the monitor Jana was wiping tears of relief with one hand as she held the phone with the other. She, too, credited the pilot for his unbelievable flying skill.

Wait until I tell her what really happened.

Shouting into her phone, Jana was making her way to the first helicopter, which had landed for another load. The president's staff filed aboard. A Secret Service agent assisted Jana into the belly of the mechanical beast. Once inside, she turned to face the camera and continued reporting.

"Even now with the children safely aboard the USS *Ronald Reagan*, despite intense pressure from the Secret Service, the president insists on being the last man to leave the bridge and that means that, since we have just reached maximum occupancy, he will wait for the next transport."

As helicopter one lifted off the bridge, President R. Lloyd Douglas turned to the handful of Secret Service agents that were left behind and gave them high fives.

Next to me, Semyaza was unimpressed. He said, "Act Three. Final curtain. Cue the actors."

On cue, Danny Noonan's F/A-18 Hornet dropped out of the dark cloud of Lucifer's army. Once again, he had the bridge in his sights. His plane trailed smoke like blood from a wound. Apparently the pursuit planes had gotten in a few licks while they were away.

"I don't believe it!" the cameraman cried.

He was the first to spot Noonan in the background while shooting Jana on the helicopter. He zoomed onto the swiftly approaching F/A-18. The jittery picture on the monitor made the threat appear even more ominous.

The pursuit planes were close behind. They riddled Noonan's aircraft with machine-gun fire.

Noonan had run out of time. Rebel angels swooped down on both sides of the Hornet, shielding it from the fire of the pursuit planes. At the same time, more rebel angels buffeted the pursuit planes, throwing off their aim.

On the bridge the Secret Service agents saw the incoming fighter. They hustled the president into his limousine, determined to protect him to the end.

"God in heaven, he's coming back!" Jana reported from the helicopter.

"Use your missiles!" the tech shouted to the pursuit planes. "Use your missiles! Blow him outta the air!"

Looking as though they heard him, both pursuit planes fired

their missiles at the same instant Danny Noonan fired his at the bridge.

Noonan's rockets slammed into the bridge midspan just as one of the pursuit rockets hit his wing. Limousines and the school bus lifted off the bridge in a fiery ballet as Danny Noonan's wing exploded, spinning his aircraft into the heart of the disintegrating bridge, where an instant later a second, larger ball of fire erupted with such force it shattered windows over a mile away.

I watched in horror as the blast knocked Jana's helicopter sideways. I lost sight of it behind billowing clouds of smoke.

The pursuit planes knifed through the smoke and climbed into a cloudless sky, having succeeded in shooting down their commander, but not before he assassinated the commander in chief.

Rubble from the bridge rained like fireworks into the bay, chunks of concrete and metal debris with smoky tails. A thick cloud covered the bridge as though history had declared it a sight too horrible to be seen.

It was Dallas, November 22, 1963, all over again. The world was stunned, afraid to take a breath for fear that doing so would be an admission life would go on.

"Did you get that?" the tech said, hushed at first, but growing animated. "Did you get that? Man! We are going to be famous! This has Pulitzer Prize written all over it!"

"Do you think so?" the tie said, sharing the tech's excitement.

"Shut up, Craig," the cameraman said soberly.

Like me, his attention was in the direction Jana's helicopter had last been seen. The smoke was thinning.

I heard it before I saw it. Rotors beating the air, sounding like a heartbeat. The helicopter emerged through the haze and steadily plodded toward the deck of the USS *Ronald Reagan* with the last load of survivors.

I began to breathe again.

The tidal winds began to clear the area surrounding the bridge, and for the first time, I saw the view that tomorrow would be plastered on every newspaper in the world and printed in every history textbook. The gem of San Diego appeared twisted and broken, its center arches thrusting upward out of the water like tombstones on a foggy night.

Coast Guard boats plied the waters, venturing into the area in search of survivors—of which we knew there were none—and bodies.

"Roll the credits," Semyaza said.

I looked to the sky. It was over. The heavens of both universes were clear. Lucifer's army had dispersed.

Across the bay where the farewell rally had been scheduled, the land's edge was lined with people wanting to get a look and a picture of history. Clusters of people stood on the deck of the USS *Ronald Reagan*, among them Christina and Jana, safe, though I couldn't see them.

Jana was no longer on the monitor. I recognized the evening news anchor. Apparently he had been on Coronado to cover the farewell rally that never happened.

It was over. The roller-coaster ride I'd been on since returning to California to speak at my high school alma mater was finally over. The suddenness with which history had turned the page was unnerving. The Douglas administration was no more. Christina was out of a job. After today, Jana would most surely be recruited by the networks. According to the clock, less than an hour had passed. But the clock was wrong. It was a new day.

Turning my back on what had once been my favorite San Diego landmark, I walked away.

Semyaza fell in beside me. "Quite a production, no?" he said. "If we really were rolling credits, do you know what they'd say? Produced and directed by Azazel."

I stopped and stared at him.

"That's right. Your grandfather put this little production together. As you can see, he learned a thing or two during his dalliance in Hollywood."

I shook my head and continued walking.

"We're not finished," Semyaza said.

"Yes we are."

I started walking again. This time he didn't follow me.

"All of this?" Semyaza said to my back. "You think it was to control history. That isn't our prime objective here."

I was tired of listening to him. I kept walking.

And then I couldn't.

My feet stopped and—just like in Myles Shepherd's office—I hadn't stopped them.

It angered me that he could do that.

In no hurry, Semyaza strolled casually until he faced me.

"Today isn't about your nation's history, Grant. That was just a bonus. Today is about you. This entire production was staged for your benefit."

I didn't believe him. How could I? He was speaking in hyperbole, overstatement for effect, it had to be. F/A-18s screaming across the sky . . . a bridge blown up . . . a president assassinated . . . lives lost . . . millions of dollars in damage. To think that it all happened because of me was . . . was . . . unthinkable. Events of this magnitude do not hinge on historians and writers, but men with names like Charlemagne, Napoleon, Churchill, and Lincoln.

"This never was about Douglas," Semyaza pressed. "Do you think we care who sits in the Oval Office? No man, not even a president, has the power to change the course of history. It takes a movement, not a man, to effect significant change. Do you really think we care how history remembers R. Lloyd Douglas? Who do you think we are? The Make-A-Wish Foundation for deluded politicians?"

"Then why?"

"I told you. Today is about you."

"I don't believe you."

If eyes were ever deadly serious, his were when he said, "Then tell me why Lucifer's second-in-command would clothe himself in vile human flesh for years? If we don't concern ourselves with presidents, why would we concern ourselves with a high school student in some mediocre California town?"

I didn't have an answer for him.

"You had come of age," he said. "We couldn't take the risk that Abdiel would attempt to recruit you or sway you to the other side. So I babysat you. Prodded you. Goaded you. I did whatever it took to get you to this place."

"My book. The White House. The Pulitzer."

"All of it to prepare you for today."

At the high school, Semyaza had boasted he was responsible for my book winning the Pulitzer. I thought it was sour grapes. For all the lies, why did that part have to be the truth?

"Do I scare you that much?" I asked.

"You present a threat we can't ignore. Your father made it easy for us. He was weak, unable to accept the reality of who he was. He neutralized himself with alcohol. He didn't even tell your mother who he really was until after you were born. We didn't have to concern ourselves with him. He was an embarrassment, never a threat. And then he killed himself."

I needed to walk. To think. But when I tried, my feet remained superglued to the deck.

"Is this necessary?" I asked, pointing to my feet.

Semyaza didn't answer me, but neither did he release me.

"All right," I said. "So . . . you're saying that all of this . . ." I waved an expansive hand at the ruined bridge and bay littered with debris. "To what end? To impress me? To win me over to your side?"

"To convince you that you cannot win," he said. "Do you know why Abdiel and the others loathe you so much? You're a bastard offspring. A freak. Not fully angel, not fully human. An embarrassment."

"While you, on the other hand, have exhibited nothing but warm feelings toward me."

"You're a mistake, Grant. Eons ago we mated with human females by design. It was thought that by uniting the two races we would unite their destinies. The Father's response was to kill our human wives and offspring by genocide, literally wiping them off the face of the earth, and to condemn their spirits to an eternity of torment. As a result, Lucifer forbade any further cohabitation with human females. However, some among us had developed an attraction to female flesh. You are the result of Azazel's lust."

That made me feel warm and fuzzy all over. "Not exactly a Hallmark moment, is it?" I said.

"A number of us have argued that the wisest course of action is to kill you outright. As a demon you are easier to control."

"I think we both know your position in that argument."

"There are others who feel you may be of some use to us."

I didn't ask. My head was spinning. How often does a guy learn that he is some rogue angel's love child, that his existence is the topic of debate at Satan's table, and that angels in the heavenlies are ashamed he exists? Of course, this after learning that a president was assassinated and a city nearly destroyed to impress him.

"What do you want from me?" I cried.

"A statement of allegiance to Lucifer."

"To what end?"

"In case you haven't noticed, you are in the midst of a war. In time of war sides are chosen, allegiances are made known. A person's allegiance with one side or the other becomes a matter of life and death."

"And if I declare allegiance to Lucifer?"

"You write your own success story for the remainder of your earthly life. As long as you do nothing to oppose Lucifer, you will not be harmed. I will leave you alone."

"What happens at the end of my natural life?"

"That is out of our hands. Your fate has been fixed by the Father."

I knew the answer to the next question, but I had to ask. "And if I refuse to pledge allegiance to Lucifer?"

"We kill you. If we cannot gain your cooperation voluntarily, we will reduce you to a demon so that we can control you."

I glanced over my shoulder at the broken bridge.

"Take a good look at it, Grant. The choice is simple. You're overmatched. Haven't you learned that lesson yet? I've been beating you at every turn since the day we first met as freshmen in high school."

"How much time do I have to think about it?"

My question angered him. "If you have to think about it, there's no hope for you. I'm ready to kill you now."

"Here? With nobody to see it? No one to cheer your final victory over me? Give me until midnight tonight. You can make a spectacle of it."

Semyaza grinned. He liked that idea.

"Midnight, then," he said. "Atop the Emerald Plaza tower where you contemplated ending your life the other day. Yes, I was there. I must say you put me in a quandary. Had you decided to throw yourself over the ledge, I wouldn't have known whether to save you or not."

Then he was gone.

There's something unsettling about people disappearing suddenly like that. But I was glad he was gone. I needed time to think.

I started to leave the *Midway*, but my feet were still glued to the deck.

"Not funny, Semyaza," I said.

The news crew had packed up and were heading toward the exit. As they walked by me, the cameraman said, "Can we give you a lift?"

When my feet still wouldn't move, I folded my arms casually and smiled. "Thanks, but I think I'll just hang around here for a while."

"Suit yourself."

"Oh . . . and guys," I said, "the Pulitzer. It's not that big a deal."

The tech snorted. "A lot you know," he said.

A steady stream of onlookers began finding their way onto the deck to see in person what so many of them had watched on television. Dallas had its grassy knoll. Now the *Midway* had one more reason to attract tourists.

As they passed by me on both sides, I nodded and greeted them. I think some of them thought I was a member of the museum staff.

Whenever I was alone enough not to be overheard, I pleaded with Semyaza, "Come on, let me go. You're not going to keep me here until midnight, are you?"

CHAPTER
30

It was dark when I left the bay, having finally regained control of my feet. I wanted to escape the crush of the curious as they swamped the wharf. But I found I didn't want to be alone either.

I considered calling Christina or Jana, but then I realized the news crew hadn't returned my phone. Just as well. If the girls knew what awaited me, they would try to talk me out of going, or insist on going with me, and I couldn't allow that. I'd already jeopardized them enough for one day.

I felt the same about Sue and the professor. I would have liked to have been able to say goodbye, but at what price? It would only bring needless anxiety into their lives. I had to face the fact that I was alone in this.

After ten or fifteen minutes of walking, I found myself in the Gaslamp Quarter, the entertainment district comprised of several downtown blocks of restaurants, galleries, theaters, and boutiques set among charming, Victorian-style buildings. It was billed as San Diego's liveliest neighborhood. That's what I needed right now, a neighborhood.

I found comfort being surrounded by people, listening to the sound of voices and loud music, while at the same time remaining anonymous. Here I could be part of the human race without anybody feeling sorry for me or asking me for a decision.

As expected, there was a single topic of conversation in the Gaslamp Quarter—the assassination of President Douglas. Everyone felt a need to tell someone where they were when they heard the news.

There was also a fair amount of speculation as to the identity and motive of the pilot of the F/A-18. I heard one guy—honest, he was serious—say the pilot was Fidel Castro's brother, Raúl. He explained that Fidel was behind Kennedy's assassination and, in a fit of sibling rivalry, Raúl wanted to kill an American president himself before he died.

At a sports bar, I ordered a soft drink and watched as Vice President Alessandro Rossi was sworn in as the President of the United States. According to the newscaster, the vice president heard about the assassination while flying to New York. The Secret Service wanted him to return immediately to Washington, but since they were already on approach to the airport, Rossi insisted on taking the oath of office in New York, just as George Washington had done.

The impromptu ceremony took place at his brother's restaurant in Brooklyn. According to the press secretary, the restaurant was selected to honor the president's immigrant roots. The newscaster questioned the appropriateness of a president taking the oath of office in a Mafia neighborhood, stating that while George Washington may have taken the oath in New York, the red-and-white checkered tablecloths of an Italian eatery were a far cry from the balcony of Federal Hall.

I remained at the sports bar long enough to see a live report from the Coast Guard station at the foot of Laurel Street at Harbor Drive as the recovered body of President Douglas was loaded into a hearse.

According to the reporter on the scene, Adrian Barbour—I knew him as the tie—President Douglas had left meticulous orders regarding the handling of his remains should such a tragedy occur, including his choice of medical examiner. However, the president's medical examiner had been delayed at LAX—something about an automobile accident—and a local examiner, Ted Dickson, an ex-marine, was being called in to identify the remains and perform the autopsy.

"Everything's playing out just as Semyaza said it would," I muttered.

You can't win, Grant. You're overmatched.

It was time I started making my way to Broadway Avenue.

Leaving the sports bar, I turned north on Fourth Street. As I was walking past a restaurant with outdoor seating, I was startled by a hand shooting over the wrought-iron railing and grabbing my wrist.

"Hey, aren't you. . . ?" He started to release my arm, but before he did, he said, "Stand right there. Just for a second, okay?"

He appeared to be in his mid-twenties. There were three other people at the table, a couple sitting across from him and an attractive redhead seated next to him. They seemed as shocked and perplexed by their friend's actions as I was.

Fishing for something under his chair, he retrieved a yellow plastic bag from a Barnes and Noble bookstore. Inside the bag was a copy of my book. He turned it over to the photo on the back and compared the likeness to me.

"That's you, isn't it?" he said.

He showed the publicity photo to the other couple and his date. They looked at the photo, at me, then at the photo again.

"It is him!" the redhead squealed.

"You're . . ." He had to turn the book over and read my name from the cover. ". . . Grant Austin! You're Grant Austin, aren't you?"

The other male at the table joined in: "Bummer! Today must have been a wild one for you, what with the president getting whacked and all."

"Were you there? In the motorcade?" his blond girlfriend asked.

"I wasn't in the motorcade," I said.

"But you saw it, didn't you? You saw the assassination?" the holder of the book asked. "Man, that must have been rough, I mean, you've talked with the man, right? Sat down with him . . . interviewed him . . . did you get to know him?"

Had he asked me that question a couple of weeks ago I would have told him I knew the president. I probably would have boasted a little about being on Air Force One, or sitting in the Oval Office, or weekending at Camp David.

"No," I said. "I didn't know him that well."

"But that must have been sad for you today," the redhead opined with a pout.

A middle-aged man sitting with his wife at a neighboring table interjected, "I believe he won an award for his book. The Nobel Prize. Am I right?"

"So what are you going to do now?" the man with the book asked. "Write a final chapter or something?"

I took the book from him, autographed it with the date, and handed it back to him. "Hold on to that," I said. "It may be worth something someday."

Reaching the fountain in front of Horton Plaza with time to spare, I took a moment to look across the street at the U.S. Grant Hotel nestled in a cozy light, its polished glass doors reflecting the passing car headlights of Broadway Avenue.

If I took Semyaza up on his offer, I could return later tonight and stay in the presidential suite, or I could take door number two and spend the night on a crowded ceiling with a couple hundred of my closest slimy green relatives.

I looked away. It was better if I didn't think about it, diverting myself instead with the sights and sounds of humanity.

The street I stood on had seen its share of history. I'd seen black-and-white pictures of Broadway on VJ-Day at the end of World War II, and while the street didn't look nearly as crowded as it did then, the downtown's main artery was pretty much wall-to-wall people.

I turned westward toward the Emerald Plaza and nearly got run over by three boys on skateboards, all wearing hooded sweatshirts. Despite their attire they seemed nice enough.

Noting my direction, one of them said, "Going down to the bay?"

"Been there."

"Kickin' president, saving those schoolkids like that! When I go down? I want to go down big time, in flames like that!"

"Careful what you wish for, kid," I said.

But he wasn't listening. The three of them had already slapped their boards down and were crossing Fourth against the light.

Five blocks later I'd reached the Emerald Plaza. Pulling open the heavy glass door, I stepped into the lobby. The door swung closed behind me, shutting out the city noise. A huge atrium of chrome, glass, and greenery, it served as entryway to businesses located in the towers.

Being nearly midnight, it was empty and as silent as a mortuary, except for a pair of bodiless voices coming from one of the adjoining corridors. One male. One female. Apparently he said or did something funny because she laughed.

Crossing the polished white-tile floor, I summoned an elevator. The doors made a ritzy whoosh sound when they opened. I stepped inside. The doors whooshed closed behind me.

For several moments I stood there like a man in an oversized coffin. I stared at the double row of buttons.

Semyaza appeared next to me.

I started at his sudden appearance.

"Going down?" he said with a smirk.

Without comment I pushed the button that would take me to the top floor.

Sue Ling lunged for the door.

"Grant?"

Jana and Christina walked in. Sue Ling threw herself into their arms, laughing and weeping at the same time.

"He wasn't at the hotel," Christina said. She was shoeless and worried. "Did you have any luck with his smartphone?"

"A guy named Craig answered," Sue replied.

"A tech at the station," Jana said. She nodded as she pieced events together. "We used Grant's phone to do the broadcast."

"He said he'd return Grant's phone to you at the station," Sue said. "Are you going out with him?"

"Who? Craig?"

"He sort of implied that you and he have something going on," Sue said.

"In his dreams," Jana replied.

From the middle of the living room, the professor watched with interest. The television set was on. It had been all afternoon.

Jana said, "We're going to drive around downtown and look for him. Come with us."

Sue glanced hesitantly back at the professor. "I probably should stay and—"

"She'd be delighted to go," the professor answered for her.

Sue questioned him with a tilt of her head.

"I'll be fine," the professor insisted. "Go with them. You need to get out."

Jana said, "Professor, you're welcome to come too. I have plenty of room. We can put your chair in the trunk."

"Very kind," the professor said dismissively. "But I have plenty to do around here."

"Maybe I should stay," Sue said.

Christina linked arms with her. "You know you want to go," she said. "You're as worried about him as we are."

When they were gone the professor wheeled over to the television set and switched it off.

He sat for a moment in the silence, then lifted his head heavenward.

"Abdiel!" he shouted.

He waited a moment, then shouted again.

"Abdiel!"

He remained alone. Wheeling himself to the hallway, he shouted, "Abdiel!"

When the angel didn't appear, he wheeled himself into the kitchen.

"Abdiel!"

He opened the front door and shouted at the stars.

"Abdiel!"

A voice behind him said, "I'm not your genie in a bottle, and I don't appreciate being treated as such."

Abdiel stood in the middle of the living room.

The professor slammed shut the front door.

"Where's Grant?" he said.

"What makes you think I would know?"

"Do you?"

Abdiel didn't answer.

"Is Grant in danger?"

Again, Abdiel didn't answer.

"Does Semyaza have him?"

Abdiel appeared beatific, as composed as a statue, and just as silent.

"Answer me!" the professor shouted.

"The time has come for Grant to make a decision about whose side he's on," Abdiel said.

"What do you mean, whose side? A few weeks ago he didn't even know there were sides. You have to give him time."

"After Grant has made his decision, I'll return to inform you."

"It's tonight? Why the rush?"

"Did I say it was tonight?"

The professor hit the arms of his wheelchair with his fists. "Do you know, for an angel you can be infuriating? Is it tonight or not?"

"I must leave now."

"Wait! What's riding on his decision?"

"I must leave now."

"Abdiel . . . I implore you . . . go to the Father. Intercede for Grant. See if you can—"

The professor was talking to air.

Fists hammered the arms of the chair.

"Abdiel!" he shouted. "Abdiel!"

He shouted until he was hoarse.

"It's not fair!" he bellowed at the ceiling. "It's not fair! Grant isn't like us! Without the Holy Spirit, he's on his own. What chance does he have?"

His words bounced back at him off the ceiling.

The professor wheeled in circles, his voice barely a whisper, pleading Grant's case. No longer addressing Abdiel, he made his case directly to God.

"Almighty Father, please, the boy deserves a chance. He's caught between two worlds. He's no match for Semyaza, and for reasons I don't fully understand, Abdiel and the others will not stand up for him. The boy needs an advocate, but you've denied him your Holy Spirit. Please don't throw him to the wolves. You've given him life. You've given him free will. Now give him a chance to choose. That's all I ask. Give him a chance."

CHAPTER
31

THE ELEVATOR DOORS WHOOSHED OPEN ON THE TOP FLOOR of the Emerald Plaza. After his initial quip, Semyaza remained silent for the duration of the ascent.

"I don't need an escort," I snapped as I stepped from the elevator.

A couple in evening dress stood waiting for the elevator. A curious expression crossed their faces. I looked behind me. The elevator was empty.

I offered no explanation. The couple stepped into the elevator without turning their backs on me and punched the Down button repeatedly to close the doors.

The stairs to the roof were at the end of the hallway. I walked the length of the fluorescent passage to the stairwell and up the painted cement steps and onto the gravel-surfaced roof.

An ocean breeze greeted me. From this elevation I could see the runway lights of the airport, the strip of residential and commercial lights that was Point Loma, and the velvet-black Pacific Ocean beyond.

In the foreground was the bay, lit garishly by banks of high-powered sodium floodlights aboard ships and the meandering spotlights of helicopters. Normally the bay at night is softly lit and romantic. This stark white glare, while necessary for men to do their jobs, seemed a rude intrusion.

A myriad of craft bobbed on the bay combing through the debris that littered the surface. Between misshaped and jagged bridge pilings, a huge crane on a barge was lifting the fuselage of Noonan's F/A-18 from its watery grave.

A huge air-conditioning unit separated me from the open expanse of roof. I wasn't prepared for what I saw when I stepped around it.

Twenty-four angels were waiting for me.

Semyaza was the closest.

"You took me seriously when I suggested you make a spectacle of this," I said.

"A word of caution," he replied. "Keep a civil tongue. When you are intimidated or frightened, you have a habit of resorting to sarcasm."

"You noticed."

"It will not serve you well tonight. Not all angels understand your humor. They interpret it as insolence."

I started to say something sarcastic, if for no other reason than to get it out of my system. But I didn't. Better to go cold turkey.

Despite everything I'd seen today, until this moment, I was never fully convinced my former rival Semyaza, aka Myles Shepherd, was really an angel, a being with origins so ancient he predated time. But seeing him here, standing in an assembly of angels, my doubts were banished.

They were all of impressive height, having assembled in a circle. Two half-circles, actually. Twelve and twelve. I recognized Abdiel. He stood with eleven others who were counted among the faithful. Opposite them were Semyaza and eleven rebel angels.

The historian within me was going crazy. The stories they could tell! Here on this roof were beings that had witnessed, and in some cases participated in, every moment of history. Not only that, the beings that stood before me were present when the foundations of the universe were laid.

I lingered on each of the angels who stood with Abdiel, wondering if I might recognize any of them by their appearance. Was Michael here, who led the battle against Lucifer and who later disputed with him over the body of Moses? Was Gabriel here, the angel who announced the birth of John to his father, Zechariah, and the birth of Jesus to Mary? I found myself looking at their lips to see if any of them looked like a trumpet player.

And the rebel side. The obvious question was, why? What was their strategy? Having stood in the throne room of God Almighty, did they really think they could win? Did they have regrets? If they had to do it all over again, would they?

From the expressions on their faces, the sense of wonder was mine alone. They glared at me with disdain. All of them. Even Abdiel.

Semyaza indicated I should stand in the middle of the circle. Gravel crunched beneath my shoes as I walked. That's when I noticed I was the only one on the roof whose feet were touching the ground.

"The mush-pot," I said, having reached the center.

"What?"

It just slipped out. Until Semyaza challenged me, I wasn't even aware I'd said it out loud.

"Um . . . mush-pot," I explained. "That's what we called the center of the circle in kindergarten. The mush-pot."

Cold, stony silence encircled me.

"Which, I guess, makes me the cheese, doesn't it? You know . . . the farmer in the dell?"

They didn't know. Or if they did, they weren't admitting it.

To help them remember I spoke the lyrics for them. "The farmer in the dell, the farmer in the dell, hi-ho, the derry-o, the farmer in the dell."

I was nervous and I was babbling and it was making them angry.

"I'm ready to announce my decision," I said.

"SILENCE, you insolent worm!"

The voice was like thunder, shaking the tower beneath my feet. It echoed to the horizon.

The command came from the angel standing next to Semyaza. His face was granite, his eyes flashed fire. "Do you have no concept of what is holy?" he said, sneering.

The circle, both sides, agreed with him. There was not a friendly face among them.

"I meant no disre—"

Semyaza cut me off. "The accused will speak only when instructed." To the others, he said, "The tribunal will now convene."

Preliminaries. Semyaza might have told me there would be pre-liminaries. I was intrigued. But then I welcomed anything that delayed the moment of decision.

Curious. How do angels start a meeting? By taking attendance? Reading the minutes? Drinking coffee and eating doughnuts—no, not doughnuts. Angel food cake.

I pursed my lips to keep the irreverent thoughts inside my head.

Solemnity surrounded me. Without exception, the angels closed their eyes and tilted their heads toward heaven. Maybe it was my imagination, but they seemed to stretch, to grow taller and even more imposing.

A low rumble agitated the gravel. The vibrations traveled up my legs and into my chest and jaw.

Because they were facing me I couldn't see exactly what was hap-pening behind them, but from somewhere around their shoulders heavy smoke poured forth, cascading down their backs like robes, hitting the ground and curling, the lengthening trains spreading until they filled the rooftop.

Reaching the ledge, instead of pouring onto the street below, the smoke stretched upward to an impressive height, then inward, peaking directly over my head like cathedral arches with the stars beyond providing a heavenly canopy.

My neck began to ache from staring upward at the incredible, smoky, transparent structure.

The rumbling kicked into a higher gear, bringing my attention back to the circle.

Beginning with Abdiel (I don't know why it began with him, maybe they flipped a coin), with his eyes still closed, his face a meditative calm, an explosion of emerald light illuminated him from within. This was duplicated by the angel to his right and proceeded this way around the circle of twenty-four. When it reached Abdiel, it repeated, each time with greater speed, like cylinders firing in a rotary engine, faster and faster until the separate firings blended into an unbroken ring of brilliant emerald green.

Everything, including me, within the interior of the smoky cathedral was bathed in a soft green light. Very nice. Very soothing.

Until I looked up.

Populating the dome, also bathed in green and staring hungrily down at me, were a thousand hideous demon faces. A shiver chilled me when I realized that to them this was an induction ceremony and I was the inductee.

The emerald light ring appeared to be some sort of communion among the angels, the sharing of a common source of energy. They seemed to feed off it and were strengthened by it.

I, too, felt it. A penetrating thrum vibrating every inch of me. Even with the demons present, I felt warm and comforted and assured and accepted. And I wondered if maybe, despite all my misgivings, somehow I was going to survive the night.

Then the emerald ring of light began to pulse with greater and greater frequency. As it did the angels grew in stature . . . eight feet . . . ten . . . twelve feet tall, looking like human pillars.

The ring grew ever brighter until it was dazzling white. The pulsing increased in pitch. It began vibrating in my head, hurting me, resonating with greater and greater intensity. I placed my hands against my skull to keep it from exploding, but the force kept building. I screamed, but it didn't help. The pressure was becoming too much for me to bear.

I felt my knees buckling and would have dropped to the ground, but a blast of light beat me to it. It hit me with force, knocking me to my knees. As with the emerald light, it began with Abdiel—a powerful, concentrated shaft of light—then continued around the circle, twenty-four angels, twenty-four shafts of the purest white light I'd ever seen. The beams focused on the center of the circle, where they met a short distance above my head and formed a single pillar of light that shot skyward as far as the eye could see and beyond.

I could take it no more. On the gravel, my eyes clamped shut, clutching my head, curled into a ball, I screamed for it to stop. The pain was so intense, I would have given anything to make it stop. I would have welcomed death.

I couldn't hear my own screams. Then, that was all I heard. The thrum was gone. The pain was gone. I risked opening my eyes. The shafts of light were gone too.

Twenty-four angels now clothed in dazzling white looked down at me lying in a fetal position in the mush-pot.

I struggled to my feet, brushing gravel from my pants, and noticed that my clothing, too, had been bleached white.

The angel with granite features spoke. "Until tonight no human has ever witnessed a convocation of angels."

He wanted me to be impressed, humbled. Maybe it was the headache and the ringing in my ears, maybe it was the ceiling full of demons licking their chops, and the renewed realization that at the pleasure of this august body I would soon be joining them, but whatever the reason, I couldn't help myself.

I said, "I'm all aglow."

Granite angel's response was swift. An invisible fist reached past my lapel and into my upper chest, fastening onto my windpipe, cutting off my breath, forcing me to my knees.

"ENOUGH!"

A second invisible hand broke granite angel's grip. It was Abdiel. I could breathe again. But another threat quickly surfaced as a scuffle broke out with me in the middle.

"I SAID ENOUGH!"

The tower trembled with the force of the voice.

Both sides backed off.

"I will not tolerate this human's insolence," granite angel boomed. "It disrespects the lives of the warriors we lost today."

"Both sides lost friends today," Abdiel replied.

"And why? Because of him!" Granite angel's finger singled me out in case anyone had any doubt. "He isn't worth it."

"I agree. He isn't worth it," Abdiel said, a little too quickly for my taste. "But if we fight we will only lose more friends and deepen our sorrow."

"Let's be done with it, then," granite angel said.

Semyaza took that as his cue. He stepped forward.

"Grant Austin, do you understand the purpose of this tribunal?"

I was rubbing my throat, though it did little to massage the pain, which was much deeper. My voice was raspy when I spoke. I cleared my throat and tried again.

"I am here to declare my allegiance," I said. "But before I do, I have a request."

The circle crackled with dissension.

Before anyone could deny the request outright, I stated it. "I would like to ask if my grandfather, Azazel, is present. If he is, I'd like to meet him."

"He is."

The voice came from near the middle of the rogue angel side. To my relief, it wasn't granite angel.

Azazel resumed normal size and stepped forward. I turned to meet him, not knowing what I would do or say. I hadn't planned this. The thought had just occurred to me and I acted on it.

The being standing before me was attractive by any standards, with sparkling eyes, a strong jaw, and confident presence. He reminded me of Douglas Fairbanks, or any number of dashing leading men of the black-and-white film era.

I wondered what he thought when he looked at me, his grandson. Was he proud? Ashamed? Indifferent? I couldn't tell from looking at him.

How did I feel when I looked at him? It was hard to say. If it wasn't for him I wouldn't be alive. But then, if it wasn't for him, I wouldn't be condemned to live for eternity as a tormented demon.

Looking him in the eye, I said, "A few moments ago, I was blamed for what happened today, for the loss of life, both angel and human. But it's not my fault, is it? It's yours. Everything that happened today happened because you couldn't control your lust."

Within seconds of Lieutenant Noonan's rockets hitting the bridge, a tsunami of phone calls had hit the San Diego Police Department. Now, after midnight, things were finally beginning to calm down. Marie Klesko, an attractive, single woman in her twenties, slumped in her chair, having survived a month's worth of activity in one shift, coordinating police units with fire and federal agencies as the city stepped to the brink of panic and threatened to jump.

With the activity on her computer screens looking almost normal again, she anticipated the end of her shift and driving home to her apartment, where she would make herself a bowl of nachos, play with her dog Beelzebub, and watch old episodes of *Friends*.

With only ten minutes remaining on her shift, the weird calls started coming in. She dismissed the first calls as pranks. But the calls kept coming. Unhooking her headset, she walked to the window. The fourth floor provided her with a panoramic view of the city.

"What's up?" Her supervisor came up behind her.

"I'm getting crazy calls about the Emerald Plaza."

"What kind of crazy?"

"That there's some sort of green thunderstorm on the top of one of the towers."

"Thunderstorm? It's a clear night."

"Yeah, so how do you explain that?"

In the distance they could see the Emerald Plaza. The top of the tallest tower was capped with smoke that pulsed with a green light.

"Should I send someone to investigate?" Marie asked.

"That's really weird," the supervisor said. "I've never seen anything like it."

"I hate sending someone after everything that's happened today. Besides, what do I tell them? Investigate a possible atmospheric disturbance atop the Emerald Plaza?"

The supervisor cracked her gum. "Send Sharki," she said. "He's into weird."

Once again I found myself kissing gravel for my insolence. Once again a scuffle of heavyweights threatened to steamroll over me.

There had been a time in my life when I thought that if I ever found angels to the left of me and angels to the right of me I'd be in heaven. But that was before I learned heaven's gate was locked to me and nobody had a key.

Once order was restored, I was back on my feet in the center of the circle. I felt like a man alone on a bridge surrounded by twenty-four F/A-18 Hornets.

"You have a statement to make," Semyaza snapped.

I took a ragged breath. The fight had gone out of me. Semyaza was right. I was overmatched. I couldn't win. A heavy weariness came over me. I wore it like a shroud.

But before I could speak, company came.

I don't know why I was surprised. If I was going to pledge allegiance to him, it was only right that Lucifer would be there to receive it.

Of greater surprise than his coming was his appearance. He didn't come as a roaring lion. A soft glow preceded him, and when he materialized his beauty was stunning.

Naturally every angel in the circle recognized him and afforded him the respect due a powerful leader. I've been in rooms when charismatic world leaders were announced. Heads turn. A hush falls over the room in anticipation.

So it was now. To say his coming took my breath away doesn't begin to describe what I felt. I found myself in the presence of beauty incarnate.

My lips wanted to sing his praises. My feet wanted to dance and my hands wave in adoration. My knees . . . my knees almost betrayed me. Never have I been so overwhelmed by such wondrous glory. I wanted to bow down to him. I started to bow down to him.

And then Abdiel said, "Lucifer."

I caught myself.

I couldn't believe what I had almost done. Lucifer was so alluring, I didn't realize what I was doing until it was almost too late. So attracted was I to his radiance, I nearly offered him an eternity of torment for a moment of it.

Does true beauty demand a price? What kind of beauty enslaves the worshipper, hurts you and leaves you poorer for the experience, and exchanges a moment of pleasure for a lifetime of regret?

A hideous beauty.

That's how the professor described it, didn't he?

Lucifer did not join the circle. He remained at an elevated distance.

Semyaza said, "The time has come, Grant Austin."

All eyes turned to me. I fought to keep from looking at Lucifer, afraid that if I did I'd sell myself out. Even then I wasn't sure how much longer I could resist. His allure went beyond visual. I could feel its tug on me.

"You've convinced me," I said to the circle. "Your argument is overwhelming. How can I compete against powers and authorities that can do the things you do? While others are protected by the Holy Spirit, because of who I am, that protection has been denied me. I stand alone."

"All you need do is bend your knee and pledge your allegiance to Lucifer, and this tribunal is adjourned," Semyaza said. "Afterward we'll go someplace and begin planning the life you've always dreamed."

"The presidential suite at the U.S. Grant Hotel?"

"If that is your wish."

I couldn't help but grin. The life I've always dreamed. And they could do it too. After what I'd seen this afternoon, I was convinced of it.

"By the way," I said, "that was quite a demonstration you put on for me today—"

"Just kneel and pledge," granite angel barked.

"Yeah, well about that . . . no. It isn't going to happen. The thing about making choices is to know your options, not only what you're choosing, but what you're giving up. And so, at the recommendation of a friend, I did a little reading in the Gospels about your competition. And I have to say, while your demonstration was powerful and flashy, when I compared it to the three-year demonstration of the Son . . . well, let me put it this way: I would rather be on the side that builds than destroys, that edifies rather than deceives, that heals rather than hurts. I want to spend whatever days are granted me making people happy rather than trying to figure out ways they can make me happy."

"Fool!" Semyaza shouted. "Without Lucifer, you have no life, only torment."

Lucifer stepped forward, instantly commanding attention. He addressed me directly. "You would choose to serve the Father who has denied salvation to you and your kind, thus condemning you to eternal torment?"

Speaking to the gravel, for I dared not look up, I replied, "It's true. The Son cannot be my Savior. But where does it say that prevents me from serving Him? That is my choice whether in this world, or in a world of torment. If I am destined to be a missionary to the demons, so be it."

"Look at me!" Lucifer thundered.

I took a deep breath. He was right. If I was going to choose against him, I should be man enough to look him in the eye when I did it.

Slowly, I raised my head, focusing hard on what I had to say, not on him.

When our eyes met, I nearly lost it. In them I saw every dream, every hope, every promise of happiness reflected. And I wanted to believe him.

A youthful fantasy flashed—how I imagined it would be to find that one perfect girl, the one I would marry. How the look in her eyes would conquer me. How I'd melt like butter at her smile, her touch. Take that fantasy and multiply it by infinity and you have an understanding of the longing I felt at that moment gazing into Lucifer's eyes. Yet, somehow I managed to say, "In ages past, you made your choice. Respect my right to make mine. If there is any doubt as to where I stand, hear this: I will serve the Son. Though you slay me, I will serve Him; though He condemns me to torment, I will serve Him."

Lucifer made no reply. He didn't fly into a rage. Why would he? What was I to him? He vanished, leaving me in the hands of the tribunal.

Semyaza was beside himself.

Overhead the assembled demons became agitated, eager for what was to happen next.

"You ungrateful wretch," Semyaza spat. "Arrogance has always been your blind side. How many times have I used your pigheadedness to lure you to do my bidding? And now it will be your undoing. You underestimate the agony that awaits you, Grant Austin. Reconsider, before it's too late."

I turned to him and said, "You know, Myles, for some reason, right now, you look smaller. You heard my choice. Do what you will."

Semyaza grinned that insufferable grin of his. "With pleasure," he said.

When I was a child I would watch old westerns on Saturday afternoons. One of the stock scenes in those old black-and-white dramas was when the cowboy in the black hat, the bad guy, finally got his due and was riddled with bullets. Replace bullets with demons and you have a picture of what happened to me next.

They hit me from every direction, clawing their way into my chest and back and face and throat and arms and legs. Penetrating my heart. Filling my mind. They squeezed my optic nerves, and I went blind, clamped my vocal chords and I was mute. I filled up quickly, still they came, elbowing and bickering for space. A myriad of anguished voices screamed in my head.

Vaguely I felt myself dropping to my knees, then my hands. The pain was incredible, but I had no voice to express it. I wanted to pass out, but they wouldn't let me. With every second I was losing control. They flopped me onto my back, racking my body with convulsions.

Though I couldn't see them, I fought to stretch a pleading hand in the direction of the faithful angels, praying that one of them might touch it and out of pity give me a measure of relief. My hand clutched air.

The next thing I knew, my arm was flopping against the gravel. I'd lost control of it. But there was a greater concern. I was being trampled to death from the inside.

How to fight them? If I struck at them, I bruised myself. If I clawed at them, I tore my own flesh. How do you fight an enemy you can't see, can't touch? How do you do battle with spirit beings?

For our struggle is not against flesh and blood . . .

I was writhing on the gravel.

. . . but against spiritual forces of evil in the heavenly realms.

You fight a spiritual battle with spiritual weapons, Grant.

My father was in me, possessing me. I could feel him.

. . . so that when the day of evil comes . . .

My chest was so full of demons I could barely breathe.

. . . you may be able to stand . . .

The voices! I couldn't think for all the voices! Covering my ears couldn't shut them out. Fight them. Think. Don't let them take your mind.

. . . and after you have done everything . . .

There were too many of them. And they were too strong. I couldn't . . . but I had to . . . I couldn't let them take my mind. Think!

After you have done everything . . . what? What comes next?

They were too strong.

After you have done everything . . . to stand.

Yes!

To stand . . . to stand!

They tried to rip the thought away. I wouldn't let them. I clutched it. Protected it. Pushed them away.

Stand firm, then. . . .

I fought them for control of my arms and legs. Ignoring other areas, I concentrated on my arms and legs. But there were too many of them.

It was no use. I couldn't do it. I tried. God knows I tried. But they were too strong. It was humanly impossible.

Stand firm then.

Humanly impossible. Humanly . . . but I was only part human. The other part of me was angel.

On the *Midway*, hadn't I seen the angelic realm? I didn't know I could do that, but I did it. I saw with angel eyes.

I clung to the thought. I was part angel. What else could I do?

Standing over me, as though at a great distance, I could hear the circle of angels chatting as though they were at a cocktail party. Renewing old acquaintances. Exchanging stories about business, swapping stock tips. One of them laughed. They were oblivious to my torment.

It infuriated me.

Somewhere inside of me was angel, and I was going to find it. I reached deep, summoning strength I never knew I had. Summoning angel strength. . . .

To stand. Stand firm, then.

I clenched a fist. Then another. It was a heady experience. With excruciating effort, I managed to do what most six-month-old babies can do, I rolled over onto my stomach. Then, winning the tug-of-war for my arms, I placed my palms against the gravel.

And after you have done everything, to stand.

The demons rallied. But they fought each other as much as they fought me, and my determination was greater. I pushed myself up onto my knees.

So that when the day of evil comes.

One foot hit the gravel.

To stand.

The battle for control of the second foot took longer. A surge of strength came to me when I realized I was still kneeling. Progress, but not good enough. I couldn't stay like this. Wouldn't stay like this. I hadn't fought this hard to kneel. I was going to stand.

My second foot hit the gravel.

Screaming with exertion, I managed to straighten up. Screaming. I heard it. I had my voice. I wanted sight as well. If they were going to kill me, they'd have to do it while I was standing and looking them in the eyes.

My chest heaving, sweat streaming down my temples and cheeks, holding off counterattacks of demons who wanted my arms and legs, I fought the battle for my optic nerves.

I saw angels. Blurred. Standing as trees. Then clearer.

The chatter stopped. They were looking at me. I looked at them.

Abdiel.

Semyaza.

Azazel.

Granite angel.

All of them.

I knew at any moment any one of them could strike me dead and end the feast of demons. But for this moment, I had their attention. I stood in the center of their circle.

With voices screaming in my head, with demons tearing at my

insides, fighting for every breath, every heartbeat, somehow I managed to speak.

Fighting to form each word, I said, "Hi-ho, the derry-o, the cheese stands alone."

There was stunned silence.

Fuming, the granite angel said, "Enough of this foolishness. Finish him."

The next instant came as a total surprise to me. I expected darkness. A sudden blow and then . . . nothing. Instead, light burst all around us like the dawning of a thousand suns. A ring of angels encircled us, a hundred count at least. Circle upon circle filled the sky, until there were thousands of them, ten thousand upon ten thousand, and with one voice they were singing:

> *Great is the Lord and worthy of praise*
> *His kingdom endures forever.*
> *Let the seas resound and the rivers rejoice,*
> *On the day of the Father's visitation.*

I felt a presence of such magnitude and weight, I could stand no longer. I sank to my knees. All around me the angels—on both sides of the tribunal—knelt and bowed their heads. Not out of duty, nor of fear, but out of the sheer energy of His nearness. Every inch of my being, every molecule came alive, charged with new life as it had never been before. The radiance I had felt in the presence of Semyaza, the glory of Abdiel, were muddy waters by comparison.

Time could not encompass Him. It bowed to its Creator. In reverence, at that moment, the universe ceased to tick.

The demons inside of me hushed and trembled at His presence.

And at that moment I felt the Spirit of the Father which permeated everything—the sky, the gravel beneath my knees, the air I was breathing—enter me in a tender, intimate way.

Leave him.

At the Father's command the demons skittered like cockroaches in a sudden light. I was free of them. I breathed freely. My mind was uncluttered. My muscles relaxed, weary from the fight.

But I felt more than just the absence of possession. I felt a communing, and with it a peace, a strength, an assurance I had never known.

Thank you, I prayed.

The Father addressed the tribunal, His voice in our minds and all around us.

The boy deserves a chance to live. See, I have set my mark upon him. For as long as he bears the mark, no one will harm him.

I blinked and it was over.

Night's natural canopy of stars arched from horizon to horizon. The tribunal was gone. Traffic sounds filtered up from the street below. The building's air-conditioning unit roared to life.

I was alone and . . . saddened. It's amazing how empty a person can feel after a nation of demons is suddenly evicted from him. But what saddened me most was that, for one sliver of a second, I knew what it was like to have the Spirit of God within me. And I wondered if I would ever know that peace again.

Shuffling my feet in the gravel, I did a three-sixty. I was standing on the roof of the Emerald Plaza tower in downtown San Diego. Not so much as a scrap of supernatural had been left behind.

I made my way toward the stairwell.

"It's not over."

I turned. It was Semyaza.

"At best, a temporary reprieve," he said.

"I'll take it."

The understatement of the year, considering without the reprieve right now I'd be clinging to someone's ceiling.

Semyaza didn't stick around. The thought crossed my mind that given the turn of events, he might have some explaining to do. I hoped so anyway.

A hand fell on my shoulder. I jumped.

"Abdiel! Don't do that!"

"You have been given a special gift," he said.

"I know."

"Don't mess it up."

"Thanks for the vote of confidence," I said. "Oh yeah, and a little while ago when I was fighting for my life? Thanks for helping. Maybe I can return the favor someday."

"But I didn't help." He thought a moment. "Oh. Sarcasm. I get it."

He stood there, and we stared at each other.

"Anything else?" I asked.

"You wielded your weapons well tonight, like a warrior," he said.

"My weapons—"

"Courage. Strength of will. Steadfastness. Spiritual weapons. You fought a good fight."

"Thank you."

"It's possible that some day I may even come to like you."

"Let's take it a day at a time, shall we?"

I started to leave.

"One other thing," he said. "Some of the angels in the circle tonight . . . on the other side. I haven't had communion with them since before time began. They were friends then. Tonight meant something to me. Thank you."

"Was Semyaza one of them?"

Abdiel nodded. "And Azazel. And it's been eons since I've seen Lucifer. He's looking good, don't you think?"

"Good night, Abdiel," I said.

Again I started to leave, then turned back. "Abdiel."

"Yes?"

"The mark on me. Is it visible?"

He nodded. "Your forehead."

My hand flew to my forehead, half expecting to feel some kind of scar. I could feel nothing. "What does it look like?"

He studied my forehead a moment. "Three digits. 666."

My mouth fell open.

Seeing my expression, Abdiel let loose a huge guffaw. "You're not the only one with a sense of humor, Grant Austin," he said. "Wait until I tell the professor!"

CHAPTER
32

I STARTED SHIVERING IN THE ELEVATOR, A DELAYED REACTION TO the night's events. Nobody was going to believe me when I told them what had happened up there.

The doors dinged and whooshed open to the Emerald Plaza lobby. I found myself staring at a police officer. From the cock of his head he'd monitored the elevator's descent from floor to floor on the lighted panel.

Blocking my exit, he looked me over. He noticed the shivering. I smiled and rubbed my arms as though I was cold. When he finished sizing me up, he stepped back and motioned me out of the elevator.

"Have you been anywhere near the roof tonight?" he asked, hooking his thumbs in his utility belt.

"I just came from there," I said.

He glanced at my pants. I looked too. The knees were soiled and still had bits of gravel embedded in them.

"What were you doing up there?"

"Contemplating my future."

"Anyone with you?"

I chuckled. "That close to heaven? Just me and the angels."

He asked to see identification and wrote down my name and contact information.

"Washington, DC," he noted. "Are you here because of the president?"

I told him I was.

"Staff? You weren't on the bridge, were you?"

"Freelance writer. I knew people on the bridge."

"Still can't believe what happened," he said, shaking his head. "Plenty to write about though."

"You don't know the half of it."

He let me go. As I crossed the lobby to the front doors I heard him reporting in. "This is Sharki," he said. "I'm going onto the roof to check it out."

I pushed through the lobby doors and emerged on Broadway. A distant din of rescue and salvage equipment could be heard coming from the bay. The streets were deserted except for the occasional car or homeless person pushing a grocery cart.

Shoving my hands in my pockets, I started toward Horton Plaza. My legs were tired, but I felt the need to walk. I figured I could make it as far as the shopping center where I could call a cab.

I didn't think or ponder as I walked. My brain was mush. There would be time to take stock of everything that had happened after I'd slept for two or three days. I might not make it that long, but I was going to give it the good ol' college try.

As I stepped from the curb the squeal of brakes and the blast of a horn startled me. In my mindless state I thought I'd ignored the signals and crossed against the light. But I hadn't. The light was green.

Car doors flew open. Women shouted my name. And the next thing I knew I was being squeezed to death by three exuberant, beautiful ladies. It was paradise.

A passing convertible carrying four sailors honked. The sailors whistled and howled and hooted.

When I am old and gray and think back on this day—the day I witnessed a president assassinated, the day I met Lucifer face-to-face, the day God rescued me from a host of demons—it is this moment, this hug, I'll remember first. I'm not sure I'll ever understand all that happened on the rooftop. Hugs I understand.

Having found an all-night fast-food restaurant, we sat in a circle in the professor's living room with empty wrappers and cartons strewn about like so many discarded bones. We'd pushed the couch against a bookcase and rearranged some chairs to accommodate us.

Christina and Jana shared the couch. Sue Ling sat in a kitchen chair next to the professor. I slumped, my belly full, in an overstuffed blue chair.

I hadn't realized how hungry I was until I got a first whiff of French fries in the drive-through. While scarfing down a couple of burgers and supersized fries, I described the battle of Coronado Bridge, the battle neither camera nor human eye could see.

Jana described the incident on the bus. Christina thrilled us with her description of what it was like to dangle out a helicopter door over the bay. Everyone on the helicopter was convinced they were going to die. Tears filled her eyes when I described how angels came to her rescue and sacrificed themselves to save her.

Not a sound was made, not even a breath, as I related the scene on the rooftop of the Emerald Plaza. A couple of times I had to pause as my emotions threatened to get out of control. I blamed it on being tired.

"I can't believe you met Lucifer," the professor said, his voice hoarse from shouting. "We need to talk more about this later."

"I can't believe I dated Satan's lieutenant," Jana said of Myles Shepherd. "Are all the good-looking men devils?"

"I can't believe I dated someone who's half man, half angel,"

Christina said, staring at me in wonder. "When am I going to see the angel side?"

"I've been a perfect angel around you!" I protested.

She scoffed. To Jana and Sue Ling, Christina said suggestively, "I could tell you stories!"

Sue Ling took that moment to play host by collecting and bagging the trash. She ignored the professor's protests that it could wait until morning.

For several minutes the professor had been staring at me. Finally, I called him on it.

Focusing hard on my forehead, he said, "It's clearest when you get angry. Six . . . six . . . six."

I shot him a look of chagrin. "Abdiel said he couldn't wait to tell you."

The professor told the girls of Abdiel's joke, and despite my arguing that nobody said the mark was on my forehead, everyone stared at it to see if they could see something.

"Ever since I met Abdiel," Sue Ling said quietly, "I can't walk down the street without wondering if there are angels watching me. How can we tell?"

"They're here in large numbers," the professor affirmed. "Like it or not, we're in the middle of a war. But then, isn't that the nature of warfare? When armies sweep through a town or a nation, they don't ask the residents if they want to be involved. If we're wise, we'll take the necessary precautions and arm ourselves in defense. As we saw on the bridge today, there are human casualties in this war."

The professor glanced at the top of the bureau at a picture of his wife and daughters. His pain was a knife to my heart. But also a warning. While I had been granted protection, that protection did not extend to the others in this room. Semyaza had already proven he would not hesitate to strike at an enemy through his loved ones.

"Grant, I'm going to start sending you additional installments of

Abdiel's narrative of angel history. It puts a whole new perspective on things."

"Abdiel is now posting guards when he dictates to the professor," Sue Ling said. From the way her eyes widened, I could tell it frightened her.

"It's a precautionary measure," the professor explained. "Abdiel isn't certain what Semyaza will do if he finds out about it."

"This isn't over," I said, relaying Semyaza's warning.

I had reached a saturation point. As the morning sun lit the front curtains, the professor, Jana, Christina, and Sue Ling continued talking. Language was lost to me. All I saw were the faces and gestures of those who had become dear to me.

I warmed myself in their presence. It felt good to be alive. It felt good to be human.

Jack Cavanaugh is an award-winning, full-time freelance author of twenty-eight published novels.

A student of the novel for more than three decades, Jack takes his craft seriously, continuing to study and teach at Christian writers conferences. He is the former pastor of three churches in San Diego County and draws upon his theological background for the spiritual elements of his plots and characters.

His novels have been translated into a dozen foreign languages, largely because of the universal scope of his topics. Jack has not only written about American history, but about South Africa, banned English Bibles, German Christians in the days of Hitler and Communism, revivals in America, end times, and angelic warfare. His novel *Death Watch* has been optioned to be made into a motion picture by Out Cold Entertainment, Inc.

Jack has three grown children and lives with his wife in Southern California.

Visit him online:
Website: *http://jackcavanaugh.com/*
Facebook: *novelistjack*
Twitter: *@novelistjack*
Goodreads: *novelistjack*